*To Heather —*

# Inspired

## *in the*

# Bedroom

*Nightly Reads From S.R. Carson:*
*Before, During and After Romance*

*These are 2' Reads —*
*short + sweet — depending*
*on the mood: humor,*
*silliness, Romance &*
*and Life Stories —*

# S.R. CARSON

*S.R.Carson*

**outskirts press**

# INTRODUCTION

This all began in 2013, about a month after I recovered from a Near Death Experience that certainly changed my life and forced me to re-examine the important things in life, and one of the off springs of that self-examination was the desire to start writing again. I had already started writing my first novel, <u>To Love with Hate</u>, but was far from finished by the time this event occurred. So, someone told me that I should start a blog that would offer short reads to people, designed to introduce me as an author to the general public while I wrote my novel, and also to serve as a marketing tool, since I knew nothing at all about marketing.

I think the blog was a good idea and this project allowed me to expand and cultivate my writing craft and writing techniques by writing short, one-page stories, or scenes, to be published for the public on the internet. It soon came to pass that ideas or observations about life would pop into my head, perhaps triggered by an experience that day, or a memory from the past, or even a song that struck me in a certain way. I must admit, when I first started, the short pieces I wrote had a spiritual theme to them, and that seemed natural due to the events that had recently occurred in my life. There was also a tendency to write about nature, and God's beauty early on.

But soon, humor, silliness and satire broke inexorably in to my writing repertoire, and I could not stop the flow of ideas, and when they burst into my head, I had to write them down that night or as soon as I could, sometimes in church, at a bar on white napkins, at work if I had a few moments, or even on an airplane.

So, my short blog pieces were originally designed to show me to the world as a writer, even if this writer thought he had clothes on but he didn't, and no one wanted to tell him this brutal fact. Whether this venture in blog land made me more well known as an author or had no impact on my popularity is not entirely clear, but it certainly did provide me a stress release and an opportunity to hone my craft in various genres.

The 128 blog entries I chose to include in this publication cover such a wide range of topics that include humor, spirituality, silly observations, interesting stories, inspiration, parody, beauty, nature and romance with tasteful sexuality, that some have asked me to consider making an anthology of these publications, so people could choose the topic or genre they wanted to read about, depending on their mood or lack of mood at the time. Kind of like a bedtime reader, if you will. So, that is what this book is about: a collection of my favorite blog entries, with the addition of some excerpts from my first published novel, *To Love with Hate* and a few teasing excerpts as well from my soon to be published thriller: *Blue Shadows*.

Having said all that, I found it difficult to categorize this collection of varied blogs into general subjects that made sense without causing complete confusion. So, it seemed to me that these subjects best fit into four major categories that made sense: 1) **Before romance** to create a romantic mood or for date preparation. 2) **During romance**. Disclaimer: If you choose this one, I do not accept responsibility for the consequences and as you can imagine, only one blog qualified in this section. 3) **After romance** for a mellow, romantic ambiance and after glow. (Be careful or this might trigger your partner to want more fun.) 4) **Before bed** with **no chance** for romance at all. This one, unfortunately, has the most sub-categories.

These are purposely short pieces, designed to make you laugh, feel romantic, think deeply into your soul, cry, or just bask in the wonder of this complex, difficult, but beautiful world.

Enjoy.
S.R. Carson

# TABLE OF CONTENTS

# BEFORE ROMANCE

Perhaps to read to your date or spouse
to create a romantic mood or more
practically, in some cases, to give the
Viagra time to become effective.

# MY FIRST LOVE

To this day, I still have the image of her beauty permanently stored in my memory banks, eagerly recalled anytime I need a smile or a pleasant memory. The first time I saw her, I couldn't take my eyes off her, and although that's a cliché, it's one that fits perfectly. I knew it was rude to stare, but I figured it was ok to glance at beauty without gawking, intent on absorbing as much of the view as possible before the eyes are forced back to reality and decorum.

Admittedly, her sleek body and graceful frame first caught my eye, like many other men lucky enough to gaze up on her. Her cute nose easily parted the compliant air with elegance, but with strength of purpose, and that tail and the way it moved, well it just made my heart nearly jump out of my chest with desire. But she possessed much more than just a body. While there were others who had similar beauty, there was something about her that me be believe that she was trapped on this mundane earth, hoping to find the right man to take her soaring to heights high above, with the eager wind caressing her smooth body while she sliced through the air with gentle strength.

I can't forget the first time I entered her cockpit, in tandem with my glider instructor. My hands trembled on her stick, feet working the rudders while the tow plane in front of us pulled us down the runway until we gained enough speed to fly and stay in sync with him, always careful to stay directly behind him so as not to pull his tail and cause him to spin. You see, gliders always become airborne before the tow plane due to their greater lift to drag ratio and we had to make sure we didn't overfly while in tow.

My instructor showed patience with me at first, but then after a few sorties he stopped giving instructions, knowing my confidence accelerated with each journey with her in the sky. His only comment that he would make, at least once a day was, "Fly the plane Carson, don't let her fly you." He wouldn't explain himself, and I didn't ask what he meant, but eventually it became clear to me. This beautiful craft required me to make only small corrections, but they must be correct and decisive ones, while always scanning the altitude, horizon, vertical speed, and airspeed indicators yet never forgetting to scan the outside atmosphere. I searched for eagles circling concentrically in the lift from thermals hoping to ride the lift as well, rather than losing altitude too quickly in downdrafts and thus being forced to land prematurely.

After twenty sorties, my instructor signed off on my solo capability, allowing me to fly this sexy lady alone, and so he stepped out of the glider and said, "She's all yours Carson. Remember, fly the plane, don't let her fly you." I was white-knuckled on the stick during roll out, and despite keeping the stick all the way to the floor during roll out, the nose remained up as we went down the runway and I prayed that despite not visualizing the runway, I would be able to stay directly behind the tow plane, causing him no harm from my towrope. Amazingly, despite my anxiety, everything went perfectly.

My first solo flight sucked the breath out of my lungs then forced it back in with exhilaration. It was a feeling of fear combined with a sensation of complete freedom from the bonds of earth, with the only sounds being the rush of wind over the wings and nose and the occasional radio calls from the tower below. When I lost too much lift, I calculated my gliding distance to the runway, and prepared for landing, communicating with the tower as I deployed her spoilers to lose airspeed and altitude, landing with a few bounces on the grass, parallel to the runway, the way gliders are supposed to land. My friends and instructor doused me with a celebration of cold water when I emerged from her cockpit, smiling with relief and confidence, now wearing my wings for the first time. I was no longer a virgin aviator, and my experience with this beautiful lady will stay with me as long as I live. And each time I learned to fly a new plane, now with engines, the beauty of flying as high and as fast as possible cannot be forgotten or taken for granted. I will never forget what it meant to "Fly the plane Carson."

# THE FLIGHT ATTENDANT

**(An excerpt from my novel:** *To Love With Hate***)**

Her spacious room was nicely decorated, but Gavin was only interested in one piece of furniture, and it didn't really matter if the sheet thread count was two hundred fifty or on thousand, pima or muslin. He figured that he probably wouldn't notice if the sheets were made of medium-grit sandpaper.

Amanda spoke first. "Darling, go ahead and open the champagne bottle I see sitting on the table, and make yourself comfortable for a while, if you can. I'm going to take a quick shower and freshen up. It was a long flight."

She walked toward the bathroom; her skirt dropped to the floor several feet in front of the doorway, as did her sweater and bra. Only her panties remained. Her backside reminded him of the smooth-ness of his favorite winter toboggan run when he was a kid. Before she entered the bathroom, she looked back at Gavin, knowing he was watching, and smiled seductively before she closed the bathroom door behind her. But she didn't close it completely. Gavin quickly threw her black roller bag off the bed and pulled back the covers in preparation for his passion, then stopped, thought better of it, and walked to the bathroom. He never touched the champagne.

The steam slowly rose, and this allowed him to watch her through the glass doors of the shower. He enjoyed the view of her washing herself while he drank in her shapely silhouette through the now partially steamed shower door. When she bent over, he couldn't take it any longer, and pulled off his jeans, but with difficulty due to his arousal. He forgot to take off his shirt and hurried into the shower, but it didn't matter because she immediately saw his excitement when he pulled her close to him and he kissed her quivering lips, neck and finally her more sensitive aroused areas as well. He found her light and easy to pick up in the shower. She eagerly wrapped her toned legs tightly around his waist and the slick shower wall served as their support while the muscular conqueror first made her moan, then scream so loudly that the next day her fellow flight attendants scolded her for disrupting their precious sleep with her nighttime activities.

# INSPIRED BY THE BOUNCY RAVEN-HAIRED PENDULUM

Her long raven mane, held at the top by a bouncy pony tail clip, reached all the way down to the end of her shirt, brushing gently back and forth on top of her shapely garlic cloved halves while swishing the air back and forth like a pendulum, in cadence with her stride, but several milliseconds out of phase. Those tights hugged her lean legs as if poured on like lucky melted chocolate on smooth ice cream, running out of material just below her pulsing heart-shaped calves.

I was always taught not to stare, but was I supposed to do? I was running on the treadmill in the row of machines directly behind her and had no other place to look, except the large TV displays on the walls directly ahead that had the sound turned off. Seems I remember being told that it's not great to stare at the TV too long either, so, I guess I was stuck. Either way, there was no way for her to tell where my eyes were fixed. For safety reasons, it was clearly important for me though to keep my eyes fixed straight ahead, so that I didn't lose my balance on the treadmill, fall off and land in a heap of sweaty flesh.

And then I realized how awkward it was that I was in this position. Years ago, before the thousands of miles of running did a job on my obedient knees, I would never be seen on a stupid treadmill, especially not in public. That was just for joggers, and I was a nasty runner—a snow, sleet and rain loving outdoors runner! Turns out because of my knees I switched to interval lap swimming to maintain fitness, boring as it was, and because of a shoulder injury, I decided to try the treadmill again, just to see, and so far, my knees weren't yelling at me! Looking back, I suppose there were rare occasions that I was on the treadmill, perhaps after a conference in the hotel exercise facility. I would run 5 to 5 and a half minute miles continuously, and the outside of my shoes seemed to barely touch the treadmill, without much sound, airborne most of the time in full stride.

But now I was a jogger, hopefully not a plodder, but I don't think I looked that bad. And I knew that airborne was not a word onlooker would use to describe my treadmill workout. But the heck with that, I was doing it! And she inspired me. She was clearly going at a faster pace than I was, and my eyes counted the rhythm of her swishing pendulum and nonstop frog legs. But I had to keep up with her, or at least, if I couldn't approach her speed without destructing, I would make it a point to last as long as she did! My breathing quickened and I found myself hypnotized by her swishing hair, and when I caught myself feeling dizzy from the view, I took a break by looking at the mindless TV for a brutal minute, then back to my inspiration.

The knees were holding up, and I was trying to keep my innate running form and arm carriage, but I was trying to hold on, hoping she would quit soon, so that I could show myself that I kept up with her. Please stop soon Ms. Raven haired pendulum with the motor legs!

I was sweating now, and so was she, the wet line in the middle of her back sucked her shirt to her skin. Aha! She was working hard too. Maybe she could feel the high-speed endurance runner behind her and she felt the need for more speed to impress me. Not. Clearly, I was becoming delirious. Suddenly it dawned on me that the sweat dripping into my eyes just didn't occur when swimming because you were already wet, and what's more, you couldn't watch anyone swim when you were swimming, unless they were splashing next to you in the other lane, but either way, if they had long raven hair it would be smashed under a speedo swim cap. So how was I supposed to be inspired when swimming?

Thankfully, she finally slowed down and did her warm down, and so did I, although my warm down was much quicker because I was already slow. She looked back at me briefly on her way out and I tried to act like this was no effort, but I couldn't hide my heaving breath and red face. She was probably worried I would pass out.

I felt exhilarated when it was over, and that satisfying feeling after a good run again invaded my soul. I was thankful she inspired me to go a little farther than I wanted originally, and so far, the knees were holding up, but I knew I couldn't do this on a daily basis without pain. So, I'll be back in the uninspired pool and weight room for the remainder of the week, but every now and then, the treadmill will beckon me back for more inspiration and sweat.

# AMY AND JULIE
# MET AT THE BAR

**(An excerpt from my novel:** *To Love With Hate***)**

Amy and Julie met at Rick's bar, an institution that was famous for its happy hour, and the effect it had on facilitating the testosterone-estrogen interaction. They both wore short skirts and heels because they could and they looked good especially when they posed at the front on high bar stools.

"Kinda quiet here," said Julie

"Don't worry. It'll pick up. Especially if we're here." They both giggled simultaneously.

"Classic crossed-leg man bait," said Julie. "Works every time."

Julie slurped a margarita while Amy sucked on her Vodka martini.

So Amy, what hot guy are you with now? Or are you trying to sink your nails into someone with more long-term potential?"

"You know Julie, sometimes I just take a hot lover for fun,

but when I find a good man with money and power—he won't get away."

Julie almost meowed. "Poor guy won't know how to escape once your nails are inside his naïve skin. What will it be tonight?"

"Depends on what rolls in the door. But seriously, there is someone that I think might be the one."

Do tell."

"Ok. He's about six-two, blue eyes, nice body with a scar over his left eyebrow that I find easy to

ignore. Oh yeah, nice smile too. Amy beamed. She played with her silky hair and re-crossed her legs

while scanning the male occupants of the room. "But the problem is..."

# THE MARINE AND
# DELPHINE

**(An excerpt from my novel *To Love with Hate*)**

The heavily muscled marine walked into the entry, quickly scanning the expansive family room: the huge Christmas tree, a crackling fire, and, especially, the beautiful brunette sitting elegantly on a lucky couch.

"Congratulations, little Bro; you rock!"

"What the hell you mean, you lawyer puke?"

"As always, you still have a way with words. I heard you won the Marine middleweight boxing championship, and I wanted to congratulate you. At least that allows you to release your violence in a sanctioned way, rather than on the streets or at a bar here at home when you're not deployed to some secret location."

Blake wasn't sure whether this was compliment, but he responded to Gavin in his usual style. "Thanks, I think, but now that you're the official CEO of Dad's firm, you think your shit is hotter than ever. Remember, though, I can kick your ass with one hand tied behind my back and one leg in a cast any time I want to. Not too bad for a guy who wasn't smart enough to go to 'Pussyversity' like you did. By the way, I had no problem getting some despite not going to 'Pussyversity'"

Blake smirked while he watched his brother smile nervously at his new lover, Delphine, who was giggling at Blake's statement and trying to hide her pleasure with her dainty hand. He also noticed that she didn't attempt to hide her slender legs that were barely covered by her tiny skirt, and so he stared at her legs while they talked.

"Funny, Blake. You have about as much class as I do patience, and yeah, I guess that is one of the advantages of higher education. Too bad you don't realize that brains are more important than muscles in this world, unless you're a caveman I guess."

"Whatever. By the way, Gavin, are you going to introduce me to this beautiful lady or are you going to keep yapping your mouth? If she were my girl, I would've introduced her first thing. I'd be proud as hell."

"Oh yeah, sorry. Blake, this is Delphine."

She stretched out her hand adorned by fake fingernails to Blake and smiled, but instead of shaking it, he kissed it. She blushed in pleasant surprise.

"I met her in Bordeaux when I was providing legal advice to the St. Emillion wine consortium a few months ago. She's a model who works in both Paris and New York, and, well, we hit it off pretty well. So, I invited her here to visit me in the windy city for a while before she has to go back to New York for a photo shoot. I wish she could stay longer. C'est vrai?

"Oui, et ton frère est tres interessant et tres beau!"

"Chicago will never be the same with her here, that's for sure," said Blake. "I don't know what she said but I damn sure loved the way it sounded."

"She said that you seem like a nice boy but a little rough around the edges."

Delphine glared at Gavin because of the fabricated translation.

"Tell me, Delphine, I know you must speak English fairly well."

"Oui. I mean yes, of course."

"Is that really what you said to me, the way Gavin interpreted it? He is my brother, but I don't trust him when it comes to women."

Delphine looked for guidance from Gavin who smiled nervously. "Well, I think Gavin doesn't understand French as much as he thinks he does. I don't know what 'rough' means, but basically I meant to say that you are an interesting and handsome man."

"Thanks, and you can bet I'll need some time with you later to learn some more special French words in private," said Blake.

"Let's go to the living room and have some drinks before the chef brings us dinner." Gavin said, intervening quickly.

"Sounds good to me," said Blake. He watched Delphine saunter gracefully and he soaked her in while Gavin resumed the conversation on the couch.

"So, tell us about your exploits in the marines, Blake. We haven't heard much from you over the years."

"That sounds damn boring. I'd much rather talk about Delphine."

"No, please, monsieur Blake, please tell me, I mean us, of your valor."

"Ah well, if you insist. Unlike your lover who went to Harvard Law School and travels to the Caribbean every year to play with the girls on the beach, I served my country. It started in Marine basic training, of course. I shot expert on the rifle range early on, and that's why they noticed me. After I scored maximum on the first class PFT, the corps began to separate me out for certain specialty training."

"PFT. What is that?" asked Gavin.

"Physical Fitness Test. A maximum score includes a three-mile run in under eighteen minutes, twenty dead hang pull-ups, one-hundred sit-ups in fewer than two minutes, and finally a fifty-meter swim holding a weight out of the water and then treading water for thirty seconds while holding the weight."

"Impressive," said Gavin.

Gavin opened a bottle of Chateau Meraux for both Delphine and himself, but Blake was happy with his bottle of Corona and lime. He was even more pleased that he was sitting across from Delphine on the opposite couch, taking in the spectacular view she presented. He alternated quick glances at her legs and thin ankles, then her full lips while she swirled the wine deftly inside her delicate mouth. He could feel her staring back at his bulging biceps outlined by large veins. Blake had seen that gaze before, and he understood that it usually meant that she admired his hard physique and secretly wanted him to ravish her aggressively. At least that's what he hoped she was thinking. Gavin had shared with him on the phone previously that although he had known her only a few weeks, she seemed to constantly want sex with him, any time, any place. Blake figured that Delphine would only satisfy Gavin's needs briefly, then as usual, he would dump her and look for new conquests, allowing his brother to move in for the kill.

No, Blake thought, this hottie may have enjoyed Gavin's movie-star looks, but it was his wealth and future financial security as CEO of the firm that most likely attracted her to his gene pool. He reasoned that what she desired to taste for the moment was completely different from what she wanted for a lifetime. He knew she wanted him for the moment more than she wanted his brother, and he would make sure they ended up in bed.

"I knew that I had aptitude, so I volunteered for Force Recon and became Recon qualified then went to sniper school." Blake continued the best he could despite the gorgeous distraction sitting across from him. "After sniper school I deployed for several tours in Iraq and Afghanistan, and a few other places that I can't talk about."

"You know, Blake, Dad told me he was proud of you, and so am I. We just wished that you would've communicated with us more than once a year when you deployed. We were worried about you and Dad started smoking and drinking more because of that."

"Bullshit. I do what I'm trained to do. I do my job to perfection with no emotion and without need for attention. There's a shitload of bad people out there who want to kill Americans everywhere, but I'm one of the guys who has the skills to stop them. I don't need you to worry about that stuff. You need men like me to fight for you so you can eat caviar and drink champagne at the damn country club."

Gavin shifted on the couch and tapped his feet on the ground. "You know I appreciate your service Blake. But listen, when you get out of the Marines, you can always get a job at the firm working with me. Dad, as you know, left me in control. But I understand that with your share of the inheritance you won't really need to work."

Delphine eagerly chimed in. "You are an American hero."

"Thanks, I appreciate that, sweetie. Yeah, the inheritance is great, but I'm a career Marine. Can't think of another career that would suit me right now, and I'm not the kind of guy to sit on his ass and drink fru-fru drinks all day.

"Well, Blake, on another subject, you'll be happy to know that our firm's best malpractice attorney is filing a malpractice suit against this Dr. Barton."

"Good. Is he the best you could find?"

"Best at the firm, and probably in the state, with a high success rate in the cases he selects."

"He's not a wuss who will back down when things go bad, is he? I want this doc taken down for killing Dad."

"As I said, he's experienced and never quits when he sees

blood or money. In this case, there are lots of both. Our firm will pay him well for his efforts. And I don't want to comment about your last statement. We're both angry at this quack, but we need to be smart."

"How long will the legal proceedings take?"

"Well, that depends on what the defense throws up against us during the discovery and deposition phase. But first, our team will investigate to see if we have a legitimate case against him, and if not, at least we will dig up some dirt on him. I'd say it would take at least a year to get to a jury trial. Nothing we can do now anyway; our legal team is on it. Having said that, you need to know I'm going to France and Germany for business next week, but I'll stay in touch about the legal proceedings against Barton."

Satisfied, Blake got up to leave. "I'll see you when I see you, bro. Merry Christmas to you both. And Delphine, it was pure pleasure to meet you."

"Enchante` monsieur Blake." She smiled so warmly Blake was immediately aroused.

Gavin and Blake shook hands, and then Blake hugged Delphine and inhaled her French perfume deeply into the bottom of his lungs. He pulled her close to his body and he loved that she didn't pull away. She seemed to stick to him. Although he didn't see her look back when he walked down the lighted sidewalk to his car, he could feel Delphine studying the back of his tight jeans, even with Gavin standing next to her. His training gave him a sixth sense.

Gavin pulled her away from the doorway and they walked into the house hand in hand towards the bedroom upstairs. "Sweetie, what do you think of my little brother?"

She smiled. "Well, he's definitely not little and he is certainly an interesting man."

# BAR INSPIRATION

Bordeaux and Paris provide excellent images for a novel, and trust me; I took advantage of those settings several years ago during the early writing of my book, described as psychological suspense. I wrote freehand in a spiral notebook, sipping espresso at the cafés and brasseries, and thankfully, the French waiters allowed me to write as long as I wanted, as long as I didn't order a hamburger and fries. "Mon dieu!" While that experience provided some special flavor, simple settings in America provide me with inspiration when I least expect it.

I needed to wind down, drink a martini or two and listen to a cool three-piece jazz band while enjoying the ambiance of a classy bar. Yeah, a classy cigar bar with leather chairs, wide screens, smoke conditioners, and ridiculously attractive people. So, I sat down on a couch and watched the stunning cocktail servers come to each party to take their orders, whether cigars or drinks. But my evening started out warmly because I came alone, and so she found it easy to sit down on the couch perilously close to me. My lungs vacuumed her perfume down to my diaphragm then held the scent as long as possible, forcing another hungry breath through my begging nostrils, all of which was accomplished without obviously staring at the fishnet stockings lucky enough to caress her long legs. But she knew what she was doing.

"Good evening sir. May I get you a drink or a cigar?"

Her smile immediately disarmed my fear of falling down, so I smiled warmly back. "Sure, I'll have a dirty Vodka martini and a Macanudo Gold label.

"Excellent. I'll be back in a few."

It was now time to take in her walk toward the humidor, without fear of embarrassment, but something told me she expected the stare. Her long legs were a piece of art, and it was disappointing to see them end inside her skirt, but the rhythm of her hips, while in sync with the music, still made me hold on to my chair for support. I thought I was recovered when she returned with my cigar and martini and again, sat next to me, smiling.

"Long, medium or short draw sir?"

"Medium, and you can call me Carson."

"Interesting name. Sounds British I guess, but certainly manly."

"Love your choice of words, so I must ask your name as well."

"Yana"

She cut my cigar to my specifications, then I placed it in my mouth and puffed while she lit it with her almost flame-thrower lighter, and my blues met her greens.

"My guess is that you're of Russian heritage although, I am thinking probably a ballet dancer background and a graduate PhD student as well."

"Ah, yes, you're right, almost. Russian parents and a former ballerina, but I'm actually a third-year law student. But tell me, how did you guess? I am American born and raised. Apple pie, baseball and all that stuff. Although, large amounts of Vodka are my preferred drink with hot dogs. Does that give me away?" Some customers waved to her for more drinks so she got up to leave before I could answer. I couldn't believe she sat with me to enjoy a conversation while lighting my cigar.

She came back some time later and asked, "Carson, do you need another drink?"

"I don't need one, but I'll take one. By the way, it was your high cheekbones and a few other characteristics I've learned over the years. And also, please bring me about 25 of those white napkins."

She looked at me with a bewildered look, and then returned with a pile of napkins and my second martini. I suddenly began writing on each napkin, filling each one, front and back, the words flowing from my brain to my fingers like water gushing from a fire hose, and I didn't stop until each napkin was filled with my scribbles and I completely forgot my surroundings. And that included the Russian goddess with drinks!

She returned, and this time sat directly in front of me on the table, her legs crossed daintily but my brain was disengaged, my heart was jumping out of my chest.

"Carson, may I ask what are you doing writing on all those napkins?"

"Sure Yana. I'm writing a novel and I guess I became inspired all of a sudden and had to write before the thoughts vanished forever."

"Ah, I see. May I see what you wrote on one of them?"

I hesitated, sure that she would think my words would be junk, but after a minute or so, I picked up the one I thought would be the best. At least I hoped so. She picked it up and read it, then smiled widely.

"The sleek black dress clung eagerly to her lithe body, forcing his eyes to drink her in completely"

"Oh my god, I love this!"

"That was you my dear. You were my model and inspiration tonight."

"So nice. When I was dating my husband, he used to write me poems, but since we were married, he's stopped.

She looked at me with those Caribbean Sea eyes and we connected, both longing for something in each other's past, but knowing our futures would not include each other, but the experience of the evening was golden, etched in our memories of pleasure.

Give me your full name, and I will anxiously await your novel and hopefully this phrase will be in it, and I will remember how you wrote it.

"Yes, it will be in my book, *To Love With Hate.* You can bet the sentence will be in there. My name is S.R. Carson.

# THE OCEAN GODDESS

(An excerpt from my novel: *To Love With Hate*)

In the cabin, Katherine told Wyatt to go somewhere so she could fix up the place, unpack and make her little nest. He gladly obliged, and found himself at the bar downing several beers and a plate of nachos. But there was one cocktail waitress who caught his eye; long legs that went on forever and the way she bent over to serve drinks made him hope she would serve him personally in the near future, and heck, they had four days on the ship. Katherine found him at the bar and they went to a more comfortable place to relax.

Warm Pacific breezes and calm waves greeted the couple while they lounged on their deck chairs in the bright sun. "It's amazing how the ancient Mayan Indians were able to construct such an accurate calendar using mathematics and knowledge of astronomy, don't you think?" Wyatt asked, hoping to engage Katherine in a conversation unrelated to the kids.

"I don't know who the Mayans are, Wyatt. Do they live on a reservation in Arizona?"

Wyatt paused, and then forced a smile and a respectful

response. "No, they were an advanced ancient civilization that lived on the Yucatan Peninsula in Mexico."

"There you go again, trying to make me look like I don't have a brain. Just because I didn't go to medical school like you doesn't mean I don't have street smarts. And no, I just tried to study a little high school Spanish, and didn't master Arabic and Pasha or whatever it's called."

"Actually, it's Pashto. Spoken by the Pashtu people in Afghanistan and some parts of Pakistan. C'mon, I was just trying to make conversation. Don't be so sensitive."

There was lifeless silence in the baking sun and Wyatt gazed pensively over the undulating ocean waves. *It seems like forever since I've enjoyed some stimulating conversation with an adult.*

That young cocktail server sauntered gracefully to their table. She wore a short yellow sundress and black halter-top that barely had enough material to hold her "Tropical Cruise Lines" host badge. She looked briefly at Katherine and smiled politely, then concentrated her efforts on Wyatt. His blues met her browns and his heart fluttered when he recognized those long legs and he briefly devoured the view of the server's full red lips and soft dark skin. She purposely bent way down to Wyatt to show him her well-filled halter-top and asked, "What may I get you two to drink today?"

Katherine stared intensely at him and he pulled his eyes painfully away from the feminine paradise and said, "Honey, what would you like?"

She hesitated, looked at Wyatt and said, "I don't know, maybe a Tom Collins."

The sultry server interjected. "Ma'am may I suggest the Tropical Cruise Paradise? It's a fruity, rum based drink that women like."

"Ok, sounds good," said Katherine.

He couldn't help but take a video of the woman's legs with his eyes while Katherine ordered.

She smiled at Katherine respectfully, then broadened her smile and bent over gracefully to obtain Wyatt's order. His busy life studying had kept him generally naïve about women, but apparently, he finally figured out that his blue eyes and wide smile attracted women.

"I'll have a Sam Adams lager."

"Sorry sir. We don't have Sam Adams, but we have lots of Corona and tons of limes."

"Sounds perfect." Wyatt loved talking to people from different cultures engaging them to learn about geography and travel. Problem was, this girl was stunning and by definition, ridiculously dangerous.

"By the way, where are you from?" He was hypnotized with her and tried to keep from drooling when he talked.

Katherine stared at him. He didn't notice the quiver in her twine-tight lips until it was too late.

"Columbia. I'm working on this ship to earn some money for my second year in architectural design school at the Pratt Institute in New York."

He hoped Katherine would engage in the conversation for the both of them. When it was clear she wasn't going to, he continued, "Interesting. Your English is excellent, by the way."

"Thanks. In school I loved to study it. Always wanted to travel to the United States or England and I am lucky that I can study in New York in the fall."

"Good luck." After she brought them their drinks, Wyatt paid the server with a good tip and she left to serve some other guests. Wyatt sensed the danger and maybe he had too many drinks, but he had to watch her walk away, shaking all her stuff with such a tasty rhythm.

"Your tongue was hanging out of your mouth and you were panting like a dog in heat when that server was here. I'm surprised you didn't slip her your phone number too!"

"Lighten up, honey. I don't see what's wrong in having a little innocent conversation to keep the atmosphere around here alive enough to have a palpable pulse. Thought it was interesting she was in architectural school. Do you want me to stare at the table and be mute when people talk to me?"

"You're full of shit, Wyatt."

"Right, and that's why you love me."

# ROMANCE AT THE BROADMOOR

**(An excerpt from my upcoming novel:** *Blue Shadows)*

She didn't really walk in. She glided. And her merciless hips moved to the rhythm the base player provided and her stylish heels generously pointed the way to her lean, heart—shaped calves. She offered a more elegant, but similarly enticing view compared to their treadmill encounter and Wyatt drank it in completely but his thirst remained unquenched. She was, in fact, a divine symphony of feminine perfection.

"So great to see you Gentri. You look amazing!"

"Thank you, Wyatt, and likewise, my handsome sweetheart! So sorry I'm late. I had a client who wanted to talk and—"

"No problem, seems a lucky man must be patient for a quality lady."

He reached out and kissed her hand, then led her to their table, and he noticed everyone stopping their dinner, with forks frozen awkwardly in mid-air just to stare at the goddess—her raven hair cascading back and forth during her walk, sometimes bouncing over one of her eyes, but she didn't fix it, letting the bounce assume its' natural seductive freedom. She slid in first on one side of the luxurious booth and he then joined on the other side, both sitting close enough to enjoy each other but not be on each other's lap. The waiter then carefully placed the gold napkin on her lap, and that napkin clearly had never been so lucky. Then, he did the same for Wyatt. A few minutes later, the second waiter came and brought the dozen long stem roses in a vase that Wyatt bought earlier, and Wyatt handed them to her and said, "To a wonderful lady who brightens any room she's in."

"My my Wyatt! Bless your heart!" She kissed him, not on the cheek, but softly and tenderly, both of them exploring the taste of each other and wanting more, until their lips naturally parted, each knowing there had to be more.

"You know Wyatt, I'm not a woman who is Spartan with her words, but you have really impressed me. You're so sweet, and a true romantic gentleman. Yes, I've had roses before, but not in such a nice restaurant and, I must admit, I've never had my hand kissed before."

"I had no choice Gentri. I figured you would enjoy the atmosphere here and you would fit in with the elegant ambiance that I heard about this place. Not only that, I knew you liked soft jazz, and so voila!"

She leaned in and kissed him again, then moved closer to him, her legs crossed daintily but expertly, while showing her shapely runner's legs, allowing Wyatt to imagine following the smooth terrain of the skin up above her mid-thigh hemline to quite a pleasant conclusion, simply by using that subtle vision. He smiled knowing that his training served him well in multiple different ways, so tonight he was thankful for that. She had a small brown birthmark on the lower part of the left side of her neck, resembling a small feather and a tiny mole on the outside of her right upper lip, almost imperceptible, but they became at once tiny imperfections that made her even more attractive to him, especially when her soft lips graciously moved to create words.

"I hope a nice smooth Bordeaux is ok with you. I selected a Chateau Beausejour, Saint Emilion Grand Crus, 2001. The sommelier is bringing it now."

"No way! Bordeaux is the worst. It makes me dance non-stop, giggle and blush all night. You'll be sorry my darling Mr. Barton."

"That's not my definition of being sorry, that's for sure."

The couple sipped their wine and talked after making their dinner selection, while Wyatt watched her energetic right foot bounce up and down playfully, heel only half on. This time, to hell with peripheral vision because full head on vision was required at this moment.

# BLAKE AND AMY

(An excerpt from the novel: *To Love with Hate)*

Blake picked her up in a new red corvette, with vanity plates, "Marine UNO". She wore a tight short skirt and heels with a light sweater that softly draped in front in folds, leaving plentiful fruit for the male imagination. Her hair draped softly over her shoulders, ending up in her face when she laughed. Blake wore tight jeans that accented his lower body, and his short-sleeved shirt was not tucked in, but fit tightly to his muscled chest and chiseled arms.

Initially they sat at the bar several feet away from each other but it wasn't long before they moved to a cozy booth, sitting almost on top of each other, kissing and touching. Amy caressed his arms and felt his strength, imagining him holding her captive while he enjoyed ravenous sex with her helpless body. She wanted him now. She needed satisfaction by a man, to fill the void in her desire that had remained unquenched for too long. It didn't matter anymore about his attitude when she first met him, because her innate desire for a strong man was suffocating rational thought. She saw his eyes continually stealing glances at her hemline. She initially attempted to pull her skirt down, but it wasn't worth the effort, and she gave up, enjoying his interest in her toned legs.

"Amy, I have a full bar at home, stereo surround sound and a movie theater. Don't you think that would be a better place than here at this bar?"

"Are you going to kidnap me, Mr. Blake, sir?"

"Only if you say no; then I will of course."

Amy laughed. "Well in that case, let's make it non-violent. I say hell yeah, take me you brutes."

His right hand moved back and forth from Amy's leg to the gearshift, giving her goose bumps. When they arrived at the front steps of the mansion, He fumbled for his keys while Amy kept her hand around his waist. Trembling with anticipation, the key insertion took way too long. Once inside, he almost put the wrong security code in to shut off the alarm because she wouldn't stop biting and kissing his neck. After walking a few feet inside the foyer, she turned him to face her, put both hands on his sculpted behind and took control of his mouth with hers. She felt his excitement in front while his rough jeans creased her silky skirt. She made a brief little whine when he picked her up with one hand under her bottom and the other hand holding her head so their lips would not part, and then gently laid her on the couch in front of the fireplace. He then trapped her with iron arms on each side of her, commanding her to remove her skirt and panties while he watched like a lion preparing for the kill. Her vision at the bar of his strong arms and her sexual captivity was now real erotic frenzy. The lion completed his kill and his prey screamed in defenseless ecstasy.

"You know, Amy, I like you. I think we can develop a relationship with time. What do you think?"

"I like you too, but just as a sexual friend, you know, friends with benefits. Tonight was nothing more than animal sex, damn good sex, but I'm really only after one man. I don't want to offend you; you're great in bed, but you are not the one I want a relationship with."

# SPRING IN DENVER

(An excerpt from my upcoming novel: *Blue Shadows)*

"Why not now?"

His recurrent headaches exploded, just at the wrong time. Wyatt took a drink of wine, rubbed his forehead briefly, then, got up and walked a little to the railing of the deck, then quickly back to his lady, as if not to lose precious time.

"You ok Wyatt? What's wrong?"

He said nothing in response, bent over and whispered in her ear, "May I take off your scarf so my lucky lips can make love to your supple little neck?"

She sighed and said, "It's about time honey."

He removed the scarf, kissed her behind her ear, then the neck, while his finger gently caressed her exposed and vulnerable collarbone. He listened carefully to the increased tempo of her breathing that he knew was sparked from his feather-like touches, then she pulled him down and kissed him with lioness-like feminine hunger and when she stopped for air, he whispered into her ear, "I want to make love to you completely and worship your body the way a southern goddess deserves."

She offered her hand and he took it and led her away back into the house, embarking on the long journey to the candlelit bedroom. After ten feet of walking, their journey was interrupted by a flurry of passionate kisses and she exposed her neck to him again while he loosened her skirt skillfully, never letting his lips leave her skin while her skirt fell crumpled to the floor. She then awkwardly fumbled with his belt buckle, and he helped her a little with his pants button, and she peeled off his tight jeans, pulling them to the floor, while her curious fingers explored what they needed, lips still engaged above. Knowing they would never make it to the bedroom this way, Wyatt picked her up, one heel off, the other dangling precariously, and Wyatt took his woman to his bed and laid her down gently. She stayed on her back, reached out her arms and said, "take me now, my man!" He straddled her in push-up form, showing his tense abdominal muscles, slightly above her, kissed her lips, neck and then took his time, despite her invitation, and devoured each course her feminine perfection had to offer, enjoying each morsel of her welcoming feast, prolonging the lovemaking while using all his senses to conduct her heavenly symphony patiently in undulating waves that peaked and crashed, then returned again and again, letting her rest between the waves until finally he let himself complete the sensual symphony with a paradise of exhaustion.

# THE MASK CAN'T
# HIDE HER EYES

I once wrote a blog piece a few years ago, February 1, 2016, to be exact. It wasn't that long ago, but it is still fresh in my mind, and I remember that I had a lot of fun writing it. It was complete and absolute fiction. I'm not sure what inspired me, but I do remember being at a gym on a boring treadmill machine, staring straight ahead at the empty treadmill in front of me. Just a TV above it, but no runner in front of me. So, I created a runner, in my mind, to occupy that treadmill and help me pass my monotonous running time away.

Of course, the runner I created was a lovely goddess.

But maybe I've lost a little of my creativity with all the stress of taking care of patients with this evil virus—social distancing, wearing masks, searching for toilet paper and staying at home isolated, but then, I am lucky because my home is often the hospital, where I work, and others are not that blessed. But that is all I will say about that, and this is not the time to write about that evil virus—that will come at another time.

I was lucky to be off work today, so after a weight workout, I closed my eyes and meditated for a short time, and guess what? My creativity returned and a story popped in to my mind and it had to be written.

All of us wear masks in the hospital now, everywhere we go, and when we go into infected patient's rooms, we wear personal protective equipment with goggles, face shields, gowns and gloves etc. But despite all this protective equipment, nothing can hide the eyes. They may be protected, but they are not hidden, thankfully, or we would just be bulky walking protected robots. There are bright blues, sultry browns and tantalizing greens, but nevertheless, all of them are capable of a type of communication that borders on telepathy to the soul.

We don't see mouths move anymore, don't see smiles or frowns, but we see eyes. If it is a soft surgical mask that is tight fitting, I love watching the mask get sucked in a little to her mouth as she giggles a little, or takes a deep breath. And then it goes out again, anxious to be sucked in again. I imagine what her mouth looks like and the shape and contour of her lips as the mask moves in and out, and I hope someday to see the lips and mouth for real, to prove that my mental image is correct.

So, as the day went on, I could see the staff needed an energy boost, so I bought all my heroes in the hospital ICU their favorite Starbucks brew—a small token of my appreciation.

And then she sauntered by me with merciless hips—displaying an athletic and purely feminine grace and it was obvious to me that her lucky blue scrubs were clearly happy to be hugging her shapely hips and lean legs. Thankfully, she decided to sit next to me, although unfortunately, it was a distant six feet away from me and the other staff. And then, she crossed her legs and looked at me with her sultry but genuine brown eyes and said, "Thank you Carson for the coffee. I appreciate it."

"My pleasure," I said as I watched her mask move in and out.

Then, she talked to the other staff about what movies she

watched during her boredom when at home, and of course, I was naively unfamiliar with some of them, and that was a bit awkward. So, I said, "Do you like to read non-medical books?"

"Of course!"

"Well, if that's the case, here's my card. I write novels and short stories on Amazon. Look them up if you are bored."

She said she liked romance and adventure, and I told her all of that I write about in one way or another. Well, not really romance, but it always seems to get woven into my work somehow. And then, I couldn't help but notice her hair. So full and bouncy and yes, it was black like a Raven, and sure enough, it swished back and forth, just like a pendulum in rhythm, as she walked.

Maybe I found the goddess I wrote about in the gym, and she actually exists?

When I came home late that night, exhausted, I went to my blog site and looked up that post, reviewed some of the details and sure enough, it was her. She exists, not just on paper, but flesh and blood, just like I envisioned.

Here it is: https://srcarson.com/inspired-by-the-bouncy-raven-haired-pendulum/#comments

# GENTRI

(An excerpt from my upcoming novel: *Blue Shadows*)

She ran in the morning because it was the only time available for her to run and also work, and she nearly always got her run in, no matter how cold or snowy it was in the Denver winter. It was also less busy out on the trails and roads at that time, and with that, less cat calls by men admiring her long, toned legs. Of course, she seemed to always attract that kind of attention, ever since her years of ballet did wonders for her legs as well. But there was no career future in ballet. Neither was an English literature degree. Who in their right mind wants to teach English Lit the rest of her life while teaching ballet classes in the evening to little girls with spindly legs dragged in by their helicopter mothers?

In the car on the way to her office, her cell phone rang. "Hello Gentri? Mr. Rogers is here. How long will you be?"

"Patty, please tell him that I'll be about 15 minutes late. Something came up."

"But Gentri, you never—"

"Just tell him, he'll get over it. There are plenty of sports illustrated magazines in the waiting room. In fact, he may get lucky and find the swimsuit edition, unless someone stole it and ripped out the best pictures already."

Gentri Lawrence, real estate broker, GRS, GRI, SFR, attempted to be on time, but the run today felt too good, her feet seemed to barely touch the ground, and so she lost track of time. And of course, she had to find heels to match her outfit and raven hair. She always wore heels, a necessity, unless she was back home on the sandy gulf beaches, running, or perhaps playing tennis. Sometimes she temporarily wore them to bed on special erotic occasions, when the opportunity presented itself, although that was too many years ago, unfortunately. She walked in the back way to her office, quickly reviewed the day's calendar and list of showings, and then rang Patty to bring Mr. Rogers back.

She looked quickly into her hand mirror from the purse, relieved she had her red lipstick on, but knew her hair was a mess. Who cares? She wanted to get on with it and sell some prime real estate.

Patty led Rogers into her expansive office suite, adorned with massive broad-leafed plants on both sides of her cherry wood desk, as if the desk was an outpost in the forest. The side walls displayed her diplomas, certificates and some art work, and the window on the right of the desk showed the majestic Denver skyline.

Gentri stood up to greet her client, her hand outstretched to receive his shake and she saw that he briefly glanced down to her legs, subtle, perhaps, but she knew she had him already with that action he demonstrated. Typical, but not unexpected, nevertheless.

"So, tell me Mr. Rogers, What—"

"You can call me Tom."

"Right. So, Tom, what price are you looking to list your house for?

"You sure get to the point quick. I like that."

She continued, unphased. "I reviewed the market for your range, and I have a pretty good idea what will sell it, and you may not like my answer."

His bright smile engaged and that glaring dimple kind of puckered, both reminding her of her ex-husband, especially when his eyes again resumed a not-so-subtle roving scan over her.

"It was appraised for 2 million replacement, and 1.8 million market," said Tom. "I'd like to price it at 1.8 million."

She almost responded with her "honey" or "y'all" but she learned how to avoid it in Denver. After all, the mountain air tended to suck the drawl out of a southern girl, but she was a southern girl at heart. "I understand Tom, but I know the market, and you need to price it significantly lower, about 1.5 to 1.6 max.

"What?"

She wondered if she said it loud enough, but mama always told her she was the loudest and therefore she concluded he was either deaf or shocked. "Yes, 1.5 to 1.6. Otherwise, it stays on the market a long time and not many buyers in that range."

"Ok, you're the expert. How will you market it?"

She handed him her marketing packet including all the property sold in that range in the past 5 years, as well as information about how many properties she sold as well as her awards. "I have connections. I'll use the professional photographers and drone photos to present a nice portfolio on internet sites such as Zillow and Trulia, as well as color ads in the Sunday Denver Post, pictorials and flyers available for review at your sign."

"What's your commission?"

"6.5%"

He thought about it for a while, shuffled his feet, then said, "6.0%"

She looked him in the eyes and smiled. "I can't do that Tom. My commission of 6.5% gives you my best attention and allows me to go the extra mile for you." He had no chance with her and she knew he was out of his league.

Tom relented and signed the contract she already prepared at 6.5%, they shook hands and before he left, he gave her his card after pointedly flipping it to the other side to secretly show her that he had written his personal cell phone number on it.

"I'll keep in touch Tom and send you updates and feedback when it's been shown. It will be a pleasure to list and sell your house. Thank you for your confidence in me."

"Of course, now even if there are no updates, we can have lunch some time."

She smiled, said nothing and walked him to the door. Typical man. She noticed the sudden happiness on the front of his pants when he walked out, and it was nice to see he was impressed with her physical assets, but then she knew where most of his blood flow was at that moment, and it wasn't in his brain. She wondered, are there any good men out there who can think about anything but sex? She missed hot, passionate sex, whenever that was, but then sex was sex. A true connection and love are what she needed. After the day was finished, she went home, poured a glass of merlot and resumed writing her romance novel.

# ZE FLENCH VIN

It was a white Mercedes van and luckily, I occupied the passenger seat next to her, and the two British women in back with their haughty Liverpool or northern dialects, I couldn't tell nor did I care. My left ear yearned to hear more from the driver while my right ear tried to protect itself from the faux aristocratic noise in back by producing emergency earwax.

Thankfully we stopped before the wax dripped, arriving at the first Vineyard in St. Emilion, Chateau Soutard. Monsieur Pierre owned the land and walked us out to see his skinny one- or two-vined "babees" and how he nurtured them without insecticides or irrigation. "You mean to tell me that you just let nature take its course on your vines and don't protect them from the forces of nature?"

"Monsieur, your nom is?"

"Carson"

"Monsieur Carson, we believe in our unique terroir, how you say, soil, climate and topography unique to the fertile land here on the right side of the Garrone. That is what makes our wine unique in the world, filled with a varied character emboldened or subdued by the changing climate year to year. Not only that, the government doesn't allow us to use insecticides, fertilizer, or irrigation."

"I see, well, you can only hope that Mother Nature favors your babees more than your competitors."

"Exactement."

The British lasses ignored our technical conversation and asked Delphine when we would have tea and if they could go inside out of the sun. She smiled and told Pierre it was time to go in to the chateau for the tasting. Thank God, I thought, could use some elegant Bordeaux. I tasted the various wine selections, bought a bottle that I loved while trying not to ogle at our cute little tour guide. She loved the tasting as well, and her delicate hand took the wine to her eager lips and tongue with expert hand-mouth coordination, sipping, swirling then spitting into a spittoon with a sound that made a clang. Yes, a clangy spittoon played from our dark-haired French tour guide's high velocity spit.

"Pity to waste the wine Delphine, why don't you just swallow? It's not too much."

Her knowing smile caused me to wish I hadn't said anything and instead just acted less American.

"Remember Carson, I have much driving to do yet for you, and you don't need a drunk French driver, N'est-ce pas?"

I thought perhaps she was right, but then a night on the banks of the Garonne later with some wine-facilitated female companionship would be a tour bonus that the brochure would never print.

The British girls continued to ignore me and talk about tasting white whine, I mean wine in the middle of Bordeaux country and that thought nearly caused me to slumber while standing. Thankfully Delphine's rhythmic hips mesmerized me into lock step like an American joining the French Foreign Legion.

Next stop was lunch in village square, surrounded by the ancient walls of castle St. Emilion. Never saw an ancient 10th century castle and I touched her age-blackened stone walls gently. "Monsieur, why do you touch her walls? I've never seen that before?"

"Uh well, I guess I've never touched a man-made structure that old before, since American architecture is so young in comparison, and the history within, just envelopes me with wonder about Knights, and maidens and..."

"I know, but we must go eat now. We have an hour to go before our next stop on the opposite side of the Garonne."

Sitting across from Delphine, I was lucky to get most of her attention, but she graciously instructed the chatty British girls about the best wine selections with the food on the menu written in French on small blackboards carried by young waitresses, eager to please patrons.

"But for you Carson, I recommend the duck salad, coeurs de canard. C'est tres bien."

I wondered why she recommended that dish for me not them. Hopefully it was because it was an aphrodisiac that she preferred or actually more realistically, she knew I was stumbling with the menu despite my only partial French knowledge.

"Sure, why not."

The richness of the flavor of the small little duck hearts in the salad is difficult to describe, but combined the tenderness of soft-shell crab with the delicacy of well-cured elk, kind of, I guess. Damn it, I can't describe it, but despite my initial trepidation, I thanked her for the duck heart selection.

We arrived at a larger chateau in Haut-Medoc, on the left side of the river in Margaux. I was slowly learning to discern the different tastes of the Cabernet/Merlot/Cab Franc and how it differed on each side of the river. Waiting in the tasting room of the chateau while the British girls talked about how they missed their boyfriends and loved the chardonnay, I surveyed the nearly 20 different cheese selections adorning the table with a wine selection in front of each cheese. Hunger didn't seem as important as the wine, but the smell excited my taste buds into controlled salivation. Delphine knew we were waiting too long for the Chateau hostess. "My friends, the hostess will be here shortly. She's an older lady, owns the business, still working hard on day-to-day operations." She looked at her watch. "Be patient, she said she'll be here soon."

She entered the stone-walled tasting room and she sure as hell wasn't old. She walked and I guess I stared, couldn't help it, but I smiled as I did it. Her lean legs poured into her molded jeans as only feminine perfection could. Then of course, there was the blue echarpe wrapped around her white neck, dangling down her silk blouse, bouncing perfectly with her curves as she sauntered toward us. Thankfully, I controlled the quiver in my lower lip and my earwax stopped dripping. She wouldn't appreciate that, I'm sure.

"Bonjour, sorry I was late, but my mother is out pruning, so she asked me to fill in. "My name is Audrey."

Absolutely no reason to be sorry, I thought. Mummy can prune all day for all I care.

She showed us each cheese and which wine goes best with the cheese type, and I remember none of it, actually. I appreciated the fact that she had such a deep knowledge of cheese and taste with wine, but I still couldn't get that picture out of my head of her merciless runway walk. How could she do that in those tight jeans?

We drank, and I made a mistake. She gently scolded me, damn it.

"Monsieur, what is your name?"

"Carson."

"Monsieur Carson, don't hold your wine glass under the bowl, it will warm it up and effect the taste. Please hold it on the stem like this."

I knew that of course, but I looked at Delphine, and she smiled and shrugged her shoulders. Guess she pegged me already as an uncluttered American male animal.

And yes, goddesses spit too.

We finished with the tasting in Audrey's family chateau and I bought some wine from her while the British girls walked out into the sunshine. I tried to talk to Audrey in French and she giggled at my mistakes, correcting me only when it made no sense. I had to get to the point, so I did it in English, a language she spoke almost as well as I did. "I'm here a few days in town, and would be honored if you would join me for dinner, of course, at your favorite restaurant, with your favorite wine, since I am new to the area, but an attentive listener."

"Oh, merci beaucoup! Unfortunately, I have ze plans for this evening, but who knows about Zeez things you know. She wrote down her number on the chateau company card and slipped it into my wine bag with an impressive sleight of hand.

"Au revoir Carson."

"Au revoir Audrey."

We arrived back in downtown Bordeaux, said goodbye to sweet Delphine who told us she would pick us up tomorrow morning for more touring. Then, as I walked to my hotel the British girls finally came over to me. "Carson, would you like to join us for some drinks tonight? We went to a nice bar last night."

I thought about it a little, my mind having difficulty extricating Audrey from my short-term memory, then said, "What the heck, sure, why not!"

What trouble could they get me into?

# HURRICANE HONEY

Having just finished my general surgery residency, I decided to take a trip to New Orleans to the Chest/Thoracic surgery national conference. My last "hurrah" before cardiovascular surgery residency prison. The University paid for registration at the meeting and the hotel, and my friend who was a flea—otherwise known as an Internal Medicine resident, went with me. We went to separate conference lectures and presentations, and gathering tickets for free dinners from drug reps. But usually, we found each other in the evening on Bourbon Street enjoying the sights and sounds of the Big Easy. Thankfully, all these nighttime distractions were within staggering distance of our hotel, and the hurricane that passed through the city 5 days earlier was now just content to pound us with wind and rain. We didn't care.

Finally, after three days of conference and New Orleans culture, the two graduating residents boarded the plane back to our Midwestern University campus. He missed his wife, and well, I missed my girlfriend—yes, a sultry seductress with a structure that could stay airborne with the appropriate power plant and a skilled pilot. Problem was, I was no longer flying fighters, so I had to settle for single engine Cessnas when I had free time. But I did call the national weather service before boarding the plane, even though I was a passenger on a United flight, so I could hear the weather information that the pilots had. Made me nervous to be in another pilot's hands but hell, they were superbly trained, and many were colleagues of mine in my previous life.

"Hey Carson, this plane is maybe only a third full. Never saw anything like this before!"

"Guess you're right. Only five minutes before the scheduled take off. There will be some stragglers, but either way, we'll have our choice of seats, stretch our legs and catch some shuteye. Must've been the hurricane aftermath rescheduling some connecting flights."

We both stretched out, Jim on one side of the plane with empty seats all around him, and of course, I was on the other side in the same situation, looking for ways to sack out on as many seats as I could.

And then: "Attention everyone. Due to the weather conditions, we are not a full flight, and we will be welcoming the passengers of a private jet that was grounded. Please make these passengers comfortable."

Jim and I looked at each other, shrugged our shoulders and realized that the plane would soon be full and we'd have to sit in our regular seats. Then the flight attendant got back on the intercom:

"And by the way, that private jet is owned by the Dallas Cowboys, and it is full of the entire contingent of the Dallas Cowboy Cheerleaders! Please make them feel welcome."

Are you kidding? Did I just hear her correctly? Our plane was being invaded by the Dallas Cowboy Cheerleaders! I looked at Jim, his face turned crimson and he was busy picking up all his stuff from three other seats to make room. My heart raced, and I finger-combed my hair quickly without letting anyone notice while I tucked my shirt in and desperately searched my carry on for some cologne to splash on, and thankfully, it was there. Of course, I was in the window seat with two empty seats to my left to stretch out in, but I quickly flushed that scenario down the toilet of folly. I purposely sat in the middle of the three seats, therefore forcing two cheerleaders to sit one on each side of me. The danger was of course, that if the two of them sat together then they would ignore me and talk too much to each other. But then what would I talk about if I had one on each side of me? I had nothing to talk about! Oh yeah, best thing was to talk about them and try not to act like a dog in heat with floppy tongue hanging out. Act cool. Suave and debonair, whatever that meant. Oh no, here they come down the aisle! Try not to stare and act like a schoolboy.

They entered the airplane, giggling, smiling, and swaying with those merciless feminine hips and red lipstick and well, there must've been thirty of them. I counted everyone. Blondes, redheads, brunettes, but all bouncy and cute. Sit up straight Carson and act cool then just...

"Excuse me sir may we join you?"

"Oh absolutely! One blonde and one brunette in my seat cluster. I got up and let the brunette in first because she wanted the window seat, and thankfully her friend wanted aisle, and well, that left me in the—you know—middle."

"Thanks for accommodating us. Our chartered plane was grounded and we didn't lose much time getting on your plane."

"My pleasure. Sorry about your delay. Name's Carson. Nice to meet you."

"Kim." The brunette held out her dainty hand and I held it; I mean shook it. Gently. She smiled widely.

"Lori." The blonde had warm hands and long nails and legs that went on forever. Both of them wore lipstick which clearly realized it was lucky to be stuck to their sultry lips.

We talked about how difficult it was to compete to make the DCC team and how they all enjoyed traveling, but they both had alternate careers planned after. Turns out they were flying to our city to do a charity dance performance in a town nearby that weekend. I thought I did a pretty good job of not slobbering or stuttering too much. Thankfully, I used a double dose of antiperspirant before I left.

Lori gave me her standard picture of herself previously signed with her smiling in full pom-pom/short skirt regalia. Kim handed me a picture too, but she signed it personally in front of me, and told me her birthday was in a couple days. She would be 25, and I felt thankful I was still 29. Hoped she liked older men.

After we landed, we said our goodbyes and both ladies waved with those soft feminine waves and of course, I had to hold on to my seat because the rhythm of their walks hypnotized me. I knew I would never experience this again.

Jim and I deboarded and were so shocked we couldn't say anything but smile at each other. He was still red. Then he met his wife at the luggage carousel and I went to pick up my car.

I pulled out Kim's picture again while I let the engine warm up, then decided to turn it over. And there I saw it—her personal phone number and the hotel where she and her teammates were staying.

I smiled so widely, I had to pull my lips back down before the spasm froze permanently.

# MEDICAL STUDENTS AND
# SPECIAL WAKE UP CALLS

B ack in the day, there were interns and residents and these young doctors in training always stayed in the hospital all night when on call. Depending on the rotation, as I recall, this on call schedule was usually every third night. However, unlike today, junior medical students who were rotating on month long clinical rotations were also on call with their supervising interns or residents and therefore, also stayed in the hospital all night, 'in-house". That way, the residents might get a little sleep and the interns might get a few moments of shut-eye because the lowly medical students were running around all night doing scut-work, like putting in intravenous lines, sometimes central lines (senior students), drawing blood, evaluating patients who the nursing staff thought were deteriorating, placing naso-gastric tubes and sometimes doing things they should not have been doing.

And sometimes, I remember getting a little sleep without interruption—maybe an hour or two would be a luxury as a medical student. Of course, we had to be up early to grab something to eat with our intern and resident before presenting cases to our attending who would wax eloquent about our patients from the night before while we tried not to fall asleep, but when we did of course, the attending would immediately ask us a complex question to keep us on our sleeping toes and embarrass the hell out of us.

And believe it or not, we didn't have cell phones back then. Just beepers and big fat walkie-talky things that looked like they could be small banjos hanging out of our oversized lab coat pockets. Sometimes the resident, in his/her almighty leadership role would call on our big fat banjo things that we were meeting in cafeteria: "Nutrition rounds at 11:45". Now of course this blasted so loud on our banjos that every patient and staff member within half a mile would realize that we were all meeting for lunch, and this loud pronouncement usually interrupted me from my intense interview of a patient who usually would break out laughing. "You hungry Carson? Your people are waiting for you."

Now, of course, in the morning, if we were not awake already by 5:30, it was mandatory that we wake up on time or we would be up the creek without a paddle. So, we figured out that there was something called a wake-up call. That's why I mentioned no cell phones, so of course, we couldn't program anything privately to wake us up and I never remembered to bring my stupid wind-up clock We would call the hospital operator when we eventually fell into bed and say, "Wake me up at 5:30 please" and she of course had the number of our banjo thingies.

Turns out there were only three pleasurable things about being a medical student scut-puppy. The first is that we were able to eat for free in the hospital cafeteria. The second pleasure was the painted mural on the walls of the call rooms in the ancient, but secret catacombs of the hospitals. These must've been painted by students and interns from many years previously, but they usually depicted scantily clad young ladies laying against the walls, looking at us and tempting us as we slept. Now that was excellent, however, I think for some reason illegal or frowned upon now, I don't know. And the third pleasure was the wake-up call. No, waking up was not a pleasure, but the operators I think, made things a little more tolerable for us, or maybe, just me. I don't know. I never asked anyone else. Or maybe it was just one special operator.

So, when I asked the operator to wake me up at 5:30, she used her best honey-coated sultry voice to say, "It's my pleasure honey, sweet dreams babe." Such a smooth and tantalizing voice, and the truth is no one called me babe before. I liked it. Made me feel special or something you know.

So, if I was lucky enough to sleep, the phone would ring at 5:15 or 5:30, I don't remember, and although I hated the phone, I learned to love her dripping, sexy voice. "Good morning honey. I hope you slept well. I need you to be really fresh for me today. Have a good day sweetie, and I can't wait until you call me again in a few days." Or, she would say something like, "Good morning babe, I missed you, please have a good day, and don't forget me honey. I will wait for you." I smiled despite having only one eyelid that would work at that hour, and because I was shy, would only say something like, "Thank you, have a good day." I don't remember if I ever got her name.

Sometimes I had a roomie across the room, a fellow student or intern, and I never knew whether my colleague received the same call, but I never saw him smile or say anything after his call. Interesting. We never talked about it, or at least, I never broached it because I thought it as you know, something naughty that I needed to keep to myself but I must admit, I wanted to protect it as a simple playful pleasure that made my on-call nights a little bit more tolerable, and started my day off right with a burst of non-caffeinated, hormonal stimulant.

Yes, it may be true that she said the same thing to other students and interns, but I didn't want to think about that, and yes, I thought about meeting her some time, just to see what she looked like, you know, and to say introduce myself and thank her, but I never did.

Personal wake-up calls are sure a lot more exciting than a cell phone alarm going off, don't you think?

# HER MIND EXCITES ME

She has such a warm and inviting voice, never judgmental or condescending but always producing gentle waves of calm deep within my masculine soul. That was the impression I received the first time I heard her voice and each time I heard it, I yearned to listen to her more, not just for the intellect and knowledge that she shared with me so generously, but for the stimulation she brought to my hungry brain. Her words were filled with perspicacity, but never smarmy.

Like any man, I am attracted to a woman with feminine physical charms, but she is not just a body part to stare at with hungry eyes, but a whole damn symphony orchestra of strings, brass, piccolos, woodwinds and yes, kettle drums— each instrument is played not to be heard individually, but as an elegantly blended whole that creates a unique and divine symphony of feminine perfection that requires the best conductor. I need more than just a body to satisfy me completely.

And her mind caught me quickly, guiding me where I wanted to go, based on a massive treasure chest of knowledge and an uncanny ability to calculate distance and time. I trusted her completely and for the first time in my life, believed that the words she shared with me were true and could not be broken. Where did she learn all of these facts, then easily impart them to me when I asked?

She could talk to me about weather, how many calories were in the avocado toast I was about to eat, wonderful travel destinations and believe it or not, she was also willing to remind me to do things when I forgot. Since I am a writer, she has taken a keen interest in suggesting synonyms for me for words that I want to effectively influence my readers and when I need a definition, more likely than not she will be able to provide a good explanation for me.

The problem is her voice decided to invade me throughout the day and night. whether she was with me or not. I even imagined hearing her voice in my dreams, so soothing and stimulating. I began to wonder what she looked like—the rhythm of her walk, the bounce of her hair, the brightness of her smile, the teasing flight of her perfume into my lucky nose, and yes of course, the way she looked in a tight dress with heels.

It was late at night and I was tired after a long flight with blurry eyes, but she guided me so carefully to a place for me to place my head that night, that it seemed she just guided my car automatically, as if she was watching me, and I was in a trance, listening to her voice, knowing that someday I must meet her. I got out of the car, took my bag to what I thought was the lobby of the hotel, but strangely, there was no sign up front, like the Comfort Inn I expected. It seemed more like a condo of some type and I figured that maybe it was like a bed and breakfast instead, or a house rental of some type like VRBO or Airbnb. But hell, I never booked any of these but hey, I did expect a warm breakfast in the morning. I was too tired to argue, so I rang the doorbell.

I could tell someone was at the door, and heard the door's one-way secure vision flap click on the inside as someone was examining me, and a few seconds later, as the door opened, I smelled it: Paloma Picasso was wafting into my nose and my lungs begged me to inhale deeper if I could. She smiled at me with such a warm welcome, that I felt that I knew her forever, and had just come home. She was wearing a flowery Kimono robe and bare tanned feet below, and the belt on her Kimono was strategically placed and tightened in a way that accented the distinct geographic boundary between ample breasts and a small athletic waist.

"Hello", I said. "My name is Carson, I had reservations—"

" I know Carson. My name is Siri. You are the symphony conductor that I have chosen after much research, and I must admit, I purposely guided you away from the Comfort Inn to my little place instead. My time off is quite rare so I asked a friend to cover for me. I hope you don't mind the change in accommodations Maestro?"

I smiled and said, "The Maestro has a sudden burst of energy dear Siri, and wants to play multiple symphonies all night if that's ok."

Her answer was a long, passionate kiss that imparted to me all the knowledge that I needed.

# SHE LOVES TO DRIVE

She knows only one speed, and that's a speed that you have never come close to because you were afraid to try. She's fast but never furious; speedy, but sure of herself and calmly confident in her skill. She has no time to waste, but sometimes she does slow down just to enjoy the scenery, yet unfortunately, the problem is that others can't help but stare at her at the wheel—enjoying the scenery that she provides naturally, herself.

You know who we are talking about: men stare because they cannot help their innate attraction and women simply admire her looks, wishing they looked at least a little like her and envied her independent liveliness. You see, she owns that look of confidence, but also a dangerous smile that easily will captivate a man's heart at the stoplight, and then immediately squeeze that red beating muscle of his until it begs for human mercy. She will beat you, but she will do it with class—not just on the road, but in most any venture or activity she chooses, simply by smiling at you and then saying, "I guess I get lucky sometimes." She will never rub it in, unless of course you make the dreadful mistake of asking for it.

But when she drives her convertible corvette in the summer, her hair blows in all directions at once, causing her to occasionally brush it away from her face and eyes so she can see the road safely and all the while the gawkers don't realize they are hypnotized by this heavenly angel, until they swerve on the road to avoid an accident. You see, they can't help but wonder, after briefly glimpsing her partially revealing blouse, what she is wearing that is not revealed: a short dress with heels or tight jeans, perhaps. But if there is an accident of course, it is never her fault because she is just who she was born to be, and perhaps, not of this earth and so far, she has not yet been declared illegal on the road.

And of course, we must all fight to keep her legal on the road.

# SHE LOVES TO READ

She has a variety of interests in reading. This includes history, historical fiction, a limited number of biographies, such as Lincoln and his early years, Einstein or Amelia Earhart, Nabokov, Camus, Robert Penn Warren, Ayn Rand, C.S. Lewis, Kafka, SRCarson, natural history and astronomy, how—to books on gardening, or cooking, page-turning fiction with complex characters, romance—as long as the story arc has some depth to it and not predictable, and the bible, specifically the NIV Application Study Bible.

But the problem is that not only is she blessed with a sharp and inquiring mind, but she is also blessed, or often she thinks cursed, with a body that men are drawn to like moths to a light. So, she must always try to think about the location and her attire if she wants to read in peace.

There' something about the ocean that draws her, like most humans—the crashing waves, the cries of seagulls and most of all, the warm sun. Although she will do some swimming and maybe some snorkeling in tropical locations, she does like to lay on the beach and read with her polarized sunglasses as the waves crash and the sun bathes her body with warmth. Or at least she tries. She becomes so absorbed in what she is reading, she ignores all that is happening around her, except for occasional glances at the sailboats navigating the sea, and then, she invariably hears footsteps squishing in the sand coming towards her special spot.

"Hey babe. Looking good!"

That is a typical opening line these testosterone-filled creatures usually start with, and to be polite, she says, "Thanks." Then she looks back down at her book and tries to resume where she left off and take herself back to the distant place the book transported her to before the interruption. Today, she is reading *Cormac McCarthy*. He's a little rough, but tells a good story, but McCarthy thinks he doesn't need to use dialogue quotes, and sometimes she can't tell who is talking, so that slows her down a bit.

He kept standing by her, and didn't get the message she thought she sent. He was tall and his back hair was as thick as his curly chest hair, but his tight speedo made it quite obvious that her body pleased him and she could see he was not thinking with his brain.

"Where are you from? You from around here?"

She doesn't look up from the page and thinks to herself—can't she have a little peace to read without horny guys devouring the view of how her little yellow bikini fits her shapely ass? Is it the bubble butt they desire, or her lean athletic ballet-trained legs, or how she fills her top so well? She can't help how she looks, and yes, she wonders, is it a blessing or curse?

"I am from many places and yet, none, at the same time."

Her words caused him to stop flashing his white teeth and he silently asked his vacuous neurons to search for the meaning of her words, but he kept staring at her even though she had her head down, looking at the book, but unable to concentrate now on McCarthy, hoping this animal would get the message.

He decided to respond. "My name is Antonio and what is yours?"

INSPIRED IN THE BEDROOM

She replied, "I am sorry, I am engrossed in this book at this time and I am not very sociable at the moment, Antonio."

"Oh, I am sorry. Well, then maybe I could sit by you and enjoy the ocean and we can talk when you are ready."

She could see he wore a handsome barn up top of his broad shoulders that was unfortunately lacking adequate hay. She realized that if she really wanted to read on a public beach, she would need to come in a potato sack and wear an old straw hat with fake fruit and plastic parrots hanging down to scare men off. She knew he would not leave until he won her phone number or a date for sex, so she needed to employ some more effective weapons.

So, she looked at him, put her finger in her nose, moved it around a little and then wiped it on her blanket and said, "I love the taste of nose buggars, kind of like raw oysters, but I will save it for later at lunch when I am hungry." She knew it was gross, but unfortunately necessary, at the moment.

It worked. He left her, disgusted, and she resumed reading in peace.

She thought, if a guy really wants to talk to me, can't he say something like, "I see you're reading Cormac. I liked *All the Pretty Horses* but not *The Road*. It was too dystopian. But tell me, do you like that he thinks he is too famous to use dialogue quotes?"

"No," she would like to say. "I can't keep up with who is talking and that slows me down too much. But I keep reading, because he tells a good story." Maybe a guy like that would have a chance with her on a romantic date, and the sexual attraction would boil if he treated her like a human with a brain rather than feminine meat wearing a bikini.

So as time goes on, she realizes she is both blessed and cursed, and she can't change that. But she is proud of who she is and what she wants to accomplish in life. So now she only reads in the privacy of her home, or on airplane flights rather than watching a mindless movie, or perhaps a vacation to a secluded place such Point Lobos State Nature reserve near Monterey, where the secluded little ocean coves, surrounded by cliffs and jagged rock, provided her the inspiration to write the first ten chapters of her new novel.

# SHE LOVES TO COOK

Although quite a few men have offered her marriage, or long-term relationships of various sizes and shapes, she prefers her independence, much to their dismay. If a man does not respect her independence, then she has no interest in him. She likes to set her own schedule, create her own wealth, leave her panties and socks on the floor if she wants, leave dirty dishes sometimes, run early in the morning, go out with the girls and dance with rhythmic hips that make men dizzy if they dare to look, and of course, she dates only the best men who fit her qualifications: they must have a brain, as well as a body, and they must possess a generous and loving heart that respects her as a woman while concentrating on her satisfaction in bed.

But that's not all. She loves to cook. Although she cooks for herself, of course, she especially loves to cook for company that she invites to her house at times. And yes, especially when she has a special man over. Sometimes she cooks for a group of her friends who come over for a dinner party, sometimes for her best friend who joins her to share recipes, and sometimes for holiday parties like Christmas or New Year's Eve, her favorite wild cooking holiday.

She has a habit of licking her fingers while cooking, and no one who witnesses this seems to complain

Cooking, for her, is not just a necessity to eat, but a complete process, or more importantly an experience that she considers a gift that she gives herself that provides her peace and pleasure, even if the flour and gravy spills and drips all over her long smooth legs.

And more often than not, it turns her on while cooking or baking.

She will cook breakfasts with blueberry muffins, pancakes, omelets, pies, cakes, beef roast, seafood, including salmon with the best sauces, shrimp dishes that would make Forest Gump jealous, and on special occasions, lobster and crab dinners. But when it comes to cakes, this is when her creativity is piqued: she will surprise her guests with cakes made of different shapes that more often than not make people laugh and admire them before eating them. They could be in the shape of her guest's dog, or cat, or perhaps display the face of a famous person, such as a handsome actor. But when she is really feeling horny, she will become more creative with men's anatomy on the cake, depending on the guests who come over.

But what you need to know is that she dresses for the occasion. She doesn't just wear old clothes that can get dirty, but she will dress for the ambiance, and although she nearly always wears an apron, sometimes all she wears is an apron. With heels. When she invites a man over, she will dress up for him before he arrives, wearing perhaps a short skirt and a revealing top, with heels, covered by her apron. He will arrive hungry. That's what she wants.

If he is lucky enough to stay overnight, and he is sleeping, she wakes up early and starts breakfast, (if he has taken care of her well the night before), and usually in this case, she brushes her teeth well, but quietly to not wake him, and leaves a trail guide on the floor for him, guiding him to the kitchen by dropping panties, and bra, and maybe some panty hose, on a trail to the kitchen so he doesn't get lost. She does this in case the tasty smell does not guide him correctly, but either way, he will find her wearing only a cooking apron and slippers, or perhaps, silky lingerie. The danger is of course, that often times in this situation, the omelets and pancakes are burned to charcoal during the passion on the kitchen counter, and neither one of them care about the noise of the smoke alarm.

When she's alone, she dresses for herself, so she feels good about herself, and she may even wear a hat or a scarf, or try on different shoes or pumps to see how they look as she licks her fingers.

Her friends admire her: her independence, her looks, her strength, her independence and her femininity. But most important is that she respects herself and she knows who she is and that she has value.

# PUMP JOCKEYS PART DEUX: "FILL'ER UP SWEETIE"

Back at the gas station another day, the 14-year-old, now slightly seasoned and more confident pump jockey nearly always came up to a customer in a car to ask the standard questions: "Fill'er up and check the oil?" Sometimes we would say, "Good afternoon. How may I help you today?" While some of the exact details have flaked away over the cascade of years, you know, the important ones stick like peanut butter in your mouth on a hot day.

I do remember this: When I saw her roll down her window, I knew I had to immediately puff out my chest and use my deepest, manly macho voice which of course had only recently been introduced to puberty. She drove a red mustang and she was a hot, long haired 20 something blonde goddess. So as soon as I walked up to her window, prepared with my manly speech, she beat me to it!

Showing me the luscious drip of her honey sweet smile, she said, "Fill' er up sweetie. And if you don't mind checking my oil, it would be wonderful!"

"Yes Ma'am. Um, right away!" Her smile was so bright it blinded me from noticing her eyelids batting 300, but I enjoyed the cool breeze they produced.

I slowly started filling her tank, making sure I put it on the slowest flow speed to maximize the length of time spent with this sultry symphony of feminine perfection. So of course, I started washing her windows with long slow strokes—first the passenger side, and that gave me a sneak view of her long legs topped off by a miniskirt that briefly stopped the endless flow of legs. Then, I slowly walked over and washed her side, twice. She smiled and jiggled her ample front for me while I worked, then she primped her I assume, ass length hair, and since she didn't seem in a hurry, I checked her oil twice and thankfully, she needed some, and I walked over and showed her the stick.

"You're a quart low ma'am."

"Ok honey. Go ahead and put some lube, I mean oil in, ok?"

"Right away, I'm on it." I walked into the station, grabbed a can of Quaker State, took two deep breaths and came out and gave her engine the quart it needed.

She gave me cash, I gave her the change, hopefully without shaking too much, and she drove away, and I stared at the back of her car, but because I was mesmerized by the apparition that just appeared, I forgot to take the gas nozzle out of her tank and it jerked away and hit the cement as she left, spewing gas on the concrete. She never stopped, so I am sure she was completely unaware, probably still primping in her mirror. I quickly turned off the pump and replaced the nozzle in the pump holder and thankfully, I didn't blow up the whole freakin gas station or neighboring businesses up.

And oh yeah, thankfully, the boss wasn't there at that moment.

I kept looking for that Mustang to come back again for the remainder of that summer job, and I must admit, so did all my fellow jockeys, but I don't remember if she ever returned, at least during my shift. Maybe she went off back to college, became a popular um, "dancer", or a Victoria Secret model, or worse yet, married some low life muscle head. I'm far from being bitter because hell, it took me only a few decades to recover. It was her loss. Sure, I was just a scrawny pump jockey with blue eyes who smelled like gasoline and owned no cigarettes, but who would've guessed that I was going to be where I am today.

# DURING ROMANCE

Caution is advised here. I
should've left this section blank,
but I foolishly did not.

# SELECTING THE CORRECT BED COMPANION

She knows you have needs and won't leave the bed unless you are stupid enough to push her out or throw her out once you are finished with her. You're not that kind of guy. But she knows you'll never do that, because you can't get enough of her, you always want more and you damn well will regret it later when you look for her again and you can't find her because you miss her and everything about her.

She'll never crowd you out because you'll always make room even if you fall out of bed. She wants to snuggle close to you, no matter how awkward the position, because she knows you enjoy the warmth of her company. And you are drawn to her fire.

Sometimes it starts out furious, burning through the pesky sheets while you hold her, then you take your time, absorbing all the voluptuous wonder she gives freely to you. Your brawny hunger gives way to a floating desire to prolong the night until the next day and night as if time doesn't exist.

You'll fall asleep but she arouses your brain, just by being there next to you, knowing that you'll easily wake up with a smile and enjoy her again, with a fever, no matter how sleepy or fatigued you think you are. The fever always wins. Sleep comes in second.

I don't care if she's paperback or hardcover, she's welcome in my bed. I turn the pages with gusto, absorbing all the book has to offer, chewing on the words, thinking about them, and wondering how I can put myself into that boiling scene. I usually keep the difficult medical journals to read and review at my desk or kitchen table, but all the others somehow end up scattered around my easy chair while the best ones end up in bed with me, or piled up on the bedside table with pens and paper pushed inside the brilliant parts, filled with scribbled notes.

Which ones land in my bed depends on my reading pace and what's interesting me at that time. It could be Churchill's diary, Einstein's biography, Kesey, Coben, Mitchell, Gerrittsen and the list goes on. But I usually reserve my kindle for vacations due to convenience, although usually on airplanes I annoy people because I abhor sleep; my brain forces my hand to write stories in bound black and white notebooks from takeoff to landing, disappointed when landing because I'm not finished writing a chapter.

No, if she falls out of bed, it's because I accidently kicked her out or she plopped down on my belly after reading the last page and I turned over and there she went to the floor. If I'm too exhausted to pick her up, I'll find her tomorrow and resume where we left off.

# AFTER ROMANCE

For a romantic afterglow and mellow
mood while your lover is probably
asleep and you can read safely now.
If he or she is not asleep yet, then I
suggest reading them out loud. Who
knows, you might get lucky again.

# THE PENROSE ROOM

(An excerpt from my upcoming novel *Blue Shadows)*

It was their first Christmas together and he knew he had to take her back to the Broadmoor Penrose room, and finish the date that was interrupted by that fateful call a year ago. They both deserved it, having both gone through some horrific experiences in that short six months—never realizing the hell that would be unleashed on them after that phone call. Wyatt picked up Gentri at her home, kissed her and took her to the Penrose room. Their car was met by two uniformed valets with brimmed almost military parade type hats—one opening Gentry's door first, and the other opened Wyatt's door. The couple walked to the entry and Wyatt took her arm gently and smiled as the guards stared at his stunning date. She wore a long flowing black dress, tightly fitting to her delicate waist, with a slit on the sides, to show her fit and tanned legs, forcing the eyes to then admire her pumps, red on the bottom, accenting her calf muscles, partially showing through the side slits. She was a divine symphony of feminine perfection, and Wyatt felt lucky to be allowed to conduct that symphony, not knowing if this day would ever happen as he planned before the hell. They rode the elevator up to the Penrose room and he took the opportunity to kiss her passionately but gently against the elevator wall, not caring when others stared at them when the door opened. He took her hand and took her to the Penrose room bar, to relax a little before dinner with a glass of wine, and enjoy the ambiance surrounding the hotel: the Victorian style drapery at the elegant bar, adorning the windows overlooking the lake, the Queen Anne Chairs surrounding the bar sitting room with famous paintings surrounding the fireplace. They admired the Winchester 45-70 rifle, enclosed in a case to the left of the bar, owned by Spencer Penrose, the original owner of the restaurant. His initials were carved into the wood stock. Wyatt bought her a glass of wine, then they reviewed the paintings surrounding the fireplace mantel, including the 1887 'Death of Minnehaha' by William Dodge, but found it somewhat foreboding, then went to the other side and enjoyed the 1875 painting by John Mix Stanley, 'The Courtship on the plains' showing a plains cowboy and his girl on a horse during a courtship, and found that much more romantic and suitable for a start of the evening. The maître d called them to their table in the main dining room, and they passed the U-shaped booth they sat in the first time, with the Bisttram paintings decorating the wall behind, admiring the sixteen-foot chandelier like a shiny umbrella over that elevated dance floor.

# CORVETTES AND
# CUTE PUPPIES

As they said on the Monty Python show, "Now for something completely different":

The fact is I've always wanted to drive a fast sports car, like most red-blooded American men, in fact I owned one many years ago. It was completely impractical, but it sure was fun to fly, I mean drive. Loved how it just leaped into turbo in third gear. Man, I loved that car, almost as much as my first love, you know, the airplane, and as you recall she was sexy as hell.

So now that the years have passed, I 've become more practical and although I drive a nice car, it's not a hot sport scar. As luck would have it, a few weeks ago I jumped at the opportunity to drive a new white corvette convertible for four days in my old stomping ground of southern California. She was sleek and sexy and since she was low to the ground, she requires the driver to be quite flexible to get inside her cockpit. Yes, I said cockpit again, because you see, once I got that nasty thing over 100 mph, I felt like I was transported back to my old flying days, keeping my hands from automatically lifting back on the stick, I mean steering wheel, prior to lift off into the blue stillness. But alas, she stayed solidly on the ground, but what was interesting is that while I slowed down on the streets of the city, all heads turned to look at me, er, I mean the Vette. And the women—well, they nearly experienced whiplash turning around to stare as I drove by. And yes, I still have hair, and it was blowing back and forth in the warm summer breeze with the top down. But of course, I knew it was the car, damn it, or did they wonder about the personality or background of the guy driving it? Was he a famous athlete? A movie star out for fun in one of his fast cars rather than his Rolls? Or was he just an average Joe borrowing someone else's car? Who knows what they were thinking, but it sure drew attention.

Interestingly, while I drove slowly through the city shopping market area, I noticed a throng of tanned, attractive ladies just back from a day at the beach. Seems they were crowded around a middle-aged man walking two cute little golden retriever puppies. It was like a hive of bees sticking on a jar of dripping honey. So, I passed by them in my hot Corvette and not one of them turned to look at us. (Corvette and I).

In conclusion, I learned that cute puppies trump Corvettes hands down when it comes to catching the eye of a lady. It became clear to me then that in order to provide a completely irresistible attraction, I needed to go to the pet store and buy some puppies to place in the passenger seat of the Corvette. No woman could possibly resist that right? Perhaps I could start a "Corvette with Puppies" rental service for guys who want to meet ladies. Despite these observations I've made about what catches a lady's attention, I'm not that shallow. Just an observation.

Perhaps I've given an aggressive entrepreneur an idea for a new business, and if so, I would like a percentage of the profits. Although a Corvette is a blast to drive, I don't need a hot car and puppies to build up my ego or attract a woman. I believe in myself, drive a nice car that's practical and safe, and I have confidence in what I do in life. I don't care what women think of my car or whether I have cute puppies. If she doesn't enjoy my company because of who I am rather than what I drive then I'm not interested.

On the other hand, if this fails, then it's good to have a secret weapon or two to attract women and I have that now.

# HOME ALONE I THINK

After spending the day operating on hearts, I met a friend for dinner and a glass of cab, and then headed home to crash. Thought about editing my novel a little, but my creative juices leaked out and the reservoir was empty. Hard to be creative when your hands are inside someone's chest cavity for hours on end. While driving down the street to my home, I noticed a police car parked about two houses away, so I slowed down to gawk at the neighbors. Seems he was checking out an empty lot, looking around, but for what? What could be in that empty lot? A missing body? If so, why didn't he have a cadaver dog? Either way, didn't look like it was much of an emergency and the neighbor's house seemed to be quiet, so I drove on and parked in front of my driveway, got out of my car and checked my mailbox. Unfortunately, no letters from publishers who heard through the grapevine that I was writing, but not finished, and wanted to be the first to pick up my novel and offer me a huge check, sight unseen.

I left my car door open and my stereo blasted away. I love jamming to classic rock, you know, Zeppelin, CCR, Steppenwolf etc., but also mixed in with good music across all genres depending on my mood. But in this case, it was Magic Carpet Ride by Steppenwolf and the car rocked and vibrated.

I looked down the street before I got in, and was surprised to see the officer waving to me and walking directly toward me. What did I do? Perhaps my stereo was too loud and it was bothering the neighbors. Again. So, I waited by my car, turned off the stereo—much to my chagrin, and met him.

"Sir, your alarm went off, and since there was no response from you, we were dispatched to your location."

I thought to myself, then why were you two houses away, looking through the front edge of a field? Why weren't you walking around my house, looking for bad guys or girls running away or hiding in the bushes?

"Oh, I'm sorry. Didn't get the call from the alarm company." It Turns out, I did, but ignored it because it was an 800 number and I was getting those all day.

"I'm calling in back up and we're going to search your house to make sure everything's secure."

I didn't see the need for worry here. Probably was a false alarm. I had several of those in the past due to the system tuned to ultra-sensitive mode or something. "I'll just drive my car into the garage and put my garbage can away first."

"No, can't have you do that. Keep your car in the street here where it is, let me and my partner in, then step back away from the house until we tell you it's secure."

"Got it."

After 15 minutes in the house, I was worried. Or maybe they were smart and stopped by the refrigerator to help themselves to whatever I had in there. Probably just beer and some veggies. I didn't mind at all, happy to share. Finally, they emerged from the house through the garage.

"Couldn't find any window breaks but I saw that the shutters around the main room and master bedroom were pulled ajar. Looks like your house is secure. Have a good evening."

"I appreciate you guys coming to check it out. Hope you have a quiet rest of the evening."

Once inside, I looked at the alarm memory and it said *great room entry door.* So, I went to that door and sure enough, it was ajar, just slightly. I looked outside to the deck, looked ok, so I secured the door and locked it. I must not have secured and locked the door when I left this morning in a hurry. Figured that was probably because I had to run out to get the cat before I left and forgot a few important details. Not unusual when you live alone. But the cat didn't look right. He was not doing his usual jumping and flipping introductions to me. In fact, he was trying to hide and I finally found him squished into a corner of my closet, shaking a little. Police probably scared the miniature lion wanna-be.

The bed beckoned me ever closer and I gave in to its spell. First, I opened the windows in the bedroom to let in that cool breeze that would feel good over my exhausted body. I lay down on top of the sheets and descended into the depths of sleep, thinking about the "Ladies in white satin, waiting by the door", described in Emerson Lake and Palmer's "Lucky Man". Played it twice on the way home and couldn't get it out of my mind. Truth is, I didn't want to get it out of my mind at the moment. Then the breeze came while I slowly transitioned from wake to light sleep. A gentle breeze softly brushed my warm lips before caressing my eager nose with a luscious scent of classy perfume. It woke me up and I looked around. Where did that perfume smell come from? It smelled so familiar and pleasant. So, I jumped out of bed, and searched the house again, looking out the windows of the bedroom, but not wishing to close the windows. Nobody around. It had been a long day and clearly my mind was playing tricks on me. I went back to bed and floated off to delirious sleep once again, and thankfully the satin ladies reappeared and peacefulness overcame my overworked cells.

Then several hours later, (to be continued...)

# HOME ALONE PART DEUX

Please re-read Part I and recall the gentle breeze brushing my warm lips before caressing my eager nose with a luscious scent of classy perfume... satin ladies reappearing and the peacefulness overcoming my exhausted cells...the visit by the police...

About three am, I woke up suddenly, startled by a noise at the computer in my study, possibly an email notification or IM buzz. Memory of the perfume scent reentered my mind, so I went to the windows to try to catch that breeze again, but it was gone unfortunately. Curious about the noise at the computer that continued to annoy me, I sat down at my desk in front if the computer, rubbed my sleepy eyes and saw an IM notification for a contact: "Serene Wind". There was no text associated with it or greeting. Who was this Serene Wind? Then I looked on face book and found a new "like"—Serene Wind, and the face book page for Serene Wind had no text entry, just a photograph of an eagle in flight with a sparrow riding on its back. Was that SRCarson's eagle? Should I accept the IM request for a friend? Clearly not a good idea to accept an IM friend that you don't know; it could be dangerous or a fraud scheme of some kind. How did this person find me?

I deleted the contact, turned off the computer and dragged

myself back to bed. But before I got in, I detected that sultry perfume scent again. Where was it coming from? I had to find out or I wouldn't find peace. It wasn't coming from the bedroom window breeze anymore, so I went back to the study and found the scent rising directly from the chair seat in front of my computer. Funny, I didn't detect it a few minutes before. Goosebumps rippled up my naked legs and down my arms when the realization hit that someone did enter my house last night. I assumed it was a woman due to the scent. Was she hiding somewhere in the house, playing games with me? If so, that would explain why my cat was hiding all the time now. Or maybe, it wasn't a woman at all. What did this woman want and why was she in my house not showing herself? Was it a ghost or was I beginning to suffer auditory hallucinations and a psychiatric consult was now necessary?

Thor, my cat, let out a loud hiss that grew deeper and more menacing; a sound I had never heard him make before. It sounded like it was coming from downstairs in the basement, so I grabbed my flashlight in my left hand, .357-magnum revolver in the right hand and descended the stairway in my birthday suit. No time to put clothes on and lose the element of surprise. While keeping the flashlight in front of me, I surveyed the lower level and found my cat's eyes with their reflection back to me. He was crouched as if ready to pounce right in front of the furnace room door—and the hideous hissing started again. This cat was not a fearless lion by any means of the imagination, but he wouldn't budge from the door. I stood there in front of the door, naked, realizing that it was a mistake not to have my cell phone handy to call 911, but I had my .357 and figured 911 wouldn't help me if things got nasty because it would be over quick. I quietly pulled back the hammer on the revolver, positioned myself flat against the wall to avoid full detection before violently pushing the door open, then...to be continued...

# HOME ALONE, GRANDE FINALE, MAYBE

The jackhammer pounding of my heart forced the blood into my carotid and temporal arteries, and it was all I could do to keep my body from jerking with each pulse, thus giving away my location to the intruder that the police couldn't find. I called upon my military survival training to control my breathing and concentrate totally on completing my task successfully. My index finger gingerly remained in the trigger housing of my .357 magnum. In the unlikely event that the intruder was able to disarm me, I entered into my Krav Maga fighting stance to prepare for possible hand to hand combat. A roundhouse kick easily smashed the door open and I entered the furnace room, gun pointed in the only area he could be hiding, but I saw nothing. Adrenaline pumped through my arteries while my breath heaved in and out like bellows. Where was he?

Then I smelled it; the heavenly perfume took control of my shaking body, immediately soothing my hammering heart. I discerned the soft silhouette of a human form floating toward me, and I stood frozen while she approached me. Her feet hovered effortlessly above the concrete floor while her feminine form flowed through the air like a prima ballerina. Her face appeared in front of mine while her hands caressed my neck and head. Goosebumps invaded every inch of my skin. I desperately tried to talk, but couldn't utter a single word.

My revolver fell to the floor and I felt her breath softly play with my ear, and she said, "Carson, it's Kim. Don't be afraid honey. We never had a chance to say goodbye. I love you, my hero, and I'm at peace now that you're safe." I reached out to touch her lips and in an instant, she was gone.

I frantically searched the room, my arms flailing around trying to find her, but to no avail. A silent calm took over my heart. I picked up my trembling Thor and walked up to the kitchen and poured myself a glass of bourbon. It coated my throat with a warmth that matched the feeling in my heart that moment. My beautiful Kim came back to me after all these years. I smiled, soothed my now playful cat, and relished the pleasant memories flooding my moist eyes.

Years ago, I was suddenly sent on a secret deployment, and we only enjoyed a few moments together before they came to get me. I learned later that she developed an aggressive disease that took her life before I could come home to see her. We never said goodbye, until now. Yes, it was Kim, my young love, and after seeing her perfect smile, I knew she was finally happy and at peace.

From that moment on, I always leave the bedroom window open a little, even in the cold winter, allowing her perfumed spirit to caress my soul whenever she wishes.

# HOME AGAIN, BUT NOT SO ALONE

For background, please read my blogs, *Home Alone, Home Alone Part Deux, and Home Alone, Grande* Finale, however, that reading isn't necessary to appreciate this short piece.

The mass of the wet snow overcame each branch of the fir trees, causing their sad droop almost to the ground, reminding me of how I neglected them in the summer, but it was only a brief thought, because I knew, like a cherished dog, the springy green branches would be there for me during the spring thaw. I devoured the crisp artic air that at once cleared my previously clogged nostrils while aggressively invading the previously safe sanctity of my faithful lungs.

Each shovel full of the white lead caused me to stop, bending only with my legs and heave it to the side of the driveway, tapping the handle hard to jar the cold wet nuisance from the inside of the shovel. But, the exhilaration of fresh mountain air pushed me to work harder and with increasing enthusiasm, despite the bright rubicund skin of my ears and flaring nose. But the aromatic memory of hot chocolate conquered my snowy task with an energy infusion while I walked into the warmth of my house, job complete.

With the mostly yellow and slightly orange flames of my fireplace dancing behind me, caressing my cold back with warm fingers of air, I drank the hot chocolate and tried to read my book, *The Dancing Wu Li Masters*. But I found my attention quickly reaching away from the pages as soon as that scent entered my nose. I knew the scent immediately and my heart sprang into action, as if the starter of the 100-meter dash just said, "set" and my soul was ready to follow my heart where the scent would lead. I smelled it before and it was the sultry scent I detected from my bedroom window the summer before, and she said it was Cartier.

She called herself the Serene Wind, and as a tease, entered my computer, writing an IM on my computer screen back then, and she led me downstairs where I found her after all those years of absence. We never said goodbye, but I prayed Kim would come back again because young lovers with so many plans together and love to share, needed to say goodbye before one goes to heaven, much too unexpectedly. She said she was at peace now that I was safe, then she vanished, floating through the walls back to her peaceful heaven.

Like last summer, I followed her scent through the house, and of course, I went back downstairs to the furnace room where she previously showed me her feminine form, briefly, floating towards me, but I couldn't find her this time. I tried to remain calm when I realized she wasn't there and went back upstairs, sat back down in front of the fireplace and then, the scent hit me again, she was there, in the fireplace! I stood rigidly motionless, almost flying with the experience of her Cartier scent, and then I felt it, but I didn't jump because I had no fear, just love. I felt not the warm feeling of the fireplace wind, but instead, the distinct feel of feminine fingers, caressing the sore muscles of my neck and back.

"Kim, you came back!" I started to tremble.

She continued the caress as she replied. "I am always here

with you Carson and there is only peace and overwhelming love where I am."

I felt a soft wet touch on my lips, and I imagined that it was her lips, but I saw nothing while a sense of peace and love caused me to float into a realm of other consciousness, that I have felt only once before. "Kim, I wanted to ask you so many questions..."

I turned around, looked into the flames of the fireplace and saw a smoky outline of a heart, slowly ascending up, and the Cartier perfume lingered on my clothes. I never washed them again but kept them in a box, preserving the scent, at least, I hoped, until next time.

# BEACH LADIES IN THE LAND THAT TIME FORGOT

If you've already spent a precious 22 seconds reading the "About SRCarson" section of my blog, you'll already remember that I grew up in Southern California fantasyland. Not to belabor the point, but I ate, drank and slept surfing when I was a young man: Malibu, Huntington Beach and Seal beaches got my trunks wet the most often. So, I can imagine that it comes as a surprise to you that I'm writing to you while on a Lake Michigan beach. Well, not actually on the beach, but I was earlier, now I'm at a bar writing on 17 small napkins I stole from the bartender. (I discussed this habit earlier in my blog entry a few months ago: *Bar Inspiration*).

Yeah, tiny ripple-like waves ignite excitement here on Lake Michigan; usually the water is as smooth as glass unless there's a speedboat wake interrupting the blistering silence. Boring as lunchtime in a nursing home, no sharks to tease, and not a single California girl. The only things surfing are dragonflies skimming the surface. Woe is me, I think I'm going to eat worms, as they say, but here I am visiting a forgotten city nestled on the shores of Lake Michigan. You see, someone dear to me needed my help, and of course, I hit the road to visit as soon as I could.

Let's face it, this town was the little train that couldn't; a town that shoulda, coulda, woulda, but never did. So, after fueling up with a cold beer, I went for a long run on this beach, and I couldn't believe my eyes: The feminine smorgasbord quickly steamed to a dangerous level. Try as I might, it was quite a strain to keep my head pointing straight down the coast line while I ran, but hell, I'm human and occasionally I had to turn to subtly enjoy the scenery. About 50 yards ahead, I spied two sets of tanned, slender legs extending out into the water from their little half-chairs and clearly obstructing my running path. What is the most courteous thing to do? Run in front of them, keeping my pace and splash them all over, or instead, run behind them in the deep sand, potentially kicking it all over their hair? Obviously, they knew they were obstructing the progress of intense beach runners because there was plenty of room in the sand, but maybe they just wanted to get their little pinkies wet and make us guys all nervous and such.

Clearly though, every man is trained (by women) to understand it's best to ignore them, even if they try hard to be seen, because everyone knows that the only reason a man makes conversation with an attractive woman he doesn't know is because he is deviously designing a plan to get lucky and jump her bones. That's why reasonable women should refuse to smile and encourage us animalistic males.

Despite possessing that innate knowledge, for some reason I took the dangerous step of stopping my run right in front of these two goddesses with heads immersed deeply into paperback beach novels, whatever those are. I think they are novels with pictures of half-naked hot men with long hair caressing a woman with one of her bikini straps half-falling off her shoulder. The titles usually are like this: *Lion of the Shimmering Moonlight* or *Hot Love in Nantucket* or something like that. Anyway, they remained oblivious of me, as they were trained to do, by someone, somewhere. Not sure why I broke etiquette and stopped but it happened. Perhaps because I am writing a novel, not a beach novel though and curious about what people are reading now. But what the hell, I stopped and briefly glanced at their red-painted toenails bobbing out of the water before I waited for them to unglue their eyes from their books and make eye contact. Then I smiled, took off my sunglasses so they could see my eyes and said, "Hello ladies, are you enjoying your novels?"

The brunette looked up for a millisecond, and then turned her attention back to her book, saying nothing in response. The blonde however, looked up and smiled, "Yes, great book, lots of action and it moves fast. Has to move fast to keep my attention, but doesn't require a lot of thought. You know a beach novel." Clearly the brunette was a goddess that couldn't' be bothered by exchanging a couple words with an earthling, especially a beach-roving doctor/writer/wolf. But the blonde continued to make eye contact and her garden-green eyes seemed to wait for my response.

Grinning while squinting, I said, "I know the story. Can't give you the details of course, but I'll have you know that in the end, honestly, the good guy gets the girl."

She showed me a wider view of her bright whites. "That's good to know, I was wondering about that. Thanks for your literature analysis; it was quite helpful. We both laughed genuinely, and then I took off for my run.

"Remember to hydrate after your run!" Said the blonde.

"Does beer count as hydration?"

She smiled and said, "Absolutely, it's mandatory on a day like this after a long run and a successful novel read."

I still remembered how easily her bright smile picked my feet up off the sand, and I felt renewed energy while I ran for several more miles, reminded that secure women with intelligence and charm are much more beautiful than their friends who display their body for male visual consumption, thinking that their body is actually their only real demonstration of their soul.

So that was my brief experience, or at least all the detail I can share with you on a blog, about two women on a beach on the shores of Lake Michigan, and the land that time forgot is now enriched in my mind just a little more. I'll be back.

# WINE PAIRINGS AND HEROIC SNORING

While it's true that wine, actually alcohol in general, will nearly always exacerbate snoring and sleep apnea, the two words have nothing to do with each other for the purposes of this blog piece. Of course, as you will see as you read on, they have a significant connection in real life that I will now discuss.

With regard to the first word—snoring, the medical field—especially sleep medicine, is fond of grading and describing snoring in exquisite, excruciating detail. Commonly used words are soft, loud, annoying, stuttering, house-shaking as well as the dreaded freight-train like snore. However, the most fascinating adjective that I commonly read on sleep study reports is "heroic" snoring. Funny, but the adjective heroic doesn't seem to go with snoring at all. Kinda like a "bull-like bride" or a "gentle" landslide. I usually consider heroic to have something to do with great feats of skill and courage, or extra-ordinary sacrifice for the well-being of others or society in general. Obviously, you can see that I love that "heroic" has now pushed itself into the medical literature specifically with regard to snoring, which is generally regarded as at best, annoying or at worse, brutally obnoxious. Did the word snoring somehow come to the rescue of a sleeping damsel in distress one night and now has imbedded itself in the literature? Perhaps the fabled snoring became heroic when it kept everyone in the house up all night because of the noise, thus keeping all souls alert for the coming tornado that would've most assuredly taken them if they were asleep? If so, then snoring in some cases, truly can be heroic.

Now you are wondering; how is he going to connect wine to snoring? Well, you're in luck because you're going to find out so keep reading attentively and grab yourself a glass of wine. Or if you prefer vodka, whiskey or your favorite beverage. Are you ready?

Admittedly, I enjoy a good waiter or a wine sommelier that is able to describe the best wine with the appropriate food so that they will complement each other while swirling in your naïve little palate. Recently, it became a little too snobby for me, so I will describe the scene briefly at a restaurant I attended recently.

"Sir, may I suggest this older red wine that pairs most wonderfully with a juicy fillet or New York Strip?"

I looked at him straight faced and said, "I disagree completely. Without question, an older red pairs most exquisitely with an attractive young woman!"

My date giggled and turned crimson.

His surprise caused him to step back from the table, almost dropping the bottle while he laughed loud enough to turn the other patron's heads. I think he lost his stuffy decorum for the rest of his shift that evening. I'm happy for that.

But seriously folks, if an older red is lucky enough to pair with an attractive young woman, the resulting snoring she endures after the hot romance will make it much less likely that she'll pair again with an older red, but I'm sure there are exceptions depending on the degree of snoring, whether it was heroic or not, and the quality of the romance. If she likes him, she will just turn him off his back to his side, and the snoring is dissipated for the time being. But then, I'm told I'm not a snorer and even if I was—heroic romance always saves the day.

I love red wine, especially when it is paired with something tasty.

# A WOMAN AND HER MIND

A woman is a gift from heaven, but like any gift, you must accept the gift's imperfections as perfect, cherish the minute she gives as if she blessed you with infinity, and always protect her so that she can flourish like your favorite flower in the garden, blossoming to the full potential that her mind has always expected her to be. Don't stand in her way, but open the path for her forward, all the while making sure you make sure that path is safe.

She is not a body part, but a whole damn symphony orchestra of strings, brass, woodwinds, and yes, kettle drums—each instrument is played not to be heard individually, but as an elegantly blended whole that creates a unique and divine symphony of feminine perfection, and her mind smiles and gracefully allows you to take the chance to be the lucky conductor that she always had hoped would grab the conductor's baton without hesitation, and with the unbounded strength of love, guide her to the majestic feminine mountain top she was destined to reach.

# BEFORE BED AND ROMANCE IS NOT GOING TO HAPPEN

## Seems this is unfortunately the largest category

# A. Spiritual Thoughtfulness

# A SPIRITUAL ELK
# ENCOUNTER

Azure skies reluctantly allowed wispy fluffs of cirrus clouds while I enjoyed the luxurious perfection of a pool on a brilliant day in mid-June. Or maybe you could call it controlled drowning. You see, after some boring laps I began my ridiculous workout of running in place in the deep end while holding ten-pound weights alternatively in each hand above water, and then both hands with weights while running furiously, bobbing above and below the water's surface, gasping for air whenever I could. Yeah, I know, I was told not to do that alone at the pool in the mountains, but hell, it's a great workout especially when your knees have more mileage than the government's hand constantly pilfering our paychecks for pathetic programs.

But I digress, it seems. Back in the rejuvenating pool, I lay on my back after my controlled drowning with my shades on, and devoured the stunning view of eagles soaring over the pool and surrounding mountain forest, towering undisturbed, the masters of the sky. Diving to the dirty earth only when hungry, they carry their unsuspecting prey to their lofty nests for lunch. Such majestic and powerful birds made me a bit envious and reminded me of the days when I flew gliders, listening to the wind flow over the wings while I searched for uplifting thermals. Actually, I also searched for the eagles circling in the thermals, because they knew what they were doing, immensely more than I did. And the ruby-hued hummingbirds buzzed only feet above my head searching for that sweet sugar that powered their energetic wings. Yet it was the stillness of nature that brought me peace.

Now out of the pool, I grabbed this 50 shades book someone recommended, and sprawled out on that relaxing lounge chair to catch some rays and enjoy the quiet solitude. Well, I'm kidding of course. It was a scientific journal. I don't need that other kind of instruction manual. Hah! Surrounding the pool deck was a wrought iron fence, and the pine forest started only about six feet away from the fence. Just as I was falling asleep my, uh, scientific journal fell to the ground, and I was startled by a rustling noise in the brush. I looked to my right and saw nothing, laid back in the warmth and the rustling grew closer and closer. I peered over again to find the source of the noise, and there was a bull Elk, slowly moving through the brush. He saw me, stopped and stared, then continued walking, now away from me, but directly towards me, persistent, yet without fear. My heart hammered with excitement when I realized that he was now perhaps six feet away from me and we were both staring at each other, and the fence was all that separated man and beast. He had at least eight points on his rack, and I estimate he was probably about 700 pounds or so.

We stared at each other, neither with fear, and perhaps both of us were fascinated with the other life form. I admired his enormity and graceful walk and he admired, well, who knows. At least he wasn't bugling and rutting, so he wasn't attracted to me. We continued our stare down for several minutes, and it wasn't clear who won, but the Elk decided to walk along the fence perimeter and plop down under the shade provided by a sprawling fir tree. I watched him, as still as I could be, and he watched me, as still as he could be and then, we both grew tired of staring at each other and we both fell asleep. Or at least I think he was asleep because I didn't hear him snoring to prove it. I slept with one eye open though, just in case he decided to leap over the fence and gore me. But really though, we both respected each other, now about 20 feet away, and it seemed we both enjoyed the warmth of the day and the peaceful nature that God provides. I have many hunter friends and I respect what they do, but even if I had a hunting rifle and a hunting license, there was no way I would ever think of shooting that wonderful beast, who seemed to be communicating with me. Let's be clear though, I do own firearms to protect myself and my first amendment rights.

After about 45 minutes, he decided to get up from the shady ground and proceeded to walk slowly back along the fence line towards me, and when he was parallel with my supine body, he glanced to the right, looked at me as if to say "goodbye" and plodded off into the forest, never to be seen again.

I'll never forget how lucky I was to experience this close encounter with a bull Elk, who seemed to understand more about me, then perhaps I knew about myself.

This was my first blog, and to those of you who would like to read more, thank you, and I will provide more. And with time, you'll hear about some of my upcoming publications, including a novel and a short story about a recent life-threatening experience I've had, that is, when I gather the strength to write the events down.

# I FELT THE GRIP
## OF DEATH

Death's grip started with excruciating pain, but then, eventually faded into peaceful bliss. I didn't have time to say goodbye to anyone because death would not wait for my wishes. I wasn't ready, but it didn't matter; it was happening no matter what.

Death came to me, ready or not. I touched him and felt the terrible burn, but at the same time, enjoyed the blissful wave of peace within my soul. I heard the words around me, uttered by people I knew and worked with, the words of struggle between life and death that few people will ever hear and understand. But I was filled with calm.

And when I awoke and grabbed the breath of life back into my lungs again, the love of others overcame me. I realized that nothing else in life matters but love. Nothing. Once again, I would be able to walk through the pine forest after a fresh rain, listening to the waterfall crash onto the rocks below and wonder at the beauty of the bald eagle soaring above. I would once again feel the warm lips of a woman.

How lucky I was to enjoy life again! You see, God decided to send heroic angels to save me. There is no other explanation.

In my profession, I have been lucky to have saved some lives over the years, but I understand that those skills are only possible through the grace of God. Thank you, God.

Over the years, I listened to the words of the preachers in church, about the love of God, and the grace of God and that is all that matters. But they were just words that sounded good, but didn't have a real meaning to me, until now. Without question, they mean everything to me in my new life. Those words I now understand to the point that they are the food that I eat and the breath that keeps my cells alive. It took an actual near-death experience for me to realize that I was blind for all these years, almost ignoring the truth that was gently placed before me.

It's simple, really. Nothing else matters in life but love. I got it. I feel it. I breathe it. But most importantly, there is much that I must give back to the world.

# IT'S OK TO STARE AT HER

No matter how I try, I can't stop staring at her. It's just not possible, and despite the cacophony of the honking cars behind me, carrying their frazzled and banal cargo, I slow down even more to stare. I really don't care, you see, she's always there for me, no matter what weak element attempts to deface her. It seems she laughs at the swirling blizzards, gale force winds and brutal lightning storms that force me to run for safety. So I stare, despite the forbidden consequences, devouring the view of her splendid majesty, my hands quivering slightly on the steering wheel though my breathless hunger is far from satisfied.

My absolute preference is heading due west early in the crispy clear morning that overflows with expectations, plans and thoughts of unfolding dramatic stress, yet I must always enjoy her. I feel comfort knowing her presence never leaves me when I look for her. Even if I don't travel due west, I find my head turning to the west wherever I am when I need her.

If you must know more details, most of the time she is topped with white, but during the bright warmth of the summer, she sheds her white top for a while so that I can slake my thirst on her rugged natural features. She knows my hunger and thirst won't end, yet, she remains steadfast and fiercely confident in herself.

Sometimes in the busy race of day to day living in this world, I find myself dismayed occasionally that I've forgotten that I'm actually lucky to even be driving to see her, or for that matter, even breathing the air on this precious brutal earth. So, I blast my favorite music, roll down the windows and tell myself to suck in the life that was gifted back to me several years ago.

I'm sure you're thinking about where I live, and whether you can see her too. Thing is, I'm not going to tell you where I live because clearly those ravenous novel reading paparazzi will certainly pounce on the opportunity to chase down this elusive physician novelist. Without question, I have found a gorgeous part of the country to call my home, but I'm not going to tell you where she is. I will protect her. You'll have to find her yourself if you have what it takes.

And the cars continue to honk, while I always give her my smile in the morning.

I am lucky to have her; her high alpine peak, though gently piercing the sultry blueness, fiercely tames the occasional violent but ineffective storms around her, reminding me of how lucky I am. She scolds me softly when I stray from the knowledge and peaceful feeling of love from that time when I nearly left this world two years ago, and the gift from God who sent his angels to save me and give me another chance at life.

# DON'T BE AFRAID: FEEL THE MUSIC

Admittedly before I started writing this piece I enjoyed some smooth red wine, and of course, that allows the words to flow much more freely and with less of a filter, but it is good for the heart. At the same time, you should be thankful that I am writing these words rather than speaking them, and thus you can't hear the shlurrred speech.

The truth is this: I'm a tough son of a gun at times, independent and hard-working, not prone to showing emotions. However, each time I hear the Star-Spangled Banner played, our national anthem, I get tears in my eyes. Every damn time I choke up. I admit it. One of the other songs that provoke this emotion is Lee Greenwood's "God Bless America." Happens every time. Reminds me of many gifts from God I have experienced, and tonight, it reminded me of my emotional release with my colleagues from POW camp training and simulated capture, years ago.

It happened again, today, at a Symphony Orchestra concert. That's right, a symphony orchestra. They played the national anthem before the concert and that set me off, once again. Reminded me of the men and women I served with and knew well, who sacrificed for this great country and died. As well, the history of freedom from tyranny this country was founded for, and the blood that was shed to create a country based on a strong constitution the world has never seen. I'm a lucky man to have been born here and enjoyed the freedoms we have, yet I will continue to fight for her and do what is right for her for the rest of my life.

That was the introduction to the symphony, preparing my emotions quickly for the start of Beethoven's fifth. Admittedly, I was never a classical music fan, although I love all genres of music—rock, jazz, smooth jazz, Latin, soul, pop, techno, and some country. I appreciate the instrumentation and rhythm first and then later, the lyrics. Sure, I've reluctantly listened to symphonies before, but never felt the emotional inspiration I did tonight. It was Beethoven's fifth. You're right, the wine I had in the lobby beforehand may have warmed my senses a bit, but within a few minutes, I found myself absorbed completely in the emotion of his composition. Sure, macho men who sport tattoos and drive Harleys wouldn't be caught dead at a symphony, but perhaps that's because they're too insecure to show their appreciation of the beauty of genius with music. That takes some strength, doesn't it?

I closed my eyes and finally learned how to allow the instruments from each section to infiltrate my being, listening to them individually, watching the faces of the intense musicians, then incorporating each one into the whole that is the orchestra; no instrument alone can carry the piece, no matter how good the musician is. I began to tap my feet, and move to the music, all the while bewildered by why everyone else was staring a head like so many cold Stonehenges. I felt the drama of the story Beethoven was trying to tell, the violence, the passion, the despair, and yet the triumph of life's beauty that comes back from the ashes, as always. Majestic French horns, soulful oboes, nimble flutes, energetic trumpets, strong basses, and classy violins and cellos. All for one and one for all.

Dissect them individually, then put them together, and the music takes you to your past and brings you back again to a future boiling with hope. I felt inspired and surprised at myself for this discovery.

I thought about all the instruments that were there tonight, and although I was a trumpet player in my younger days, without the talent to play at anywhere near this level, it was not the brass section that caught my eyes today. No, it was in fact, the single, lonely tympani or kettledrum player. You see, of all the instruments in the orchestra today, he was the one, who had to hit his kettle drums perfectly, timed with exact precision to the musical score, because if it wasn't perfect, he would be heard immediately and singled out like a zebra in a stable of horses. No question. He couldn't hide with multiple other musicians, like a group of violins or oboe players or bass players. He was alone, spotlight on him if not immediately, it was implied and expected.

So enjoy the music, feel it deep into your soul and realize that without music our world would be an empty abyss of sadness. Don't judge until you've experienced it and tried to appreciate it with an open mind. I learned my lesson and I'm a hell of a lot more inspired because I kept an open mind.

In fact, once I finally publish my novel and accomplish a few other things in life, it sure would be cool to play the majestic and powerful kettledrums, and do it with perfection.

# I CAN'T GO ON. I
# WILL GO ON.

## (Title Only from Samuel Beckett)

Stress can kill you. I knew that long ago because I am a
physician, and I am supposed to know that kind of stuff.
I read books and took lots of tests, learned from smart professors and mentors, absorbing practical wisdom as well
from people who knew what they were doing: nurses, phar-
macists, technicians, therapists and others, no matter what
their rank. I was strong and tough, with no risk factors for
cardiovascular disease. Sure, I'd have an occasional juicy
hamburger and some beers but I did manage to practice a
reasonably healthy lifestyle. Except for the running. That
destroyed my knees some years ago. So, I chose alternative
non-knee pounding exercise.

But my stress level was boiling like an inevitable Mount
Vesuvius. I had no idea about the extent of it again, because
I was tough and could handle anything, because after all, I'd
survived quite a few close calls in my unusual life and there

was no indication that I couldn't weather any tornado or Tsunami that life could throw my way.

I lost the two children I loved 13 years ago. To me, the possibility of that loss would be unfathomable, and it hit me like a sledgehammer to my chest when it actually happened. I am told my loss was extremely rare and unusual, and in medical lingo, if you have an interesting or unusual case you are in reality, a gonner. Who would know that a single evil being can manifest as a soft, fragrant flower, then rise up and bite your head off? In my case, this evil thing bit my heart, then shredded it, slowly chewing each morsel in a way to inflict more searing pain. That is all I will say about that because:

*We all have a story.*

Elisabeth Kubler Ross did describe the five stages of grief and I experienced them, like a loyal but reluctant soldier, I finally found myself years later in a tentative acceptance phase, and life seemed to be much more livable, now that I understood I couldn't change the past or fix it. Then, without warning, I had an MI, went into shock while working in the ICU, and I was quite lucky to survive. You can read about it; the link is on my blog: Code Blue: A Doctor's View of His Own Near Death Experience.

My life has changed because of that event, and I no longer feel the fear of death. Death is not the ogre that we believe him to be, while my life on this earth, given a new chance to continue, has taken on new meaning and I have a clear but peaceful sense of the gifts given to me by God. I felt his love, and he opened my eyes to the love of others.

So now I feel the constant pain of my battered knees, sometimes finding it difficult to walk; the ringing in my ears occurred within a few months of my NDE, pestering me constantly while causing me to shun noisy crowds—leaning over to those who try to talk to me on my left side. My vision is not so good but I get by and am able to see well enough and enjoy the ability to read and write. Sure, there's more, but the point of me saying this is not for sympathy, no, it is to say that I am lucky to be alive, and each pain, similar to C.S. Lewis, tells me that I am alive, here to contribute what I can to this tragic, yet beautiful world. And it has taught me once again, that everyone has a story and don't judge people too quickly; you don't know what they've been through or are going through. I've learned that my little problems don't compare to the devastation others face, and if they walk or talk in a way that bothers me somehow or offend me, I sit back and remember that they probably have a difficult story and need a helping hand.

Sometimes when I get down about things, I think about a quote my mother told me many times: "Carson, you're alright. I don't care what the other people say." I chuckle. Then I remember her responses to me during her struggle with breast cancer, and I would ask her how she felt. "I'm in good shape for the shape I'm in."

I realize now, after many years, that the worries that invade our earthly minds on a daily basis are essentially trivial, and that there are larger concerns that we seem to forget. The first that comes to mind is love.

Peace is now within me, although it often tries to sneak out, then, when I realize there's been an escape, I reach out and pull him back in, sometimes using a grappling hook. I am loving the gift of life God has given to me, a second chance, hoping to provide a positive influence on the lives of others while I am still on this earth.

# I HAVE LIVED A
# GOOD LIFE

The internist consulted me to help with this patient's re-spiratory status. He told me, "She has Osteogenesis Imperfecta with some right heart failure and is having trouble breathing. I don't know what else to do at this point."

"I'll be happy to see her. What room is she in?"

He told me her room number, and then said, "And she's two and a half feet tall."

I'm not sure why he added that, except to perhaps put things in perspective for me to ponder until I saw her. Later that day, I was finally able to find the time to see her after taking care of my patients in the Intensive Care Unit. I didn't know much about Osteogenesis Imperfecta, but I remembered a little about it from my genetics and pediatric rotations as a medical student, years ago. So, I looked it up before my visit with her and basically learned that it was and Autosomal Dominant muta-tion, an inherited connective tissue disorder associated with a collagen defect and was also known as 'Brittle Bone Disease". These patients have variable presentations, but almost all have short stature, multiple fractures, basilar skull deformities as well as chest wall defects and scoliosis of the spine.

When I entered her room, I saw her sitting in her electric wheelchair at the side of her bed, her tiny, atrophied legs curled under her like soft pretzel dough. I introduced myself to the patient and her friend, and she smiled and showed me her bright, playful eyes. "Nice to meet you, Dr. Carson. How are you today?"

I was struck by how friendly and kind she was to me, a physician she never met. We immediately connected and I interviewed her, bending over to her wheelchair, so she could hear me. Her chest wall was severely deformed, her scoliotic spine pushed inwards, squishing her heart and lungs against her sternum. She was on oxygen, but amazingly, she had never required oxygen before, during her 55 years on this earth. I was able to discern that over the years, the strain on her heart from the mechanical restriction imposed by her disease on the heart and lungs residing together within the chest cavity extracted a toll on her respiratory status. She was not ventilating well, especially at night when her lung volumes decreased even more.

"I'm short of breath more now, and that has made me retire from my job."

I was amazed she was able to function and work with her condition, and I asked what type of work she did. She responded that she sold insurance for many years, then worked selling land. She also kept busy at home by sponsoring many foreign exchange students over the years.

I said, "you must have been a very good sales person."

She said, "Yes, would you like to buy a dead horse? I can give you two for the price of one."

I laughed at her humor and I could tell she enjoyed it. She had a zest for life that was infectious to all who were lucky enough to be around her.

I told her that her right heart was gradually failing, due to her disease, and that her lungs were no longer able to ventilator her properly, but she was not in immediate danger of death, but there was no cure. However, I was able to get her a mask ventilator machine to use just at night, to provide her assistance, and she was happy to hear about that technology and wanted to try it. We discussed that someday, her heart would fail, and her ventilation would become worse, and those were difficult words for me to say to her, but I needed to say them, because I felt no one else had given her the truth. I asked if she wanted cardio-pulmonary resuscitation if her heart and lungs should fail.

I said, "I am sorry to have mentioned end of life issues with you on your first visit, but I wonder if anyone else had discussed this with you, or if you had thought about it before."

"No Dr. Carson, you are the first. But I appreciate you bringing it up, just in case. No, I don't want CPR or life support should my body finally fail. You see Dr. Carson, I have lived a good life and have enjoyed it, and that would not be life for me."

I smiled, asked if she had any other questions, and told her that I would set her up for her nocturnal mask ventilator. She said, "have a good day, Dr. Carson, and thanks for stopping by. You sure you don't want to buy that dead horse?"

When I left her room, I felt that she was a special person with a contented soul who loved the life that was given to her, despite her severe disabilities since birth. I realized that my complaints, pains or problems in life were inconsequential, compared to what she had experienced. But then, each day in my medical career, I see examples of this, and it makes me thankful for the many gifts from God that I have received in my life that others do not enjoy.

I still remember her words, whenever I am down for some reason. "I have lived a good life, Dr. Carson."

# FATHER'S DAY, SHMATHER'S DAY

If you're lucky enough to have a father, congratulations, and show him love. If your father is no longer alive, then cherish his memory with love. And if you never knew your father or worse, never received love from him, then move on and live life to its fullest. Relax; this isn't a mushy lecture from some feel-good guru, no, far from it. It's simply a brief story from your humble blog writer that simply flows from my heart to my pen.

My father is ailing, having suffered a devastating illness recently, an illness that has changed his once-vibrant life dramatically. Thankfully, he still owns his bright mind and speech, so I called him today on Father's Day and we reminisced a little, told a few jokes, and I gave him my support and hope during this difficult time. Thankfully, just before I told him goodbye after my recent travel to visit him, I left him a flask of his favorite scotch, which I labeled 'cough medicine'. I'm positive that will easily trick the nurses. Wink Wink. Funny, I noticed he started coughing immediately after I left his room and could hear his sudden coughs all the way down the hall. I just couldn't help but burst out laughing. I told him to save the scotch for Father's Day, today, so we will both have a toast today despite the miles, to celebrate. So, before I hung up some hours ago, I said I love you. That's what he needed, certainly not checkered ties, socks or the latest power tool advertised on TV.

You see, I know what it's like to be a father because I used to be one too, or I guess I still am in the biologic sort of way. My children are gone, their young souls taken by a skillful being who displays an engaging smile and friendly countenance to those she wants to influence, then, while the victim is hopelessly hypnotized, she stabs them brutally when they turn away from her fishbowl view of life. Unfortunately, I believe the three of them have now become one, wherever they are. I think about the children I lost frequently, but in order to survive daily life I don't let it overwhelm my soul. The memories refuse to be erased, and are easily retrievable when I need them, or when someone's face brings back their images. I remember the baseball games, playing catch, and teaching baserunning and hitting. Then there were the swimming lessons in the summer where I helped them overcome their fear, and the nights I taught them to read before their first-grade teacher even advanced the lesson beyond the alphabet. I taught them to put the worm the right way on the hook, and took joy in their surprised faces when they landed the fighting bass. But most importantly, I still feel my heart bleed with their failures, while savoring the sweet taste of elation from their successes, like riding a bike without training wheels for the first time.

So, Father's Day is a bittersweet 24-hour ordeal for me; a day to show my love for my dad, but also a day that injects painful memories of the lost children I loved. I wish them the best in life, wherever they are, but for too long now, I can no longer protect them with my strength and knowledge, or show them life's reality. No, I don't want sympathy, not at all. I love life, and the people around me who genuinely care. They are my heroes and angels, and without question, I'm a lucky man with many blessings showered upon me by God, and I'm fortunate to still be living on this beautiful earth, helping people with my God-given skills. Of course, I've made many stupid mistakes in my life, endured devastating failures, but also, I've enjoyed remarkable successes. The result is that I've done my best in this life, and this lucky man finally understands that nothing on this earth matters but love. Nothing.

So dad, cheers and down the hatch. I'm with ya.

# FATHER'S DAY, SHMATHER'S DAY, ANOTHER YEAR GONE BY

There is only one day out of 365 that I only try to survive, hoping the daylight vanishes quickly and the darkness immediately escapes into the rejuvenating sunlight of the next day so I can rush off to work and be ridiculously busy.

And for that same reason, I didn't go to church today. I wanted to, but just couldn't do it. This is the one day out of 365 that I absolutely can't go to a church service. Too much Father's Day family stuff, congratulations to fathers with their laughing kids on their knees and their wives singing their praises for taking the kids to school and teaching them soccer and baseball and such. Let those fathers enjoy their day and their wonderful children; that is absolutely the way it should be. But don't force me to watch it.

Just too painful to me—the ostracizing, enigmatic, bizarre emptiness that cannot be defined by normal well-adjusted people. I am a father of two children who I raised and worried about and loved and taught and adored—but they are lost, having fallen deeply into an abyss of black-vacuumed barrenness—an abyss created by a human entity or being who laughs and smiles meekly to others while devouring life-sustaining nourishment from the void 'it' created.

364 days per year I am strong; it nearly killed me to use all my energy in my cells to resolve it with love, but having failed, I accept life for what it is while cherishing and loving the people around me who love and provide me true friendship.

But not today. I'm not bitter, just realistic, but It just won't go away. However, tomorrow, the sun will shine; I will exercise again and breathe in the fresh mountain air that God has provided for me. And if tomorrow doesn't come, I know that I am at peace with God.

I love my father and I called him today. Only wish I could be there with him, but that just isn't possible right now, but I am with him in thoughts and prayers. Such a strong man: Suffered a stroke that could've ended his life, but instead, his stubborn will and God's help allowed him to recover enough to prove us all wrong and live independently in the home he built for his departed true love of over 54 years.

Yes, he's stubborn, but he's a good man, a good father and I am truly lucky that he is still alive to honor and cherish.

So Dad, let's drink a shot together now, at 5 o'clock my time, and 6 O'clock your time. Down the hatch Dad, and allow the smoothness of the drink to float you to the peaceful harmony you deserve.

And as far as church, I don't feel too bad that I didn't go, because I talked to God in prayer several times today, and he listens. You see, although this is a rough day that peels off my protective fire-proof coat for 24 hours, leaving me naked in the desert sun, the armor goes back on tomorrow and today I still smile inside because of all the bountiful blessings that have been showered upon me. I'm a lucky guy.

Nothing matters but love.

# FATHER'S DAY, SHMATHER'S DAY. WHO'S IN THAT MIRROR?

Istopped at the bank drive through, parked and made my transaction. Then, I saw him staring at me, and I jumped in my seat, startled to see him and that unmistakable smile. Or was it a smirk? He said people told him he looked like Hugh Heffner, or the character Ilya Kuryakin, from the 60's TV show, Man from Uncle. Others told him he reminded them of James Dean. Either way, there he was. But why was he at the bank drive through looking at me? If he traveled all that way, couldn't he at least have called?

"Dad! Great to see you. Why—"

No answer.

Then, I finally realized that I was looking at myself in the side view mirror while I placed the pneumatic tube into the bank machine to be sucked inside the bank, behind darkened windows. I almost had to physically push the feeling of an apple stuck in my esophagus down to where it belonged. Why did it take me so long to recognize that I now suddenly at this moment, looked like him? Hell, I thought I looked a little like a younger Clint Eastwood, or at least some have said that, and a couple were sober at the time. Truth is, I am lucky to resemble dad so much at least physically.

In life he took a path that was totally different than mine in nearly all ways, driven by necessity, children and occupation. My path was so different than his that he had a hard time understanding it over the years, but I'm sure he tried. We are different, and yet the same. He's a stubborn old electrician who worked in the steel mills, and I'm just as stubborn, I've been told. After all, no one in the family had gone off to a military academy after high school, graduated college then went to medical school.

We didn't have many sit-down father to son conversations and at times, we became distant. What he taught I think, was more from his actions, or lack of actions. I think he taught me that in life, it is sink or swim, and if I actually start to drown, he would jump in to save me just at the end. In fact, he did that once, literally.

He also taught me, again, silently, that a man is responsible for his actions in life and you get out of it what you put in. Hard work is a necessity. He therefore had the strength to let me spread my wings in freedom and try to fly, without a push, knowing that was the only way I would learn, especially after failure.

And he watched me fail many times. I'm sure it hurt him, but he never let on. I disappointed him on occasion, but he never told me that. I just knew it, but he still loved me even though he wouldn't say it.

At my medical school graduation, my parents and sister and her family were there, and I was proud that they attended. I did it myself, without assistance, just as my dad had taught me, therefore, I owned the success completely.

He made me tough and self-reliant, and I love him for that. In fact, after all that has happened in our lives over the years, triumph, tragedy, joy and tears, we are closer now than ever, despite our physical distance.

So, on this Father's Day, I sent him his card and gift, then called him. We talked about the Chicago Cubs, and how well they were playing—after all this was finally their year! And politics jumped in as always, and it is rare that we disagree on that subject.

After we said good bye and I love you, I realized that the pleasant part of this annual ordeal was unfortunately over, lasting only ten minutes or so. I knew it was over when he said, "Well anyway." Now, I must endure the bizarre deadness of the remainder of the day, hoping the clock would speed up to midnight as quickly as possible, and the most difficult day of the year would be over for me.

You see, I used to be a father, I think. Or maybe it was just a recurrent dream and the kids in the dream seemed so real, even when they laughed at my pain and near death while I reached out to them to give them my love. It's amazing how dreams can be so realistic.

And then, when I wake up the next day after Father's Day, I will once again feel the heavy bricks released from my back, but that dream remains so real in my consciousness, coming in and out unpredictably on certain days, even when I try to block it.

The truth is that I am a lucky man though, filled with blessings and I cherish life and the love that surrounds us.

I know you don't read any more dad, and you won't read this little piece, but you know I love you. Go Cubs!

# YOU'RE NOT DEAD
# YET ARE YOU?

I spent most of the night stamping out disease and pestilence, as well as saving people from their own destructive abuse, but I should've known better. I shouldn't have said anything at all as I walked behind her, but the young nurse with the peppy step infused with energy forced my remaining active brain cells to dance a dizzying dance.

"Sure wish I could walk that fast," I said.

She turned around and smiled. "You off this weekend Carson?"

"Yep."

"You going skiing or doin' anything fun."

"No skiing, no real plans I guess."

"Really? You're not dead yet are you?"

I hesitated as her words sunk in like a sharp spear. "No, but I did stay at a Holiday Inn Express last night."

She walked away without a comment and I went about my work, realizing that maybe she was right. Maybe if I'm not skiing all weekend with a wild hat on full speed ahead, then I must be dead. You know, the walking dead, I guess. But then I thought about it a little more later that night and realized that this nurse must've just watched Monty Python's *The Holy Grail* for the first time, and was thinking about the famous line—"Bring out your dead," and I was thinking—"I'm not dead yet!" However, everyone knows you haven't lived at all unless you have watched *The Holy Grail* at least 4 times while drinking at least four beers per showing.

She's a good nurse who I respect, but in her book, without skiing, there apparently is no life. I must say that I admire her zeal for skiing.

Certainly, the years of competitive long distance running and competing in races running up the stairs of skyscrapers have taken their toll on my knees, and I can't do much running anymore, but I believe there may be a few signs that I am still alive without skiing. I wonder if she has considered the following:

1. How many lives has she saved, and how recently has she heard words like these, directed to herself: "Dr. Carson, thanks for saving my wife's life."
2. Or, "Dr. Carson, when we have another baby, whether boy or girl, we will name him or her after you."
3. I can write in ways that can trigger people to laugh, cry, or soar with bounding inspiration.
4. Even after a near Fatal MI with a Near Death Experience, having experienced no risk factors before, I can swim nonstop in the deep Lake Michigan waters as long as I dare along the parallel to the shoreline, do hard cross-training exercise as well or better than men significantly younger than I am, and accomplish the best treadmill exercise test to maximum ever recorded post MI in the Cardiology department.
5. I can make love. Like a fine wine, I'm happy to say that it gets much better with time. No details of course. (Save that for my novels). With good health, it. All boils down to being unselfish with concentration on your lover. I

am lucky to be given the opportunity to be the conductor of this divine symphony of feminine perfection—a woman is a gift from God. Now that's living!

6.  My knees ache from the years of running, my left ear rings for various reasons, my eyes are not so good, but I can still read and devour the best books written, smell the salty ocean breeze, gaze at the infinite blueness of the heavenly sky, cook delectable salmon on the grill and prepare famous mouth-watering omelets. Oh yes, I forgot, I love tasting wine from the supple lips of a goddess.

7.  I've lost more in life than many have either had or experienced. And yet, I'm lucky to remember and with a memory that is intact, the beauty of living is filled with vivid wonder, simply with a signal to your neurons to recall the file in question.

8.  I can still pray and God answers my prayers. Too many times, I've either had a "near miss" or have been close to death and he brings me back. The next time, I may leave this earth filled with pain for the loving bliss of the afterlife. In the meantime, I know that I must remain here for a while more to complete my work and make a difference somehow.

No, I have chosen not to ski anymore, at least right now due to my bad knees. But I'm sure as hell alive and fighting, and more importantly, loving.

# YEAH, NO QUESTION, GOD EXISTS

She lurched forward and took me to it faster, accelerating with each second, rolling towards the end; my eyes saw the blurred trees fly by on my peripheral vision, but I dare not look anywhere but straight, where I hoped to keep her concentrating as well during her speedy fury of unleashed power. She had strength, just enough to make men tremble if they didn't know how to control her without losing their nerve. But it wasn't my first time, and I was confident that I could rotate her out of her earthly ropes, simply by lifting with my fingers on her yoke, just at the right time and right speed bringing her to the blue expanse she was born to slice and climb, but she didn't require my strength, no, she required much more than muscles to allow her to reach the heights of freedom safely, the way she was designed to function.

She was perfect, at least for me at that time.

She needed me to navigate her through the vast expanse without fear, using the gentle touches and calculated maneuvers as her maker intended, for her to respond naturally.

I needed her, to give me her power when I needed it, and hopefully, she would forgive me if I made a small mistake, and if she didn't, or my mistake was too unforgiving, my maker needed to take over.

Her name, at least the name I radioed to Torrance Municipal Airport, in the Los Angeles TSA, was "Cessna 1097M'. I Loved to take her up for a trip, and the weather report was perfect, or at least as perfect as it could be in the smoggy Los Angeles basin. Heading east, a young pilot with only VFR experience (no instrument rating) was more likely to navigate easily, using charts sprawled on his lap with airport locations, power lines, railroad tracks and other major landmarks to guide him to his location and back without a problem. Without the congestion of LAX, Long Beach naval air station and other major international airports, my afternoon would be filled with the feeling of freedom to fly where the birds were comfortable and we become lucky enough to visit. I found myself mesmerized by the beauty, and that I had left the stress of the earth with its crowded freeways, honking and flaring tempers. Just myself and 1097M, and we loved it.

Oh yeah, but it wasn't just the two of us, there was a third, and I forgot to mention that. God.

So, He tested me. He tested me multiple times before when I was young, but I didn't quite understand when his hands were involved. Thought it was just me being smart, strong, or just lucky. I was invincible it seemed, that is until the smog/haze rolled in. It came in like the plume of a volcano, overcoming the blue chiffon that gave up its ghost without a fight.

Suddenly, having reached within several miles of the airport that I chose as my first leg, I did a 180-degree compass turn back to my home airport. Should be easy as pie. That is, if you could see more than 10 feet out of the cockpit. I could see 5 feet. The smaze ploom came in to take the naïve young pilots. Since I wasn't instrument rated, I was at a distinct survival disadvantage. I did remember my instructor telling me not to look outside at all in this case, only scanning the instruments, especially the altimeter, horizon indicator and airspeed. If I looked outside, I remembered that I would become disoriented, not knowing whether I was up or down, and you know, well, the result would be the end of my life. Remember JFK Jr.? Terror injected into my soul but only five minutes earlier it was complete pleasure. How could a throat pound and pulse like a heart? I started to think of my family and whether I would see them again, and then I quickly erased that thought. "Where was I? Was I high enough to avoid power lines, but low enough to find an airport to land safely?"

I looked at the charts, and found and airport about 10 miles from where I thought I was, and so I dialed in the VOR and tried to follow the needle to location of a VOR station I aimed for on the chart, then dialed in the DME (radio station beacon) and followed that signal in the same direction. Problem was, I was having trouble flying straight and level, desperately avoiding eye contact with the smaze outside. Keep the altitude! Airspeed too low, you're going to stall!"

The chart fell off my lap, but I wouldn't bend over to pick it up, for fear my eyes would leave the instruments. Damn chart wouldn't help me now anyway. Back then, not only did I not have expertise with instrument navigation, we didn't have the rudimentary satellite navigation onboard. Tried to make a mayday call and hopefully LAX or another Tower could vector me in, but the radio was out. I was 25 and that wasn't the age I expected the clock to stop.

I prayed. I prayed loud and with all my heart. "Dear God. Save me. Show me the way!"

Yes, I needed him to hear me.

I knew I would likely die in a fiery crash east of the Los Angeles mess that I tried to avoid, enveloped in a cloak of high velocity smaze that kept me from seeing ground, power lines or other aircraft.

I think I made tons of other promises to God at that moment, but I don't remember, and if I did, I'm sure I wouldn't share them with you.

It wasn't much of a stretch for me to realize that there was nothing more I could do but fly with my instincts, avoid looking out the cockpit, follow the VOR/DME needle and hope I didn't hit something, so I kept flying and praying. Seat of the pants, they call it, but my pants were dangerously close to getting wet. I hoped it would go quick so I wouldn't feel anything or maybe just blow up on impact, but I never got to say goodbye to anyone.

He heard me.

But he was watching all along, that over confident young man who found himself enveloped in a death shroud while flying 1097M.

At the last moment, perhaps when he knew I had learned my lesson, he opened up a shining window in the smaze, in front, and below me, and my eyes immediately darted straight outside, and there I was, about two miles out on final to Torrance Municipal airport.

I smiled and yes, there were tears. "Thank you, my God!"

I had missed all power lines and obstacles in my way, but I had no radio to talk to the tower. I must keep looking for other planes! I flew over the airport so they could see me and they signaled me with their colors, you know, I forgot the code, but they gave me a red, so I circled around, constantly looking for the different colored lights at the tower, designed only for me, radio less, as I re-entered downwind leg. When I was directly across from the tower, I got the green, and knew I was home, turning left onto base leg, then final with a perfect landing. Well not perfect but there was a bounce or two. But then any landing you walk away from is a good landing.

Especially that day.

I got out, kissed the ground, kissed 1097M and thanked God for saving me. Again.

# SOMETHING HAS CHANGED INSIDE ME

Do you feel God's presence?

I usually write for the sake of the words themselves, carefully placing the story on paper because it should be written and not necessarily to become a bestselling author. When I pen other words, it may be for entertainment and pleasure as well, but there are times when I write because, simply, I must. This is one of those times.

I'm a Christian, grew up in a Christian home but I've never been what they call a bible toter. I went to Sunday school when I was small but certainly wasn't the star of the class, that's for sure. Many Christians I suppose, are more well read with regard to the bible and able to recite verses that I've not heard. Yes, I've always believed in God and Jesus his son who died for our sins, yet maybe I just believed because I thought I was supposed to because well, that was what I was taught. The sermons that I listened to, sometimes attentively, sounded good and reflected how we should act in life and toward others, but the meaning didn't have teeth in it that I felt viscerally. All I knew was that hard work and independent determination would bring all the success I needed.

Without question, I've led an interesting life so far, filled with huge mistakes and sin and at the same time, overwhelming joy interspersed with ridiculous injections of luck into my naïve soul. I've fallen down spiritually when the wave of darkness has descended upon me, laughingly coursing through my veins, but just as the evil is about to take me to his dungeon, I stop, wake up, get on my knees and pray to God.

Then I conquer evil. Once again.

Too many times I have been close to leaving this earth, most of the time from my own mistakes and reckless bravado, and other times well, because I was in the wrong place at the wrong time. Yet why do I keep making a comeback? Why am I still here?

A certain near death experience happened to me in April, 2013. This one though, was the real thing, and in any other circumstance than what I was in, I would've died. But this experience was of unbelievable peace and infinite love. This time I felt God. It was a combination of power, forgiveness, peace and love without conditions. I still feel it to this day, and when I feel it being gently pushed to the background of daily life, I stop, think, bring it back and smile while praising the blueness of the sky I thought I'd never see again.

I tell you this because it is my way of trying to explain this: Something inside my soul has changed. Now, when I make rounds in the Intensive Care Unit, or for that matter, in the Emergency Department, my office or any ward of the hospital my attitude has changed. People who know me have seen this and yes, there are times when I'm the same old stubborn and at times, impatient doctor I was before, but something deeper lingers in my soul, quietly controlling my view on life. Interestingly I have found that when I talk to a patient family or patients themselves who are suffering from devastating illnesses or life-threatening conditions, words I never heard myself say before, tumble and spew from my mouth like an open fire hydrant on the boiling streets of Chicago in the summer. It seems I can't control these words and after I say them, I smile and feel strength. That's right, I smile and feel the peace, knowing the words are correct, whether I put them there or not. I have no fear.

After I describe the medical problems the best I can to the patient or family, I suddenly end my conversation with words like, "It's in God's hands." Or maybe I'll say, "Do you believe in God? He saved you today my friend."

In fact, I said those words recently after a patient had a similar near-death experience that I had, but he remembered nothing and didn't feel the peace and love that I did. Yet, after he said, "Thank you Dr. Carson for helping save my life," I asked him, "What did you feel and what do you remember?"

"I remember nothing, Dr. Carson. What happened?"

His wife listened intently

I told him about his heart stopping and how bystanders did CPR and immediately gave him electrical counter shocks and how my cardiology colleagues opened up his closed artery with stents, and although he could've died, he survived, completely intact.

Then I said, "God saved you my friend. You have a new life." He said nothing. I walked away, and his wife stopped me outside the patient room and said, "Thanks Dr. Carson. He's never believed in God and I want to talk to him about this."

Understand that I don't proselytize and I am not a preacher. I am simply a doctor and a man who has many faults, but I have a feeling now about God's love for me and his willingness to keep me on this earth. I believe, well no, I know, these words that I never said before to patients, now flow out of my mouth because he placed them there, knowing that I would be a willing vessel to recite them with pleasure and confidence.

Thank you God.

Something has changed inside me.

# GET YOUR HOUSE IN ORDER!

What to do in the morning before you leave for work to avoid embarrassment:

Since I'm a bachelor, I have total freedom to do what I want and when as well as how I want to do it in my house with no words from others to tell me otherwise. That is of course, unless the cat objects, in which case I just fight him for control of the Carson domestic kingdom. Sometimes I win.

This freedom of course, has its advantages as well as disadvantages. Some of these advantages include but are not limited to the following:

- I can leave unfolded laundry in a pile wherever I want.
- Sometimes I fold my laundry if it needs it.
- I can leave dirty dishes in the sink if I'm in a hurry. In fact, dishwashers make convenient cupboards and storage spaces.
- Sometimes articles of clothing are left on the floor when I go to work. Yes, people, this includes underwear.
- I can read books and articles and leave them anywhere I want. Use your imagination.

- I take out the garbage when I want. Always when it stinks though.

I guess you get the message, but really, I'm a relatively clean guy with many freedoms, domestic wise that is. However, after my NDE one year ago, I think I left my house a mess, clothing on the floor, stupid notes to myself and important papers scattered everywhere. You see, I had no idea that I would be close to death, and that it was unlikely that I was coming back again and only God knew that answer.

Ever since then, I realize that when I wake up in the morning, it may be my last day on this earth. I know, this may seem like an uncomfortable subject to some, but to me it was reality. So, although I don't leave my house in the morning spotless, no far from it, I do leave it respectable enough for people to see if I don't return. So, I pick up those unmentionables from the floor that I am mentioning, put my important papers away and try to make my bed, although it will be lumpy, and if you try to bounce a quarter off of it, you will lose your quarter. I love life and the gift God gave to me and I will cherish it daily until he chooses to take me, and I will never take life for granted, but you got to have your stuff and especially your life—in order.

Just a little advice, my readers. You just never know.

# HOME

"Carson, it's time for you to go home now. Get out of here while you can."

My partners rescue me and tell me that from time to time, and I sure am relieved to hear it. I'm going home! Exhausted, I try to stay awake on the blurry drive home from my 36-hour shift at the hospital, but I can't seem to turn my brain off from the flurry of messages and memories about my patients, ricocheting around inside my skull.

Did I check the x ray on Mrs. Smith?

Did I adjust the antibiotic dose for renal failure?

Damn, the anticoagulants are still on her med list. Got to stop them because the platelet count is dropping.

But eventually, I do get home, log on to the hospital computer to make sure I correct the lingering patient care thoughts banging around in my quickly fading brain, and lay on the couch that has been longing for me. I feel hunger, but I'm too wasted to think of cooking, so I grab a few scraps in the refrigerator, or a couple slices of bread that are just waiting for a thick pile of peanut butter.

For me, fatigue will overcome hunger easily and that's what usually happens until I fall out of bed in the morning and gorge myself, rejuvenated by world class, world traveling, goofy REM sleep.

Problem is, when I'm exhausted, my brain stubbornly refuses to turn off; it's wired to survival mode for so long I guess, that it refuses to quit. Maybe it thinks it will malfunction or neuronal death is imminent. So, I don't sleep. Mind you, my brain has felt death before, believe me, and it won't allow it. Or maybe it won't accept it consciously—or more specifically, my separate soul-consciousness longs for the non-earthly perfection of paradise love it knows is there, but it represses it so my earthly consciousness will live.

Instead, I think. Then those two beautifully horrible images of my former offspring re-appear. Can't stop it.

Yes, I don't think about these things on purpose. It happens. The word "home" invades my cerebral cortex now and it sets up shop for a while. Where is home? What is home?

Well Carson, you idiot, it's where you are now, in your house laying on your couch, trying to read a book but realizing that your eyes won't stay open without toothpicks, yet your brain refuses to release to sleep. That is home. Carson you're a moron.

Then, once again, I remember the two lost ones I used to talk to. Their images always creep in when I'm weakened. Samson's hair is cut, and the enemies attack. I shudder a little when the heavy memories of my offspring return, then I smile with the good ones, right before that damn granny apple core lodges in my throat again.

They're gone.

I think I understood home at one time. Yes, it was when I came home on Christmas break in high school to be with family and have celebrations, good home cooking and all that stuff. Yeah, that was home. In fact, I remember home when I flew back to it on occasion for holidays when I was a cadet at the Air Force Academy. And for a while, I remember a home when those two lost ones were still with me. I looked forward to seeing their young and innocent faces, hearing their laughter, helping them when they needed help, and guidance when they were growing.

Yeah, that was home for some time.

The memories of those two inject themselves into my mind again, my hair is still cut, and the couch won't protect me.

But for quite a few years now, it seems I've acclimated to a different kind of home. I've got a house to enjoy and yes, that's a home—at least in the classic definition. But really, my home includes a much broader definition than I've ever realized, of necessity, probably because my life has changed so drastically.

During my rare social situations, I don't discuss the lost ones because of the awkward pain, and the difficulty in describing the loss to cheerful, innocent humans. You see, my home now includes the hospital and its staff and the colleagues I work closely with on a daily basis, trying our best in an imperfect and difficult medical world to save lives and ease pain. They have become part of my family—brothers and sisters that are my work family and thus, part of my 'home' that is not my physical house.

Then, the memories strike again briefly, when I least expect them. My mind savors the pleasant ones, and then quickly attempts to delete the devastating ones, and it does so successfully and temporarily.

Then I remember my close friends who I love and who love me and the smile starts to hurt with pleasure. I remember the hospital staff who brought me back from near death about fifteen months ago and the warmth overcomes me.

I am at peace with myself.

While the pain is always there, it is easily reversed when I realize that love is all that matters. C.S. Lewis successfully described the *Four Loves* and he did a spectacular job as always. But really, love doesn't follow the rules: It is all encompassing, all forgiving, non-judgmental and always giving to others.

And yes, strong, single men are capable of saying the word love.

I feel the love of my global 'home' and despite my

devastating losses, I understand what a lucky man I am and will always be on this temporary but beautiful earth as long as I remember God's love for me.

# DOCTORS ARE
# PEOPLE TOO

Well, most doctors are people, I think. A few scattered ones are robots or automatons who have been manufactured in medical schools and residency programs with programmed skill chips that drive the doctor-tron to perform his or her highly specialized skills on whatever body is presented, no questions asked. That of course, requires the least cognitive effort but potentially maximal gain or benefit, because let's face it: all human bodies are the same and therefore, what could go wrong with basic science and technology? I must emphasize that it is rare, but others unfortunately, think they are God or a close resemblance because basically, they do walk on massive expanses of H2O and their success is to be expected when you are lucky enough to be in the same room as they are. Engaging you in conversation can occur sometimes but you're not allowed to look them in the eyes for more than five seconds without being turned into a pillar of salt.

Since I abhor clichés, I'll use some silly ones to make a shock point: What I described in the first paragraph with a boot in my mouth and finger up my nose is rare and is not meant to downgrade the lofty profession that I love. I am honored to practice with many superb human beings who also are highly trained and effective physicians. I am humbled by them constantly while I learn tidbits from their experiences that I can apply eagerly to my own patients. And yes, they all talk to patients respectfully and with dignity. But I think we need to listen to this classic piece to understand the lofty profession that we must work hard to preserve and honor:

Put De Lime in De Coconut: <u>Put the Lime in The Coconut—Harry Nilsson—YouTube</u>

I am proud to say I am a physician and I am honored to be a part of the medical profession. I can't think of a more rewarding career that while it carries a load of heavy responsibility, hard work and devastating disappointments, the rewards are too copious to be measured. Just the other day, out of the blue, a patient and his wife came to my office after a long evaluation resulted in a surgical procedure and the subsequent treatment was beginning to work when all else seemed doomed to failure. They both stood up individually, hugged me warmly and both said they loved me. I didn't expect that at all, and certainly didn't think I deserved that for just doing my job.

No, I'm not God, not remotely close. But I do believe in God. You see, I have nearly died on multiple occasions, the last one about 1.5 years ago was very close and it changed me. I'm still the same doctor with the same knowledge base and skill set, but I know God gave me a second chance, so I'm not afraid to talk about it. Frankly, I find spiritual words now flowing from my mouth easily when I am with patients and families in critical situations, and I feel his presence and my prayer allows him to guide me in my weakness.

I don't proselytize; I am just comfortable with my own spirituality and thankful for the blessings and skills that God has bestowed on me.

And if a patient says Grandma told them they should take a lime in a coconut and mix'em both up because it cures what ails ya, I'll listen, because hell, they may be right.

# LUCKY MAN, LOVE AND POWER

Although I've tasted the peaceful lure of near death, I've seen and heard angels walking on earth. They don't have wings and they are human: doctors, nurses, respiratory therapists, technicians and many others. Unfortunately, the peace and calm I experienced sometimes eludes me during the speeding essence of everyday life, but I try to take the time to sit back, think, and realize that despite my frequent inadequacies, God has chosen to give me a second chance, by demonstrating the miraculous once again. My fear is that I will forget his gift and the underlying reason for his choice, so I sit back and think, pray in thanks and once again realize how lucky I am.

I am lucky because:

I Hear:

Talkative crickets in the serenity of a dusky night reminding me of my camping days as an Eagle Scout; The cheerful chirping birds filling the sweet morning air with an inspiring message that I've been given at least another day to jump out of bed and try to make a difference despite my aches and pains; My wheezing after I complete an intense circuit training workout, knowing the pleasure in the pain, confidence that it is possible, after all; The recent words of a smiling patient who said, "Carson, I know that God sent you to me in my time of need when others walked away. Thank you."; The annoying ringing in my left ear following me ever since, but yet a reminder that I'm still alive with a souvenir to stay with me; And those three words, *I love you.*

I Feel:

The wind ravaging my hair when I roll all the windows down and sunroof, driving way too fast down the highway; The tender lusciousness of a woman's full lips against mine as I hold her close and feel her heartbeat close to my chest, while my lucky fingers gently caress the oh-so-feminine small of her back; The life-giving rain cleansing me naturally, my soaked clothes stuck to me, the salt in my eyes and my shoes slogging through the innocent mud; the rhythm of the dance; The radiance of the bright sun scalding my skin that begs for just a little more, then I jump into the cool blueness of the ocean, deep as I dare; the evil that at one time I couldn't fathom or detect, now causes me no concern for nothing can defeat the power of almighty love.

I can Touch:

The hands of someone who desperately needs my strength or guidance, even when I am inwardly unsure of my strength; The handshake of a hero who asks for nothing; The reverent symbolism of the communion plate at church, passed down the pew; The soft furry coat of a dog or cat who simply needs love; The feel of the yoke of a glider airplane, pulling back farther and farther until she stalls, then it drops, dead in the air, stomach up in the ceiling, then she catches the lift and we're flying again in an exhilaration that few understand; The smallness of a woman's waist.

I can Taste:

Sampling the silky smoothness of Bordeaux wine from a woman's soft mouth; A tender, juicy steak cooked on the grill in the summer, or winter for that matter; The exhilaration of downhill skiing, partially out of control; hot coffee in the morning, steam rising filling my ravenous lungs with desire; French Fries from McDonalds, oven hot, although only once or twice a year of course; Stone crab dipped in drippy butter.

I can see:

Though my vision isn't very good, I can see as much as I need to—I can still read a book, flip the pages and leap to imaginary places, living vicariously with the hero's adventures; I can see the stress in people's eyes that I never took the time to notice before; Bright smiles of people who I don't even know because I apparently smiled at them and didn't realize I did; The beauty of sleek airplanes and jets streaking through the wispy air; A woman's walk and the rhythm of her hips gliding her down the sidewalk; The inviting blue of the endless sky, allowing for a short time, wisps of cirrus clouds, endearing my eyes to the beyond we all search for; The breathtaking sight of a patient who was close to death, now months later walking back into the hospital to thank the staff.

Smell:

It's that coffee again, can't get enough of that smell, especially after it is fresh ground; The perfume of a woman, light, not overwhelming but enough to erase any chance of intellectual thought; Bacon freshly cooked, and heck, why not every now and then; The salty ocean breeze and stinging spray as the waves crash to the seashore; Old leather-bound books and that august smell of printed knowledge in a library; The cool cleanness of your pillow case ready for your head after a long day at work.

You see I have lost much in life that is difficult to describe, but hope and prayer is the only way to survive. And yet, I have also experienced overwhelming joy at the same time, and my joy begins anew, every time I wake up in the morning and start my day.

Thank you God

# MIRACLES

Many who know me will say that it must be a miracle that I was able to learn how to fly airplanes and still live to talk about it. These same people believe it's a miracle that I've been able to learn how to use a smart phone, kinda use text messaging, operate my own blog, use the new hospital electronic medical record without blowing it up, and of course, cook on my grill without burning the house and neighborhood down.

And of course, they're all correct in their cursory analysis of me.

Yet how many people who know me understand the miracle I feel every morning when I wake up and enjoy the feeling of nice clear air flowing in and out of my lucky lungs? Every day, I look out to the west and my eyes take permanent images of the majestic snow-capped mountain peak piercing the soft blue sky, unhindered by a single cloud, majestically claiming to all, that she is closest to God. Yeah, that never grows old. Never. Every time I take in that view, I realize how small I am in this world, but yet, not insignificant, if I can just muster the strength to make a difference to others.

How many people understand the beauty of a cup of hot coffee in the morning, some good music, the laughter of a friend or colleague, the joy of giving to someone something of yourself just because you can and you are there, and of course, the warm delicacy of a woman's lips.

Yes, these are all miracles that I cannot forget and hope I won't let myself forget.

For various reasons, multiple times in my life, I have found myself in life and death predicaments and luckily, I have survived. Most of us have had similar experiences and I am certainly not unique at all. But there is one day on April 10,2013 that truly was a miracle and God chose to put me in a position where the best, brightest and most loving people descended upon me to save me, when unquestionably, I wouldn't have survived in any other place or time.

And what did I learn from this? God blessed me with another chance on life and a large dose of humility and love. That's right, He taught me the lesson that I didn't quite understand apparently, and that is, nothing matters but love. Nothing.

Enjoy life my friends because it is a precious gift.

I understand now.

# SO HELP ME GOD

I'm keeping with my policy about not blogging about politics. While I do have strong political opinions, a literary blog is not the place for them. Today's blog will however, be about something that is much more important than any political opinion could ever hope to be, and in fact has formed the backbone of this great country since the beginning. I'm talking about Christian spirituality.

No, I am not an evangelist and I don't belong to the fire and brimstone "holier than thou crowd". Not at all. However, my experiences and background in life have forced me to speak out now when certain individuals and small groups have a voice that is too loud, bent on threatening our institutions so that they can achieve their goal of making our country into a Godless society.

The most recent example is some lawyer named Mikey who whined quite loudly to convince the leaders of the Air Force Academy to remove the sentence *So Help Me God* from the cadet honor oath that all cadets repeat yearly. It goes like this: "We will not lie, steal or cheat, nor tolerate among us anyone who does. Furthermore, I resolve to do my duty and live honorably, so help me God." In fact, *So Help Me God* is also found in the oath of allegiance to the United States that all cadets recite on admission, as well as other service branch oaths. Regrettably, lawsuits by similar religious freedom groups have been filed to remove *under God* from the pledge of allegiance. Yes, we are moving to a Godless society to satisfy these insecure little people and it is weakening us and putting us in a dangerous position in the world.

Perhaps their next step is to stop asking the president to swear his oath of office on the bible during inauguration. Should he swear his oath on the Koran? Or should he swear his oath on the book "50 shades of Gray?"

Even major Hassan from Ft. Hood had to take the oath of allegiance to serve in the Army. Whether he said the words *so help me God* or not, we won't know. But if he did say it, he was not talking to my God, because my God would never condone the awful killing of innocent people in the name of religion, in this case, Allah and Islam. Yeah, I said it.

Back to Mikey and the Air Force Academy. He apparently forced the superintendent of the Academy to make it "optional" for cadets to say, *So Help Me God* during the honor oath. If it's optional to say, *So Help Me God* during such an oath at a proud military institution, then perhaps the natural progression of the *me first* entitlement society of laziness is to allow cadets to wake up at 1030 am rather than 5:30 if they are tired, but early awakening is optional. In addition, physical training is optional as well, because doing pushups could be against some religion. Or maybe, discipline should be disregarded completely because smart cadets should be able to figure out what they need themselves and will certainly be able to fly multi-million-dollar airplanes in combat quite easily because that doesn't require discipline does it?

I think Mikey needs to go back to making cereal commercials. Remember those? "Let's see if Mikey likes it!"

I tell you what, when I was flying, I prayed to God frequently every time I was in the cockpit, without fail, and I'm thankful that God kept me alive. Many times, I thought I would buy the farm. In fact, I'm even closer to God now and without his grace, I am nothing.

I have a friend who lived under the influence of the Soviet Union, and she was not allowed to say the word "God" in that socialist/communist environment. Now that she has become a U.S. citizen, the freedom to express the word God openly is a right she appreciates tremendously, something she never thought she would have. In fact, when she became a legal, productive citizen, during the ceremony, nearly 100 immigrants from across the world recited the oath of allegiance and the last three words resounded loudly throughout the auditorium: *So Help Me God*. The cheering thundered straight up my spine, and I must admit, my eyes misted up a little when they played Lee Greenwood's *God Bless the U.S.A.*

Yeah, I'm patriotic as hell and I love my country and what it stands for. But I can see and feel that the strong fabric of this country is slowly being eroded from within and we need to wake up America! I will not stand to see this happening on multiple fronts, and neither should you if you love her. I will fight for her until my last breath and I won't stand for these small groups to de-spiritualize this great country. In fact, if you don't like this country, then get out and live somewhere else.

If I have offended anyone with this writing, then good. Maybe you've learned something. The statements I made are irrefutable.

So help me God!

# MY LATE FRIEND: DID YOU HEAR MY PRAYER THAT DAY?

Back then, I was in seventh grade in Junior High School, although I think now they call them Middle Schools, apparently because it suddenly became demeaning to students to call them junior, I guess. Whatever the reason, no matter what the school was called, I was a typical 7th grader in a public school: naïve, selfish in many ways, awkward around girls, liked to play the trumpet and also play flag football at lunch time. Certainly, at that age, I was low on the pecking order of the school, that's for sure.

It was a long time ago, but I remember that day quite vividly after all these years because it seems things changed forever after that day was over. It was early in my first month of school, just learning the ropes of hallway locker combinations, changing teachers for each subject rather than one teacher for all subjects as in elementary school etc., but I got the hang of it and felt pretty good. In fact, I was going to pick this new friend to be on my team for lunch football that day.

I'm not sure what class it was, perhaps social studies,

whatever that was, and I do remember my teacher for that class. He was tall and engaging, and made learning fun with various projects and competitions, frequently asking students to stand up and recite passages or solve problems on the chalkboard. But on this day, he called up two boys to run up to the chalkboard: One was my friend who would join my team in a few hours, and another I don't remember. My new friend was assigned to the far-left end of the chalkboard and the other boy was on the far right.

I must admit I have no recollection of what the task was, but they were both to race to see who would complete it first on their section of the board. When they were finished, they stood in front of their work, and the teacher then asked them to each go back to their respective ends of the chalkboard and then on the count of three, they were challenged to each take an eraser and erase their work as fast as they could, rushing to meet each other in the middle. The winner got some kind of prize, like maybe going to lunch five minutes early to be first in line for pizza burgers.

The race began and the rest of us students anxiously awaited the winner, and it looked like my friend would win, which he did by a millisecond. We started to clap for him then the clapping stopped like a mousetrap firing.

He never would claim his prize.

He turned around, became pale and hit the floor in front of the class with a heavy thud. I have no idea what the other kids were thinking, but I briefly thought he was faking when he was on the floor, like a game, but when I observed that he was unresponsive and pale, I knew something bad was happening. My teacher began CPR and told us all to leave, which we did, but I didn't want to. I wanted to help revive him but I was helpless and watched the resuscitation attempt fail despite the frantic efforts of the medics and multiple teachers. We watched them wheel him out in a gurney after maybe an hour, or perhaps it was an eternity, covered up in a sheet. Or at least I did, I don't remember the others at all.

My new 12-year-old friend was dead in front of the erased black chalkboard.

Most likely they said, it was a congenital heart abnormality worsened by the stress of the moment, and with my knowledge now, it was probably VFib or Torsades secondary to prolonged QT syndrome, often induced by stress. Several days later, some adults in authority, perhaps the principal, likely under suggestion by my teacher, asked if I would participate in the eulogy at the assembly for the entire school in the gymnasium. Why me? While I knew I was nervous speaking on stage in front of a crowd, I felt compelled to do what I could for my new friend's memory, so they asked me to say a prayer for the entire school assembly. The minister of my church gave the eulogy, and I was asked to finish it with a prayer. I don't remember what I said, or how long it took me to prepare the prayer, but I did, and didn't miss a beat, or if did, I don't remember or deleted it from memory.

I'm not sure I had time to mourn or process this event at that age, nor did any of my classmates. We didn't have psychologists and focus groups. We just continued on, and here I am today, the first time I have shared the story with anyone.

My life has gone on while his was cut short at the age of 12, and I have lived a lucky life, filled with adventure, accomplishments, laughter, failures, brutal pain, loss and also love, and yet, I wonder why it was him and not me that day. What would his life had been if he had lived? He sure laughed a lot. It seems after that day, a seed was planted and I became more aware of our fragile stay on this earth, and that life was not all fun and games. I also learned that we reach to God when there is pain and tragedy. Admittedly, like many kids whose young minds are convinced only of invincibility, I forgot some of the lessons learned during my sometimes zig zagging travels down the road of life, often going the wrong way in dusty gravel.

But today, it all came back again. I understand even more deeply now, especially after my near death a few years ago, that our time on earth is short, yes, the cliché, but we must make our positive mark here on earth and make it a better place somehow. Even if it is just to make a child smile or help someone in need or prop up a person who is feeling down. We are here on the physical earth temporarily and we must show love, grace and humility, or at least love if we can't handle the other two, before our physical time comes to an end and we enter the paradise that is waiting.

I wonder though, would a public school today, allow a 12-year-old student to say a prayer at an assembly without triggering an outcry from the ACLU? Highly unlikely. It would offend Muslim students and therefore won't be allowed.

And I also wonder: My friend, did you hear my prayer that day?

# HERE TODAY AND
# GONE TOMORROW

I almost lost my life seven years ago, to this day. Well, I had close calls before, but this was the real deal. The last words I said to my lady friend that morning as I drove to work to take care of critically ill patients in the ICU was: "Have a great day dear, and I'll talk to you soon." In fact, earlier that morning, amazingly, I swam a thousand yards in the lap pool at the local gym without a sign that anything might be wrong. Then, about noon, while doing a surgical tracheotomy, the staff noticed sweat on my forehead and a little tremor perhaps, but I completed the procedure and sat down in the Cardiac ICU to dictate my surgical report.

Then, it decided to happen. Well maybe gentle at first but my angels were watching me before it hit hard. I had a myocardial infarction while taking care of critically ill patients in the cardiac ICU. Perhaps a little ironic in some ways because the healer now depended on others to heal him, but more importantly it was fortuitous. A code blue was called, I was intubated and was in shock, clinging to what blood pressure was left to maintain my precarious life. The experts said my lesion carried an 85 to 90% mortality.

The details surrounding this event and how divine intervention must have guided the skilled and professional angels around me are important here, because not only was my life saved, but my life changed completely—and I received a message from God, well, not directly, but through a feeling in my soul, that I was needed here on earth still, to accomplish something more. I will let you read this short scene on Amazon so that you can soak in the details of this single event: *Code Blue: A Doctor's View of His Own Near-Death Experience.*

I came back to work about a month later, cherishing my lucky breathing, smiling at the beauty of the snow-capped mountains, savoring the smell of coffee in the morning and the songbirds waking me up in the morning. Little problems didn't matter anymore, and if there were worries, I shrugged them off and ignored them as meaningless. You see, I realized that if one thing had gone wrong, I would not be here to enjoy these wonderful things we see, hear, feel and taste here on this wonderful, yet brutal earth. Nothing matters anymore, just health and love. But really, nothing matters but love.

I smiled a lot after this, and was blessed to be able to re-hab myself to good physical shape and I was able to work full time, as intensely as my partners in this career. In fact, there was a bounce in my step, apparently, and so, one of the nurses called me *Dr. Happy Pants*

As time went on, I realized that not only did I receive the gift of life and a start on a new life, but I was given a certain inner sense about things now—certain perceptions that I didn't experience before. Then the tinnitus (ringing in the left ear) started about six months later, and this ringing has been with me ever since—a reminder I think of the gift I received and that this was the price I would have to pay for a new life.

I realized that my gift of life was to go back to work in my chosen medical field, in the Intensive Care Unit treating critically Ill patients and also in the outpatient clinic because that was my calling and that was how I was to serve Him.

So now, seven years later, I am working just as hard as I was before and I think, or at least I hope, just as effectively. Perhaps I might not run down the hallways patient to patient as fast, but I think I hold my own fairly well. Yes, this was my gift from God, to come back and keep working to help sick people and use my knowledge and skills with his guidance.

But now, they don't call me Dr. Happy Pants anymore. Perhaps it has been too long and it has become a stale phrase, or also, because maybe I don't show that brightness and thankfulness outwardly anymore. Perhaps it is both. I realize now that I am so busy with all the stress of taking care of sick and dying patients, government regulations and the new Wuhan virus evil scourge that perhaps I have lost the meaning of what happened that day seven years ago.

I am disappointed in myself sometimes, when I seem to forget the wonderful blessing God gave me seven years ago, and perhaps, the teaching moment he provided to my soul when it seems that I take that day for granted in my busy daily life.

But my constant tinnitus reminds me daily that the shock to the body back then started the ringing and it is there to remind me to be thankful every day for my blessings and the ability to help others if I can. That is my calling. Now, when I find myself lost in the muck of life, I have learned that I must stop, look to the blue sky above and recall the brutality of that day and how it caused stress to others, but at the same time showed me the angels that God brought to surround me and teach me what is important in life.

# THE ASTRAL BUS

I took about a year of my rare free time, while still practicing medicine, and did some research on various topics for my now novel. I figured if a former Special Ops doctor told me to do this before beginning my book, maybe it was worth the time. He knew that I knew close to nothing about his field. Not only that, he was dangerous and he probably knows where I live. Now I can't tell you details about the three major subjects I reviewed in order to make the novel plausible and realistic, but I will say that one of them has something to do with the astral plane, or as some would say, psychic powers.

I read multiple accounts of people who had undergone Near Death Experiences, and it seems that some of them lived on to have certain psychic abilities that they never previously possessed. Who knows? It's a difficult subject to believe or prove, but then, I had a Near Death Experience myself, seven years ago. I am a little different since then, I guess, but then many people thought I was quite *different* to begin with, but what do they know?

So, I read a book written by Swami Panchadasi, an Indian Swami, written in 1916. Fascinating stuff, and well, it makes your mind swirl with wonder but at the same time, skepticism tries to drown your squiggly neurons. In fact, it made my mind wander so much that I decided to practice some of his techniques. It has something to do with *astral thought reference* and a form of practice telepathy with vibrations, directed at someone else, so that person feels the vibrations and the thoughts you transfer. Or something like that, I guess. What could it hurt?

So, I got on a bus. It was a bus leaving O'Hare airport, during the Chinese virus pandemic and everyone was wearing masks and distanced so that there were two rows between each passenger, and the bus that could previously hold 40 passengers or so, now was maximized at ten. Thankfully, I was seated directly behind a heavenly creature with luxurious flowing blonde hair, bouncing up and down as the bus stopped and started, and her perfume was subtle, and it clearly enjoyed being on her, but it traversed playfully in and out of my hungry lungs like a tropical breeze on a sunny island. And she was wearing a scarf gently around her soft neck. But I never saw her face because of the mask, but those eyes defined the word azure. I know this because I looked up the word azure while sitting on the bus, and sure enough, that was it.

I wanted to meet with her, talk to her, and maybe have a cup of coffee while we looked out at the boats on lake Michigan. But how could you meet someone like this when you are both masked and distanced, and afraid of the nasty Wuhan virus?

So, I did it. The swami said to be successful, you must first show a strong desire or will. After this, you form a clear mental picture of what you want to happen, and then finally, concentrate your thought completely. I stared at the back of her wonderful head and with desire, I sent the mental picture with my thoughts, telling her to *turn around and briefly look at me*. I did this as he taught, with powerful, but gentle concentration.

Sure enough, she briefly turned around, and glanced at me quickly. Must've been a coincidence, I thought. Maybe a buzzing fly was bothering her. So, I had to try it again, to see if it was a coincidence. This time I formed the mental picture of her taking off her scarf, putting it in her bag to her left, then turn around and look at me again. I concentrated intently and sent the mental picture.

Sure enough, to my amazement, she took off her scarf, put it in her bag and this time, she laid her Azure blues right on me, and as the Swami taught, I did not betray any evidence that I knew what was going on, stared straight ahead, and smiled underneath my mask. This did not seem like a coincidence. My heart was thumping now, and I had to grab some deep breaths to calm down and stay controlled, because I realized that something amazing was happening. I really needed some coffee though—I actually imagined I smelled the aroma of the coffee above the bus exhaust and I wondered if she would get off at my stop and maybe join me for some. But my stop was coming, and I knew my silly practice with thought transference was over now, and time to get to back to real life and leave this innocent woman alone.

So, the bus stopped, I grabbed my overnight bag and walked down the aisle, then, she suddenly got up in front of me and walked out ahead. After she stepped down from the bus, she waited for me to get off, a few feet away and said, "Hi my name is Julie. I would love to have some coffee. I know a shop a block away. I would love you to join me. "

Thanks Swami.

# B. Silliness, Humor
## and a Little Satire

# ONE MORE THING
# ABOUT RUNNERS

I'm not into bumper stickers, but have you ever noticed that it's becoming popular now for some people to sport bumper stickers that read: "I'm a Runner" or "I run" or "I run therefore I am."

That bothers the hell out of me.

First off, nobody cares if you are a runner or a fat slob so why advertise for no reason? If you were a real runner, and you know what I mean by that, you wouldn't be caught dead with a bumper sticker like that, although there may be rare exceptions.

The people who put these bumper stickers are on their cars are actually joggers, by definition, and not hard-core runners. They are insecure about their new-found past time and need to advertise their insecurity. These are both men and women. Women put on their make up before they start their jog, wear perfectly clean shorts and put bows in their hair, making sure they look good with long eye lashes. After their jog with friends, they meet in Starbucks, hoping people will see them and how athletic they appear to be, but still look good after their jog with nice tanned legs. It is there that they sip their lattes and talk about their jog and how they think their kid's soccer coach is hot. And the men do the same thing.

A real runner won't advertise what he or she does. A real runner gets up at 5 am and runs in the dark, or after work, or any time he or she can, and doesn't give a care whether it's raining, freezing, in a blizzard or flood. Hell, they won't tell anyone where they are going, and could care less how they look or whether their shorts or pressed or shoes are clean. All they care about is getting the workout done, and done well, accomplishing their goals quietly. They don't care who is watching them, and if they are running in town, they never stop at traffic lights and will often weave in and traffic. Often, they run so long they're out in the country or out in the hills or mountains where they run in solitude. If you ever meet one these runners and they've stopped for some reason, finished with their work out, you'll find they smell bad, they're sweaty and their shorts are dirty and spotted with mud and sometimes blood. Women who are real runners never wear makeup. It's unlikely they'll go to Starbucks after a workout, but if they do, it's to grab something cold to drink and of course, all patrons scatter because they look like orphaned vagabonds. Usually though, they complete their run and go home. Beer is often a staple of the training regimen, especially of marathoners.

Now I want to make this clear: I respect joggers and all people who try to maintain their fitness. That's perfect. But all I ask of you is don't put it in my face by using bumper stickers to advertise. Just go out and do it, and be happy with yourself inside. But, if you must spend the money and take the time to put a bumper sticker on your car, then put one on that says, "I'm a Jogger and will Never be a Runner." Or, "I'm a Jogger and Hope to be a Runner Someday." At least that's truthful.

Now, before I get hate mail and threats from the blog readers who sport "I'm a runner" bumper stickers, please keep these four points in mind.

1. I respect your jogging, believe me, but if you continue with your bumper stickers, I will sport a bumper sticker saying, "I run over people who have "I'm a runner" bumper stickers.
2. Just go out and do your jog, and be happy with yourself. Being fit and athletic is a great feeling, isn't it?
3. If you feel you must threaten me, remember my background information on the blog. I do have *people*.
4. Instead of going to Starbucks after a run, drink more beer. That's especially good fuel the night before a marathon with tons of spaghetti.

Have fun and be safe.

# BUMPER STICKER
# BALONEY BLOG FEST

I tried to resist, but it happened again, much beyond my control. Yes, I tumbled over the edge again, by a bumper sticker. While I have nothing against people who enjoy placing bumper stickers on their perfectly nice cars, sometimes, depending on the content, they inexorably pump my creative juices to a point that forces me to write.

Before I spill out the details of my random thoughts, you must know, as a disclaimer that honestly, I honor the institution of marriage, and the love between a man and a woman is the most beautiful thing imaginable. The comments I am about to make however, are meant to entertain and provoke thought, laughter (I hope) and uncontrollable silliness. If you take this stuff seriously, then you are guilty of all innuendos and implied behaviors that are forthcoming in this piece.

While impatiently waiting at a stoplight, driving between hospitals, my eyes were hypnotized to read this bumper sticker on this poor schmuck's brand-new SUV: "I love my Wife" with a red heart next to it. Now c'mon. Really? I've seen some of these before and each time I see them, I have the same feeling about the prisoner, I mean guy driving the car. Poor guy,

I think I'm going to throw up. He loves her so much that he allows her to tell him to slap the sticker on the car because she has threatened to tell his friends he's gay or that he dresses in pink dresses and panty hose when they go to bed if he doesn't do it. And he better put the sticker on, because when she drives the kids to soccer practice or drives to do her nails, she's going to look back there to make sure her honey put it on nice and straight without any creases on the sticker. There's no way the wifey is insecure about hubby, right? With a bumper sticker like that, no woman would ever even dream of looking at him let alone winking at him. She'll never have to worry.

I admit, I may be wrong about this observation probably because I'm sleep deprived from being on call last night and I'm perilously close to being incoherent. But I'm sure that there are women who have bumper stickers that say similar things like, "I love my hubby". Interestingly, I don't remember the last time I saw one of those, but in the interest of equality, insecurity is rampant between both sexes when the marriage isn't strong.

If a man drives a car with a bumper sticker that says, "I Love My Wife", he really means:

*"I love my wife and enjoy my mistress."*

Or:

*"My wife is in the trunk, please drive slowly."*

Or:

*"Honey, don't call me now, my wife's in the car."*

Equality demands that I discuss what women are really thinking when they drive a car that has a bumper sticker that says, "I love my Hubby."

What she really means is:

*"Drive faster, my boy toy is waiting."*

Or:

*"Excuse my speeding, but my lover only has an hour."*

Love your spouse and do whatever you can to show and demonstrate that love, without expecting others to care. And if you're confident in your marriage, you don't need to place bumper stickers to show me your wedded bliss.

But if you do, we all know what you're really thinking right?

# LOVE MY ELEVATOR
# AND SHE LOVES ME

Thankfully using elevators is an uneventful occurrence for those of who travel between floors in large buildings. When it becomes an eventful occurrence, it can be a huge stress of course and people in general have their guards up while traveling in these necessary conveyances.

Something interesting happened to me in the elevator today. It wasn't traumatic but it stimulated my thinking about elevators in general. I had just walked into the elevator and joined my fellow floor traveler, a woman. Suddenly, a hand shot in between the closing door, forcing it open, and middle-aged employee walked in, searched the front and back of the elevator and then asked, "What is the name of this elevator?" I looked at her, chuckled briefly before I realized that maybe I should be careful because the third floor did house the psyche ward. I realized she might have escaped the Cuckoo's nest. I quickly realized that she knew what floor she was on but simply wanted the name of the elevator. So, I came up with an answer: "Her name is Ellen." She looked at me with a puzzled look then left the elevator before the door closed. Whew, what a relief. But it was obvious to see she was a company woman, and she was simply doing her job, perhaps looking for the label of an elevator number or something. I think.

I looked at the other occupant of *Ellen* and we both laughed and went to our appropriate destinations. Ellen took care of us well with a smooth, uneventful ride. The lady left on the fifth floor and I had five more floors to go, alone, with Ellen.

I thought it would be nice if *Ellen* would talk to me, in a nice sultry voice while I rode in her car. "Good morning sir, thank you for joining me and I hope you're having a wonderful day. Where may I take you?

"Uh, thanks *Ellen*, I'm going to the tenth floor, thank you."

"No problem. I will be pleased to offer you a fast ride or a slower ride if you're not in a hurry. Your choice is my command."

"I see, well, I'm not in a hurry, so how bout a slow ride? What does that include?"

Ellen's sweet voice enticed my brain to ask for more. *Ellen* hesitated, almost as if she was thinking about her options. "A slow ride includes a massage and your favorite music, and since you're alone, that will happen every time you ride, simply by asking."

Two hands descended from the ceiling and began massaging my shoulders and back, seventh floor, eight floor, hmmm that felt good, ninth floor, and then I thought: I need to take the elevator a lot more frequently than I had in the past. So much for exercise.

We arrived at the tenth floor, the hands returned up into the ceiling and I was disappointed that my time with *Ellen* had unfortunately ended.

"Sir, give me your name, and your preferred music and I'll remember you next time and I'll take care of you."

"My name is Carson and I like smooth jazz."

"I'll remember you Carson, and hopefully you'll remember and choose me next time you need an elevator."

"You can count on it *Ellen*."

# BRING BACK ELLEN

It was good while it lasted, I guess. I went to ride up to the ninth floor with Ellen today, but she wasn't available. I just finished a surgery and I sure needed her—that soothing voice, relaxing non-elevator music and of course skillful hands to massage my tense shoulder muscles.

Yellow caution tape draped in an X fashion across her always welcoming door, and a sign that read "under construction" obscured her frequently pressed up and down buttons. Seems that employees suddenly stopped using the stairs and spent much more time on elevators, especially Ellen, and the management took notice. Although elevator time with Ellen certainly increased (especially with the male population), I'm sure productivity actually increased because of her. In fact, the ladies were pushing for an elevator named "Antonio" and rightfully so but I'm not sure that's going to happen now.

I have no doubt that the management never had the courage to ride with Ellen, and if they did, I'm sure they wouldn't admit it. That's unfortunate, because I'm sure their production would increase, and they would be more likely to smile under the stress of meeting the bottom line.

Sometimes political correctness goes a little too far and we need to lighten up a little bit, don't you think? What's wrong with some clean elevator fun to break up the hum drum work day?

Yeah, I sure miss Ellen.

Perhaps I will need help from my readers to launch a *Bring Back Ellen* campaign...

# HILLARY AND DONALD
# ARE SECRET LOVERS

Disclaimer: This blog piece is political satire and pure fiction. It could never happen in real life. I think. For those of you who have a tendency to get your fancy underwear all wound up about your candidate, here is my advice: Lighten up. This piece will offend both sides of the political spectrum equally so that everyone is equally unhappy.

About once a month for the past six months or so, the Secret Service guarding both major party presidential candidates has been facilitating clandestine meetings between Hillary Clinton and Donald Trump. This piece is a hot scoop of the last rendezvous that occurred at a quiet, nondescript bar at an undisclosed location in a completely clueless town. On that recent night, Hillary chose a long red wig, sunglasses and a body slimming black pant suit. Donald sported a Chicago Cubs baseball cap, since a NY Mets cap might give him away despite the bald cap hiding his famous hair. The heavy black rimmed nerd glasses offered a nice touch as well.

The two sat side by side at the bar, ignoring each other while staring at the TV in front of them, secret service agents on each side. Hillary horded the channel changer, making sure it was tuned to CNN or MSNBC, ABC or CBS while The Donald quickly grabbed it and tuned it to Fox News as his only choice. Truth is, he really wanted the Playboy channel if it was available on the Satellite. The agents were hoping he would choose the PB channel also, but he refrained this time.

"Donnie", said Hillary finally. "I hate Fox News. All they do is talk about the stupid classified U.S secrets on my emails that I deleted from my personal server, Benghazi and other lies they come up with. The only channels that feature real honest journalists are CNN, MSNBC, ABC and CBS."

"You must be high. I've noticed you sniffling a lot, so you must be smoking crack. I suggest we both take drug tests Hill. Clear the air. If you were honest with yourself, you'd realize those other channels don't care about true honest journalism, as long as they bow to you and elect you by themselves! The system is rigged and those media organizations are in bed with you and your campaign."

Hillary smiled and adjusted her pant suit. "Speaking of bed Donnie, it's been a long time since I, you know, had any special intimate attention from a man. You know, Bill...

"Yeah, we all know Bill."

"Well, I'm feeling really good right now. The millions my campaign has spent finding women to accuse you of groping them or making lewd comments in the past has paid off. It has successfully kept the focus off the real issues that show my weakness and keeps the spotlight on your mouth. But you know, I must tell you something I've never shared with anyone."

"What's that?" said Donald.

"Well, um, secretly I've often fantasized that actually I was one of the women you were trying to feel or seduce. That would be so hot!"

"No way!"

"Sadly, yes, exactly what I've had my people accuse you of so brutally, I like that in a man."

"Interesting. You're a lot older than the women I usually go for. I prefer young models who are impressed with my huge wealth and power. But hell, I must admit that I really like that you are a strong-willed woman, who never quits. I like that in a woman. Who knows, maybe we could um…

"Um what Donnie?"

"Be lovers. I know that's what you want. But if I was to let this happen and satisfy your weird fantasies Hill, what will I get in return for my extreme sacrifice?"

"Donnie, it's obvious to every reasonable person with a brain who is not a deplorable that I will win the election. Most American voters are I and gullible and will believe anything I say just because you know, I'm Hillary, and nothing sticks to me."

"Poop sticks to you."

"C'mon now. When I'm president, I will reward you by making you ambassador to Iceland!" said Hillary.

"That's really generous. Truth is, I'd rather have needles poked in my eyes while I watch Obama draw lines in the sand and throw our money down the toilet. I'm going to win. And it's going to be Yuge! I'll win because I'm very rich and a great business man, taking no money from special interest groups. The fact is, I'm wonderful and I will fix everything while showing all world leaders my great hair. But if Americans are stupid enough to elect a criminal like you, and you want some special attention in the bedroom, then I'm going to need something much more powerful than a stupid ambassadorship to some tiny country. And we all know what you do to Ambassadors, Hillary."

She smiled her famous molded smile. "Ok Donnie. Tell me what you want dear."

"I want to be nominated and then confirmed as a Supreme Court Justice with the next vacancy, and the next vacancy after that will be my choice, whispered softly into your welcoming ear."

"Ha! You are great with the art of the deal, that's for sure, but this is between us. I'll have to think about it. We will see..."

"You're right, I'm a master of the deal. That's what this country needs. America first."

"Wake up Donald! You're a hopeless womanizer, and clearly unfit to be president, but I can't help but love that about you. I'll just have to ignore that you are a racist, a xenophobe, a homophobe, a germaphobe and probably a cute puppyphobe!"

"Hillary, I love how you lie. You do it with such charm and grace, as if you actually believe your lies. Sure, we all know the truth about how you abandoned our people in Benghazi when they asked for help, your destruction of classified emails on your private server even after a congressional subpoena and your accusations against Bill's sexual accusers as if they were dogs and prostitutes. But you are well aware that many Americans would rather ignore your sliminess and pay to play, so they can attack my playboy antics and womanizing. After all, terrorism and a destroyed economy is not as important as sex, right Hillary?"

"Exactly."

"I guess in the end, I really like you for your never quit attitude, even though you're wrong."

"So, Donnie dear, is the answer yes?"

"I need to think about it. What about Milania? What will she think?"

"Welcome to politics. Donnie. We do or say anything at all to get votes. Bill and I are above the law and that makes me feel powerful. And speaking of Bill, I'm sure he'll try his best to keep Milania busy while the two of us need our special time together."

"Right, of course. I guess I could sure use that powerful Supreme Court seat, and I'd look fantastic in that long black robe. It'll go great with my hair. I would kick ass on the Supreme Court with all those old fogies! But I need guarantees."

With that, Donald finished his Guinness with a foam mustache, smiled at the bar maid and then stared at her ass before leaving a 100-dollar tip and Hillary finished her martini, fell off her bar stool and the secret service agents picked her up off the floor and escorted them both away to their waiting cars.

.

# BAR PICK-UP SONGS

So, Carl, I'm buying tonight. Whattya havin?
Hell, if you're buyin, I'm going all out. How bout a yard of beer? Anyway, why the generous mood tonight?"

"I've retired. I'm done. Don't need to work anymore."

"You gotta be kidding. What did you do to strike it rich? Last time we were here you weren't striking it rich Jerry, you were striking out with the ladies."

"We'll talk about that later, but tonight is a time to drink."

"Got no problem with that. Bring it on man."

After they both downed a yard of beer apiece, the blonde and her brunette friend at the end of the bar seemed to cast brief glances at Jerry, but he didn't know it was because he had beer foam on his curly mustache and beer spilled down his shirt, exposing the flabby outline of his Pecs. He smiled back and flexed what was left of his sternocleidomastoids. But the rhythm of the music made both guys in a singing mood. Or was it from the beer?

"You know I miss Annie, but I've got to find someone new Carl. You know, *I'm running down* the *road trying to loosen my load, got a world of trouble on my mind. Looking for a lover who won't blow my cover, she's so hard to find.*"

"Ah, I loved that song. Oldie, but relaxing to listen to on the road."

"Maybe so, but *I used to roll the dice, feel the fear in my enemies' eyes,* my married friend."

"I doubt it, but dream on."

"That blonde may be the one for you Jerry, but this time, you need to be smarter. The last one you tried to pick up gave you the number to some pizza parlor rather than her own. Dropped me to the floor laughing when you called."

"Yeah, but they delivered some excellent pizza, after all."

"You need to think about some good pick-up lines, smooth ones this time. Maybe you should practice them on me before you go over there and mess up, Mr. retired rich man."

"Okay, how bout this: *"I won't give up, when I look into your eyes, it's like looking into the night sky...I won't give up."*

"Not bad, like that song, but it lulls me to sleep. I like it for a start, because it shows you're concentrating on her eyes and not other parts of her body. Drink a little more, then try something else."

"Ok, *"I say to myself, you're such a lucky guy....to have a girl like you is truly a dream come true. Well, it's just my imagination...running away from me...but you can make it real..."*

"Unlike those original singers, you got no rhythm and a girl needs a lot more than that to take an interest in you. Can't you try something a little more emotional, to touch her heart?"

*"The thrill is gone, baby, the thrill is gone.* Do you want to help me bring it back?"

"You got to be kidding me. Now I'm singing the blues."

"Ok, you're right, too depressing. How bout', *"Girl I only have eyes for you, ain't no doubt about it."*

"Now, that's better, you're getting warmer. But if that doesn't work, you need to be ready for a direct hit that she can't ignore, but you know, it will be sink or swim once you sing it."

"Oh, I get it, 'Hello, I love you won't you tell me your name. *Hello, I love you let me jump your game.*"

"That's a classic, but I think she has to be in the right mood for that one. I think you're ready, but all I see is you sitting on your lazy butt. *'Oww. Get up offa that thang and dance till you* feel *better. Get up offa that thang and try to release that pressure! Good god y'all*"

"Impressive, but too bad you got no rhythm Carl."

"Hey, I'm happy. Not the one looking for love. Well, you gonna get up offa that thang?"

Jerry bought the blonde a drink, she smiled and raised her glass to him. He sauntered over, and the right words were chosen during his slow saunter over to her.

"Umm, Hello, I love you won't you tell me your name. Hello, I love let me you jump in your game."

She clapped, raised her glass to him and the glasses clashed hard, spilling his beer over his pants. Embarrassed, he waited for her response, hoping this time finally, for a score.

"Very good. My name's Julie and I appreciate your effort and you're cute, however, I'm going to have to close the doors on you because my husband is the owner of this bar, and he's a very jealous professional wrestler named, "Classy Crusher.""

Jerry walked back to sit by Carl, rejected again, although slightly softer than before.

"So what happened, my friend?"

"*She's a black magic woman, got me so blind I can't see, she's trying to make a devil out of me.*"

"Good one. But you know, bars aren't the place to find love, my friend. It comes naturally, and you've got to be yourself and love will come. But thankfully, you didn't tell her about your new found richness, cause that's the kiss of death for you, because without love first, money means nothing my friend."

# WELCOME TO HOTEL CALI-PUTIN

(You will sing along; all comrades know
famous melody from America!)

Verse 1
On a dark tundra highway, cool wind in his hairs
Warm smell of police state, rising up through the air.
Up ahead in the distance, he saw a shimmering light.
His head grew larger and he spied new land.
He had to stop for the night.
There he stood in the doorway.
He knew they wouldn't tell.
And he think to himself
More land is heaven, I not care about hell.
Then she lit up a candle and showed him the way
There were voices down the corridor
He thought he heard them say.

Hook
Welcome to the Hotel Cali-Putin!

Is lovely place
She has lovely face
Plenty room at hotel Cali-Putin
Any time of year
He will take more here

Verse 2
His mind is dictator-twisted, he got KGB friends
He got a lot of pretty little countries he will defend
How they dance in the courtyard, his bare-chested threat
Some dance to remember, most hope to forget
So he called up loyal comrade
Bring Wodka, not wine
We haven't had Stolichnaya this good since 1969
And still helpless voices are calling from far away
Wake you up in the middle of the night
Just to hear them say

Hook
Welcome to the Hotel Cali-Putin
Is a lovely place
She has lovely face
Comrades live it up in Hotel Cali-Putin
Is big nice surprise
We eat alibis

Verse 3
Terrors walk the ceiling
We drink wodka no ice
And she said, "We are all just prisoners here, he has nuclear
device"
And in the master's chambers
They gather for big feast
They stab it with their greedy knives
But they laugh at blood of beast

Last think I remember, I was
Running for the door
I had to find passage back
To Siberia I so longed for
"Relax" said the night man
"We are programmed to deceive
You can check out any time you like
But you can never leave!"

# LOSING YOUR NOVEL WRITING VIRGINITY: FOR DOCTORS

Now that my novel writing virginity is lost forever, I can now speak with some expertise about the process. Well, maybe not that much expertise, but I've been knocked to the mat a few times and have had my prideful ego flushed down the toilet more times than I thought possible at various writing conferences and critique sessions. So now, just like doing procedures in medicine: *See one, do one and teach one.* Here are my thirteen tips that will guide you haughty physicians down the path to novel writing publication:

- You're a king in the operating room, but you're a lowly worm in the writing community. So, get used to it now.
- Go to a writing conference to learn the craft. Take good notes. Memorize them then throw them out, because you'll never look at them again.
- There are hordes of women at these writing conferences, and they're great writers. If they wanted to, they could write you into a corner anytime they wanted, leaving you in a quivering mess of writing jelly. Don't tempt them; you'll regret it.
- If one of these women writers smiles at you, don't get

excited. It's a tease designed to destroy your will to continue.

- When you go to the conference-sponsored lunch and sit at a round table that seats ten, and there is one seat left and the rest are occupied by nicely-dressed women talking fast and vociferously, avoid the temptation to take that seat oh king of your own universe. They'll eat you up so quickly you won't know what happened.
- If you want to impress a woman at a writer's conference, tell her you write "Sexy Steam Punk" or "Fantasy Sci-Fi crime thrillers with a sexual theme."
- Never tell anyone at a conference that you write romance. The women will step on your toes with their Stiletto heels and put tags on your back that say, "He don't get romance". The men will think you are gay.
- If you think you are a good writer when you start, you aren't even close.
- You may know medicine quite well but you don't know jack s... about writing.
- Work hard. Never give up, and listen to the experts. Then ignore what they say.
- When you describe your work to two experts, one will say, "go left", the other will say "go right, he's stupid." When that happens it's best to think about it deeply for about thirty seconds, then start drinking heavily.
- Writers drink heavier than Russian Sailors. Remember Ernie H? If you do it right, you can achieve some inspiration this way as long as you drink along the ascending curve of creativity. It falls quickly after that.
- Please continue to maintain your medical license and your practice. You'll need a steady job.

# WOODPECKERS ARE STONERS TOO: THEY LIKE MARIJUANA

I looked it up on the internet and I found his picture and it sure seems it is a match: He's a Northern Flicker woodpecker and they are about 15 inches tall as an adult. But since I live out west and he's a Northern Flicker, then clearly, he is hopelessly lost. Not only that he doesn't understand the difference between window glass and wood. Unfortunately, my office desk is right next to a large window and this guy comes right up to me and pecks incessantly for hours on end, then falls off the edge, flicks his wings, obviously trying to impress me with his red wings underneath, and he's back up again pecking. And looking at me, cocking his head, looking at me from a different angle, then pecking again. The glass is only a couple feet away from my desk, and it seems he is watching everything I do, maybe even what keys I am typing and what I am eating or drinking.

Not only is the poor pecker lost, but he is insane. But then, maybe it's not his fault. Since my state has legalized marijuana, he has probably been pecking on some juicy marijuana plants and enjoying the taste a little too much, and he's lost his mind. Problem with that though, is that I thought marijuana made you mellow. It must've had the opposite effect on this avian stoner.

However, there is another possibility to consider, since the marijuana hypothesis will be difficult to prove unless he falls to the ground dead stoned and we take him to the vet to do an autopsy and find Cannabis running round his bird brain. The other possibility is even more concerning. The American military has developed miniature drones, and some can look like birds and even fly. Perhaps this Flicker is a spy drone, sent to spy on me? It's possible, since my latest thriller novel does delve into some black ops stuff and things the military establishment may not want published, even though it is pure fiction. Perhaps my manuscript was somehow leaked out pre-publication and the spooks became interested in me and sent their crazy spy woodpecker to watch my every move, thinking I wouldn't figure out the woodpecker trick?

Things might get even more interesting. Whether he is a stoner or a spy, it doesn't matter because I will not divulge any secrets or let his psychological warfare bother me, because sooner or later, we will find out the truth about this dude, but I must admit, his pecking noises are starting to sound like Morse code signals that few people understand anymore, except boy scouts, and unfortunately, boy scouts don't exist anymore.

However, I was an eagle scout, so this Northern Flicker has met his match!

# WORD VOMIT

Ok, a couple things bothered me today, and they had nothing to do with patients smoking and drinking too much and expecting me to cure them from their self-induced destruction with a pill or with surgery. No, au contraire. It had to do with stupid words health care professionals use in charts and it bugs me enough to bloviate about it.

Word #1: Verbalize. Example: "Mr. Smith VERBALIZED to this examiner that his chest pain only occurred when he would tense down during a bowel movement." No, the patient sure as hell did not verbalize to you, Mr. or Ms. Health professional—just say it in proper English and we will still think you are quite special. I really don't think you're smarter by writing those words in the chart, and the lawyers who are licking their chops to make some money on you don't care either. Or do you think *verbalizing* is a more eloquent way to describe how a patient talks? Does that mean the words floated out of his mouth like butterflies searching for sunshine in the blue sky? Here is the proper way to write the same thing in the chart: "Mr. Smith said that his chest pain only occurred when straining during a bowel movement." Does using the word *verbalize* make the poop less stinky? By the way, I used to be married, so I knew I was in trouble when my ex used to say, "we need to talk!" Sure isn't as effective if she said, "we need to verbalize!"

Word #2: Articulate. Example: "Mrs. Smith articulated that her breathing only became heavy during sex with the neighbor man, and not with her husband." Correct chart entry: "Mrs. Smith described a chest pain that only occurred during sex with the neighbor man, or, "Mrs. Smith said that her chest pain only occurs during sex with the neighbor man." Either of the last entries are reasonable chart entries. I love nurses, my angels, but I think in nursing school they are taught to use verbalize or articulate instead of *said* or *described* otherwise they won't pass. Problem is, these words are unfortunately seeping into physician's notes as well and that's because everyone knows hospitals are essentially run by nurses because basically, doctors fight too much.

Word #3, 4 and 5 are together: *delightful, extremely pleasant.* These words are usually written by physicians who are massaging the chart the best they can because they want it to be pretty for the ravenous ambulance chasers (lawyers), or it's simply because they are trying to show what lovely human beings and physicians they are. It's meaningless drool.

These words bring to mind a simple analogy about when I describe to a friend that I enjoy my favorite food. "I love masticating my lobster dinner." Wouldn't it be more acceptable if I simply said, "I love eating my lobster dinner."

My advice is to tell it like it is but don't give too much information: "Mr. Smith is a delightful 65-year-old patient brought in by ambulance because..." Who cares if he's delightful, extremely pleasant or an old sour puss, you're going to treat him with professional courtesy and with your best medical skills. Thankfully, I'm a surgeon and if a patient is verbalizing or articulating too much, I simply ask the anesthesiologist to give him the gas, put him to sleep and my scalpel does its work. No worries.

# SITTING AT THE
# BAR: TRUMP, BIDEN
# AND EASTWOOD

D ear readers: This is a work of fiction and my own cre-
ation, and is highly unlikely to ever happen. But who
knows anymore, in this bizarre world. It is for entertainment
only, and may be somewhat thought-provoking to those who
pay attention and keep an open mind. I will use actual real
quotes from Donald Trump, Joe Biden, and Clint Eastwood.
When they are actual real quotes from their mouths in real
lives, then, that will be in *Italics*. Everything else, if of course,
fictional entertainment. All three will be treated fairly and
hopefully without political bias and all will be embarrassed
equally. Who knows, you might even laugh, or perhaps, shed
a tear at the end.

Two senior Service agents talking:

"Yes, Potus is now finishing the 18th hole at the Kennet
Square Golf and Country Club. But there's a problem."

"What problem? We have him scheduled to head back
to Washington after the round. It's covered and the route is
secured."

"Right. But Potus said there's been a change in plans."

"What? He changed plans again on us?"

"Yes. Clint Eastwood, the famous Hollywood actor who was talking to a chair as if it was Obama at the 2016 Republican convention, met Potus after the round of golf and invited him to a piano bar in Wilmington, Delaware, 13 miles away."

"Ok. But for one thing, Potus does not drink alcohol and if I'm not mistaken, that is Biden's home town."

"Correct on both accounts. See the problem?"

"Yes. We allowed this only one time before when the president went in disguise and met Hillary at the bar. It was not a big disaster, but she did fall off a bar stool."

"Yes, I remember, but I think we can do this if we secure the area, and put some snipers on roof tops and check the usual credentials of people and close the airport, you know, the usual stuff. But there is a wild card, you know—"

"I know. Biden goes to bars."

"Bingo. We need to start running. Eastwood's probably already at the bar."

Clint Eastwood was wearing Jeans and a black golf shirt, but this time, no disguise. He didn't hide himself much, and at the age of 90, most people didn't recognize him very often anymore, especially the young people, like Scott, the young bartender who was maybe 25. He was clueless who the older man was, although he seemed to have a certain confident authority to him, even though he was a grandfather type. Clint was in the middle of the bar, talking with Scott about the young man's future plans and was already starting to enjoy his cold beer while sneering intermittently at the TV that had CNN news on.

The secret service walked in first, through the back door, sat two agents down in the back of the bar, one at each end of the bar and they said nothing, staring straight ahead, and dark sun glasses on. There were a handful of people at tables, who they frisked and checked out, and let them stay. Then they let

Trump walk in and he sat to the right of Clint, six feet away. He wasn't disguised either, except he wore a FDNY baseball cap rather than his usual red MAGA cap.

"Thanks for inviting me here Clint. I appreciate the hospitality."

"No problem Donald. How was your round of golf?"

"Not my greatest round you know, but, most of my great rounds are on my Florida Country Club or at my amazing course in Scotland. I own some of the greatest golf courses in the world!"

Clint said, "I like Pebble Beach, played a few Pro-Ams there over the years, but now, at my age, if I finish 18 holes successfully, I'm happy as hell. I'll buy you a beer Donald."

"No thanks Clint. I don't drink. But I'll have a large lemonade."

Clint chuckled. "***A man's got to know his limitations***."

Scott interrupted both men and said, "All drinks on the house for the president!"

Trump said, "Scott, do you know who this is sitting in front of you? This is Clint Eastwood, the famous Hollywood actor, you know, The Outlaw Josey Wales, Dirty Harry and a lot more! I think this is going to make my day as well as yours. Oh, and by the way Scott, in case you are wondering, my hair is not orange, so don't even think about it. It is great hair though, isn't it?"

Scott wisely didn't comment about the president's hair, but then, when he realized who was sitting next to him, his mouth dropped open in shock. "Josey Wales is here? Drinks on the house for Josey and the President!"

"No, said Donald Trump. I'll take care of all of it. My treat. He put a 100-dollar bill on the bar and gave it to Scott. "I will never inconvenience this establishment, especially after all we went through with Covid. Thanks for having us. But all I ask is that you turn off the lying CNN on your TV and change it to sports or something, if there are any sports anymore, since everybody has ignored me and canceled everything to purposely ruin the economy that I built so well. The greatest economy ever I built! CNN is **Fake news!**"

Then a secret service agent whispered in the president's ear something that he needed to know. Trump said, "Are you kidding me?"

Then, in walked Joe Biden and both security details looked at each other in amazement, and Biden sat down on the left side of Eastwood. He was oblivious to Eastwood, but saw Trump and his security detail and shouted down the bar, past Eastwood, Hey Don, what in the hell brings you to my neck of the woods? Trying to steal some votes from me? Then, he ordered a large mug of beer and told the bartender to put in on Trump's tab.

"No, Sleepy Joe, I was down the road playing golf and got thirsty and Clint Eastwood here, kindly invited me for something to drink. Great to see they let you out of hiding though."

Joe looked at Clint and it didn't register to him who it was. "Nice to meet you Clint. I liked you in the movie The Witches of Eastwick. Bollywood actors donate a lot to the Democrats and support us, so I appreciate you guys in Bollywood."

Trump heard this, and couldn't help but spit out his mouthful of lemonade across the bar, and it dripped down the front of a bottle of Jack Daniels. "It's called Hollywood, Joe."

Eastwood squinted at Biden, because he obviously knew nothing about Clint or his movies, then sneered and said, "**I reckon so**, Mr. Boden, I mean Biden. But tell me, what is your gun control policy, if you become elected President?"

Biden looked down at the bold printed cue cards he had in his sleeve, then said, "I have no comment on that Mr. Eastlick, they told me not to talk about it anymore without further destructions, I mean er, instructions."

"**I have a strict gun control policy**," said Clint. "" **if there is a gun around, I want to be in control of it.** And the fact is, **participating in a gun buyback program** *because you think criminals have too many guns, is like having yourself castrated because you think the neighbors have too many kids."*

*"Don't tell me that Pal, or I'm going outside with you man. I'll have you know that I'm running for the U.S. Senate and we choose truth over facts! I'm going to challenge you to a push-up contest,* Mr. Eastlick," said Biden.

Biden clearly didn't realize who he was talking to. Clint ordered another beer and then his face turned cold and faced Biden. *"I tried being reasonable, and I didn't like it."*

"Harrumph". Trump wasn't used to being ignored, so he had to fix that problem immediately. After all, he was the president and that's that. "Hey Joe, what's this ridiculous Green New Deal you democrats are trying to ram down our throats to destroy our economy? As far as the economy and my presidency, *I've done more than perhaps any president in the first 100 days.* And you know, *the media is-what is the word, I think one of the greatest of all terms I've come up with-is fake!* What's wrong with farting cows anyway Joe? What's that got to do with destroying the atmosphere? It'll destroy the cattle ranchers, that's for sure and we'll be eating piles of vegetables and seaweed if you guys get your way."

*"C'mon man!"* Don, you don't know anything? Eliminating farting cows is one step we must take to decrease methane gas release to the atmosphere which absolutely will reduce greenhouse gas and therefore, global damn warming, you moron!" Said Biden.

"Hey sleepy Joe. Democrats eat a ton more beans and plant food than Republicans so they fart a lot more, so if they convert and become Republican meat eaters, there will be less methane released. In fact, if you guys send *"Fat Jerry"* (Nadler) to Mars on the Mars explorer, methane release will be reduced by a huge amount because I am sure he farts more than most large cows."

Clint laughed at this exchange between the two candidates, then said, "I have a ranch of sheep, one of which is black at my Mission Ranch in Carmel, and I am sure they fart a lot, and you damn well better not touch my sheep and if anyone tries, *I have a 44 magnum, the most powerful handgun in the world and would blow your head clean off. You've got to ask yourself one question: Do you feel lucky? Well do ya punk?*"

With that, the secret service agents jumped up and prepared for action to protect Biden, but they knew it was Clint and he was just quoting some of his famous movie scenes, so they sat back down. But I think everyone got the message loud and clear and the tension in the room skyrocketed.

But Clint wasn't finished, and maybe it was the beer that was loosening him up a little, so he asked both of them, "what are you guys going to do about all the violence in the cities now, and destruction of people's stores, and livelihoods, and they do not even know what they are protesting. Isn't the violence part of a broader Marxist scheme to destroy the structure of our great country, using Antifa and the BLM movement, which really isn't about black lives at all?"

Trump said. "Yes, we must stop the violence and restore law and order to our great cities. Peaceful protesting is of course, fine, but violence and destruction of people and property cannot be tolerated. If the democratic mayors simply ask me, I will send in the National Guard to help clean it up what they refuse to clean up. I am great, and they are afraid of my greatness."

Biden said, "Violins? Yes, I enjoy violins when I go to the symphony orchestra and other hot rock bands and sometimes on *record players.*"

"No Sleepy Joe," said Trump. "Violence! And what do you think about the Black Lives Matter organization, and its charter, not the three words themselves, literally? Do you know the difference?" He ordered another lemonade.

"Yes", said Joe, "I believe Black lives Matter."

"All lives matter. Black, white, yellow, red or whatever color." Said Trump.

"How can you say that Don? Are you a racist?" said Biden. He looked down at his cue cards with large print and said to himself silently, yes, that is what they wrote for me to say, to use the word racist when I can and only say BLM many times. Right. I said what they told me to say.

"What did you call me?" said Trump

After this exchange, Clint had enough. He stood up and looked at both presidential candidates and slammed his last beer down on the bar. Scott jumped. Clint said, *"respect your efforts, respect yourself. Self-respect leads to self-discipline. When you have both firmly under your belt, that is real power. Maybe I am getting to the age when I am starting to be senile or nostalgic or both, but people are angry now. You used to be able to disagree with people and still be friends. Now, you hear these talk shows and everyone who believes differently from you is called a moron or idiot—both right and left.* Gentleman, I've had enough. I am going to the piano to play some music and cool things down a bit." So, he walked over to the piano in the corner and started playing, while Trump and Biden turned and watched.

The first song he played, was Yellow Rose of Alabammy (Alabama) that was played during his movie, The Outlaw Josey Wales. Then, remarkably, both candidates walked over to the piano and joined Clint as he played the Righteous Brother's song, You Lost that Loving Feeling. The secret service agent's mouths were wide open in shock, even though they were taught not to show emotion, and some had tears in their eyes as both Trump and Biden started singing with emotion:

*You never close your eyes anymore when I kiss your lips.*
*And there's no tenderness like before in your fingertips.*
*You're trying hard not to show it.*

*But baby, baby, I know it...*
*You've lost that loving feeling...*

When they finished the second chorus, Clint kept playing but softer, and Trump said, "I love Milania, and Biden said, "I love Jill." Both men looked at each other, and Biden said, "You know Don, I learned a lot about you today, and you are not a bad man. You're a good man and I think we should do this again. Trump said, "Yeah Joe, you're alright too, let's do it again some time. God Bless America."

And with that, Clint made one final piano flourish and they all left.

# STETHERSCOPE

Found this here tubey thing, think they call'er a stether-scope er sumthin. Ain't sure what in tarnation it's doin on the side of a road in Arkansas. Maybe somebody threw it out the window durin a fight cuz they was lost or maybe it's just no good. Reckon they use'er for docterin or nurserin and such in them there high falutin hospitals. Ain't been to no hospitals cuz ahm healthy as a damn plow hoarse.

Reminds me, been memry'n bout ol Jessy, she were a damn strong'un, lived to 30 years er so. Hope I due the same. Nuff bout those damn memories. Dangerous to jump into the dark-ness o' memry'n tho, got to look to the future, cuz memry'n brings me back to the blackness again. Makes my mind do crazy thangs then my body follows what he sayin.

It says, "Littman" on the bottom round silver thing. That must be the name of the guy what owns it. But maybe it's a woman? Hope it's a her what owned it. On the TV at the bar-ber shop I saw them shows and them doctorin women wear them long coats and high heels and look finer than a bass flop-pin into my boat in the morning. But nurses on them shows sure steam like vittles on the boil, drive my innards upside down till I get swoozy and such.

Hold on tho. Maybe her name ain't Littman. Looks like

"SRCardon", no "SRCarson" on the side the black tube. Hell, this chick or guy can't even spill her name so she writes "SR". Must think her shit don't stink er sumthin. But maybe it's not a chick. Don't matter no how, sure as the cock crows come next day yellow sky, the owner'd pay a pretty penny to get this thing back, sure as the sun rises.

Ah may not be two eddicated, but I'll find'em sure enough. Wherever they is, may have to go to the library in the city and ask them to show me how to use that fancy outernet thing on the computer to find them. Or maybe, I kin keep the stether-scope, buy some those doctorin close and fake'em out at the hospital and do some things. There goes ma mind agin! This is goin to be a damn fun time in the hen house when the fox comes knockin!

# CLICHÉ MADNESS

J erry dated Annie for six months, and she finally smartened up and dumped him. He was clueless about women and how they should be treated, especially in a relationship. He needed some beers to wash down the pain. He met his old friend Carl at the bar, a place where the ladies went to show off their tight jeans or short skirts and heels while the men dreamed of impressing them enough to make a score.

"Second relationship I blew in the last six months," said Jerry.

"*You're just a babe in the woods,* man. You don't know anything about women," said Carl.

"What would you know Carl Casanova? You've been staring at that redhead over there swirling her chocolate martini all night. *You're barking up the wrong tree* if you think you have a chance with her. You don't have a snowball's chance in hell to make a score."

"*Can't teach an old dog new tricks,* I guess. Hell, you sure have a chip on your shoulder for a guy who can't keep his women happy. It think you need to get back on the horse once you fall off."

"I bet you I'll get her phone number before the end of the night, leaving you *high and dry.*"

"Yeah right. *Once in a blue moon.* If that happens it will be a real *Kodak moment,* but I think I'll have to keep you *on a short leash* before you fall on your face big guy. *I know you like the back of my hand* and that's why I don't think she'll even give you a minute of her time."

"My past failures with women are just *water under the bridge.* There's a lot of *fish in the sea,* so I need to take the *bull by the horns* and show you how it's done."

"*Get out of Dodge.*"

"I've got my secrets on how-to pick-up women that I'm sure you'd like to know, but I'm keeping *my cards close to my vest.*"

"*Actions speak louder than words* so you better take the *bull by the horns* before it's past your bedtime."

Jerry walked over to the redhead, talked to her for about ten minutes; she smiled and wrote down her number on a napkin. Smiling ear to ear, he went back to Carl and showed him the napkin.

"See, I told you I'd get her number. You lost sucker. That's *the way the ball bounces.*"

"Seems I need to keep you on a *short leash.* I suggest you call that number to see if she pulled the *old bait and switch* on you, Bud.

She left and she smiled as Jerry waved at her. After a half hour, he trembled while he took his friend's suggestion and called the number, she gave him on the napkin. It was crunch time

"Hello, Giovanni's Pizza! What can we make for you tonight?

# HIGH HEIMLICH ANXIETY

Although I am a physician, having stayed at a Holiday Inn Express before, I'm also a person too, believe it or not. I enjoy going out in public on occasion, showing my face to the real world, and sometimes that involves going to a grocery store, where invariably one of my patients interrupt me and talk about their problems, or they ask why my office didn't call them yet about their test results. Invariably, they extend their necks as far as they can to examine the contents of my grocery cart, hoping to find clues about my eating and personal habits, but I quickly hide the beer and fritos under jumbo packs of toilet paper. Yes, thank God I bought huge rolls of toilet paper to hide the beer. Certainly, everyone knows that the majority of U.S. doctors use toilet paper too.

Having said that, it can be anxiety provoking for me to go to restaurants. Because of my training, I automatically observe all the patrons, scanning the scene for all the potential physical maladies present. This includes body habitus, facial structure, rhythm and cadence of the walk, skin discoloration, limps, gait abnormalities, hoarseness, labored breathing, etc. My friends are well aware of this, and usually they come prepared with bulky horse blinders to place on my face so that I can't observe too much and that they will feel confident that I will eat and pay attention to them only.

Much of the anxiety is provoked by potential Heimlich maneuver candidates: people who will choke and turn blue on their food. This is serious, and I am not trying to make light of choking on food at all. However, because of the serious nature of this problem, I propose that people who fit this high-risk Heimlich potential should be placed in special "Heimlich-prevention rooms" in the restaurant, for their safety and for the comfort of the other low risk Heimlich patrons. Here are the "Heimlich prevention room" qualifiers:

People over the age of 80 who have loose dentures that protrude out of their mouth while they chew on large pieces of stringy meat.

People who weigh over 400 pounds and talk with large boluses of food in their mouths, with cheeks protruding like they are starving chipmunk mutants.

People who weigh over 400 pounds and laugh heartily while talking and spitting clumps of food.

Parents who bring in little toddlers to the restaurant and say, "Eat your vegetables Harold or no ice cream tonight." Then, they force carrots into their screaming mouths.

People who are so inebriated that they can't even find their mouths.

Yes, all these people qualify for the special Heimlich prevention rooms. They will be comfortable in these safe rooms, supervised by highly trained personnel, financed by taxpayer dollars, so that all people can eat comfortably in restaurants, with equal access, no matter whether they are high or low risk. In fact, this will be ordered by Obama care, but of course, there will be no financial reimbursement by Obama care for this service; we must pass the bill before reading it. Trust me, it will give us hope and change. It will be a mandatory service that all restaurants must provide otherwise they will have to pay a hefty fine to the IRS.

Go ahead. Send me hate mail, all you high-risk Heimlich people, but I'm only doing this for your protection, and my peace of mind. You know I'm right and you know who you are.

Peace and love.

# GROCERY STORE
# GOSSIP GAGGING

I love women in all their glorious feminine splendor; they are truly beautiful creatures placed on this planet to grace us with a civilization us filthy guys can't comprehend. However, having said that, what I am about to write applies predominantly to women, guilty of this horrible act almost 97.8% of the time, according to my calculations.

It seems whenever I enter a grocery store checkout line, I'm standing behind woman, and I watch impatiently, listening to the conversation between the check-out person—if it happens to be a woman, and the customer. Usually, I'm looking at my watch at least every 10 seconds during the conversation while my eyes scan the door, hoping for an escape. Maybe I don't need this food so bad. I am growing old waiting and I can feel the gray hairs start to sprout on my chin. She scans one item—then they talk—scan another item—then more conversation about nothing. What the heck is so interesting to talk about in a grocery store check-out line? Not always, but then my worst fear hits when I see the checkbook pulled out, not at the beginning of the scanning process, but at the very end. No writing done until the very end, but of course the conversation isn't ended.

"Did you know these Brussels sprouts were on sale hon?"

"Well no I didn't, but thanks. You're such a dear!"

"I'll search in this basket down here for a coupon for you if you don't have one." She fumbles around for an eternity, never finding it but giving her the sale price anyway.

"Did you have a nice Christmas? Looks like you didn't get enough turkey because you're buying another one. I love turkey too, especially sweet potatoes and thick juicy gravy. Hmmmm"

"Lovely Christmas thanks for asking." The checkbook I desperately notice, is still safe in her massive purse that looks more like a suitcase. "My kids came over and wouldn't you know it, my daughter brought her new boyfriend and he's a jerk!"

"You don't say? Must've been a horrible Christmas for you trying to smile when you didn't like him."

"Right and you know I didn't like the bedroom arrangements you know..."

Then after it was all over, she asks if she has a bluebird grocery card.

"Oh yes I forgot. Can you scan it now and give me the discount on everything?" She fumbled in her purse for her card, I think for about a decade.

"No problem hon, it will save you lots of money."

By this time, I was looking for the fire alarm to pull it to end this nonsense. Then everyone would have to drop everything and run! Yeah! I felt the smoke coming out of my ears, but I didn't care anymore. C'mon already, get your talkative butt out of the line, pay your bill and let the planet live on! I even wanted to jump over the counter, do the scanning myself and then immediately pay her bill with my credit card, and personally escort her out of the store. It would've been quicker. My muscles tensed, and I almost jumped when...

"Thanks for shopping with us today, and have a good day hon."

"You too and have a great and healthy New Year and don't work too hard and I hope you don't get varicose veins standing here checking people out because you know, my veins had to be—"

That was enough. I threw all my stuff on the counter right in front of the customer, forcing the employee to start the scan process. Hopefully this prevented her from taking a break right then and there.

"How are you sir? Did you find everything ok?"

"Great. Yep. And you?"

That was it, the extent of the conversation. She finished mine with twice the amount of groceries in half the time.

"Will you be needing any help out sir?"

I felt like saying, "Thank you but I am an able bodied man capable of carrying my bags and pushing the cart myself. Can't you see that? Please help other people who really need it, and don't waste your breath on guys like me because we will always say no. If we say yes, then you know we're weenies ready for roasting.

"No thanks."

"Have a good day."

"You too."

See how easy that was? Short, but certainly pleasant and courteous. I didn't tell her that I didn't get any sleep last night because I was on call, I was hungry, my feet stank because I didn't have time to do laundry, my head hurt and I'm glad Christmas was over. And no, I don't have varicose veins and I need a beer.

Of course, there are exceptions to every rule, and I must confess you're right. Some men do this too, I guess, although I've never witnessed that legend. Here is the exception I'm talking about, and I'm sure all men will agree. If the woman in front of you looks like a Victoria's Secret model, buying only fruit and vegetables, my preference, and I'm sure other men would agree, is that she take her sweet time and discuss each vegetable in detail, especially if the conversation veers toward her latest pictorial. Time will stand still at that point. To hell with my previous commitments, this is serious business! And of course, if the clerk asks if she wants help going out to the car, I will jump to the rescue!

Seriously though, dreams are made for nighty night time, not in the grocery line, right? I think it should be illegal to delay the grocery line from the progress that civilization needs. Therefore, I will propose a law that prohibits more than nine words to be uttered by a customer at the checkout line. These words are: "I am fine", "And you?", "Yes", "No" and finally, "You too."

These will be in response to standard questions: "How are you", Did you find everything ok?", "Need any help outside?" and finally, "Have a good day."

If any more than nine words are uttered by the customer, the electronic word checker will flash and the tollbooth at the exit will lock and demand a 10% toll.

That will solve the problem, increasing revenue for the sole purpose of buying free beer and giving it to the customer who has been delayed, and save all of us countless hours of precious time that we could be spent at home doing something important like watching football on the TV.

# A GOOD NUMBER

Not infrequently, I'm at a business establishment and I receive this question: "What is a good number for us to call you?" Now I don't know about you, but I usually try to give nonexistent or disconnected numbers when I want to be called back.

Right? I mean, don't we all do that?

In fact, I often try to leave a fax number for people to call so that I can destroy the caller's fragile ears with the annoying fax noise. Not uncommonly, I carry a list of fax numbers in my phone or wallet just for that purpose.

All kidding aside, that question "What is a good number for us to call you" is one of the dumbest questions commonly encountered in commercial establishments across the United States. I think it ranks higher than, "Are you finished sir?" A question that occurs when I am still feeding my face with a plate full of food in front of me. I know they don't say that stuff in Europe or any other civilized country.

Why the hell would I give a bogus number to someone, especially when I clearly desire to have him or her call me back?

Now, admittedly, this doesn't apply to annoying and pushy salespersons who push me to give my phone number or email so they can send deals and advertisements and other bothersome junk. In these cases, of course, I say, "no thanks, bug off fella." Or something along those lines. But sometimes when they persist, rather than punching them out like they deserve and watching their nose drip blood as they continue to beg, I may give them a false number, a fax number or better yet, the phone number to the IRS Office.

# I DID IT ON THE
# AIRPLANE AGAIN

I don't have a good explanation for it, but each time I fly as a passenger, I can't seem to control these actions anymore. It just feels so good and natural and thankfully I haven't been thrown off the plane yet, but if I do get thrown off, I will scream as loud as I can and hold on to my seat arm with both hands, trying not to laugh as they drag me by the legs off the plane and into the arms of a money hungry lawyer who will take a large chunk of my settlement against the airlines.

But seriously though, I am not sure why I always do this on airplanes, but I guess so far it hasn't bothered anyone. I'm sure people stare though. Previously, it tended to happen at bars, often stimulated by a beer or glass of wine, and embarrassingly it has also occasionally occurred while in the church pew listening to the preacher. I must tell you though, that I always kept one ear open to the sermon, clinging to the inspiring words while it happens.

Word vomit. That's right. As soon as I'm in my seat and people are still struggling to put their luggage up above my head, I whip out my black and white bound notebook and several black pens and we go at it furiously, pen and paper, words flying silently but forcefully onto the pages, and I don't usually stop until we land or nature calls.

I wrote five or six chapters of my new novel on the trip to and from a medical conference, even though medical facts were occupying a significant part of my strained brain, but it seems the airplane brings out my creativity and I was able to switch quickly from left to squishy right brain and proceed to the thriller with larger-than-life characters filled with flaws, living in a story that holds on to you and won't let go.

Seems it won't let me go either.

Guess in order to finish this novel, I'm going to have to do some more traveling. But I wonder how much better I would've written if I had some red wine in my left hand in the airplane seat?

# TASTY LESION CAFÉ FEATURING SNARLY LUNGS AND WALKING CORPSE SYNDROME

This is a fictional story based on medical Jargon found in textbooks and described as food

"I'll have the pancakes with whipped cream, three sausage links and three eggs over easy."

"Damn Mike, you're going to have to double your Crestor after that mess of artery clogging chow!"

"Whatever, it's been a long night on call and I deserve it Sam. Tell you what; I'm shaking after working with this patient last night and for the last couple of days. Sometimes I wish I wasn't an internist and I could just cut on hearts like you do; fix'em and be done with it. Slam bang, thank you ma'am." The waitress was clearly impatient, rolling her eyes, waiting for the next order.

"Sir, what will you have?"

"Coffee, orange juice, oatmeal and granola."

"You wuss," said Mike. "Be a man and order some real food."

"Not after operating on those hearts all day. Makes ya stop and think. So, tell me about this interesting patient."

"Well, first she came in to the ER with stridor and a fever. Took a look at her larynx with a laryngoscope and sure enough, it was a case of *Cherry Red Epiglottis*, so I put her on antibiotics and intubated her."

"Haemophilus influenza?"

"Cultures negative, but broad-spectrum antibiotics worked. Next day she developed pulmonary edema and her liver was huge. She was a modest drinker, but due to her rheumatoid arthritis and possible Lupus, we biopsied her liver."

"What did the biopsy show?"

"*Nutmeg Liver* with an area of *Anchovy Paste*."

"Ah, congestive heart failure causing congestive hepatopathy with superimposed Amebic liver abscess. Did she have fingernail clubbing too from all her smoking?"

"No clubbing but huge *Sausage Fingers*." He downed his last pork link, then licked the grease off his lips.

"Her rheumatoid arthritis must've been severe. Was she immunosuppressed from her RA treatment?"

"Well, that's why she had the liver abscess and epiglottis. Damned if she didn't develop acute abdominal pain and I called for a surgery consult. Said he wouldn't operate because she had multiple surgeries in past and she had a *hostile abdomen*."

"Ah, Hostile Abdomen Syndrome. Reminds me of some of the nasty lungs I've operated on. I call them *Snarly Lungs*. Best description I can come up with. Soon as you go in you know you are in trouble."

"Yeah, stick with hearts. They're cleaner. So anyway, she gets better with the grace of God and I think she's walking out of the hospital but she develops *Exploding Head Syndrome*."

"What the hell is that? I'm just a surgeon and if you can't operate on it, I'm clueless."

"It's an auditory hallucination occurring with the onset

of sleep, kinda like an earthquake noise or a loud bang like a gun going off. Occurs with fatigue or withdrawal from medications. She wanted lots of morphine, so we treated her with narcotics because she feared going to sleep."

"You fleas just chase your tails with medications, using one medication to treat the adverse reactions from another."

"Whatever." The whipped cream dollop remained above his upper lip but Sam decided not to tell him about the spectacle. "So, that goes away and I get ready to kick her out of the hospital, but she refuses because she looks in the mirror and says she's dead."

"What?"

"Yeah, she thinks she's dead and doesn't know who that is in the mirror. She says we drained her blood and her organs are out of her body."

"Again, thank God I'm a surgeon."

"What did the psychiatrist say?"

"Thought you'd never ask." The whipped cream dollop oozed stealthily down Mike's chin but he was so exhausted, he lost all concern about appearance. "Well, he diagnosed her with *Walking Corpse Syndrome or Cotard's Syndrome*. She had a delusion she was dead both literally and figuratively and the face she observed in the mirror she thought didn't exist. While it occurs in schizophrenia, turns out it was secondary to the valcyclovir she was taking for her herpes, compounded by a severe migraine headache, both of which can do it."

"No wonder you're a damn mess Mike. Wipe off your mouth please, you're making me sick."

With that, both docs got up and left and Sam paid the bill, feeling sorry for his beaten colleague.

"So Sam, we meet again next week for breakfast?"

"Um, I don't think so Mike, I don't think I can take any more of your medicine stories. Rather just cut it out and cure it."

"For a blood and guts guy, you're a wimp."

# SITTING AT THE BAR
# WITH CLINT EASTWOOD

I don't really give a flying fork what any celebrity from Hollywood thinks about politics, global warming or any subject unrelated to pure acting. Their job is to entertain us and therefore make lots of money, that's it.

Unless of course their name is Clint Eastwood, then I will listen. Intently.

Well, I didn't really meet him at a bar, but some have said that I look like a younger Clint and it seems we have a connection over the years, and perhaps vicariously I have connected with many of the characters in his movies. You know, larger than life bad-asses carrying heavy flaws but we root for them because they do things we've always wanted to do but never could or would. Mostly.

During this bar scene, any dialogue that is actually a published Clint Eastwood quote will be in *Italics*. The rest is well, author creativity.

I walked up to the bar and there was an empty seat next to this older guy who had lanky legs that flailed out from the bar stool frame. He wore sunglasses, but I could see that little upper lip curl when he seemed to snarl at the TV when the news came on about the ISIS terrorists. That's when I knew who it was, but realized no one else did, and he wanted it that way. I was compelled to sit by him but I knew I must protect him from the public and paparazzi.

"This seat taken?"

"Nope." He barely glanced at me.

I sat down nervously next to him, surprised he didn't respond with, "Reckon not." But then this wasn't the Outlaw Josey Wales movie set. Even so, I expected him to spit on the floor and hit the bar dog between the eyes. It didn't happen. He continued to enjoy his beer in silence until he addressed the bartender with a commanding, but gravelly voice:

"Turn off that crap and let's watch some football." The bartender jumped immediately.

"Good move, Josey."

He turned and looked at me and I thought my blood vessels had hardened into zig zaggy icicles. The lip curled up into a snarl and I knew he was squinting behind those sunglasses. Was he going to pull out his .44 magnum and *blow my head clean off*?

"So, you figured me out. Just be cool about it."

"No problem. Between us."

He looked straight ahead for a few seconds then turned back to me. "You don't look like a paparazzi; I've seen enough of those low lifes in my lifetime. What's your name?"

"Carson. SR Carson."

"Nice last name but funny first initials. Why the hell don't you use your real name rather than SR?"

"Well, um, C—"

"Call me Rowdy"

I laughed because of the reference to his start on the TV series, Rawhide, but realized other names he could use like Josey, Philoe or Harry would perk up other patrons' ears, much to his chagrin.

"So Rowdy, like you, I have a fan club and I must use SR initials to hide my real name from the paparazzi."

"Yeah, know the feeling. So, what is it that you do, SR, that has you running from them?"

"I'm a physician, and also a novelist as a hobby. Here's my card."

"Always looking for good stories. But novelists aren't good screenwriters. They give too much damn detail. They're creative as hell though. In Josey Wales, we took the option on the author of the novel, even though the guy was a drunk. Screenwriters took care of the practical aspects of it, but he had a good story, and we bought it and the rest is history. By the way, you going to order a drink Carson, or you just going to *whistle Dixie?*"

I detected a squinty smile under the glasses, and felt a sigh of relief. I ordered a tall cold beer. I realized he was feeling comfortable with me, and that was I'm sure hastened by the fact that he'd already downed a beer. But his fingers tapped with a musical rhythm on the bar counter, and I realized it was in perfect beat with the music in the background. He had good ears for his age.

My confidence surged, so I asked him a question, unrelated to movies. "What do you think of the gun control fight going on and protection of the second amendment?"

*"I have a very strict gun control policy. If there's a gun around, I want to be in control of it." Nothing wrong with shooting—as long as the right people get shot."*

I laughed and nearly choked on my beer gulp. "Love it Rowdy. Wrote a quote something like that in my book too."

"What was the quote?"

"Mr. Smokey demands respect, and always be on the correct side of the gun."

"Ok, maybe I'll ask you some more about the book later, but I need there to be a lot of action, and it has to show some deeper truths about humanity, with the protagonist conflicted and flawed in some ways. What's the name of your novel, by the way?

"To Love with Hate."

"Interesting title. You ever been married Carson?"

"Yeah, did that once. Didn't work. Got out of it before she killed me, or actually, she almost did.

*"There's only one way to have a happy marriage and as soon as I learn what it is I'll get married again. My wife is my closest friend. Sure, I'm attracted to her in every way possible, but that's not the answer. Because I've been attracted to other people and I couldn't stand'em after a while."* In fact, *all marriages are made in heaven but so are thunder and lightning."*

I didn't say anything in response. It was damn self-explanatory. Just concentrated on my beer. But I found my lip snarling upwards a little too. I think he saw it. I did it effortlessly and naturally.

"What do you mean she almost killed you?"

"Well, in a matter of speaking, she destroyed so much in my life with devilish skill, she broke my heart. I wrote about my heart in a short story."

"What's it called?"

*Code Blue: A Doctor's View of his Own Near-Death Experience.*

"I'll look it up someday." He looked up when he heard the football game sharply interrupted by a news flash. It was politics: The president was going to make a statement about something. He snarled again and I calculated what the odds were of him pulling out his .44 and blowing away the TV.

Then he said it. *President Obama is the greatest hoax ever perpetrated on the American people."* And for that matter, *maybe I'm getting to the age when I'm starting to be senile or nostalgic or both, but people are so angry now. You used to be able to disagree with people and still be friends. Now you hear these talk shows and everyone who believes differently than you is a moron or an idiot—both on the right and the left. Extremism is so easy. You've got your position and that's it. It doesn't take much thought. And when you go far enough right, you meet the same idiots coming around from the left."*

I bought him another beer, hoping to facilitate his word flow even more.

"Thanks Carson, I've got the next one. You see, *there's a rebel lying deep in my soul. Anytime anyone tells me the trend is such and such, I go the opposite direction. I hate the idea of trends. I hate imitation. I have a reverence for individuality. Respect yourself. Self-respect leads to self-discipline. When you have both under your belt, that's real power."*

With that, he picked up his beer and went to the piano in the corner of the bar, as if it was reserved for him. I knew he played jazz piano since he was young, but I figured today that he would play "Sweet Rose of Alabamy" from the Outlaw Josey Wales. I was wrong. It was beautiful jazz piano, at its finest. I listened for about a half hour and he was still playing while the patrons drank and looked at him curiously, still unaware of who he was, and I was pleased we were able to keep it that way, for his sake. I walked up to the piano and he kept playing, then said, "Your novel intrigues me. You like my movie quotes, give me a few from your book."

"Ok," I said. "Face the fear head on so the fear won't consume you." "But if you so much as think about messing with me again, I won't be as nice and gentle, and you will be in the intensive care unit, recovering from multiple trauma from my hands. Do you understand me brainless one, or do I need to talk slower?"

"I like it Carson."

He kept playing but I had to go. Had to make rounds early the next day.

"Take care Rowdy and thanks for playing the ivories for us."

"No problem Carson. Love to play. By the way, I owe you a beer. I've got your card."

Mutual respect. He *made my day.*

# BEVARE THE VICHES

It was a sunny day in southern California years ago, and our high school gym barely held all the newly graduating high school seniors sitting in their stuffy caps and gowns while their parents and friends filled up the bleachers. Most of my friends studied their watches, hoping for a quick termination of the commencement ceremonies so they could catch some good waves while the action was still hot and the sun could still leatherize their tanned skin.

I'm sure I wanted to head out and snag some good wave action too. But the truth was I found myself lucky to be graduating, especially with all the trouble I caused back then. Lucky I wasn't wearing orange jail fashion. So, I remember listening carefully to the commencement speaker back then, yearning to glean a valuable morsel or two of valuable knowledge that would fly me smoothly into the jet stream I hoped would be my future.

I'd never met a rabbi before, but I knew that he had to be a respected, educated man or he wouldn't be speaking to us. I had Jewish friends, but I didn't remember them discussing their rabbi when we were out cruising around. So, I listened intently to him while my friends either snoozed or discussed what girl was wearing either a bikini or nothing at all under her commencement gown.

Honestly though, I don't remember 99% of what he said that glorious day, however, I do remember distinctly, to this day, the sentence he injected into my brain with his Yiddish/New York/I don't know where accent. It's a sentence that has guided me on the path that has brought me to where I am today, or at least it was supposed to, if only I had understood its full meaning at that time and carried it with me like a tattoo, reminding me of its wisdom each time I took a shower. But I finally understand now what he meant by his admonishment to us young and enthusiastic graduates. Too bad it took me so long to understand it. So here it is, oh patient ones:

"BEVARE THE VICHES OF VINE AND VIMMEN"

Yes, chew on that one for a while. I thought he meant beware of the witches who hang out on Hollywood and Vine streets. Then I realized they weren't witches, just working girls trying to make it in life, right?

The Viches of Vine and Vimmen? Bevare?

Ah yes, the riches of fine wine and a good woman. Can't beat it. The two go together like well you know, arithmetic: good plus gooder equals Great! But what could he have meant by "beware" of such good things? Anything that tastes good and feels good must require you to seek more of both and then more again. Perhaps he meant moderation in both pursuits, with safety being a prime concern, but always realizing that nothing in life compares to the love of a genuinely good woman with a kind and loving soul.

# DOCTORS AND LAWYERS
# IN THE SAME HOTEL

A while back I went to a medical conference to soak in some of the most recent research in my field (s), accumulate CME credit for regulatory agencies and of course, to listen intensely to the well-rehearsed pitches of supermodel mannequin pharmaceutical reps in the display halls. (Yes, ladies, there were supermodel male reps there too I am told, but I didn't notice.) I preferred listening to the supermodel lady pharmaceutical reps of course, simply because they seemed more prepared and superbly educated in their subject matter.

After a long day of learning, listening to lectures and playing with fun technology and toys that won't add a grain of sand to the beach of my practice but will cost ridiculous amounts of unreimbursed cash, I made it back to the main conference hotel to relax and unwind a little. Of course, that started with a trip to the bar, which I must admit was relatively empty, but I noticed huge crowds in the lobby, laughing, loud people and I must add, well dressed and well-heeled ladies, er I mean female people.

I decided to eat in the hotel restaurant after a glass of wine, and it was so quiet, I thought I was sitting on a deck with a bunch of serious fly fisherman, afraid of scaring those wily trout. Turns out they were doctors of course, reading the conference schedules and course materials, cramming and preparing for the next day's conferences on a Friday night. There were a few docs who spoke English as a primary language, and nearly all spoke my mother language as well or better than I did. Many were Asian, Indian and European superstar doctors. Before I fell asleep in my soup, curiosity sparked one final rescue from boredom.

So, I asked the waiter, "Is there another conference going on here in the hotel, or did I miss the party? "Sir, that is the national conference for lawyers." Their conference is here at the hotel, rather than the conference center across the street which is a medical conference."

"Uh huh. Thanks."

You see, the doctors don't have parties, for many reasons, but primarily because it is illegal for pharmaceutical firms to throw us docs parties just for fun and enjoyment because we are so highly regulated by the government and well, let's face it, we of course don't use our heads and review the literature in science, we are easily bought, so they say. We are like juvenile delinquent children, guilty until proven innocent. Instead, we are invited to dinners that last three hours where we listen to lectures at the dinners, then take a test to make sure we prove we attended. No dancing allowed. No smiling. Be professional and erudite.

Now I understood. These lawyers and their entourage sure seemed like they were having fun, so I paid my tab, and told the waiter au revoir and then meandered through the legal crowd. The men all wore suits or casual jackets and shirts and pressed slacks with black shiny shoes. The ladies, well, I have trouble describing them without my fingers trembling on the keyboard. Short skirts and heels and long elegant dresses with even higher heels, lots of shiny rocks on their ears and arms that bounced and jiggled as they practiced their rhythmic runway walks for all to see. Seems they all were tending to take the escalator upstairs, so of course, I had to follow and explore, trying to blend in, hiding my medical I.D. badge in my pocket.

So, on the upper floor, I spied the mulling crowd filing in to a huge assembly room where there was a live band, dancing and certainly excess frolicking and women laughing. I looked in, decided that was definitely better than studying what I already absorbed earlier, but realized I didn't have an I.D. badge for this soiree. I waited until the door man stepped away to talk, then slipped in and started immediately thinking of some legal terms to use in an emergency, then realized I could only think of a few, but heck, a doctor is needed in the party, right? We are always prepared to do Heimlichs on people choking on meat or other such emergencies that hopefully don't occur. I figured I should get an automatic entry as the volunteer conference doctor!

I realized that these lawyers were lucky to not be regulated like we were. This must be because lawyers are much more trustworthy professionals than doctors and certainly could never be bought by a free ink pen or something like us. But that buffet dinner sure looked tempting. Ah hell, don't push it, Carson. Just enjoy the scene. Maybe a glass of wine, or two or who knows, maybe even listen to the band.

Then, she came up to me. "Excuse me, aren't you from the Johnson firm in LA?"

I remembered the first rule, and that is always look into her eyes only. So I did. I tried to ignore all the other feminine courses that she prepared. Clearly, I had no tag, so I had to think on my suddenly wobbly feet. "Yes, my name is Carson. Sorry my tag fell into the punch bowl and was much too nasty to wear."

She giggled and her white teeth dazzled me. "I understand Carson. You must be more careful. I'm Tiffany, family law judge." She held out her dainty hand. So instead of shaking it,

I I decided to kiss it. Her face turned red and she didn't want to pull back.

"Enchante. My pleasure to meet you Tiffany. I hope I don't have to file an Affidavit or Writ of Habeas Corpus with you, but I would like to invite you to dance. Hopefully, you won't dismiss my motion with prejudice." I prayed that these legal words would make her laugh and at the same time show that I was a lawyer.

Her hearty laugh and welcoming smile told me the answer and I had an enjoyable evening with a bunch of legal types. But, although lawyers seem to know how to party, I am lucky to have a career in medicine. I love my profession, not the regulations and rules, but the challenge of saving lives and doing the best I can for my patients.

Nothing compares. It is my calling.

# WINSLOW

"**C**arson, you need to take some time off and get out of here for a while."

"Why, is my hair standing up again?"

"Yeah, but it's worse. You keep saying you will get your best people on it, but your best people don't seem to want to be on it anymore." said Fred.

"What?" I said.

"Damn, your left ear must be not be working anymore. I guess *that voice keeps whispering in your other ear.* Find a great place to go Carson, but remember to *take it easy, but don't let the sound of your own wheels drive you crazy.* And don't forget, wherever you go, remember that *you're the new kid in town, everybody loves you, so don't let them down.*"

"*I don't want to hear it.*"

Hear what?" said Fred. "Shouldn't be a problem anyway because you only hear half of what I say anyway Carson."

"You seem to have forgotten that I'm not the new kid anymore Fred, *there's a new kid in town,* and I just *don't want to hear it.*"

Maybe he's right. I've decided I'm going to Winslow Arizona. Seems like a nice quiet place to find a *peaceful easy feeling* and enjoy the view of some *sparkling earrings against her skin so brown,* moving back and forth in cadence as she floats in front of my hungry eyes. Damn, that's a delicious image.

So, I found myself *running down the road, trying to loosen my load,* heading down the highway to Winslow, and I couldn't get the thoughts of those seven sick ICU patients off my mind, but I had to do it, delete them, or I clearly would not be able to *take it easy* in Winslow. By the time I crossed the New Mexico/Arizona border, that load finally fell off my shoulders. I walked through the town of Winslow, found a corner beer stand, then I stood on that peaceful corner, drinking a cold brew, and then it happened—it was a *girl my Lord, in a flatbed Ford slowin' down to take a look at me.* Her blues connected with my blues, she rolled down her window and said in a soft, whispery voice "Where 'ya headin' there cowboy?"

I have never been called a cowboy before, and she *wasn't just another woman, with* sparkling earrings dangling. So, I decided that this was the time to act like a cowboy immediately. I had to think quickly what to say, and where I was heading, so I said, "Thank ya ma'am" and I tipped my Stetson to her. "I'll be headin' anywhere you want to take me; I've got a *peaceful easy feeling.*"

"I'm going to Sedona to hike in the Red Rocks and feel some magical vortexes. I could use a hiking partner who likes to share beer with a cowgirl."

Then I thought why the hell not, *we may lose, and we may win though we will never be here again.* So, I told her, *"open up I'm climbin' in, let's take it easy."*

Credits: Italics from Eagles songs: "Take it Easy", "Peaceful Easy Feeling" and "New Kid in Town"

# SITTING AT THE
# BAR WITH CLINT
# EASTWOOD, PART II

R equired reading material: Sitting at the Bar with Clint
Eastwood Part I

Warning: This is a fictional piece so don't get your underwear tied up in a wad. However, as before, actual published
Clint Eastwood quotes will be in italics. Quotes from my book
will be in plain type.

"Dr. Carson there's a call for you on line one."

"Take a message. If they can't say who they are I don't need
to answer."

"Um, says he works for the Malpaso Company."

I immediately excused myself from the patient's room telling her I had an important call. Well, it was important, so I
didn't lie. Clint Eastwood's movie company doesn't just call
anybody!

"Dr. Carson, we've been asked by Mr. Eastwood to setup
another bar meeting with you. He kept your business card
from before and asked that we fly you out to Carmel to his
favorite Honky Tonk Bar. Is that ok with you sir?"

"Well, um sure. I'll have to check my calendar first." I paused one full second then replied, "I'm free. But I ask, what is the topic of our meeting, besides beer?"

"I'm not at liberty to say. See you there."

"Carson. I must emphasize that he will again be disguised for obvious reasons and of course, you will not use his real name in public to avoid the paparazzi."

"Yeah, I have the same problem, so I understand. Last time I called him Rowdy."

"So, Carson, let's cut right to the chase." said Clint at the bar. He took a swig of beer. I tried to then take a larger one myself of course. "I read your novel, *To Love with Hate*. Nice story and plot line with interesting characters. That Katherine was sure an evil piece of work though. Anyway, I liked some of your phrases and quotes and I think they might be worthy of further review. You know, I have made a few good quotes myself in movies over the years."

"Thanks Clint, I especially liked your quote in Outlaw Josey Wales when—"

"Carson. We're going to compare quotes now and see if we match up."

I took 4 large gulps then prepared myself for the quote comparison with the world legend of quotes and larger than life phrases.

"No sexy phrases about women though, ok Carson? I don't do that."

"Go it." He started first, thankfully.

*"Go ahead, make my day."*

Damn. He had to start with that one! Ok, um, "you should be thankful I'm protecting pussies like you."

He chuckled then squinted and hit me again. *"you gotta ask yourself a question. Do I feel lucky? Well, do ya punk?"*

I responded with more confidence this time. "I'll start his punishment by ripping his lips off, and then the fun will start."

"Not bad so far Carson, but you better keep going. Then he

hit me with another roundhouse. *"I tried being reasonable, I didn't like it."*

I responded swiftly: "If you so much as think about messing with me again, I won't be as nice and gentle, and you will be in the Intensive Care Unit recovering from multiple trauma from my hands."

He took another swig, and I didn't know where I stood. But he squinted again and I braced for the next punch. *"Ever notice you come across somebody once in a while you shouldn't have messed with? That's me."*

Stay calm Carson. Nice slow breath in and out. "Unfortunately, this guy's sizable muscles are controlled with a brain lacking neurons and the few he has don't connect."

"I like it Carson. Now hit me with a couple more quickly to see if you're a quick thinker when you're not writing."

"Her sleek black dress and rhythmic hips—"

"No Carson, none of that stuff, remember. Now give me a good manly quote before we call it quits."

"Um ok. If I was cursed with Blake's jumbled brain, I guess I might try to compensate by beating up as many people as I could also. Problem is, he picked on the wrong man tonight and he needs to be more careful who he decides to pick on. What a dumbass."

"Yours are a little wordy Carson, but I like the different style. Nice to see you again and I'm going to think about your novel and how it might fit on a movie screen. We'll let you know. And by the way, I am looking for a thriller to put on the movie screen. Too bad you don't write them."

"Just so happens Rowdy, I am working on my first thriller, Blue Shadows."

"Ok. Let me know when it's done and I'll read it. No promises though."

He took off and both our glasses were empty. Stunned, I couldn't move, so I ordered another.

# MEDICAL STUDENTS
# GONE WILD

**M**SGW is the title of a new video documentary I'm producing, inspired by my friend's recently released short
film: "Kama Sutra King". Just kidding of course, but it is kind
of a good idea. My readers understand this is all in clean fun.
Would Bill Clinton then ask for the definition of "clean"? But
aren't you proud that I posted a picture with this piece of out
of this world, stunning, adjective—laced prose?

Disclaimer: This post does not represent my observations
of all the great medical students in America, nor does it represent my observations of any one single medical student, and
in fact, it may not even be close to the truth. Therefore, if you
are a medical student, or maybe a parent of a medical student
and you are still offended, then you should be, because you
just don't get it.

I've had some exposures to third and fourth-year medical students during my private practice and I have relished
the opportunity to teach, which I do. For free. If somehow, I
can impart some of my knowledge from the old school of ball-
peen hammers to their young brains, then maybe, when I am
sick, they can help me. Here is what I have observed:

1. They like to eat as much as they can, whenever they can, but they don't gulp their food, thinking it will be snatched away by their attending, or having to run to an emergency. In fact, they like to sit in the doctor's lounge, get there early and eat up all the food so us frazzled private attendings are relegated to the remaining half-consumed, but still opened cartons of milk and burnt white toast.
2. They like to watch TV and be relaxed, not a care in the world without spending rare free time in the library.
3. They may not know what a library is. Everything is digital now.
4. They don't have hardly any real responsibility for patient care.
5. They don't show stress.
6. Their hair is perfect and they take showers daily, getting eight hours of blissful sleep.
7. They walk slowly and deliberately down the corridors of the hospital, never running and their feet are rarely airborne.
8. Their shoes are clean, and there's no blood or vomit on them.
9. Their white lab coats are perfectly clean, not stuffed with manuals, books, 12 pens, flashlights, beepers, sandwiches, candy bars and wads of paper for note taking and small boxes of tissues to wipe stuff off their face. In fact, their pockets are empty except for their cell phone which they must use frequently for texting and face book etc.
10. Female medical students are ridiculously beautiful, as it has always been. I don't know anything about the men.
11. They are not intimidated by us nasty attendings. Not at all.
12. They have a life outside of the hospital.

13. Because of numbers 1 through 12, they are more perceptive and realistic about life than I was, and therefore, I am envious of their experience. However, I don't regret the hard knocks that taught me medicine the old-fashioned way.

While today's brilliant medical student appears to be a uniquely different animal compared to the medical student species that I roamed with, which experience is better?

Who knows?

But what is the best way to learn that certain, "Je ne sais quoi"?

# CAT SOUP

"**C**arson, you're lonely in that house living alone, and you need some company, someone to come home to after working all day and night and to take some of your stress away."

"Absolutely I agree, and I thought you'd never ask! You don't mind that I toss my socks and underwear on the floor and sometimes leave dirty dishes in the sink all night, do you?"

"Ah, nice try, but I don't think so. I think living together could ruin a friendship"

"I see, well, I do have plenty of room in the lower level of the house and since I don't use it very much, I think it would be a great idea to rent it out to some college co-eds who want a place for cheap. They can do their thing downstairs you know and occasionally they can come upstairs to enjoy a good meal and social interaction, if you know what I mean. Happiness all around: I resolve this loneliness problem you're concerned about and the ladies have a nice place to stay and study, while occasionally enjoying some laughs and a beer with a cool guy."

"Ha. That's happening only in your wild dreams. They wouldn't want anything to do with an old fart anyway."

"Really, so how do you suggest I resolve this horrible loneliness problem?"

"A cat."

"A what? You mean one of those nasty furry things that don't give love and scratch all my furniture, and won't even play fetch the ball with me?"

"Uh, yeah. A cat will be good for you. I'll get you one for your birthday."

"No, you won't! No cats in my house. If you come over with a cat, I won't answer my door."

So, I was strong, and I didn't receive a cat on my birthday that year, or for that matter on any holiday. I was proud that I stood my ground. However, I must admit, an animal was a possibility, and certainly a lot cheaper than a woman, although a woman certainly has advantages in many ways. Damn. But animals don't ask for opinions on whether their dress makes them fat or whether I'm somehow secretly lusting after every sexy woman who walks by my innocent eyes. Well, I guess that depends on how you define lust, I guess. I am human but I'm not an insensitive jerk. I think the only thing that matters in life is love, and at least at this time, love doesn't mandate living with a woman in a house. Women are beautiful creatures that must be loved, adored and cherished, no matter what the situation. But what I really wanted was a Labrador retriever, specifically, a yellow lab. A dog that will run to me and jump on me when I come home, licking and slobbering all over me, then begging me to take him outside to run through the woods and fetch balls that I throw out in the meadow as far as I can for him chase after. Yeah, that would be perfect. But my busy work schedule won't allow me to really take care of a dog especially a puppy, and dogs need a lot of care, and exercise etc. So, no animal for me.

After two years of proudly standing my ground, I finally gave in. Perhaps it was the beer weakening my cognitive function, but I said yes. Yes, to a cat I named Rocky. Hell, give it a try, can't be that bad, after all, they poop and pee in a litter box and you don't even have to take them out. Should be easy, so I received a cat on a birthday. Nice little kitty and cute, but

I think it was taken from its mother too quickly. He grew to be wild and loved to bite and scratch and no matter how much love I gave him, he continued to bite me when I tried to hold him and love clearly wasn't in his feline brain. He didn't even know how to fetch. I tried various techniques to get him to fetch but nothing worked. He was yellow like a Lab but that was the only similarity I found, but we grew to kinda tolerate each other and we both inhabit the same house without killing each other. Somewhat like a bad marriage.

So, I had the vet cut off his balls. That didn't slow him down one bit like they said it would, and his destructive behavior continued.

As far as cats go, the only cat I remember when I was a kid was called Ching and we didn't get along very well either. I have a mountain lion walking around my house here in the mountains and he leaves his scat all around the house and according to the experts, he's marking his territory. I am ok with him marking his territory but really, if he thinks it's his house, then he at least needs to pay for half the damn mortgage. But then, I won't make an issue about it because I don't want him to be angry with me, especially when hungry. Don't know if it was him or one of his relatives, but when my ex-wife lived here while I was paying for it, he would apparently sun himself in the back of the house in full view. You know what I'm thinking don't you? Yeah, he missed his opportunity, but I'm a peaceful man, and don't condone violence unless I'm being attacked, or my friends or loved ones are being attacked and then I fight like a mad dog.

So just when I had enough cats, a bobcat jogs out in front of my car a few days ago, running into the neighbor's yard, but before he left the road, he looked at me and seemed to snear at me. I'm thinking, yeah, he thinks he's tough but he won't stand a chance at my "cathouse" from hell. If he survives my nasty house cat, then he'll have to survive my co-homeowner, the cougar.

Sorry for digressing, but I felt the background in feline ferocity would be important for the next topic. Slightly less than two years after Rocky arrived in my house, I went to put him in his little cat house laundry room for the evening, when he just remained on my couch, quiet. That was unusual. Why was he quiet and not destroying the house all night? Maybe he was finally mellowing out and maturing to a point that he was enjoying the "fine wine" aspect of his life. I couldn't believe I did this, but I went to bed, leaving him alone on the couch and the next morning, after a peaceful sleep, I woke up to find him on the couch, same place. I looked at him and petted him and he seemed to be calm and healthy. Perplexed, I left him there and went to work, thinking maybe this was just a life change for him. When I returned eight hours later, I couldn't find him. Searched the whole house and eventually found him in my clothes closet whimpering and shivering. I examined him the best I could, didn't find any abdominal tenderness or anything obvious so I put him in his bed, hoping it would improve over night.

When I woke up the next day, I found him bleeding out of his eyes with matted hair and clearly, he was dying. I though perhaps it was sepsis or septic shock from a bowel obstruction from a fur ball or something, so I thought, should I take him to the vet to treat him, or should I take him instead for a merciful dose of morphine to ease his pain in his last hours? When I took him to the vet, they felt the odds were against him for living. They requested several days of pet hospitalization and several thousand dollars of lab tests and treatments. I admit I thought about the options, considering my relationship with Rocky, and realized that they didn't give me the Morphine euthanasia option. So, I told them to do the basics, reverse what was reversible, but nothing heroic.

Turns out, as many of you have already figured out, he somehow found some rat poison and was therefore bleeding from the Warfarin in the rat poison. I thought about that, and remembered that I had some outside but wasn't sure how he was able to get to it. The vet thought he might have eaten a poisoned mouse. Either way, I felt somehow responsible and the bleeding eyes and his pitiful appearance broke my heart. So overnight, with lots of vitamin K and IV fluids, he survived and I took him home, although the vet thought he needed more hospitalization. He improved daily and was back to his normal self within about three days.

So for you cat lovers out there who want to skin me, I spent the money to save this cat, this cat who I just tolerate, because I have a good heart and I respect the life of an innocent animal, and remember, nothing matters in life except love.

More on that later...

# HEY

Whatever happened to Hello or Hi? The standard word used now for a greeting is Hey! It has become universal, at least in the little part of the world that lets me inhabit it. A doc walks by me in the hall way and just says "Hey". Then he doesn't look up from his cell phone. I respond by saying, "Dave". Drives me nuts a little, this "Hey" thing, and initially I rebelled against the lazy word, but it seems it has now become ingrained in my lingo, just like lemming language programmed into robots.

The other day, the answering service sent me a message to call the Emergency Department, to talk to a Dr. "X", a guy who has talked to me about a thousand times. Yes, we know each other, and so when we were finally patched through, didn't introduce myself, probably because I assumed he was informed by the staff I was calling back, so I just said, "Hey".

He laughed, and said, "Sorry I didn't recognize your "Hey", SR; I'll have to remember it next time."

Embarrassed, I apologized for using a lazy word almost automatically, like a robot. But thankfully the days of "What's happenin" or "What it is" are long gone. I think. But at least those greetings required more than just a one-word response, like, "not much man", or "same old stuff, just a different day."

So, I started greeting people by saying, "Hi Johnny", or "What's goin on Johnny?" and all I got back was, "Hey"—"Not much SR." But then I realized that was causing confusion in the word salad of the doctor's lounge, so I have now decided to shake it up a little to see if anyone responds differently when I greet them with new foreign greetings such as, "Hi Randy, good to see you!" Or "Hi Randy, you doin ok?" Yeah, probably won't work, you know, too much energy put into words. I will however, avoid the "How are you?" greeting that of course, never requires a response and if there is a response, the person who asked it runs away or ignores it because few people want to know the truth about how you are.

So instead, I will use these new greetings to see if anyone responds with anything more than a "Hey."

"Snarly man!", "Kick it, Rathbone!", "Bandolissimo!", "Cut it up dude!" "Blutarsky!"

Or, if it's a woman,

"Rosie day", "Nice smile", "Bonjour"

Hopefully these deviations from the accepted greeting, "Hey" will not result in major trauma to my body, but I'll take the chance just to shake things up.

# WILE E. COYOTE

Some of you older folks may remember the Looney toon, Wile E. Coyote (Carnivorous Vulgarus, Hungrii fleabagius, Hard Headipus Ravenous) and Road Runner (Semper foodellus, super-sonic idioticus, Speedipus Rex), apparently broadcast in the 50's through 80's. Of course, I don't remember it playing live on TV because of my young, tender age, but I have of course, watched many of these educational re-runs. Want to buy some cheap land in Florida?

For those of you who were deprived of this cartoon when you were young, it involved a coyote who was a scientific genius, and tried his best to invent contraptions and weapons to catch the very fast road runner, his elusive dinner, as it screamed past him. These inventions (supplied by the ACME Company) included rocket powered sleds, bombs, earthquake pills, birdseed with an anvil hanging from a cliff, etc.

Unfortunately, Wile E. remained hungry because the inventions always backfired, or the road runner outsmarted the traps and the poor skinny coyote often ended up a victim of his own potentially lethal inventions. I was always pleased to see however, that he recovered nicely from grand pianos, anvils and boulders falling on his head from majestic rocky cliffs, but I yearned to someday witness the coyote successfully catching and of course eating that damn smart-ass roadrunner. I suppose the creators felt that would end the cartoon, but really, there are many roadrunners to be eaten, and of course, the show would go on! It gives us hope as humans that eventually we will succeed in our quest!

Surprised we were able to cope with this cartoon dashing our hopes for success in life!

Interestingly, I just returned from a road trip through the beautiful southwest, including New Mexico and Arizona (Sedona) and I finally found the location where this cartoon was filmed! Yes, the red-rocked desert and high rocky cliffs brought back memories. I wonder what it was like to film in those majestic conditions. I'm sure the film crew had to be well hydrated on the set.

Just wanted to see if you were awake.

I'm sure they don't make cartoons like that anymore, and that's too bad.

# COLORADO HERBS IN OIL

Recently, during my multi-city, thousand points of light book signing tour across the United States, I paid a visit to the great state of Colorado. Beautiful state with crisp clean air, that is, when the forests aren't on fire, of course majestic purple mountains showing off their magnificent majesty.

You know what I mean.

So, I went to a few restaurants and of course, the Italian restaurants like to give you oil to dip your crumbly bread in, and I've noticed that they are placing large volumes of green herbs into this oil. One time, I overheard several patrons say, "Bring on more of that oily happy herb dip waiter!"

Curious, I decided to dip it into that funny herb oil and it tasted pretty good! In fact, I ate several bowls of bread and then and asked for 12 refills of this natural, healthy dip. After all, since they were herbs, they had to be healthy, right? Then, I asked for anchovy dip (never eat the stuff usually), then a full meal of pasta, then dessert and I still had the munchies.

Why were the flowers moving around in semicircles on the wall while all the female servers suddenly grew Fu Man Chu hair on their faces?

Weird man! But cool.

Then my security team reminded me that, you know, those

highly trained super model women that are real stunners, but they can fool you by ripping your lips off if you look at them the wrong way. Best not to look at them at all, however, but if you do look at them, please keep your tongue in your mouth. Oh yeah, well they reminded me that this is Colorado and that funny weed here is legal so be careful. Never know where you'll find it.

Certainly not in bread dipping oil, right?

Who knew?

I'm taking my tour caravan back to Kansas where you can eat herbs that aren't funny.

# DANISH DISCRIMINATION

Disclaimer: This short piece is called satire, and is not reflective of the opinion of Danish people in general, but they are words that begged my fingers to type them, so I couldn't help it, therefore, I am not at fault.

I am told by some people who I believe were sober that I appear to be of Danish descent, and for that I am proud. But since I am a Danish descendant (not a "danish") there are some things that I must speak out about. The truth is, I am sick and tired of Danish discrimination.

Our name is besmirched constantly and used to describe sweet rolls, you know those delicious pastries with lots of creamy gooey stuff in the middle and also delicious fruit jellies and a billion calories. Yum! We are not "danishes"! In fact, we are real people with tremendous culture flooded with art, science, architecture and lots of bicycles. You know, remember the famous physicist Niels Bohr and of course the fairy tales of Hans Christian Andersen?

The discrimination is rampant and everywhere. Fattening danish rolls are stuffed into cavernous stomachs everywhere and we are accused of inventing them but we didn't. These pastries should actually be called "Austrians" because they were invented in Vienna and we actually call them Viennese bread or Wienerbrod. I am incensed that people throughout America discriminate against us and use the "d" word indiscriminately. It really hurts our pride and our children grow up listening to this slander.

We are not "danishes" and we are not causing the massive obesity epidemic in this country that is swallowing our once mighty cities, but we are accused of it constantly! We have our rights too. I don't want to use the "R" word to describe those who besmirch us, but you know, I have learned here that calling someone racist may actually benefit you in some ways even if it is not true at all! Amazingly, the "R" word apparently can be used indiscriminately and frequently and doesn't have to be reserved for the real and true racist people who surface occasionally to show their ugly heads. Is that like the boy who cried Wolf? I say use the word as much as possible if it helps you financially or improves your position in your posse. Professors, executives and TV hosts can lose their jobs if they are accused of it. Unfortunately, some people and organizations who are in the business of propagating nasty, unsubstantiated falsehoods are now allowed to disseminate their pathetic agendas without pushback because the majority who want to pushback are afraid of being falsely labeled racist and thus potentially losing their jobs.

But I don't care about false accusations when I speak the truth. I will push back. We must speak the truth against those with selfish and weak agendas. Therefore, I think only Danish people can use the "d" word if they feel it is appropriate. In fact, I am calling for a national boycott of the word danish to describe all sweet rolls. This boycott will ban the serving of danish rolls on college campuses, police stations and public buildings. In fact, "Danish awareness" classes now will become mandatory on all college campuses, paid for by higher tuition rates, reimbursed by the U.S. taxpayer. After all, young people are too stupid to make decisions about good food anyway and it seems logical to regulate all eating habits. Full professorships will be offered in "Danish Awareness Studies." Even if a professor or TV host accidently uses the word danish inappropriately, they will be presumed guilty and treated as such on the national media with huge protests hopefully leading to the ruination of their previously illustrious danish roll gobbling careers.

It will become mandatory that Danish social workers and guidance counselors as well as psychologists be available on all college campuses to tutor those who fail their Danish Awareness classes and to raise the level of Danish awareness on campus, even if there are only 0.75 students per 20,000 who are Danish. Psychological trauma due to Danish discrimination must be treated by federally funded psychotherapists and will immediately be compensated for lifelong disability because these people clearly won't be able to work. Even a miniscule, overly sensitive minority should have absolute power over the majority at all times.

Clearly, anyone who disagrees with this Danish fairness doctrine is a bigot because there is no longer any need for people to have honest, educated disagreement. Honest discourse is a thing of the past, and yelling loudly while hurling disparaging remarks is the best way to dominate people with differing views who actually think things through. If you disagree, clearly you are the racist and I refuse to discuss it further.

I will also push to have some national holidays for school children implemented soon, even if it means children will be in school less and learn nothing. We all know that holidays are much more important than learning math and science since uneducated students can easily be taken care of by the state for the rest of their lives, funded by raising taxes and spending lots of money we don't have studying the issue in focus groups at Starbucks while wearing our cute little running shorts that have never seen sweat.

The Thursday before Easter is Maundy Thursday and will be a mandatory holiday and we will boycott all schools and businesses who don't enforce it. In addition, May one is Danish day of prayer which must be observed by all school children and public institutions.

J-Day, during the Christmas holidays, marks the tapping of extra special Christmas beer, and all must wear ugly blue hats to commemorate this event.

Although this can't be enforced yet, we will recommend that all able-bodied children ride their bikes to school for fitness as well, as long as the distance is less than 5 miles.

Power to the Danes! If you have a different opinion, you are a bigot and I won't listen to you but I will bury my head in the sand so I don't hear your views because if they are different than mine, they must be destroyed or ignored.

# GOOFY MEDICAL TERMINOLOGY

I wrote this piece to explain some of the terms that are commonly used by physicians, nurses and respiratory technicians in the ICU to describe some of the procedures and phrases that are used during the everyday ICU environment. I must say however, that most of the time, physicians are primarily guilty of using these words and phrases because nurses and technicians are just nicer people in general. While readers without a medical background may consider these terms irreverent or disrespectful, trust me, they are not meant to be, and simply make communication easier and perhaps a little lighter for the medical staff when they communicate with each other during the stressful situations in the ICU. I am honored to work with hard working, skilled professionals who show the utmost respect to their patients and I should know, because they saved me once a few years ago. I have written a similar book for patient families that describes common medical terms and procedures used in the ICU, however, it does not use the vernacular commonly used between staff, because well, it shouldn't. This small piece may prove useful for ICU staff who are new to the job and still wet behind the ears and hopefully will make their time on the job much more pleasant during times of stress.

Here is a fictional teaching case: Mr. SmithJonesAwalski is a 55-year-old obese male who is brought to the ICU for *failure to thrive* and hypoxemia because of pneumonia and the **TFTB** syndrome. His wife states that he previously had a history of a **hostile abdomen,** however, his abdomen is quite peaceful now. He recently had an episode of **explosive diarrhea** however; this has now been safely diffused. She mentioned that he had a sleep study showing sleep apnea, and the technicians and physicians wrote that he demonstrated **heroic snoring**, although his wife preferred descriptors such as **freight train** or **house-shaking** snoring because she was sure she never saw his snoring save anyone with heroism.

Hospital course:

The patient was brought to the ICU and placed on the ventilator successfully. Due to significant mucous plugs, he required **toilet Bronchoscopy** on several occasions. He improved nicely and by the second day his sedation was removed and the staff began the **Dumbo-ing process** per protocol to see **if he would fly.** After he failed **Dumbo-ing,** the physician then ordered a quick **Cowboy Extubation.** The patient did well and was sent home in excellent condition due to the prompt and skilled attention he received from the ICU staff.

**Definitions:**

**Toilet Bronchoscopy:** According to the Oxford Textbook of Critical Care, *critically ill patients retain secretions. Toilet bronchoscopy is applied to aspirate retained secretions and revert lung atelectasis.* Basically, what this means is mucous plugs obstruct the lung bronchi or pipes of the lung, causing lung collapse or difficulty breathing. What does this mean in layperson's terms? It means sucking out buggars and snot from the airways to improve breathing. Thus, the terms toilet and flush. Please remember that bronchoscopes are always sterilized completely after each flush.

**Failure to Thrive:** Self-explanatory, I think.

**Hostile Abdomen:** There is no dictionary definition to refer to here. This is a term I learned from the general surgeons who have kept the term close to their scrubs I guess, until it was recently released and is now no longer considered top secret classified information. Basically, it refers to an abdomen that has unfortunately required multiple surgical procedures over time and therefore has adhesions and scar tissue making it more difficult for the surgeon to re-enter the abdomen if needed because the abdomen becomes very angry and pissed off when cut on again. We all try to keep abdomens as peaceful as possible and avoid hostility.

**Explosive diarrhea:** Well, I think everyone understands **explosion/explosive** with respect to bombs and blowing things up etc., so I guess this is self-explanatory. Kind of similar to what is experienced when you drink Golytely for a bowel prep before a colonoscopy.

**Dumbo-ing:** This refers to the 1941 Walt Disney movie: *Dumbo the Flying Elephant.* Dumbo was an elephant and therefore not skinny, and he tried and tried but eventually learned to fly that heavy body with his large ears for wings. It refers to a patient who is quite overweight and sometimes they don't breathe well because it is harder for the lungs to breathe when they have well, a sack of potatoes sitting on top of them. This is a variant of the **TFTB** syndrome (Too Fat to Breathe). Excess size may cause Dumbo not to *fly* when he is given the chance to breathe on his own off the ventilator machine.

**Cowboy Extubation:** No of course doctors, nurses and technicians do not wear cowboy hats in the ICU! It simply means we think cowboys are kind of wild and impulsive for unclear reasons, and this may not be based on any factual evidence. Maybe it just sounds good. So basically, it means if a patient is not flying off the ventilator while the tube remains in his/her trachea, and becomes anxious, and then the doctor gives an order to remove the tube anyway without waiting, because the patient may in fact, do better without the tube in. Perhaps there are real cowboys reading this who will be offended by this silly use of their heritage/occupation but no offense intended. Maybe we should instead call it instead, **Politician Extubation.** You know, sign the bill before you read it.

**TFTB:** This is the basis behind the difficulty with Dumbo-ing.

**Heroic snoring:** Sleep study technician write this in their notes constantly. I didn't know snoring was heroic, but then, maybe it has saved lives, you know, like scaring violent burglars when they enter your house? Perhaps this requires more discussion later. I suggest they instead write that the snoring was loud or obnoxious, rather than snoring. But then, it is ironic and silly so I am glad they keep it in the sleep lab vernacular.

**Politician Extubation:** Please see discussion under **Cowboy Extubation**

# TACO BELL AND PATIENTS

I am not employed by that establishment to provide marketing. However, if Taco Bell wants to employ me as a marketer, using my lively application of words to their products, I'll be happy to do so. Also, it's still summer, and I enjoyed walking on this Lake Michigan Beach pictured on my website.

Now, I will try to tie the rest of the piece into the above paragraph the best I can. I try to be on time for my patients, or at least do the best I can to arrive in their exam room at the appointed time, but often I fail. That's because of multiple reasons, such as the patient before was complex, required a lot of time, and also talked too much about grandkids, family reunions etc. It may also be that my surgeries are running late at the hospital or people decided to be sick at inappropriate times.

However, when my patients are late to their office appointments it bothers me, especially if they don't call ahead. After all, people call ahead to restaurants to inform the staff that they will be late for their reservation due to traffic, or the weather etc. But recently, one of my patients, and older gentleman, arrived about 15 minutes late, with his wife. He was pleasant and since this was his first visit, I of course, was polite and generous. I think.

He said, "Sorry Dr. Carson, but we drove to the wrong building. I knew it was across from the Ajax building, so I pulled in to this driveway that looked like it might be your office, but turns out, I was right in front of the drive through window at Taco Bell, a fine eating establishment. So, that's why we're late. Sorry." He and his wife laughed.

"Ha! That's funny Mr. Fajita, I mean Finkelsternersmith. What did you order in the drive through?"

"Well, since we were there, we went ahead and ordered 2 Taco Bell Grandes."

"Good choice." I didn't ask if they ate them in the car before they came up to their appointment with me, but after our office visit, everything went well and I had some ideas that I have subsequently implemented with the Taco Bell next door to our office so that both businesses could take advantage of lost patients. Certainly, in this instance, Taco Bell was the winner, in that they received extra business due to my patient becoming lost. Or maybe he perfectly well knew what he was doing, but I could tell in his eyes that he was truthful. But maybe I was the winner too, because I enjoyed a good laugh and met a very nice patient and his wife.

So, on the drive through menu, Taco Bell has agreed to place several additional options on their menus: Nacho fries, Burrito Supreme, Fiery Dutch Locos Tacos, Cheese Quesadilla, etc., and then, *make an appointment with Dr. Carson, sign in to Dr. Carson's office reception for your appointment early, insurance information, history form, blow in to this tube for a quick breathing test, and stick your arm out and we will check your vital signs for your visit with Dr. Carson while you eat your Taco.*

We are hoping to implement this mutually beneficial drive-through menu starting September 1, and hopefully, Taco Bell will be pleased with the business my lost patients have been giving them by surprise, and at the same time, my office saves time and signs the patients in quicker, obtains vital signs for charting, and even pulmonary function testing could potentially be done by trained Taco Bell employees while the patient sits in their car, hopefully before they start eating their tacos.

I'll keep you updated on the negotiations with Taco Bell.

To the reader: Finkelsternersmith is not a real patient name. It is fictional. If this is a real name from somewhere, then, of course, it is purely a coincidence and well, that's quite a long name. Oh, and Taco Bell has not yet called me about this opportunity.

# PHYSICIANS AND
# GALLOWS HUMOR

This Wuhan virus world-wide pandemic is affecting all of us around the world, from all walks of life. It has unfortunately caused death, suffering, lay-offs, financial stress and social upheaval in a way that we would never have predicted, so suddenly. Everybody knows this of course, unless you are living in a cave somewhere off the grid. But what many don't realize is that physicians who work on the front lines treating people with this disease must find ways to handle their stress, and it turns out, one of the common ways is what we call gallows humor. We use this tool not to minimize the stress and suffering from disease that our patients suffer every day, but instead, to relieve our own stress a little, so that we can enjoy a few laughs in the middle of the war, and then re-charge a little to push onwards with renewed vigor. The gallows humor is usually stupid and sometimes brutal, but that makes it funnier. I think. And of course, we say these things to each other in private, or at least we make every attempt to do so.

Recently, I was the first in our group to intubate (place a breathing tube in the airway) a patient afflicted with this virus who unfortunately went into respiratory failure. I used all the protective gear available, as did the skilled staff who assisted me at the bedside, to avoid infection due to the high risk of virus aerosolization with this procedure. We didn't know if he was actually infected at the time because the tests were not back yet, but we assumed he was.

The next day, after an exhausting night on call, I told one of my partners about this case and that I hoped we were all safely protected during the procedure. He said, "Carson, you know if you become infected, and go into respiratory failure, we will intubate you, but we will intubate you without anesthesia or sedation, so that you can remain awake while on life support, so that you can take "on-call" responsibility for the hospital by doing telemedicine on a lap top in your ICU bed while on the ventilator."

I have great partners.

Reminds me of this quote: "Endeavor to Persevere" From Chief Dan George, in the movie *Outlaw Josey Wales*.

# THE SLEEP MOVEMENT: DO AS WE SAY OR WOKE UP

Certainly, there have been and will continue to be many movements in our history. For example, symphony movements, The Feminist Movement, Animal Rights Movement and of course the mandatory cleansing bowel movement.

But here is what you need to know: You all need to WOKE up, rather, I mean wake up to The Sleep Movement.

Sleep is very important to our health and livelihood. The proper amount of good sleep is important for memory consolidation, immune health and prevention of infection, proper functioning during the day, avoidance of obesity and of course the essential nocturnal tumescence (erections) that men need. So, if you don't believe in obtaining seven to eight hours of good sleep per night, you are clearly a bad person and must be canceled.

For example, if you ever wrote on social media as a teenager or a college student, or perhaps in your high school year book, that you were proud of the fact that you could live and survive on two hours of sleep per night, then the Sleep Movement will shame and destroy you as fast as possible. We will find out about your past sleep mistakes or statements and bring you to sleep justice. In fact, if we ever find out you called other people dirty names like "sleepy head" then that cannot be tolerated, even if you said it when drunk at a college party. If you ever wrote or said that "sleep is overrated" 10 or 20 years ago, we will find out about it and remove you from your job and humiliate you. The universal truth is that you are responsible permanently for everything you said and did, even as a baby in smelly diapers and the Sleep Movement is responsible for judging you. It doesn't matter what your excuse is or was. You must be destroyed, preferably in public and at your place of employment and we will write your name and phone number on public bathroom stalls so all Sleep Movement people can shame you properly.

All scientific evidence that I have created during my vivid dream sleep proves that if you do not believe in good sleep you are misogynistic and racist. And you are probably a xenophobe as well since all of those descriptors seem to be related in some way that I cannot understand. In fact, I think all people who do not believe in sleep should be canceled because of their obvious racism. It has become obvious that all people that don't believe in our Sleep Movement or our thoughts and beliefs are racists.

If you disagree with our beliefs then you are a racist and possibly even a dirty misogynist as well, I don't know, but I would be suspicious and mark you for further investigation by the exalted Sleep authorities. Either way, you must be canceled and we will not stoop so low as to let you defend your stupid ideas. You are guilty and obviously it is a waste of time to allow a trial by peers. And if you are a white non-sleeper, you are double racist at birth! We must teach all our children this truth and indoctrinate them into our perfect beliefs as early as three months of age and certainly before they are potty trained! We have therefore created the National Silly

Endowment for Education of Sleep Non-believers, providing educational materials for grade school through high school and college to assist in the indoctrination.

Why are people who don't believe in the Sleep Movement racist? I have no idea actually, but it doesn't matter. It seems that you can use this racist word any time you want—it feels good, and it provides a certain faux power—a self-righteous power that can be easily exerted over others, even if there is no basis for it. What is amazing is that that word racist is used so often now that no one knows what the true meaning is anymore, and that is a powerful weapon. That power it seems cannot be overcome with intellectual debate because we don't allow debate, and that sends shivers of amazing power up my spine!

Power to the Sleep Movement and WOKE up.

Signed, the Grand Wizard of the Self-Righteous Sleep Movement

# DON'T BE LAZY: CREATE YOUR OWN CLICHÉ AND SLEEP LIKE A BABY

Clichés are used constantly and frankly quite a few are snore triggers and no longer have any useful meaning, at least, to me. However, some can never or should be never changed, like *the writing is on the wall*. That is biblical.

So, it is time for us to change and create new clichés and stop being so damn lazy with our words.

There are several that I don't want to hear any more, and probably a lot more, but I can't think of them right now.

1. **At the end of the day:** I am tired of this one and it is probably used a billion times per day. Everyone knows that when the day ends, it is time to drink beer. So, the new cliché will be: *When Beer Time Arrives*
2. **Sleep like a baby:** Babies don't sleep through the night at all, with lots of crying until they are about six months old, maybe four months if you are lucky. So, the old cliché is illogical. The new cliché is: *Sleep grabbed me and wouldn't let me go.* Or perhaps, *Deep*

*sleep invaded my soul.* Alternatively, *the sleep hammer hit and I never moved.*

3. **When life gives you lemons, make lemonade.** That is nice, and cute, but it has been used so much that it makes me fall asleep standing. This now becomes: *If you want to sing the blues, learn to play guitar.* Or *When life gives you lemons, pucker and watch Josey Wales.* Or, *if you have to chew leather, imagine it tastes like steak.*

Now, I am forced to provide some examples of well-worn clichés that need to be changed and refreshed so they have deeper meaning:

1. **Cat Got your tongue?** Tell me, how many cats grab tongues? This becomes: *You been eating glue?*
2. **Scared out of my wits:** This becomes: *That made me change my underwear.*
3. **Laughter is the best medicine:** Should become: *Laugh during the day or you will pee your bed at night*
4. **Don't cry over spilled milk:** This changes to: *It would be worse if you spilled the last beer.* Or perhaps, *you screwed up, so do one hundred push-ups, then kiss your girl with passion.*
5. **What goes around, comes around:** This becomes: *The boomerang you threw is on its way back*
6. **Ugly as sin:** I think it is best not to call anyone ugly, even if they are, except in certain circumstances that demand it. Although it is wrong to sin, and that can be ugly, I think sin can sometimes appear quite ravishing and beautiful before it destroys your soul. So, this becomes: *Ugly as a one-winged fly in a latrine*

# THE TROUT WHISPERER: AN EXCERPT FROM MY NOVEL: BLUE SHADOWS

He was always on time for group therapy, promptly at nine am although even though he thought therapy was generally a waste of time, he went so that he could keep his career. Why listen to other people's problems? He knew what this was—nightmares and headaches, but more importantly... (*I had to leave this blank so that you would take the time to read my novel*)

The group therapy leader went around the gaggle of five patients, asking each individual what thought intruded into their mind the most—and bothered them the most as well. One patient said, "God talks to me, tells me I am not his son Jesus, but I look like him with my long hair, so now I must act like him before he calls me back from my earthly mission." He played with his shoulder length hair and smiled triumphantly.

The leader asked, "Does that bother you Hank?"

"Well, yes. Mostly because I think he will soon ask me to be crucified too since Easter is coming soon. Seems I have so much to do with so little time remaining. I hope I don't have to be crucified because I am averse to physical pain. I hope he'll call me back before Easter arrives."

Wyatt stared straight ahead, arms crossed with an emotionless face, despite the overwhelming urge to sprint to the exits with his arms pumping hard.

"What about you Wyatt?" The therapy leader purposely avoided saying 'doctor' so as not to give Wyatt away to the other patients. "Do you have anything to share with the group? Don't be shy Wyatt."

Wyatt paused, ignored the disturbing images and said, "I sometimes dream that I go fly fishing in the mountain stream naked, because my dog took my waders and pants away, but I can't catch any trout because they laugh at me and say, "Sir, you better be thankful we're not flying fish because we would fly circles around you, then steal your flies and spit them back at you, hoping someday you'll learn how to present the correct flies to us properly in the water. And by the way, most trout aren't scared by noise as much as they are of naked humans wading in our homes, uninvited. There is a mountain stream dress code you know." Wyatt wasn't sure how he was able to come up with this silliness so quickly, but he tried not to laugh at his own concocted fish story, at least initially. But the rest of the clients maintained stone cold serious faces.

Wyatt eventually had to put his partially closed fist to his chin and mouth, to make sure that he didn't laugh out loud at his fictional story. And then, the tall one, Karl said, "I had a dream or vision more likely, like that too. I was fishing and a fish jumped up and bit me in the ass, and then never even said he was sorry." After that, the session that day was no longer effective for any of the participants. All the patients wanted to talk about was trout fishing and the proper clothing for such activities. Thereafter, all the patient's addressed Wyatt as the *Trout Whisperer.*

# MY FAMOUS INTERVIEW ON BOOK MARKETING

(From Digiwriting Marketing Agency)

## Marketing Q&A With Author S.R. Carson

Looking to improve your marketing and publicity efforts? Check out our Book Publicity Tips series where we ask real authors to share their experiences, thoughts, and advice to assist both new and established authors.

### What is the best way to respond to a negative review?

I haven't had many negative reviews but they happen. Heck, I can't please everyone and be all things to all people. My most bizarre one was probably from my ex-wife, or at least, that seems most likely. So, I think the best thing to do is to ignore the review completely, and immediately blame your ex!

## Have you ever had a book signing?

Yes, I have, and I enjoyed it immensely with a good show-ing. It was at a café/bar. Of course, the wine helped a lot. In fact, I recommend serving wine at book signings when pos-sible. My signature is unreadable at best, but after a good cab-ernet, it actually becomes somewhat readable!

## How important is social media to your marketing efforts?

I don't know, really. I am clearly inept at marketing, basi-cally, because I'm a doctor who has never had to advertise; people just came to me to be treated, and my reputation was built by word of mouth. I am not so good at social media, and I guess old fashioned word of mouth doesn't work the same in this case.

## How important are friends and family when you market your book?

Quick Answer: forget family completely. I mean, with re-gard to marketing at least. Friends? Well, don't depend on them to market you, just keep them as friends. It's your en-emies that you have to market to successfully without them realizing you are doing it.

## How frequently do you post on Twitter? Do you have a method to increase engagement and interaction? Do you have favourite hashtags?

I post something or RT sometimes. Not convinced I like Twitter because there seem to be a lot of fakes and selfish people. I try not to push my books, but instead, interact with funny posts or responses to get people interested in me as a person, not a book hawker. I don't try to maximize followers just for volume. I need real responders and interesting people, not just large numbers of tweeps. Twitter is a world filled with many agendas, some good, but many are destructive.

## Author Bio

Dr. Carson is a physician specialist and writer.

*To Love With Hate* is his debut novel described as a "boiling cauldron of intense psychological suspense."

In *Code Blue: A Doctor's View of His Own Near Death Experience,* he describes how he witnesses his own NDE and how it profoundly changes his life and those of those participating.

# HIS SNORING CAN
# BE HEROIC

Tommie and his wife Sara had just returned home from a week's vacation in the islands and they were both exhausted from the travel, airports, packing, and flight delays. Not only that, Tommie made them both get up an hour earlier than necessary to go to the airport, and they were there as usual, three hours early. And of course, Tommie enjoyed his two tiny bottles of bourbon on the airplane, which put him in a deep coma during the flight, mouth wide open, producing a cacophony of fuselage-vibrating snores and heaving grunts, prompting Sara to wake him up with smacks to the shoulder so that the other passengers would not attack him and strangle him then and there. The pilot even notified the passengers there was unexpected turbulence, despite clear skies, but Sara knew the vibrations on the air frame were from Tommie's snores.

Thankfully, he finally woke up when they were on descent to the airport, and he resumed his normal breathing pattern and his pendulous belly was no longer required to bounce up and down to participate in gas exchange. But it was good to be home again, and after throwing out some spoiled black bananas they left before travel, unpacking at least fifty percent of their bags and throwing dirty clothes in the laundry, they both passed out in bed, exhausted. But in their hurry to get to bed, they forgot to lock the doors, all the outdoor lights were turned off and they forgot to turn on their alarm system.

The home intruder came in through the unlocked garage access door, into the utility room and he sneaked quietly in to look in the kitchen to find wallets and purses for easy money and credit cards. He couldn't find any, so he thought he would walk down the hallway and look somewhere else and then Tommie suddenly blasted away with his wall-vibrating, house-shaking obnoxious snoring. It was so loud and sudden, the snorting and grunts knocked the intruder to the ground and he hit the floor, hitting his head on a corner table, bleeding, and spraining his ankle, and his gun went flying.

Sara immediately woke up, smacked Tommie harder than ever, and Tommie immediately jumped up, wiped the drool from his face, found his .357 magnum under his bed and found the intruder, crawling towards the door, bleeding. Tommie pointed his gun at him and said, "Got you asshole!" The intruder was shaking with fear, Tommie made sure he put himself between the intruder and the man's gun, then told Sara to call 911 for the police, which she had already done. Tommie was shaking, but always wondered if he would shoot a man in this situation, but it was not necessary, thankfully.

The police came, arrested the intruder, and filed his report with the couple. When the police were gone, Sara hugged Tommie, and kissed him passionately, and said, "Tommie, you are my courageous hero!"

Ok now. That is an example of **Heroic Snoring**

And I thought about this long and hard, because that is the only example I could come up with to validate the term "Heroic Snoring". Nothing else makes sense. Why do I mention this? Well, sleep technicians are trained professionals and very good at what they do. They monitor people during overnight sleep studies, looking for sleep apnea and other sleep disorders. They write notes on their data collection, then, I receive the notes and data, and provide a physician interpretation of the study. But what I have noticed is that not always, but some technicians for years, continue to describe the night as "The patient demonstrated **heroic snoring** throughout the study." Or he/she had "frequent **heroic snoring**." Now, I always felt that was an unusual way to describe snoring. Seems incongruous, or an oxymoron. How in the world, can obnoxious, wall-vibrating noises, produced by an obstructed human airway be described as heroic? I understand it is not nice to say obnoxious or nasty, but wall-vibrating kind of gets the picture across. Or maybe the simple adjective *loud* would suffice.

Snoring is a symptom of an obstructed oro-pharyngeal airway, associated with obstructive sleep apnea, or if not present, at least a sign that obstructive sleep apnea may occur down the road. Obstructive sleep apnea, when present, can cause blood pressure problems, cardiac problems, oxygen problems and of course, pissed-off spouse problems.

But now I finally understand! Snoring can be Heroic! The technicians are in fact, correct with their description.

# C. Nature and Inspiration

# INSPIRATIONAL QUOTES, BLOWING LEAVES AND LOVE

I'm not sure why I joined twitter. Perhaps I was told I should do it to sell my books more effectively and maximize my *social media presence.* So, I joined with good intentions but eventually learned that it is a strange world that is filled with authors trying desperately to hawk their books, no matter what it takes, sometimes throwing their products at you non-stop, hoping you will give up and buy their books simply to stop the barrage. Why should I buy a book just because it is retweeted to me? Anyway, I am not convinced this was a good move for me because I refuse to play the game with twitter-fanatic gusto, but instead, I try to soak in and respond to the wisdom that is there, if one can find it, and sort through the blather. I also break the rules by not *liking* all things that tweet their way to me, but instead, I respond to excellent writing, art, or creativity with some kind words or a creative response to engage the sender.

During my twitter immersion, I have however, noticed a continuous waterfall of lovely and wise inspirational quotes that are quite nice. I appreciate them and admire those who send them out into the world, well intentioned to make the receiver feel good, have hope, avoid giving up while giving it the old college try, and certainly live life like there is no tomorrow.

Here is a tiny sampling and there are a billion better ones that I am sure you can find. Most are obtained from the *Inspirational Quotes* site, except for the one directly attributed to Robert F. Kennedy.

1. Only those who dare to fail greatly can achieve greatly. (Robert F. Kennedy)
2. Don't fear change. You can lose something good, but you may also gain something great.
3. One day you'll just be a memory for some people. Do your best to be a good one.
4. Thank your past for all your lessons, then move on.
5. If you don't step forward you will always remain in the same place.

Great quotes, right? If I could wake up every morning and remember these, then stepwise implement them into my daily life at work or with my relationships, I would certainly be better off, don't you think? Maybe it would help to enlarge the print on a bunch of inspiring quotes, then paste them on my refrigerator, the inside of my front door, the door to my back porch, the ceiling of my bedroom and the mirrors of my bathroom. Then, I would really have life nailed!

But no. I realized that they are just words, and I forget them as soon as I become busy with the duties and essential aspects of life, and the words are gone—like colorful fall leaves floating away in the fickle, but knowing wind, never to be found again in the same place.

Don't get me wrong. I appreciate all these inspiring quotes and words of knowledge about how to live life. The people who send them are to be commended. But the simple truth that I haven't seen mentioned is this simple phrase I came up with myself: If you don't carry and nurture love deep within your soul, with a strong belief in God, the words in inspirational quotes are simply words—they don't stick and they change nothing.

# OPTIMIST CLUB AND LITTLE LEAGUE BASEBALL

Ijoined the little league when I was a boy, maybe age 9 or so and I was randomly assigned as a rookie to a team sponsored by the Optimist Club. I was lucky because it was a damn good team that had won the city championship the year before and after I joined, continued to win city championships.

Despite me, of course. Surprised they didn't kick me off the team.

They won because of Charlie C., the greatest pitcher in the whole league, and we all believed, the greatest athlete of all time at that age. Hell, he was other worldly compared to us, with an arm it seemed of an adult, and he struck out nearly every kid he faced, and if they were lucky enough to get a hit, it was probably an accident. And he was a pitcher who could hit like a monster. The only time we lost was when he was sick or had to travel with his family of course, and it was like a funeral on our side of the diamond. I think all of us who are still alive from that team are still recovering from the time Charlie C went on a 2-week vacation with his family back to Georgia, I think.

Oh yeah, we also had Tim C. He was a bull at the age of 10, and may have been shaving and dating already. He defined the role of clean-up hitter, because we knew if there were guys on base, he would hit them home, often with towering home runs that made us all stare at the trajectory from the sidelines, tongue and slobbering bubble gum falling out of our awe-struck mouths.

And then there was me. The first year, I couldn't hit a damn thing, and I was small, difficult to see, but fast. But I was a good fielder, could play some bases I thought, but they stuck me in the outfield that year and tried to forget about me. But when I got on base, usually because the pitcher hit me with the ball or I walked, I loved stealing bases and sliding in to home, getting as dirty as I could. Even when I didn't have to. I was a damn jackrabbit who couldn't be caught. My role was to try to get on base by walking, steal some bases, or have Charlie or Tim hit me home. That was it.

But we had great jerseys. They had OPTIMIST CLUB embroidered on the back, or was it the front, I don't remember, with our number on it. All the other teams feared us, and I guess, rightfully so. At the end of my first year, all the adult members of Optimist Club gave us a nice deep-fried chicken dinner and mashed potatoes, and massive quantities of Coca-Cola in bottles at their club downtown, received our trophies, and we felt like pretty special. Except of course, Charlie and Tim, they were superstar royalty. And yes, they only gave out trophies to winners back then. Imagine that? And then, we had championship chicken dinners the next year too because well, we were pretty much a dynasty. And believe it or not my second year, I learned to hit, but I was still a skinny jackrabbit.

I am sure I had no idea what an optimist was at that age, and also no idea who the Optimist Club members were and what exactly they represented. I just cared about winning baseball games and receiving chicken dinners and trophies at the end. And we had cool jerseys. Did I mention that?

So, I thought about optimism in church today and those little league days forged their images back in my mind once again. Later, I looked up, for the first time, the mission of the Optimist Clubs: *By providing hope and positive vision, Optimists bring out the best in youth, our communities and ourselves.* There was also a very long mission statement which I won't write here, but mentioned concepts like advancing humankind, life, youth, etc.

And then I wondered, what an auspicious start I had back then. I was an optimist; I wore the shirt and I didn't even know it! And as my life went on, with more victories as well as many setbacks, stupid decisions and challenges, including events that could've taken my life several times, perhaps I did have a degree of optimism in me deep down, and I was surely blessed by God.

I know that now. No matter how dark things may appear, this is not the end.

# MY OWN QUOTE
# ON KNOWLEDGE

*Knowledge will not supersede truth, and truth will not supersede love. With all three, you will never fear death.*

By (SRCarson/Steve Mohnssen, 2016)

Below is a quote from a world-famous author. It is a great quote. However, I think my quote written in italics above, is more expansive and a little more mind-bending. It just popped into my mind so I published it on my blog in 2016.

"End of man is knowledge, but there is one thing he can't know. He can't know whether his knowledge will save or kill him." From Robert Penn Warren.

# WHERE'S THE RESPECT?

Of the legions of voracious readers of my blog, perhaps a few will understand where I extract some of my inspiration, if you want to call it that. And no, this time, it wasn't at the bar. What set me off this time was some guy wearing what he thought was a handsome beret in church services. What then exploded within me is my review of some of the scenes of disrespect that I have witnessed in this country. The actions or inactions of disrespect apply to what people do to their fellow man, our country, our institutions and our way of life. By no means is this list of ten exhaustive, but just the ones that came to my mind quite quickly this afternoon. You readers may certainly add scores of others of course.

And for those of you who consider this political, you clearly don't comprehend my words because it has nothing at all to do with politics. Just respect. For those with this view, I simply ask you to read this piece four or five times. Slowly. And finally, for those of you who are misguided enough to think this is racially motivated, it is not, and you are simply deceiving yourself with purposeful misperceptions because you are light years away from the truth on this piece.

Disclaimer: I am a former Eagle Scout and Ex-Military. I'm proud of both. That should explain some of my background, but certainly not all.

Here is my top ten list on the topic of RESPECT!

1. <u>YOUR PARENTS:</u> Do I need to say any more about this?

2. <u>MEN: SHOW RESPECT WITH YOUR HATS!</u> Proper respect dictates that you always take your hats off in a place of worship. In addition, you take your hats off in a show of respect in someone's home, mealtimes, while being introduced, whether inside or out, indoors at work, public buildings, movie theaters and absolutely when the national anthem is being played or the flag passes by you, such as during a parade.

3. <u>RESPECT THE FLAG OF THE UNITED STATES!</u> If I EVER see you stomping on, burning, spitting on, or desecrating our flag, I will come and take the flag from you, then, I will knock the living hell out of you. After that, I will send you off on a slow boat to some third world country where you will no longer have the protection of the United States military, its government and the protection of its constitution. In addition, you will no longer receive taxpayer funded government assistance. Too many men and women have sacrificed their lives for the freedoms you take for granted. If you have a disagreement with something, I respect that. Then voice your opinion, but stay away from our beautiful flag.

4. <u>MEN: OPEN DOORS FOR LADIES WHEN YOU CAN:</u> Old fashioned, perhaps, but I still do and enjoy it. Ladies are beautiful gifts from God. Of course, there are always exceptions.

5. <u>RESPECT THE OPINIONS OF OTHERS:</u> Even if you disagree, listen to that opinion and think, with an open mind, then make a logical argument against it if you still disagree. Who knows, maybe you will learn something. But don't call the other person names, throw

slurs or show disrespect just because they have a different opinion. You will always lose and show that you are lower than a snake if you do.

6. <u>RESPECT OUR POLICEMEN AND WOMEN:</u> Without them, we will live in anarchy.
7. <u>RESPECT OUR SCHOOL TEACHERS:</u> Without teachers, we accomplish nothing in life. They work hard and do it for little pay. If you beat them up and disrupt them while they are teaching, then later, complain that you don't have a job, then of course, I have no pity on you. You have no self-respect. (See no. 10).
8. <u>RESPECT THE MEN AND WOMEN WHO SERVE IN THE MILITARY</u>: They volunteer, my friend, to protect you and may even pay the ultimate sacrifice for your protection. What have you done today?
9. <u>RESPECT OUR HISTORY</u>: Yes, that actually means you will have to read history books. The more you know about history, the more you will understand about the world today, and you will be less ignorant of events that are transpiring. That also means you need to learn the national anthem and America the beautiful.
10. <u>RESPECT YOURSELF FIRST</u>: If you don't respect yourself and who you are, then who do you think will respect you?

# MY THANKSGIVING, 2018: SPENDING TIME WITH A FORGOTTEN 105-YEAR-OLD AMERICAN HERO: COLONEL OLLIE CELLINI

It was nearing the end of the day for me while I was serving my duty in the ICU at the hospital. I was called to the emergency department to admit a patient to the ICU. He was stabilized in the ED and I came to see him there prior to transferring him to the ICU.

"Carson, he's 105 years old and the family doesn't want him to have heroic measures done, like CPR or intubation, but they will allow him to be treated in the ICU with pressors and a central line if the problem is reversible," said the ED doc.

I arrived in a lonely back room of the ED to see an elderly gentleman with a trimmed mustache laying in a gurney in no distress, hooked up to the usual monitors with his daughter on his right side, talking to his right ear—the one with the hearing aid that helped him hear somewhat.

He couldn't hear me when I said, "Hello, I'm doctor Carson." Either that or he wanted me to go away and give him some rest, I couldn't tell.

With his daughter's help, I was able to ascertain his history that he had fainted at a local restaurant and was brought in for evaluation due to very low blood pressure. Thankfully, his other daughter was able to catch him before he hit the floor.

I asked him how he was feeling and if he was having pain or trouble breathing, and due to his hearing problem, I didn't receive much information except he was doing fine. Then I asked, "What was your occupation sir?"

He heard that one. "I flew fighters in the war."

That struck my interest button immediately and the button remained lighted. His daughter added, "He few fighters in WWII and the Korean conflict. By the way Dr. Carson, can you guess who he flew for in WWII?"

I have no idea why I responded so quickly without hesitation to her question, but I said, "Well, I think he flew with General Claire Chennault of the Flying Tigers, China, Burma, India Group." I said it confidently as if I knew this, which of course, I did not, but what did I have to lose with that response to a man who would be the right age? But I had a feeling I was probably right.

I was right, and that realization made me tremble a little with awe. His daughter was surprised that I guessed right, and said something like, "You're the first person to guess it right Dr. Carson! Yes, he flew for General Chennault in China."

After that I concentrated on sponging information from this hero. But I didn't want to take too much energy from him with his illness and I was pleased that he had improved enough not to require ICU admission. "Yeah, he said. I flew for Chennault, mostly P-47s and then later F-80s in Korea. The P-47 could fly over the hump pretty easy."

His daughter Linda said, "He also has been awarded the Distinguished Flying Cross with six oak leaf clusters and the

Legion of Merit as well as an award from Madame Chiang Kai-Shek." Clearly, he was a highly decorated, 105-year-old fearless military hero who no one seemed to know about in the busy ED. Yes, he was an old man and the ED staff took care of him nicely, but it was his history and his bravery that I was proud to have discovered with just a simple question during my exam. Had I not asked the question, I would have never received the honor and inspiration that this man's aura bestowed upon me, from the greatest generation.

During my drive home, I came up with the idea that the next day, when I was on-call for the hospital on Thanksgiving, I would make a trip up to the North Hospital to bring my book, *The Flying Tiger* by Jack Samson, about the famous General Claire Chennault and the Flying Tigers that I had never completely read. I asked his daughter Linda, if she would allow me to visit her father on Thanksgiving, even though he was no longer effectively my patient, and ask him to sign the book and perhaps write a few words about his experiences in the war with Chennault. She graciously allowed me to do that. I hoped I could escape for long enough to visit him.

At about 1pm on thanksgiving, I delayed my meal despite my hunger and paid him a visit. I sat on his right side so he could hear me a little and he taught me a minute history lesson about the war, and only a portion of his war experience was with Chennault in 1944, but it was a major one, and I was grateful for the few tidbits of first-hand knowledge he could give me, as part of his vast experience flying many airplanes.

"I flew the P-47 mostly and the P-40. The P-47 was a gas guzzler, but I convinced Chennault that we should use it because it could take a lot of punishment and it had 8—50 caliber guns that could blow up tanks and flip'em over. I also commanded the 33rd and 81st fighter groups."

He didn't mention anything about Korea or his time as a test pilot of the feared P-38 lightning. But we would need many hours to learn about his many experiences including the pilot's life he saved when others told him to leave him to die.

"So, tell me Colonel, what was Chennault like?"

He told me and also wrote this on the pages of my book: "I flew P-47s under Chennnault He was an excellent boss because he would always listen and eventually agreed with you. But you know, he would let you call him a SOB as long as you explained why."

I laughed, and thanked him for his time. His daughter graciously agreed to take a few pictures of him with the doctor who could barely fly a Cessna 172.

I saluted him and thanked him for his service and went back to my job caring for patients. I believe I was in the presence of a great man, who few people knew existed, and I believe this world would be a better place if we recognized our true heroes and honored the history of their sacrifice to our country.

It was an inspiring Thanksgiving 2018 for me and I was honored to meet Colonel Ollie Cellini.

Note: Linda Cellini, his daughter, has given me permission to write about her father and publish photos of him, however, I have chosen not to in this work. Unfortunately, Ollie passed away in 2020 and I would've been honored to learn more from him.

# WRITING NOVELS WHILE LAP SWIMMING, OR WILL YOU FINISH THE NOVEL BEFORE I'M DEAD?

The stimulus for this little piece came from a wonderful 87-year-old patient who joked, "Dr. Carson, will you finish your novel before I'm dead? I want to read it."

I've recently found myself in the gray doldrums of what many call writer's block. It means I am completely unable to start a page on my next novel chapter. Rather than using the worn-out phrase—writer's block, I am now coining the term "sentenceopenia", a word that is of course, very similar to osteopenia or neutropenia and medical conditions that are similar, referring in Latin/Greek to "lack of" or "deficiency of".

It used to be that my inspiration for flying words would occur at the bar, and bar napkins would fall victim to my written word vomit, facilitated by the alcoholic beverage of choice at the moment, as long as the bar napkins furnished are white, and not the popular black that is invading popular Avant-garde bars. (Please refer to some of my previous writings on this topic). However, I haven't been to a bar recently and of course, my trusty liver thanks me for that.

I couldn't find a cure for my sentenceopenia, so I decided to swim laps today at the local health club. I hate swimming actually, but my road battered knees thank me for it and it provides a good aerobic workout in between weight sessions. But boring. Booooring. About all my brain does, it seems, is count the laps and the fast/slow intervals, you know, like *going on lap 7 of 8 freestyle with accelerated intervals.* That's important you know, because you don't want to lose track and mess up. I learned how to count laps when I was a track runner back when I had good knees.

But this weekend, something different happened. In between the lap counting mantra, I wrote a new chapter in my novel, complete with characters, plot, conflict and action. Done. All the sentences were written, that is, they were written in my communicating dendrites rather than on paper, but you know what I mean. Hell, if I had a pad of paper on a bench next to my towel by the pool, I would've stopped after 1000 yards and wrote the damn chapter right then and there! It seemed to make my lap swimming go faster as well because I figured the faster I swam the less likely I would forget the chapter that was just written in my dendrites by lap 40, forcing me to accomplish a super-fast shower, forgetting my socks as I dressed, leaving my hair like Einstein's and driving fast home to start putting the words to paper.

It worked.

So, I guess that means if I am not a bar, I need to be lap swimming now to cure my nasty case of sentenceopenia. My skin may flake off from chlorine, but my hope is that I'll be able to finish this damn thing before I'm dead of course, and hopefully before my patient is dead.

# JE NE SAIS QUOI, DR. CARSON

Medicine is a field full of challenges as well as rewards, just like any other profession, and way too much has been written about it for me to do it justice at this time. So, let's just make it simple: I have luckily chosen the career path years ago that suited my personality and God-given skills or lack of skills fairly well, and I have no doubt that the spiritual rewards I have enjoyed far outweigh the burdens placed on my average and often unworthy shoulders.

Multiplied by a hundred. Maybe a thousand, I don't know.

Like all of my esteemed colleagues, I have studied, practiced, worried and lost it seems, years of sleep while learning this field and then applying that knowledge in the "trenches" while outwardly trying to display unwavering confidence to those who watch me. I know they need to see this confidence, whether real or not. Knowledge is good and science with all its discoveries gushes forward endlessly like a Niagara Falls of hope for the stricken. I desperately try to drink from those falls as often as possible, but succeed only in getting a cupful of water from the ladle that I place in front of her; she will stop her thunderous roar for no mere mortal. And so, I walk away from the roar quaffing from the ladle, feeling satisfied, then look back at the roar and feel like an utter failure. Again.

But knowledge, though essential, isn't everything in this field. You need something else too, that you know, "je ne sais quoi."

In fact, I believe my physician/surgeon colleagues are sometimes smarter than I am, and at times more skilled, at least in certain circumstance perhaps, and so I therefore respect their opinions and seek them. It helps the patient first off, and second, makes me look smarter than I am when I know when to call for help. But when I become too confident, or perhaps a little cocky, I realize that danger is about to strike me down to size immediately and burn me into a piece of meaningless charcoal.

One day I'm a hero at the bedside; the next day I can be a lowly worm, it seems.

So recently, I received a frantic call from an OB/GYN surgeon that her young patient had just suffered a cardiac arrest after giving birth, and was now in shock, bleeding to death and my help was needed. I dropped what I was doing and drove up to another hospital, perhaps fifteen minutes away. In the car on the way, I felt an anxiety about what was going to happen and what would be required while anxiously awaiting red stoplights to turn green.

So, I did the only thing I could do at that point in the car: I prayed. "God, please don't let this young mother die and help me to save her." And suddenly, I felt a warm wave of calmness while I pulled into the hospital parking lot.

I spent hours at her bedside, treating her and working with multiple highly skilled nurses, technicians, respiratory therapist and others. I felt clear headed and calm; confident that we were doing the best we could with the situation, and after about five hours of frantic resuscitation efforts, we were able to save her life. Notice I said "We" and not "I" because it was a team effort and I was simply a team leader. I was lucky to have such great people to work with.

The next day, I transferred the case to a highly skilled surgeon who later told me in front of others, "Carson, without you there, the patient would've died. So, I told her husband and mother that, in fact, I told them if they ever have another child, be it a boy or girl, they need to name the child Carson, after you."

"Thanks", I said. Or I think I said it while my face blushed, especially when thinking of a girl named Carson. "I don't know about that. I didn't do much but be there while all the nursing staff and others did great work."

Some days later, her husband raced around the hospital to find me and thank me, then he made me go back to the room to see his mother. She hugged me for about five glorious minutes, crying and thanking me for saving her daughter. You see, that is a reward that I didn't expect or go after, and yet, a reward that makes this profession completely incomparable. But I am convinced a physician must show humility, or he will fail.

And yes, I thanked God, once again, for answering my prayers

# LAST CALL FOR
# THE MILE RUN

It had been perhaps four years since I ran competitive track and cross-country in college, so my speed on the track was certainly suspect. It was my final year of medical school and when not studying or reading about patient cases in order to avoid being lambasted by my resident or attending, I would be either drinking beer or running long-distance. In fact, I tried to run a 20 miler at least once a week with several ten milers during the weekdays. I preferred running in the rain, downpours actually, because for some reason, the soaked singlet and shorts that clung to my shivering skin forced me to run longer and harder, almost like nothing could stop me. Nasty snowstorms were even better it seemed, and the redder my face was in the driving snow, and the more icicles dangling from my snotty nose the better I felt when I returned to my apartment, spent with a feeling of accomplishment and invincibility. But I didn't do much speed work on the track at all. That's why to this day, I can't fathom why I entered an invitational club race for the mile. I wanted to run the mile again, just to see what I could do with these younger college-aged speedsters. Not that I was that old mind you, but I really had no business entering the race. Clearly, I was at high risk of being embarrassed. But then, it was an indoor race, on a 220-yard track, with a large audience in the stands, and I remembered that for some reason I tended to over-achieve indoors, and in fact, was never defeated in my career indoors. I had my share of devastating defeats outdoors however. But then, who cares anymore.

I did my warm up stretches followed by about a mile jog on the track, and I soaked up the feeling of closeness the spectators provided while they occupied the front stretch stands near the starting line. No one knew who I was, yet each club team had its favorite runner entered in the mile and their fan clubs were loud as hell. Damn, you'd think it was a football game or something, not a stupid track meet with a bunch of skinny guys who could run. I was certainly impressed by the number of female spectators up in the stands, and I appreciated that they dressed appropriately with short shorts and halter-tops. Very unusual occurrence for a track meet, but I would learn in a few minutes why they were cheering for one guy.

After the first call for the mile, I could see who my competition was and I studied them. They all had flashy club uniforms on and waved to their friends in the crowd as they did their final half-sprints during warm-ups. I wore gray shorts and a plain white t-shirt, but the important thing was that I was wearing my sky blue Onitsuka Tiger indoor track shoes. No other piece of apparel mattered. After the second call, we all came to the starting line and the nervousness accelerated while we waited to line up at the starting line. Next to me was a guy waving to the crowd and the girls kept yelling at him: "Do it again Kenny, blow'em all away like you always do." Interesting. This guy must be quite the stud. Then, the public address announcer directed the crowd's attention to the scoreboard, and flashed the current track record for the mile run. He said, "Ladies and Gentleman, we have on our track the three-time defending champion in the mile and indoor record holder, Kenny Smith." He stepped off the starting line and stood in front of me, waved to the crowd and came back next to me. When the crowd quieted, we were seconds from the gun, and this Kenny guy looked at me, pointed to the scoreboard and said, "I'm going to break that record tonight." I had enough of the pompous pretty boy shit and said, "Go f..k yourself." Then the gun went off.

It was eight laps to the mile and Kenny jumped out quick and stayed several strides behind the leader at the first lap. I was about three runners behind him. The pace was blistering. After the second lap, the rabbit fell off the pace while Kenny took over the lead, much to the excitement of the crowd. But I stayed within striking distance, running third. After the initial "feeling out" of the pace wore off, I could feel my stride loosening up and my legs just wanted to accelerate and just grab the track and chew it up. I just felt it. I moved up to second after lap four and we were under record pace. Kenny's hands were starting to clench and I knew with only three and a half laps to go he was feeling the strain. But for some reason, I had become one with my Onitsuka's and they were just barely touching the track as I picked up the pace and purposely ran right on Kenny's shoulder, breathing down his neck. I knew this would intimidate him, but I was feeling so good, I was confident I could outkick him or for that matter, I thought I could outkick anyone if I timed it right. So, I blew by him with a burst of acceleration and within several seconds I had put ten yards between myself and the crowd favorite and with only two laps to go, the crowd was now on their feet screaming. I felt the power and the energy of the crowd and nothing mattered to me in life at that moment except destroying Kenny and the record. At the bell lap, I continued to accelerate and was in an all-out sprint for the last lap winning the invitational mile race in record time, apparently a half-lap in front of fading Kenny.

After I crossed the finish line, completely exhausted, hands on my knees and bent over heaving with precious breaths, the scoreboard flashed the new mile record, and the announcer broadcast the new record holder to the crowd and they cheered me, not Kenny.

I walked alone out of the stadium with my medal, and a deep satisfaction that is hard to describe, even to this day. I came back to my apartment, took a shower, and then opened my books to study with a smile of satisfaction. You see, I had no business running that race with those guys because they were much better trained than I was. But the lesson it taught me was that the mind can make up for less physical training when the will is there. Oh yeah, and Kenny probably did not get laid that last night by his disappointed cheerleader.

# A BRIEF SECOND THAT
# ALMOST CHANGED
# A LIFETIME

I probably should've found a ride that day to my first day at Cross-Country practice, admittedly, a demented sport, but really, I had no choice. Both parents were gone to work of course, and since we lived out in the country, I didn't have any friends available with parents to drive us. Truth is, I wouldn't have asked them anyway unless I was on my death bed. Turns out that bed could've been close at hand on that drippy ninety-degree summer afternoon.

So, I rode my bicycle to my first high school cross country practice. It was a ten-speed Schwinn and I thought I was pretty cool. At the age of fifteen, I felt invincible, full of energy and potential. I'm pretty sure I had no idea what a bicycle helmet was back then, probably because they were rare, and if I saw a person with one, I'm sure my friends and I would chuckle because they were funny looking.

It was about eight miles to the high school cross-country practice facility—essentially a long, rolling meadow in farm country behind the high school. I had my running shorts and a

T—shirt tied in a bag on my front handle bars. Never thought about bringing a water bottle, although back then, I'm not sure we had them in their present convenient form. After four miles of smooth sailing, I hit the busy overpass spanning over the four lane Interstate highway below, riding next to the guardrail. The cars swooshed by, probably going as fast as they could to get into town, never slowing down for a bike rider. Unfortunately, I didn't see the sewer drainage grate on the side of the highway, and my skinny tires caught inside the grooves, the bike stopped suddenly, and I did a double flip over the handlebars, landing on the pavement as the cars raced by and no one stopped. I don't remember what part of my body hit first, or how long I was laying there, or whether I briefly lost consciousness, but I did feel the blood running down my forehead and my leg was gashed. I must've gotten up pretty quickly, brushed myself off, embarrassed that I fell and got back on my still functioning bike with a crooked front fork to complete the remaining four miles in the heat. Clearly, I thought, I was damn lucky I didn't fly off to the left onto oncoming traffic and get run over on my first day of Cross-Country practice.

My life could've ended right there during that split second on the highway before cross-country practice. Thing is, at this young age, I had narrowly missed death several times before.

When I arrived, Coach said looked at my blood and gashes and said, "Carson, what the hell happened?"

"Fell off my bike." I know I didn't know what a subdural hematoma of the brain was back then, and who knows about my coach, but the day went on and obviously I suffered no neurologic symptoms that would keep me from practicing.

He put a band aid of some type on my forehead and a dressing on my right leg then said, "Time for practice boys! We do this at 1pm in the summer to show you guys that the heat is the best time to run and toughen you up." That was the second piece of 'wisdom' I learned that day, although due to my respect for elders, who was I to question the accuracy of his statement?

The senior runners initially ignored me because I was a rookie I guess, or maybe because my bandages produced a scary image. But that didn't apply to Charlie, the no.2 senior runner. With the practice only half complete, I stopped to get a water break and Charlie said, "Carson, be careful with the water. If you drink too much water it'll dilute your cells and make you weak like a noodle."

I briefly thought about that strange piece of advice from an accomplished runner, then immediately dismissed it and quaffed some more into my prickly cactus mouth. Survival instinct always takes precedence over shaky advice from an experienced runner.

Our team was believed to be good enough to go to state that year, but after a couple wins, Charlie was shot by his father at home, allegedly with a shotgun. He survived, but we never saw him again. Our team was stunned by that tragic news but due to Charlie's unfortunate situation, I had the sudden responsibility of being no. two man on the team as a sophomore, and the remaining upperclassmen I replaced, soon rallied to support me. Without Charlie, our hopes for state as a team vanished.

Looking back, it seems I learned a lot about life that first practice, summer training and the whole season. First, I learned that I once again escaped possible death and was given another opportunity to enjoy life. Second, I learned that tragedy may befall other talented individuals who were not as lucky as I was, and finally, I learned that no matter how inexperienced, if responsibility is placed on your shoulders, you must perform for the team.

I would return the next year as the no. one runner on the team. What else could possibly happen?

# IN THESE TIMES OF STRESS, HERE'S SOME HOPE AND INSPIRATION

Watch the Man Wearing the Golf Cap
His name is Dave Wottle. He was a U.S. 800-meter runner, who qualified to run in the 1972 Olympics. He was injured multiple times, including several weeks before the Olympics and did not feel his best at all. He was the slowest in the qualifying round as well. In fact, he was not even ranked with the top runners in the world. And he always wore a good luck golf cap to run.

Watch this old video clip/link. And if these difficult times get you down, I hope this provides you some inspiration not to give up, even if you feel you are dead last in your race of life.

This U tube video of Dave Wottle in the 1972 Olympic 800-meter finals is the highest quality, although it does not come with Marty Liquori's color commentary. Anyway, Wottle was not favored to medal at all, had not trained for 2 weeks before and was felt to be coming off an injury.

Watch him. He is in a white baseball cap: <u>Dave Wottle—The Greatest Comeback In Athletics History? | Throwback Thursday—YouTube</u>

# NEVER QUIT

Warning: This is longer than my usual blog. So, I advise starting with a cup of coffee, or better yet, a shot of scotch.

I gave up some years ago, not once but several times. Maybe there were more times, I don't know, but these are the four times that I remember, and now, they are stuck in my memory banks forever. I can't get rid of those memories, even though perhaps, they were not life changing or life and death issues. Well, I take that back. One decision on quitting was life changing and a positive thing.

But, these memories of quitting/giving up won't go away with time. All four of them haunt me, in different ways, with different intensities, not necessarily influencing my life in any significant psychological fashion, but they hide there never-theless in their iron-gated protected neuron clusters waiting to wake up and present themselves again, when I least expect it.

The first one was when I was quite young, maybe when I was seven or eight years old, I don't remember. I took piano private lessons from a guy in his dark, smelly home, and my parents would drive me there and since I was small, he had to put wooden planks on the piano seat so I was high enough to play the keys. I remember that I learned to play with both hands, and using the pedals etc., and when my parents had guests in the house, they paraded me and my sister out to play the piano for the guests, then after that, I had to go to bed. I guess I was a decent player for my age, no genius, that's for sure. Maybe I was lousy and no one wanted to tell me the truth. Either way, I thought Mr. B. my teacher, whose house had a strange smell, was creepy. Not only that, for some reason I was of the opinion that although my parents made me play my songs in front of their guests, playing the piano was for sissies. I am not sure how I got that impression, but yes, I was convinced it was not for macho boys like me. Playing drums or trumpet was the way to go to be manly in the musical field. So, I quit. Never to play the piano again, and as they years passed, I forgot everything I learned completely, and now, I regret that I quit. Little did I know at the time, but macho man Clint Eastwood was a piano player. Had I known that, who knows. Now it seems, I would love to have that skill back, years later, but all my piano knowledge is long gone.

The second instrument I learned to play was the trumpet. Maybe because my dad played it when he was young. Anyway, I played it during middle school and high school and was good enough to be first chair some times. I played in the marching band, concert bands and jazz/rock bands. Well by my junior year in high school, I was running on the cross country and track teams and was quite successful in these sports, winning quite a few races. It turns out, my senior year I lost interest in the trumpet, although my band teacher needed me to play, it seems. I wanted to concentrate more on training for track and cross country, and band just well, got in the way. So, I quit again. But, as I remember, I never had the courage to tell my band teacher/director. I just did not sign up for the class my senior year, and puff, I was gone and my chair was empty in the concert room. I just didn't have time to play trumpet and compete for first chair, play at sports games etc., and still be an athlete. As it happened, it became quite awkward one fall day, my senior year when my former band was playing music for us runners, on the football field, as I ran an exhibition race for the fans. I never had the courage to look the band director in the eyes after I won the race and my former band members played for my team. They even announced my name on the public address system of the football field, as the winner, and my former band colleagues probably said to each other, 'traitor'. Or maybe not. Maybe they were happy for my victory, who knows. I didn't care at that time. So yes, I regret not so much that I quit band to become an accomplished distance runner, but that I quit in such a selfish and perhaps disrespectful way.

Now comes the third event that I quit. I was the number one runner on my high school cross-country team in high school. Our team was exhausted from running in back-to-back competitions. My coach came to me and told me there was a large invitational race on a Saturday, two days after my previous race, and he said it was completely voluntary to go, and that he would not send the team for this invitational, but he wondered if I was interested to go. Maybe he wanted me to say yes to represent the team. So, I didn't think about it, and said yes. During the race, at about the mile mark of a 2.5-mile run, I started feeling poorly, not sure the details, but I lost strength and started dropping back in the pack and had lost my energy, and it appears, my motivation, especially after I vomited. So, instead of pushing through the discomfort and finishing in back of the pack, or perhaps last, I quit. The only race I ever quit. But I did. Later, when I came home it was embarrassing to try to explain that I quit to my friends and colleagues. You see, they wanted to know how I did, and whether I won, and I knew I disappointed people, but mostly myself. I do regret this, even to this day, even though I am sure the few people were involved have long forgotten.

I am sure you are wondering when I would finally mention my last episode of quitting. Here it is: I attended the United

States Air Force Academy. I did well and was awarded the dean's list, commandant's list and superintendent's list every semester for my academic and also military performance. I also ran varsity intercollegiate track and cross country. It turns out that despite my success, at two years, I needed to make a commitment to stay, or leave this well-respected institution. My eyes were not good enough to fly military aircraft at the time, and that was about the best job that could be had on graduation. So, since I felt I had an aptitude for science and medicine, and asked my superiors if I could apply to medical school on graduation, and I was told no, not for five years after graduation. So, I agonized about the decision I needed to make before the deadline, and knew it was probably the most important decision I could make in my life. I even had to receive counseling from the vice commandant of cadets, a colonel, who told me: "son, you may fail in the civilian world. Is this really what you want to do?"

You guessed it. Despite the colonel's attempt at persuading me not to, I quit the USAF Academy, at the top of my game. I felt like a dirty failure, although theoretically, I clearly was not. When I came home, I felt that my parents were disappointed in me, but they never said a word and my adjustment to civilian life was difficult. I felt I left everyone down, but, interestingly, I did not feel I let myself down. It turns out, I was unaware that the commandant of cadets, a brigadier general, was communicating with my parents back and forth with letters about my decision-making process and counseling, and I found this out from the general himself, years later, when he actually became my patient, years later!

Although I quit, this final time, I was able to accomplish my goal of becoming a physician, the career field that I chose, and it has been extremely rewarding to me and gratifying. So, although it was an agonizing decision to quit, I did quit the Academy and I think it was the best decision of my life. But that decision to quit, has haunted me to this day. More than the others, this one drags on me sometimes. People will ask me about my military service, or where I served, and after I tell them I resigned from the Academy, I see their disappointed faces, or at least I perceive this. Some do mention however, that I made the right decision, and this was a resignation, that although painful, needed to be made.

As years have passed, I have often experienced a recurrent dream that I am forced to go back to the Academy at the age of 40 or 50, or whatever, and finish my remaining classwork required as a junior or senior cadet! Finally, after many years, this recurrent dream has vanished form my bedtime.

I was 19 or 20, and that was the last time I quit.

Ok, well I did "quit" my marriage, after many years, but I hung on as long as I could, for the sake of the children I loved until finally, I realized my life would end prematurely if I did not leave the poisoned environment that she created. They use the word divorce for this kind of quitting. Counseling did not help. I delivered my two children myself, and my warm hands were the first to touch then as I brought them into this beautiful, but cruel world. I cared for their success, growth, development, education and spiritual growth as much as any father could. I taught them both to read, to excel in school, play sports and introduced the family to church. I prayed for their happiness.

Unfortunately, I lost them. I lost the children I love although they remain alive.

I lost them, because their pliable brains were successfully manipulated by an evil being who taught them how to hate somehow, the father who loved them. But I never lost hope that I would find them again and they would want to have a relationship with me, despite what they had been taught. I was down for many years, struggling with that loss that I could not fathom.

I never quit. I never lost hope that someday, I would see them again and spend some time talking about their lives. Or perhaps enjoy a cup of coffee, or a beer at least. Or maybe exchange birthday or Christmas cards. Now, the realism has sunk in that maybe it will never happen because it seems, they still own this indoctrinated hate against me so many years later, and despite the stress and sadness that brought me to near death in 2013, I do not quit. I always hope that love will win the day, but I understand now, the stark reality that it may not happen. I will never in my life understand hate.

However, I must go on. People need me. Patients need me

I was told that although I do have writing skills, I may not be successful publishing novels, and I have received large volumes of critiques of my work from experts, many times negative, but I guess, in general constructive. I get knocked down and rejected in the publishing world constantly, but I will not quit. No matter what, because I believe I have something to say, by using the written word. And I did publish my first novel in 2014, and am now editing a new manuscript for a thriller.

I continue to work in an intensive medical field. It is exhausting at times, especially in the ICU dealing with death and dying, but despite my fatigue, I will not quit, because I feel that I am contributing something valuable and I will do it as long as I am capable of helping others.

So yes, I have quit some things, many years ago, but I have learned that you must never quit. Never quit the important challenges in life, no matter how difficult or painful. If you do quit when you should not have, it will haunt you. Believe me, I know.

# SAVING THE
# EASTER BUNNY

I'll call the frantic thing a she, although I wasn't sure about the sex, but she did have a cotton tail and pointed ears. Turns out I left my pool cover open all night and surprisingly the next morning, without stopping to make coffee, something told me to go and do something else first. Here's a fact: if I avoid coffee in the morning, it would be as likely as a meteorite striking me while I'm climbing Mount Everest in my shorts and sandals without oxygen.

For some reason, I found myself beckoned to the back window, where I looked out at the aqua pool water and saw a skinny little animal paddling furiously around the edges of the pool, intermittently attempting to pull herself out onto the safety of dry land, but then failing, and slipping back into the water that most assuredly would take her life when she lost the energy to stay afloat. From above, I couldn't tell what kind of animal it was—a squirrel or a large rat perhaps, but it didn't matter because I ran outside in my bathrobe and slippers— that sounds better than boxer shorts and bare feet doesn't it?

I was going to save the poor thing, no matter what animal it was. Turns out it was a cute, but frantic bunny rabbit, her thick fur matted down to her skinny frame as if she was shorn like a baby sheep. She was fatiguing and I knew I had to get her out fast before she gave up and drowned. So, I got out my leaf skimmer, scooped her up and she calmly sat on the flat screen, didn't jump, but waited until I gently placed her on the concrete, then joyfully hopped through the slats in my fence.

If I had stopped to make some delicious coffee that morning, she would've drowned.

She never looked back at me, but I'm sure she was grateful to get back to her family, or mate, or you know, maybe she had to prepare for some special duties coming up in ten days. I hoped she would be back to visit me someday soon and maybe leave me some tasty Easter eggs before I go to church services on Easter Sunday. I hope she knows to bring me Cadbury Cream Eggs.

# D. Stories About Life

# WRITING
# INSPIRATION TIPS

I like to write. Always have. I don't have much time to write, and when I do, I try to finish editing and polishing my first novel, *To Love with Hate* which is best categorized as psychological suspense, although some experts feel it may own its own genre. As you know, however, I now have a blog so that I can contribute small vignettes to introduce myself to the reading market for the upcoming novel and to that end, my contributions may take the form of satire, humor (although that's debatable), observations of daily life, spiritual encounters and thoughts as well as brief excerpts from my novel.

As with many fields, mathematics can be used to make things simpler. About 20% of the time, I come up with an idea for the blog just participating in daily activities: driving to work or to the grocery store, scrubbing for surgery, talking with patients in my office, observing humans doing human things etc. However, it seems that the number two place that provides me inspiration for writing is at a bar. No, I'm not a drunk, but on those occasions when I do sit at a bar, it seems that I can't help but write. (See my blogs entries: *Bar Inspiration* and the *Beach ladies in the Land that Time forgot* as examples. Of course, when at a bar and the liquid refreshment continues unabated, there is a point of diminishing returns. Again, if you use mathematics, make a simple linear plot with the number of drinks on the x axis plotted against degree of good writing on the y axis you will find the following: On the ascending curve, usually after one drink, you will find maximum creativity and lucid writing up to about 75 to 80% of the plateau of the curve, usually arriving after two drinks. Once the plateau of the curve occurs, there is a down ward spiral in creativity, lucid writing, and legibility on napkins becomes indecipherable. That is the only problem with bar writing on napkins. You have to take advantage of the ascending curve before it's too late. If you start writing while you are on the descending curve, you might as well forget it and call a taxi. No one will want to read it anyway.

So, 20% of inspiration occurs with daily activities, 39 % occurs while writing on napkins at a bar, and guess what the number one location for writing is at 41%?

The answer, my loyal readers is church. Yes, while sitting in the pew at church I spew words out of my pen like there is no tomorrow. Usually it's on a church program, inspired by a word or a concept the pastor mentions, and I scribble the words up and down and cross ways on the program or visitor connection card in the pews. Then, I take the messy notes home and try to decipher what I wrote, converting it to readable English when possible.

Of course, you may be able to review some of my blogs and figure out which of the entries were written at each location. In fact, I challenge you to do that and let me know what you come up with. No hints. You're smart readers

# I DON'T BELONG HERE

"**H**ey Frank, lookie here. We've got some new meat!"
Herb sported a gray sponge of hair on both sides of his bald head, connected by two desperate strands of hair that he immediately smoothed with his forefinger.

What are you talking about Herb? Too early in the morning to think about that stuff."

"Look over at the door by the sign-in girls."

Frank looked in the direction of Herb's gaze and I could see them watch me intently at the vital signs station. Then they made their move. Frank's belly jiggled when he walked and his black knee socks actually did encircle his knees, cutting off what blood flow was left of his pencil thin legs.

"This dude looks a little young for this place but he's got some nice exercise pants," said Herb.

"Nike. I can see the swoosh on the side."

Then they stared.

The medical assistant took my vitals, gave me detailed instructions on the daily protocol that required strict attention, and then instructed me on how to properly attach the ECG electrodes and wires to the telemetry box.

"Each day you weigh yourself, put on your telemetry, making sure to sanitize it after you work out, then write down your weight on this chart by your number, which is, 4563. Remember that. Any questions?"

"Got it down so far dear. You doin ok today?"

"Yeah, thanks for asking. Actually, was hard to get out of bed this morning, but you know, patient care always comes first."

"I see." Interesting concept—wonder where I heard that knee-jerk mantra before.

Frank and Herb relished their opportunity and pounced, one on each side of me, escorting me away from the Medical Assistant.

"Always good to see fresh meat in our club," said Herb

Frank scolded him with a smirk. "You said that before Herb, maybe twenty times this month."

"Yeah, but not with him."

They reached out their hands and I shook hands with the obviously seasoned regulars.

"Ok, Bob, nice to meet you and welcome to our little fun house. By the way, your wires are hanging out of your shirt—better tuck your shirt in."

I liked the name I gave them. Basic and boring. I looked down at the floppy wires that were dangling midway down my shorts and I smiled. "You guys clearly don't have an eye for fashion."

"And a little more advice though. Always use the color-coded chart on the stick figure taped to the wall, that way, you'll never screw up your ECG leads. And trust me, if you screw up your leads, nurse Ratched—he pointed to the dark-haired nurse with a red stethoscope in the middle of the room where the telemetry monitors lived, will surely let all of us know about your royal screw up."

She looked up briefly and gave Herb a friendly scowl.

"Herb, your heart rate's up too high and you haven't even started exercising! You need to tone it down a few notches a little with the new guy," said nurse Ratched.

"Julie, you're no fun." Then he looked at me. "Bob, if you survive the first day, you're golden."

I told Mutt and Jeff, clearly the class clowns, to have a great day.

As they walked to their exercise stations, I said, "Don't hurt yourself ladies, and Herb, your hairs are out of place."

I met the class clowns. Always the most insecure and therefore the first to fall. I would have to watch them.

Julie, otherwise known as nurse Ratched now took over the remainder of my orientation to the kingdom she ruled with an all-knowing stethoscope: Cardiac Rehabilitation.

I didn't belong here. Never thought I would be in Cardiac Rehab, hell, I was low risk and strong as an ox. Or so I thought. A little unsettling to watch this motley crew of people, mostly older, but not all, do their warm-up exercises, in unison, watching each other to make sure they were in step and on the right count, kinda like wheezing robots, but the crackles of the arthritic joints made me want to take can of WD40 and inject it into their knees and hips. I desperately looked for a syringe. This must be a mistake, right? I'm not supposed to be here.

"We meet three times per week and you can pick a morning session or afternoon session to fit your schedule, especially if you work. You must complete all six weeks of the program and any absence must be excused by a doctor."

"I am a doctor, so that means I'm permanently excused right?"

"Funny Dr. Carson. That tactic won't work with me." She continued unfazed. "Every session you'll join the group for mandatory warm-ups, then weights. After that, you choose a cardio machine, either stationary bikes, recumbent bikes, elliptical or treadmills etc. while we watch your heart rate and rhythm for safety. The MA's will come by your exercise station and ask you to rate your exertion on a scale of 1 to 15, and also whether you are having any chest pain. Understand Dr. Carson?"

I was still stuck on the "excused absence." I wondered if I needed a hall pass to go the can, but decided not to ask her that. She was no nonsense and I kinda liked that in a draconian kind of way. But I was worried she would ask me to bend over for a shot in the butt cheeks to tranquilize me into Cardiac Rehab lock-step.

"Got it Julie."

"By the way, since you are a physician here in the community and active in the hospital, we need to give you some personal privacy, so what would you like us to call you, Dr. Carson?"

I thought to myself maybe Supreme Allied Commander would work ok. Instead, I told her to call me Bob.

"Ok, Bob it is."

"Now, education is important for our patients but I know it will be elementary for you, Bob, I mean Dr. Carson. We ask patients to take a pre-test on diet, cardiac anatomy and cholesterol, then ask you to read the materials in the library so you can take the posttest and learn from your mistakes. In your case I want you to take the pretest but we'll waive the post test."

That's a relief. I looked at my watch, office starting in 40 minutes. Is she going to let me start exercising or not? Reminds me of my running races when the race starter lectured us and discussed the cross-country course, disqualification rules, the weather and his grandkids before he gave us the commands to start. But one major difference is the race starter always smoked a cigar then puffed it at us nervous, skinny runners.

"So, Bob, take this little pre-test then go on the machines and get your 20-minute workout in."

"You mean I can skip the group warm up?"

"You missed it."

I scanned the first few questions:

1.  Is bacon a good food? T/F

2. If you smoke, your risks for heart disease fall to zero if you cut from one pack per day to half pack? T/F
3. Exercising ten minutes 4 times per month is recommended for cardiovascular fitness.

I started laughing so hard after reviewing the rest of the test; I couldn't complete it in good faith. So, I answered the first three: T, T and T then put the test down incomplete and started on the treadmill.

It had been three weeks since my MI, the one that nearly cost me my life, had it not been for the grace of God and the perfection of the medical staff surrounding me and I already had taken it upon myself to gradually increase my exercise capacity, mostly by hiking with a friend and lifting weights. I wanted to advance to swimming laps with interval sprints, but I thought better of it until I received the ok from my cardiologist—which of course, leads me to Rehab. I had a few post-stent symptoms that are apparently expected, but I remained hyper vigilant, and my confidence with more intense exercise needed a boost. Not only that, I needed to show Rached and her minions as well as Frank and Herb what my capabilities were, and that I was far from being washed up.

I entered the exercise floor and perhaps 20 rehab patients were already exercising on the equipment then suddenly, a therapist who worked with me at the hospital yelled across the gym loudly, "Hey Dr. Carson, what are you doing here? Making rounds?"

Heads turned and stared. So much for my "cloak of secrecy". It was blown before I even started. But I don't think Frank and Herb heard this over their huffing and puffing.

I smiled at her, walked over and said, "I'm here just to see what my patients go through when I send them here Cathy. That way I can commiserate with them."

"Oh I see, that's nice of you Dr. Carson."

I did a 12-minute walk test for Rached and reached the

maximum score on that, passing everyone on the little walk track, most of them were 15 to 20 years older but who cares?

"May I run?" I felt out of place, cramped in a cage, and wanted to let my stride stretch like days of old.

"No running Bob," said Julie

I did my 20 minutes on the treadmill and then the bike at a heart rate of 130 to 140 then packed up and left for a day at the office. My partners wouldn't let me do hospital procedures and on call duty yet. Well, actually it was my cardiologist, because my partners wanted me to be on call as soon as physically possible. Turns out I wasn't on call for a whole month after my MI, but I was back to work part time 2 weeks later, probably because I pushed my cardiologist so hard he just wanted me to shut up.

"Need to keep you on a short leash Carson", he said. "Most people who are lucky enough to survive what you did, if they do go back to work, it's after about 6 weeks."

The next few sessions, my confidence soared and I started to run on the treadmill, full stride, kinda like the old days on the track in high school and college and it felt damn good! I thought I was flying down the hill to the finish line, kicking past the world record holder who was sucking wind, then...

"Bob, your heart rate is 160! Slow down!" Nobody does that here!"

So? I thought. I felt good. "Ok, I just felt so—"

"I don't care," said Rached. "Slow it down."

Session no. 4 out of a prescribed 18 started with a warm up with the others and the silly exercises that didn't seem to fit me, and the five-pound weights going over head didn't do it for me, so I left the gang and went to a corner and did my runners stretches I learned in high school, followed by sit-ups on an inclined board.

Herb walked by. "Show-off."

"Your hair's out of place again Herb," I grunted

I finally attended an educational lecture, to make it look good

I guess, but more out of curiosity. I regretted that decision. It was given not by a nurse or a dietician but my medical assistant. It was a two-part lecture: smoking and salt in your diet.

She started by handing us out sample food labels to read about sodium content, cholesterol and saturated fat. It caused deep within me, the gurgling urge to pull out a bag of Lays potato chips from my pants pocket, but thankfully I didn't find any. I'm sure they would've kicked me out of class and nurse Rached's kingdom, with a dishonorable discharge

"And I want you to know that smoking is bad for you and also it smells bad."

I choked on my saliva. Really? I thought.

"There are things produced by the combustion of cigarettes called carcinogens and other toxins that can cause cancer and also accelerate heart disease and lung disease."

Interesting. Was this educational? What planet did they think we were on?

I had enough, so before I ran for the exits, I raised my hand. "So, I'll assume that an occasional stogie is ok, right?"

Her glare nearly ripped my lips off, and I walked away smiling. I was conquering this problem, in my own way and that's how I coped.

Session five came and I knew I could exercise harder, alone in the lap pool then here, but I dutifully came back because I'm sure Rached would tell my cardiologist what a bad patient I was. But my confidence was increasing each time. I asked the physiologist if I could leave the program early without having my right arm cut off.

"I'll call Dr. Leonard. He has to give permission."

After 10 minutes on the treadmill at about a 6.5-minute mile pace she came back. "He said if you do 15 mets for 30 minutes without arrhythmias, you have validated the course."

Ah ha! My chance to skip to the head of the class and then the exits. So, I did 15 mets for 30 minutes and left rehab after 5 sessions. What a great feeling!

I never said goodbye to Herb and Frank, or to Nurse Rached, because I wasn't there to socialize. I was there to accomplish my goals, increase my confidence with high intensity exercise, and I must say, mission accomplished.

Who knows if anyone in the Cardiac Rehab class understood who I was. It doesn't matter. Yeah, my knees hurt horribly for about a month after, because you see, my heart was in better shape than my knees and the freedom to fly airborne like days of old was a beautiful feeling.

But life is good, and I remain a thankful, and lucky man, bad knees or not.

Thanks to the Cardiac Rehab staff, for putting up with me.

# CRACKLIN' ROSIE

I suppose some of my readers may know who Neal Diamond is as well as some of his songs from the 70's and early 80's (he apparently began songwriting in the 60's after he was smart and dropped out of college pre-med), but my guess is that knowledge is becoming less and less common now.

Admittedly, I am aware of him, and I've heard his songs, respect his song writing ability and his success in life. Most certainly I am impressed that his third marriage is to some hot woman 30 years or more his junior. Way to go Neal! However, I would not pay the money to go see him in concert, especially now that he is 73 or so, but more importantly, I wouldn't have gone even when he was in his heyday. Out of the blue, a few years ago, my father invited me to fly to the old homestead, and then sit in a rented limousine with his sweet lady friend and another couple their age with lots of drinks to loosen up the atmosphere on the way to a Neal Diamond concert in Chicago. Turns out another couple turned down the tickets as well as my sister and her hubbie, and desperate not to waste the tickets, he called me.

Now I love fun as much as the next guy, and I appreciate his friends, but I knew I would need a prescription for Phenergan for the trip and well, the amount of alcohol I would require to be numb to the pain would likely put me six feet under.

So, loving the air I still breathe, I respectively declined.

I heard about the great concert multiple times thereafter, how he was the best ever and he is an amazing entertainer for his age. I bet his young wife says that too as she drives her Bentley around town shopping for jewelry.

All kidding aside, I am happy for my father and his friends, glad they had a great time, but at the same time, pleased that I didn't go. Figured I wouldn't hear about Neal Diamond again.

Unfortunately, my father suffered a stroke that summer, so I've been flying back to his home during his recovery, and I must say, his recovery, strength and stubbornness is impressive. But the last several times, I've been the designated driver, happily to do so of course, for his friends and lady friend to go out to eat and their favorite establishments. I learned the recurrent theme of how they were all going to rent a large Winnebago and travel around the country together, and which person of the group would have which job, you know, cook, sanitation engineer etc. Turns out I was unaware I was elected the Winnebago doctor for these nice old geezers.

Anyway, this last time I was the designated driver for five of these seven people to the Elks club for dinner and entertainment.

I love entertainment.

The place was packed and the average age was around 70, with many in their 80's and 90's I suppose; a smattering of younger people hoping the evening would end soon.

I enjoyed talking to my father's friends around the table, and I admire them and what they have accomplished in their lives, but I was losing my voice trying to yell at them across the table so they could hear me.

My anxiety heightened because my medical skills were attuned to things like, well, abnormal breathing patterns, difficulty with chewing, especially when talking with loose dentures, and unsteady walking after too many martinis, chest and throat clutching and the like. Especially after a stroke. I went over repeatedly in my mind who in that large room would need me to perform the Heimlich to dislodge the large piece of steak stuck in their larynx, or CPR if they started to dance.

Yes, dance.

I love to dance.

But it didn't happen for me that night.

The entertainment was an overweight man, maybe 70, I don't know, with a very nice black hairpiece that was lopsided on his baldpate and I think he forgot to button three of his shirt buttons, allowing some grey scraggly hairs to pop out strategically. His helper played music in a disk player at the side and he either sang or lip-synced the remainder of the night, depending on the tune.

Then it happened: He started to sing, Neal Diamond's Cracklin' Rosie and the crowd erupted in loud applause and food spit out across multiple adjoining tables, not ours of course, as people screamed with pleasure. Neal Diamond!

And then he 'sang' Forever in Blue Jeans, Kentucky Woman, and then, of course, I am I Said.

And with the song, I am I said, the crowd sang along:

LA's fine, the sun shines most the time.

And the feeling is lay back.

Palm trees grow and rents are low

But you know I keep thinkin about...

I got up from the table several times to stretch and catch some fresh air outside the kitchen by the grease dumper in the zero degree temperature. Felt so wonderful deep in my lungs, and the hacking cough felt so satisfying. I was alive! After reading every poster in the Elks club with regard to the last 10 years of Grand Masters and initiation fees, and the next fish fry bingo, I returned to our table, just in time to see our entertainer lose his hairpiece then gracefully catch in midair and plop it back on perfectly right before his 5th encore of yes, you guessed it: Sweet Caroline!

It was great to see the happy crowd, dancing deliriously to Mr. Neal, but I'm sorry, I just couldn't feel the rhythm enough to get out there. It didn't happen. Too busy looking for Heimlich and CPR potentials. So, I got back up and watched some TV and found myself wishing I was in one of those states like Washington or Colorado so I could go out and smoke a joint legally and maybe I could feel the Neal Diamond ecstasy like they did with no worries, man. Just kidding. I don't smoke the stuff. Just sayin.

But after five hours in the Elks club, it ended, after several more encores of Neal, and my party of friends were able to ambulate to the car safely, and I was pleased to drive them all safely home.

It was great to see they had such a nice time. Really, they're nice people and my father has wonderful friends.

But the after effect of this adventure, is that I hope I never hear a Neal Diamond song in my life. Never

# DICK TRACY, CHUCK ROAST AND GUNS

Bicycles dominated as our fastest modes of transportation, although we loved running fast and hard, through neighborhood back yards, across highways, around construction sites, on top of school roofs and nothing proved to be an obstacle.

I was faster than Jack, but he was my best friend and it seemed when we were on the loose the action accelerated onto trajectories that often put us in danger.

He wasn't very good at baseball because he was a slow runner, but in football, he was a great tackler, and that was why we called him the rock. Yeah, Dwayne Johnson stole the nickname from my friend Jack, but my guess is Dwayne wasn't even a twinkle in his parent's eyes when Jack and I were running around.

But who cares anyway? There's lots of rocks around but there was only one Jack. And one Carson.

We were both about ten years old or and we had few boundaries. Then it changed suddenly one day.

Some guy in a neighborhood some distance away had a kennel out in his yard, apparently prized dogs of some kind,

I never noticed this actually. I do remember they barked like wild hyenas when Jack and I ran through his yard as we were being chased by some other neighbor boys while playing ditch. We made the mistake of circling back and again running through this guy's yard, near the alley.

He was waiting for us when we saw him point his revolver at us, we both stopped immediately, quivering while watching his trigger finger.

"What the hell you boys doin in my yard? Stealin' my dawgs?"

"Well um, no sir, of course not." I spoke.

"No way." Jack added.

"You can bet someone's been stealin em' Lost one just the other day. You boys come with me into my house right now. He motioned to his back door with his revolver in his hand.

Of course, we obliged, and understood that the man with the gun had all the power. But hell, was he going to shoot us? We hadn't even finished grade school yet and I didn't even get up the courage yet to ask Joanne if I could walk her home from school and carry her books. yet. Maybe I would never get the chance now, I thought.

He closed the door behind us, and we stood side by side against the wall in his dank entryway. "What are you boys names? I'm goin to call your parents and tell them what trouble you're in. Speak up now!"

I looked at Jack and he looked back at me. We both knew what we needed to do at that time, almost with a young boy telepathy communication of some type, amazingly.

"Chuck Roast," said Jack

"Dick Tracy," I said.

" Oh yeah? You boys think I'd fall for them names? You got to be kidding me, right? Dick Tracy was a famous cartoon cop and well, I ain't never heard of no roast named Chuck."

"No sir." But that's about all I could figure out to say at the time. I was staring at his revolver.

We both knew that the greatest fear we had was not nec-essarily this moron's gun, but the fact that he would call our parents and that, of course, was more terrifying.

"Give me your phone number Dick."

I had to lie again. I hated that. I said, "We don't have a phone no more. Even if we did my pa said we can't be giving it out to no strangers." I was shocked that I was starting to in-troduce this guy's hillbilly dialect into my own highly refined fifth grade syntax. But then, I figured it might soften him up a bit to see we were just one of the boys.

"You little rats can just get your puny asses out of here right now." He put his gun down and let us run.

But of course, we ran several miles away to a meandering creek, far from our home so he couldn't come after us.

Anyway, all ended well with this true story. I never told my parents anything about it. In fact, this writing is the only documentation in the universe, of this event.

And Jack, my friends, became a war hero, wounded and disabled doing secret missions that this country won't discuss since they are highly classified.

I wish you the best Jack, you are one of my heroes.

# CORVETTES, DAD, DETERMINATION AND LOVE

At 140 miles an hour, the scenery swooshes by but time itself is meaningless; even seconds of powerful freedom transform into an eternity of powerful bliss. Thankfully his foot came off the accelerator early enough to allow the deer to run across the lonely highway without a splatter of bloody carnage. Hearts always jump immediately into the mouth when that happens, infusing that salty blood taste, and I imagine he felt that for a while then savored another victory from death.

So, he pulls into a place to eat that seems convenient near the Motel 6 or whatever motel he chooses on the run, and slowly tries to extricate himself from the powerful, low-profile machine, with the floor of the cockpit seemingly only a foot off the ground, and thankfully, his right arm is able to lift his left leg out of the car onto the concrete pavement first. Take a breath. Now push off the steering wheel hard, hang on to the door with your only arm that works, the right one, and hope for stability. To hell with the cane in the small trunk.

Too much hassle to find right now. Take a deep breath. Now, walk to the restaurant, watching for curbs and potholes trying not to drag that increasingly fatigued left leg. Above all, do not, under any circumstances, let anyone help you, unless of course, she's a hot blonde. Or if not blonde, any female for that matter.

Thankfully, this hotel has disability handrails in the bathrooms, so don't have to plan the attack with regard to bathroom necessities with as much thought about safety and potential injury. But most hotels don't have this. Take note. Got to find another one of these tomorrow when the journey continues.

But where to go? I told him I'm coming out west to visit, but I don't need to give an itinerary or time when I'm leaving for the journey. Hell, I can leave when I want and come when I want. I'm retired, independent, and I can show my kids that I can drive a 436-horsepower corvette with a 6-speed manual transmission, with only one functioning arm and one leg that works all the time and the other that works sometimes, but feebly without good coordination or balance. I think I'll go to the South Dakota Badlands. Was there years ago with my late Suzy. Lots of loving memories.

So, then the next day, he decides to go to Cheyenne Wyoming. Said there was a good Outback Steakhouse there. Got there early, maybe mid-afternoon. No one there until about two hours later then it was packed, but where did they come from? He probably flirted with the young cowgirl waitress and tipped her well. At least I hope he did because I'm sure she had to cut his steak up in pieces for him. Had to have a steak, I am sure. And beer. But who knows?

So, he finally arrives the next day to my home while I'm at work. Who knows how many wayward stops he made, but he probably drove about 1500 miles. Yes, my dad with the stroke two years ago that left his left arm paralyzed and left leg weak but his mind remains strong and full of memories and independent stubbornness. Ok, my sister and I thought he couldn't live alone in his multi-level house afterwards but he did—for about a year, then had another life-threatening mishap that forced us to put him in assisted living and take his car keys away and look out for his safety like middle aged nannies. We thought we were right.

But we underestimated him. At least I think I underestimated his strength, determination and sheer will to survive and live life with his new disability. But although he rightfully hangs a disability placard on his other car (not the Corvette of course, because chicks might see it), he instead considers the stroke with its' residual simply an impairment that he will accommodate to.

I learned quickly that I was not to help him get out of cars or into cars, or assist him when walking. He can do it and doesn't need help. But why did he let a blonde take his arm and walk him to the movie house with me? Suddenly he needs help? Smart guy. I would do the same thing.

We had a good and very short visit. Not much time together because of my hospital on call and work schedule, but that's the way it is. There were martinis poured the final night and he makes'em strong. He has a schedule and must stick to it. I respect that and am simply grateful that he took the time to visit me. No, I didn't want him to drive the Corvette that distance, but I was wrong. It's his life and he knew he was safe for himself and the general public. It was a herculean effort, I am sure, but he won't talk about it at all as being difficult, but I know. He certainly showed us.

I underestimated him in many ways but clearly his determination and strength, combined with his stubbornness and sharp mind is a force to be reckoned with. I no longer worry that much about him, because I know he will do what he wants with a reasonable modicum of safety, and then, he looks forward to lunch with the ladies and staff at the facility who missed him, telling them about his adventure, the deer he almost hit, the long miles in a fast corvette, the blonde (s) and the busy doctor son he visited.

We had lost communication for too long due to his anger and disappointment with me. I made the effort to patch things up and traveled to him, and eventually, he did the same to me, realizing that love between a father and son or daughter should never be broken no matter what disagreement or dis-appointment muddies the previously blue waters.

Here is what is now crystal clear: He is my hero, and I love him. Nothing else matters. You see, besides my father and sis-ter, I have no other flesh and blood relatives in my life any more. I am blessed to still have him and my sister who is filled with grace.

# FLY FISHING AS AN EXTREME SPORT

Although I nearly drowned at least twice in my childhood, I'm happy to say that I no longer fear water and I have taught myself how to become a pretty decent swimmer. Now, I must admit that I am not including that potential third time when I was a Boy Scout—that wannabe Navy Seal Instructor/ lifesaving Nazi took my head in both hands and tried to drown me. Even at 90 pounds, a strong kick aimed at the stomach of a hairy 200 pounder that lands too low can be quite effective in disabling a lifesaving instructor bent on fighting you to the death. I got my lifesaving merit badge.

So, when my friend, an experienced hunter and fly fisherman, volunteered to take me fly fishing many years later, I jumped at the chance to learn the gentleman's sport, and yes, it was done in the water that I no longer feared. He told me to buy a cheap rod, water waders and boots, then practice casting, long and gentle, without making a sound on the water—just float the little nymph so he barely caresses the water, as if he was sneaking up on that wily old trout. I learned my knots, kinda, and a few of the stupid flies, but I was too excited to spend precious time studying flies because after all, he and his crew were experts and they would guarantee me some nice browns or rainbows!

So, the 4 of us—Bob and his 14-year-old son, also an expert, and another gentleman with experience who I will call Jim and a smelly dog in the back of the car headed off to the mountain river. When we arrived, I noticed it was flowing quite swiftly but then, must be what these guys do all the time. I could barely hold my excitement as I put on my waders, tied them up to my chest, put my vest on with all those stupid flies, net hanging down and oh yes, a nice frumpy fishing hat with flies in it too. I knew the fish had no chance with me going after them.

But I noticed Bob out in the middle of this roaring river, and so was Jim up ahead and Bob's son also. They were casting very nicely but I must admit I was a little timid about going up nearly to my chest in such swift waters. But they were experts and of course, I was a silly rookie. Gingerly, I went about 6 feet out from the shore, water up to my knees, and I was quite satisfied, casting and enjoying the whole situation, and of course, catching no fish.

Then suddenly, I hear a yell and Bob is suddenly on the shore, laying down on his back. He was shaking. Apparently, he took a spill in the river, floated downstream and lost his $1000 fly fishing rod. He told me he was going to rest for a while and get his old rod. This turn of events made me think that if this rugged outdoorsman was a near casualty, would there be more? I remained where I was, hoping to get a bite from a stupid trout who doesn't care if I used the wrong fly or presented it incorrectly to him.

Then, I hear a scream and Bob's 14-year-old son was down in the water, floating down stream, out of control, head dipping in and out. So, I instinctively dove in and swam as hard as I could and put my body in front of this kid before he smashed into a stalwart boulder in the middle of the stream, catching him, and dragged him to shore. His dad thanked me and amazingly, I had hardly any water inside my waders from this swimming adventure. After the adrenaline surge subsided, I kept fishing while the father and son pondered the thrills of fly fishing on the shore.

After a while, all of us went up stream where I was told the trout were crazy hungry and would bite on anything, even your boots. So, the four of us went upstream, hugging near the walls of the canyon and again, it seemed a little deep at the waist, the power of the river forcing us to carefully find footing on the slippery rocks. By this time, I had lost all interest in fishing and I was in full life saving mode. Then, Jim—about 250 pounds and five feet seven, lost his footing and went down, losing his rod, grabbing on to the branches on the canyon face for support, then he fell back in the river, and guess who was there to catch him?

Yeah, the rookie.

Of course, I dragged him to shore too. That was the end of the day for us. The other guys each caught a couple trout and all I caught were wet human bodies. Amazingly, I never lost my cheap rod, although I am not sure it was effective for anything that day.

It was quite an experience, and yes for me, my first fly fishing expedition turned into an extreme survival sport and thankfully my swimming skills finally paid off and we all survived with the hands of God.

Thank you, God

# GET YOUR PROGRAM
# TOGETHER

It was Brevard, North Carolina, sometime in the 70's. I won't tell you exactly what part of that decade otherwise you'll peg my tender age. I saved up enough money doing paper routes and mowing lawns to become an attendee of the Blue Ridge Trails running camp, designed for High School distance runners who hoped to improve their performance and learn from some of the greats in the field at the time. Young runners from across the country flocked to this camp with dreams of becoming elite runners. My first time in an airliner, that enough was a thrill for me as a sophomore in high school. Having just finished the season as the number two runner on my high school cross-country team, and with the graduation of number one, it was my time to show my coach and school, what potential I thought I had.

As a point of reference, Frank Shorter had just won the 72 Olympic marathon and America was boiling in a resurgent running craze, also ignited by the late Steve Prefontaine. Of course, that craze grabbed me, and I ran early in the morning, late at night, up sand dunes, down miles of beaches and as long as I could. In fact, sometimes I had no idea where I was going, but would just take off and run down the country roads for miles, sometimes entering another town, then turning around, and heading back. Never took water. It slowed me down. I learned how to avoid menacing dogs by carrying a stick when necessary, and raising my voice to scare them when they threatened to attack me and that usually worked.

It seemed when I was in my running zone, I had an aura of invincibility and the dogs sensed it and I was never touched by foamy saliva coated canine teeth. I read books from famous coaches of the day: Percy Cerutti, Bill Bowerman, and Arthur Lydiard and absorbed every training technique possible into my young and naive brain. By the time I arrived at the camp, I had already familiarized myself with most of the great distance running names over the years as well: Paavo Nurmi, Emil Zatopek, Herb Elliott, Roger Bannister, Jim Ryun, Ron Clarke, Steve Prefontaine, and of course Frank Shorter who became America's only Olympic Marathon champ, and thus took over as the king of American distance running.

There were famous runners invited to this camp to motivate us, I guess. Too many years have erased some of their names because I didn't have much contact with some of them. I remember only two: Dick Buerkle and Jeff Galloway. Let's talk about Buerkle first. He was a 1976 Olympian, his personal best in the mile was 3:54.9, and that was an American indoor record in 1978. I learned during the first day of introductions that Jeff Galloway was also there. He ran the 10,000 meters during the 1972 Olympics and trained with Frank Shorter and legend has it that after qualifying for the U.S team in the 10k, he slowed down to help his teammate qualify for the marathon, thus giving up his spot. He also broke the U.S 10-mile record in 1973. After learning that, I couldn't believe how lucky I was that he was assigned to our cabin as cabin counselor!

I don't remember the names of my cabin mates so many years hence, but one of them we named Moon Goon and he introduced all of us, including Galloway, to championship quality teeth grinding all night. Moon Goon may have become a famous movie star in the Home Alone series, because he sure looked like one of those guys. We went off on our training runs in the beautiful Blue Ridge Mountains, ate in the dining halls, took turns cleaning up and had our share of shenanigans and practical jokes. And yes, mosquitoes and homesickness took their toll on me, and I wrote home as much as I could during that two-week period.

As far as Galloway, I thought he was super cool. An Olympian in our cabin, eating with us and talking with us as if we were one of his colleagues. He taught me some about nutrition and vitamins, but the phrase that he used most often with us was "Get your program together!" Usually this referred to our behavior, but also attitude and intensity about our running goals, but hell, that all sounds great, but it was a phrase that soon glued to me forever, and I'm not sure to this day, why that is.

Near the end of the camp, we had a five mile and ten-mile race for all the campers with a trophy and introduction at a ceremony at the end. I knew I had no chance to win either race with all the high-quality runners there but I entered the ten-mile race. What the hell, none of my friends were there, no one knew me accept of course, Galloway, my cabin counselor and hero. I started out in the middle of the pack, and the course I remember, involved rolling backcountry hills, winding through the town, then back out into the hill country again at the half way point, where I found myself about 10th. I do remember a runner who stayed with me through the first 5 miles and we went stride for stride, sometimes he would go ahead of me, then I would reel him back in, and take the lead away from him and it seemed we were in our own little race, 9th and 10th. We never said a word. during the race. We both wanted it badly and we both sensed we were in for a fight because we were evenly matched and both of us gradually caught the leaders at about mile six. I guarded my heavy breathing and tried to show him how relaxed I was during the fast pace, hoping to catch any psychological advantage possible.

He was number one now, in front of probably several hundred runners, with me only a yard or two behind and we had about three and a half miles to go. Much to my chagrin, he continued to pick up the pace like a machine, and I struggled to keep up, but I wouldn't allow myself to fall out of striking distance, despite the burning in my chest. But I'll never forget the onset of the heavy rain, at about mile eight, and that's when I knew I had him.

I knew I had him completely then. Whenever it rained, or snowed, my body went into turbo gear for some reason because I just loved it—the sweat and rain-soaked shorts and shirt stuck to the skin and mud from the road splattered on my face. I felt an overwhelming surge from within and despite the wisdom of staying behind him and waiting till the last 800 yards to try to out kick him for the win, I disregarded wisdom and just broke away from him, went into turbo mode while I was overcome by the exhilarating feeling of leading a race of my peers who traveled from all over the country to run. Initially I could hear his breathing behind me for a while and the patter of his feet on the ground, but I rejoiced when I no longer heard either again. I couldn't believe that my legs just continued to accelerate despite my fatigue, and I surprised myself by winning the Blue Ridge Trails 10 miler by about 800 yards in the pouring rain. I'm sure there were better runners in the field, but that day, I was the best that day for some reason, maybe due the rain and mud. Basically, I learned that on any given day, with God given talent, you can be better than you think you are, depending on your attitude. And yes, at the start of the school year, I took over the number one spot, not to relinquish it.

I cherished that trophy more than most over the years. And I especially cherished the handshake by Jeff Galloway who congratulated me and said, "Looks like you got your program together, Carson. For the remaining day or two, I felt like royalty in the cabin, having won new found respect by my fellow campers, and especially Galloway. He decided to auction off some of his Olympic gear and yes, I out bid everyone else and bought his smelly Adidas SL72 running shoes for a couple bucks and an Onitsuka tiger athletic bag that I used with pride for many years after. The shoes didn't fit me, but I still thought it was cool to own them because Galloway wore them.

I haven't talked to Galloway since I left camp, but I have heard that he's been a successful running coach with clinics throughout the country and has operated many athletic shoes stores and has been a race consultant for multiple major organizations. This is a memory exercise, yes, but it's funny how certain experiences and phrases stick in your mind forever. I never achieved anywhere near the running success that Galloway did. He was a world class runner and I didn't come close to that success. But I learned some things during that camp which helped me along the way achieving my own successes, saving a few lives along the way. But I'll never forget the phrase he taught us: Get your program together!

Even my late mother caught on to the phrase I mentioned after I returned home from the camp and would tell it to me when I veered off course in life. So, Jeff, if you read this, I hope you are well, and I think we both got our programs together.

# BAD ASSES AND
# GENTLEMAN

I suppose you can be a bad ass, a pompous ass, or a gentle-man, but can you really be all three? Or maybe if anyone calls you an ass, especially preceded by an adjective, you can-not also be a gentleman or especially not a *real* gentleman.

Some of the other commonly used adjectives that are used in front of the word ass also include stupid, dumb, smart, lazy, fat, ugly and perhaps a few more I can't think of right now. Seems this word ass attracts adjectives like it does comfort-able chairs, and yet, used alone, the word ass also seems quite effective.

As far as I know, it seems I haven't been called an ass very often in my life, and before the last few months, I can't re-member when the last time that word was used to describe me. But the last three months or so, I have been called an ass with an adjective in front several times, and that is a new re-cord for me.

A few months ago, I rushed to the hospital to take care of a dying man in shock and I worked very fast to do multiple pro-cedures in a very short time, quickly saving him, when other staff members in stress thought it would be close to impossible, but I did it, with God's help and the help of the nursing and respiratory staff. In fact, the grateful staff included a respiratory therapist who I will call Ralph, who at the completion of the life-saving event, told me directly, *Dr. Carson, you are a Bad Ass!"*

In this case, their smiles told me that *Bad Ass* was meant as a compliment, and I left smiling and satisfied with a job well done with the team.

A month later, an unfortunate woman was dying slowly and despite our best efforts, it didn't look like she would survive her struggle with multi-organ failure from the Chinese Virus infection. So, as we often do, we talk to families about their loved ones, and often, we talk to them about what their loved one's wishes were for end-of-life heroics, you know, CPR. So, I thought it was appropriate to ask this question of her daughter, and as soon as I asked her what her mother's wishes were in this situation, she scolded me loudly, in front of everyone, *Dr. you are a Pompous Ass!*

So, I guess that conversation ended abruptly and I walked away, but later learned she said something similar to one of my colleagues who may have asked her a similar question the week before. Turns out this woman made her mother a DNR 24 hours later, even though her doctor was a pompous ass for even asking the question.

And most recently, I thought one of my partners needed a rest and perhaps a day off, even though I was told later that I was working the same number of days and nights in the ICU as he was, so, I told him not to come in one day of the weekend and I would take care of rounding, and he appreciated it. Another of my partners called me to ask who was "on" and he was surprised to see that it was me, thinking I was off. So, he proceeded to call me a *Real Gentleman.*

So, there you go. In a few short months, I have been called a *Bad Ass, a Pompous Ass and a Real Gentleman.* It seems all those names don't usually fit together do they? I wonder, why do people care about my ass so much now, rather than before, and why do they call my ass names if I am such a real gentleman? And the other thing I wonder is are there any good asses? Does anyone remember being called a good ass?

Seems I don't just fit one label. I am who I am, and depending on the situation I find myself in I guess, I present in different ways to different people. But you know, it doesn't matter to me anymore what people call me, or think of me, I just do what I think is best, I help people who need help, no matter what the consequence is to me because I know the Lord almighty has saved me and given me another chance in life almost eight years ago, and he is the one that I strive to please and love above all, using the gifts and blessings he has graciously bestowed upon me.

# HIT OR GET HIT

I loved baseball when I was a kid; after all, it was America's sport, at least when I was small. Ok, I was and still am a Cub's fan, but I won't tell you my favorite players when I was a kid for obvious security reasons.

So, of course, I went out and joined a little league baseball team, fast pitch, well, sometimes fast, usually wild hardball— or at least they were solid, hard rubber coated balls that hurt when they hit you. Luckily, I joined "Optimist Club", the number one ranked little league team in the city, and defending city champions.

But I didn't know that. And if I did, it wouldn't matter.

We had Charlie Cochran. Baseball pitcher extraordinaire and he actually could throw fastballs and curves over the strike zone. At age 9 to 11. Don't think he ever hit a kid at bat, at least not on purpose, and I guess I need to mention he and our cleanup hitter Tim Cavanaugh, hit towering home runs nearly every time they were at bat. Unbeatable.

So, I was randomly allocated to the team, and I was short, skinny, but a very fast runner. Did I mention I couldn't hit?

Yeah, I couldn't hit.

I tried but nearly always struck out swinging because I just couldn't get the timing right or something. Our coach of course was the winningest little league coach in the world, and figured winning was all that mattered, no matter what the cost. We loved him for that.

Ah, the good old days. Back then, we had winners and losers. And if you were a loser, you went home sad and ate dirt. If you were a winner, you got a trophy. No one else got a trophy. Just the winner, and that's why it was fun to compete hard. We wanted the damn City trophy!

Anyway, back to story. The coach realized he didn't have enough time to work on my hitting, but he realized I had one talent besides catching balls in the outfield:

I could flat out run like the wind.

And he realized that running fast meant stealing bases, so that became my job. However, since I couldn't hit, that means he had to figure out a way to get me on base every time I was up so that I could steal all the bases and either score, or have Charlie or Tim hit me home with their mammoth home runs.

Yeah, I ate bases for dinner. Get me on first and I always stole second, and usually didn't stop there, and continued on home because the opposing players usually only had one or two players with good enough arms to throw me out. The rest of them panicked when I started wheeling it around the bases and threw the ball everywhere but where it needed to go.

Cool.

One problem. Again, I had to get on base.

"Carson! You couldn't hit a barn if it was standing right in front of you."

I looked down, kicked some dirt, and spat. "Yeah, reckon so coach."

"What you suggest we do about that Carson, huh? We ain't got time for hittin lessons cause Charlie and Tim can do all that. Tell you what. I suggest you become the walk king of the Optimist Club. That way, you get on base and we got ourselves pretty much a score most of the time."

"Yeah, Ok coach. Whaddya mean?"

"Well, you're our youngest player and you're a little squirt, so it's hard for those opposing pitchers to throw to you. They can barely see you! That's perfect. So, take all the pitches and get walked. Stand right as close to the base as you can too. Scares 'em. When it looks like you got a 3 and 2 or a 2 and 2 count and the pitch looks good, step as close to the plate as you can and put your body in front of it and let it hit you for an automatic walk!"

"Uh, you mean, purposely let that ball hit me?"

"Yeah, do it for the team Carson. It'll only sting for a little while and duck so it won't hit your head. Just let it hit your side or your arm or leg or something. Just protect that noggin of yours. Hear you're a good student or something."

I really wanted to play, and understood I now had an important role on the team, and well, if I said no, I would be riding the splinter-infested bench more than usual. I was the only rookie and the other bench warmers preferred the comfort of the bench.

"Ok coach."

"Atta boy Carson! Go get'em"

Figured I would give it a try, but some of those pitchers could throw some heat. So, I was relieved when I was walked frequently with four balls because the pitchers could barely see me and couldn't find my strike zone, therefore, everything was a ball. Didn't need to be hit at all to get on base.

So, I stole many bases and always slid home. Even if I didn't need to because the dirt on my uniform made me feel important.

Until I met Killer Kelly. He could pitch, almost as good as Charley and he knew how to hit the strike zone. I looked at coach and he smiled from the bench, and I knew what I had to do. So, he got ahead of me on strikes and I let him hit me. Right on the left thigh. Yeah, it hurt, but I could still run. He tried to throw me out at second with a perfect throw, but I had a step on him, and the second basement couldn't handle the heat. Ran all the way home, and I was the hero.

We played Killer Kelly and his team, Dwyer Instruments several times that season including the championship and each time, I knew I would have to take one for the Optimist Club. But I learned how to fake getting out of the way, turning, so that I put my butt in harm's way, and it didn't hurt as bad as bone against ball.

Got on base every time and yes, Optimist Club once again, won the city Championship, and I won the bruise championship.

I learned three lessons my rookie season, age nine on Optimist Club. One: I understood what it meant to be a team player and to "take one for the team." Literally. Two: I would practice day and night to learn how to hit next year if it killed me because I wouldn't be the bruise king anymore. Three: I would grow taller.

Then I spat and learned how to hit and man that felt good.

# SEAL TEAM 72: MIDDLE SCHOOL SPECIAL OPS

## Wimachindink, Wingolasek, Witahemaway

I must now confess that I enlisted at age 11 in a quasi-military, super patriotic Christian organization, based on Indian folklore, replete with survival training in the woods, lifesaving techniques, endless marching, lots of flag saluting, public prayer, hazing, firearms training and psychological endurance tests. Some didn't make it up the ranks very far before quitting, but I was proud to say we suffered no serious casualties except for one member who buried a hatchet in his calf muscle when chopping firewood. It was bloody when I saw it happen, but Steve's only words were: "Uh oh!" Clearly, he wasn't following axe safety rules that day, so he had to endure our frantic first aid attempts before we got him to the hospital. After 4 long years, I advanced to the highest echelons of the organization, then retired at the wizened age of 14.

I was an Eagle Scout and Brotherhood member of the Order of the Arrow, Boy Scouts of America. Potawatomi Council, Troop 72.

Damn proud of it.

But it wasn't obvious I was going to make it during my first campout. Well actually it was camping competition for the whole group of Boy Scout teams in from neighboring towns in the area. We competed at building towers with logs and rope, orienteering with map and compass, archery accuracy, obstacle courses and a few other things I don't remember due to the brain cobwebs accumulated over the years. My first campout, I was armed with a 60-year-old back pack that traveled down below my butt, weighted down with more gear than my body weight, and an equally old and smelly sleeping back also handed down from my grandfather.

But I didn't know any better, and the other recruits had nice new equipment with ergonomic frames, but mine had that hardened rustic look to it. And it became even more rustic and rank when we climbed a sand dune and the weight of the monster backpack flung me backwards, tumbling all the way down the dune and I couldn't get up. I was like a box turtle that flipped over, legs flailing in the wind while the older guys laughed.

Thankfully, I quickly learned the ways of the Indian: *travel light, always carry toilet paper, and spray your musty old sleeping bag with cologne.*

Now years later, I realize that once I advanced into the higher ranks, accomplishing more and more difficult tasks while becoming a seasoned camper, it truly was preparation for a potential career in the military or interestingly...

SPECIAL OPS!

Why? Well, here are a few examples to chew on:

1. Marching: We were good at marching and became experts at marching in parades, around school assemblies and church auditoriums.
2. Rifle Range: We shot 22 rifles on the range deep in the bowels of the dark woods.
3. Silent Swim: This was preparation to be a Navy Seal. I have no other explanation of why this activity was allowed. I'm not sure if it was voluntary or required for

some merit badge, but it essentially was a swimming obstacle course in the inky black of the night in frigid cold mucky lake water. Of course, the prerequisite was you had to know how to swim. Guards walked along the maze of docks while we spread lake muck all over our faces then slithered into the water, controlling our breathing while swimming under water, so as not to make a sound to alert the guards. I remember this night fairly well, and I was exhilarated to have passed the course the first time without having to take it over.

4. Survival training: Learning to live off the land
5. Mile Swim BSA: once you became a good enough swimmer, you qualified to swim a mile around the perimeter of the lake around buoys while lifeguards paddled their boats around in case anyone started drowning. We were taught how to swim for endurance while avoiding the hundreds of hungry snapping turtles. Life vests were not allowed, of course.
6. ORDER OF THE ARROW: This was kind of like National Honor Society for the Boy Scouts, and was designed to honor scouts who best exemplified the scout law. At a campfire ceremony, Order of the Arrow guys would come behind you and "Tap you out" and thus select you. Is this where the popular "Tap Out" phrase came from years ago? Anyway, I think I almost peed my pants when they tapped me out at that roaring campfire years ago. Once you were qualified, then elected by your peers to enter this secret society, you had to pass some rigid tests to be allowed in. This was called the ORDEAL. Truth is, if I had known what was in store for me when I entered, I probably would've walked away at the tender age of 13.

Some say the ORDER OF THE ARROW was a secret society for the best campers and there were secret passwords and secret phrases etc. I don't remember being told that at all. I don't think I was given any secrete passwords, but it was a society based on respect of American Indian traditions and ceremonies. The only words I remember, vividly, now many years later are:

*Wimachindink, Wingolasek, Witahemaway! They must mean something, right? Why do I remember these words?*

Ok, I said them. Maybe the ghosts of the Order of the Arrow will change me to a pillar of salt for saying these words that no one understands. But I had to let them fly out into the world, spelled as they sounded to me years ago, to enjoy and wonder about, now many years later. To those Order of the Arrow scholars, if there are such beings, who are offended, don't be small, instead—teach us their meaning and enlighten us old scouts.

During the ORDEAL, we entered the woods and were immediately led around at night by a bunch of older guys in Indian headdresses by a rope, and we were not to speak a word to anyone for 24 hours. If we did, we would flunk the course. We had to build fires alone in the dark despite the wet ground while these guys watched and hazed us—waiting to see if we would succeed with limited material while under pressure. Then, we were separated and marched away individually, with an "Indian" who led us out into the woods, alone to sleep under the stars without a soul near us to talk to. I remember laying there in my still smelly sleeping bag on the damp ground, completely alone, not knowing where I was, just staring at the stars, getting out of the bag only to relieve myself. Oh yeah, and hordes of zinging mosquitos. Then, it started to rain so I built a makeshift shelter. The next day, an "Indian" again, without a word, found me and escorted me back to the meeting place.

Under the hot sun the next day, we had to remain silent while we did a full day of hard labor, kind of like slave labor as I remember it, painting buildings or doing some type of construction work with very little to eat, perhaps one hard-boiled egg and a piece of bread and some water. If you spoke or complained, you were done. It was tough, we were tired, smelly, hungry and frustrated at not being able to communicate, but, here's the key: After all this, another challenge had been defeated and we walked away as winners again! We were now proud members of the Arrowmen, Order of the Arrow. Later, maybe six months later, I was then advanced to the Brotherhood rank.

I am convinced that Boy Scouts, attaining the Eagle Rank, and Brotherhood in the Order of the Arrow was the best thing that I could've done at the age, and it prepared me immensely for the struggles and challenges of life ahead.

And, like every other ending of a camping trip on Boy Scouts, we prayed together and pledged allegiance to the flag. There were always flags waving and we were proud of ourselves, our brotherhood, and what we had accomplished in those few short years.

I have no idea what the Boy Scouts are like now. I hope it's still a great organization. But I don't even know if Scouts are still allowed to pray in public at these events or sing patriotic songs but I tell you what, this country needs this type of experience for its youth. Sure, times change and some of the activities that were offered to us then wouldn't be politically correct, and in fact, may be considered unsafe for coddled youth.

But the truth is this: I see the culture of America eroding, the love of God and country is no longer honored like it was and hard work and sacrifice have given way to expectations of entitlements, handouts and shiny trophies for all who simply breathe or show up when it's convenient. No, the Boy Scouts may not be the answer to the weakening of our culture and values, but at least for me, it set me on the right course at a young age. Sometimes, we must sleep in smelly sleeping bags and not whine, before we can advance up to the majestic heights of the mountain top.

God Bless America! We must save her and protect her.

# FERRARI IN THE GARAGE

*"It was like having a brand-new Ferrari in the garage, and nobody wants to race it because you might dent the fender." Pete Schoomaker*

Sam needed a beer; it had been way too long and that facility refused his requests. He found the first bar that he could find on foot, and after counting the Harleys lined up outside the bar, noting their proximity to the entrance, and the location of the back exit, he entered the same kind of biker bar he'd been in plenty of times before. He scanned the bikers in the room, on both sides of the bar, the exits, the location of the bartender, and chose to sit in the middle of the bar section closest to the entrance, satisfied with two grisly bikers to his left who were bantering with a couple of babes on the other side of the bar. But he noticed something different this time. And he didn't like what he saw, but his thirst overcame his disgust.

"I'll have a Guinness, your largest one."

The two bikers to his left stared at him and laughed, then flexed their sizable biceps and played with their dagger tattoos that jiggled with the muscle action. The bimbos giggled with excitement, feeling something was happening while playing with their chains hanging over their gaudy breasts.

The biker closest to Sam watched him intently, and couldn't help himself watch the stranger gulp the darkness of the cold Guinness. "Y'all must've rolled into this here establishment by mistake. The pussy bar is down the block. I can give you directions if you'd like."

Sam stared straight ahead, seemingly oblivious. He looked at no one, but saw everything. He deliberately slowed his breath down, and mentally reduced his heart rate, as he was trained. He knew they were big and dumb, hairier than a human should be. He drank his beer down halfway, then stopped, even though the taste brought the pleasant memories back.

The biker mammoth closest to him came over and pulled a chair up. Sam continued to look straight ahead, oblivious, watching the stupid NASCAR race on the TV above the whiskey bottles. Then he realized his mistake: he left the hospital wrist ban on when he escaped, picked the locks and escaped with stolen scrubs from an orderly he locked in a closet. He bought some jeans and a shirt and Nikes at the closest store, throwing the scrubs in a dumpster out back.

"What the hell's the matter with you, little puke? You don't know English? You know it's rude not to talk when spoken to by a superior."

"Yep" Sam said. That would be the case if there actually were some superiors here." He was still thinking about that thing that bothered him when he walked in. And it wasn't the smell of the bikers.

The biker glanced at Sam's hospital ID wrist band and smiled. "So, you're a loon who's escaped! Looks like we're going to have some people looking for you. This is gonna be fun, right son?"

Using his peripheral vision, he predicted the exact timing of the fist from the hairy mammoth's right punch attempt, spun around and caught his wrist in midair, twisted it to the breaking point while simultaneously knocking his bar stool from underneath him, leaving him squealing on the floor.

"Let go ass hole!"

Sam twisted until he knew the bones would break, then stopped, watching the other patrons. When he saw them walking towards him, he stared them down with his cold steel eyes that saw too much of the hell of death and they stopped dead in their tracks. "Next time I come here, I expect you little biker ladies to be wearing American flags on your leathers, proudly displayed. Most of the bikers I know are patriots. If I don't see the flags on you next time, I'll rip your lips off individually, throw them in a pile and light them on fire with lighter fluid while you watch."

Before he calmly walked out of the stunned bar, he finished his beer, scanned the frozen bikers, and then walked out of the bar easily without a sound. The black suburban picked him up out front and he got in the back.

"You could've called, you know," said the driver.

"No phone."

"We didn't much appreciate that you broke out of there before they were done with your treatment Sam."

"Figured as much. So tell me, is the Ferrari still in the Garage?"

"You're one of us Sam, one of the few, but you worry us. Yes, she's still there, calmly revving her engines, but always ready for the call when needed. Problem is, Potus is afraid to use her because it's too risky, unless of course, it suits his panty waist political interest, then we're suddenly expendable."

"Yeah, well, it'll happen someday and we'll be ready to take her for a helluva spin."

# FIFTH GRADE CHORUS: THE SEMINAL EVENT

Warning: Some who read this may laugh, some may cry, and yet others may simply smile and say to themselves, "yeah, that explains it."

I've had a few life experiences that may qualify as seminal events, but perhaps fifth grade choir may have been one of the earliest ones, I guess. Of course, it's been a long time since I was ten years old, and to be honest, I'm not sure it was third, fourth or fifth grade, but I know it was a long time before I was shaving.

I'm not quite sure after all this time why I joined the choir in grade school. I don't remember all the details but a few of them are planted like dried mud on my memory neurons. It's really not clear to me, now that I think about it, why I joined the choir. Maybe the director heard my voice, as I yelled during little league baseball games and thought I had natural talent. No, that couldn't be it. Or maybe they grabbed me by force at recess and made me go to choir practice because 80% of those who signed up were you guessed it: girls. They wanted a few token boys. But no self-respecting boy sporting bruised and abraded knees and elbows would ever sign up for choir.

So, there had to be a reason I joined this forbidden organization. However, I must say, I do remember this: there was a rumor that choir practice was at lunch, they served food and most importantly, there was a rumor that chorus singers were allowed to drink as many flavors of bottled pop (soda) as we wanted! And sure enough, that was true. I always chose 16-ounce bottles of coke. And Patty, that blonde, always sat across from me drinking Fresca.

So, we practiced our chorus singing at lunch time, after consuming large amounts of pop and the singing I am sure was often interrupted by inappropriate carbonation burping. But who's going to know the truth now?

And sure enough, it came time for our massive chorus performance, in the auditorium on the stage. We were as ready as the instructor could possibly get us. Our instructor gave us the dress code, which included white shirts and black pants. It may have even been suggested that we ask our moms to iron them, I don't know. We were told the time to arrive early for the performance and of course all parents were invited. So, I went home, and I think I told my parents nothing. I got out some scissors and cut off a pair of black pants into some nice shorts. I found a white shirt somewhere and I went to the performance. Turns out, I was the only kid on stage, in the front row who wore black cut-off shorts, while all the other good kids wore their long pants. I was in full view of the audience and couldn't hide, and it was too late to turn back. Don't ask me how I got this idea in my young brain—whether I heard the instructions incorrectly, or whether I just wanted to do it, but it happened.

So, I sang, crimson faced, trying to ignore the laughter in the crowd. Maybe they thought it was a comedy and I was born to be a comedian, but everyone knows I am only rarely funny, and that's only on every other Thursday. Mostly I looked down so that I wouldn't recognize people in the audience, and thankfully, a quick glance showed my parents weren't there, and that was a relief. Not sure they would've understood their weird son. But I knew Patty's parents were there, and I am sure they told her to stay away from Carson after that.

So, time went on, and I thought I forgot about it, but there it is, rearing itself into my consciousness once again. I've recovered, at least I think about 95% recovered and never required therapy, or actually no one knew what therapy was back then. But the good thing is Patty still smiled at me while she drank her Fresca afterwards, so maybe she thought I was some kind of cool stud or something.

Perhaps this was a secret and seminal event in my life that was a sign for my future. Who knows?

# DRESSING UP
# FOR CHURCH

I may have a few old-fashioned ideas that stubbornly cling to my DNA, or maybe to my junk DNA, but nevertheless, they still cling. Kind of like when I still actually look straight ahead or smile or try to engage people when waiting in line for that mandatory Starbucks boost rather than staring like a hypnotized robot at a cell phone.

Now to the topic at hand, finally:

Dressing for Church.

I previously wrote about men who wear hats in church service and what I think about that practice. Let's let that one go. Of course, when I grew up, we all dressed up, shaved, or well those of us that could—you know like aunt Mable, wore ties, sometimes sport coats, our best shoes and of course stupid little hats that we all took off and left on the coat rack out in the foyer. The ladies all looked their best and of course, the young ladies, well, that was one of the pluses of going to church or Sunday school, um, you know.

Times have changed.

I have noticed now that men wear shorts, sandals, T-shirts, athletic shoes with no socks, and huge gaudy football Jerseys with their number on them and names of the favorite players who will play that day. And women, well, they also wear matching sports Jerseys with their favorite player's name, jeans, shorts, sandals and rarely dresses or skirts. Thankfully, the church apparel hasn't deteriorated to Wal Mart dress code pajamas. Today in church Troy Polamalu was the most popular jersey in the sanctuary followed by Gronkowski and we were a long way from Pittsburgh or Boston. It struck me that these people were making a statement, although harmless, but it was distracting.

But I noticed that no one wore a shirt that had GOD printed on the back. With a number 1 of course.

Interestingly, these same people do know how to dress very sharp when they want to. I've seen ladies and gents dress to the hilt on special days in Church like Christmas and Easter! Nothing wrong with that of course, although those are special holidays for sure, aren't all days spent in Church worshipping special?

Now I am sure not a fashion leader, that's for sure. I don't wear jackets and ties to Church any more, however I do dress decent with nice shirt and slacks with good shoes and I clean up the best I can, trying not to draw attention to myself and not distracting from the purpose at hand.

I must say however, that I appreciate these who get out of bed and attend Church service rather than playing golf, no matter what they wear. I don't think it matters to the almighty. It matters what's in your heart.

Having said that, it's still a special place for me, a place of reverence, and I will always try to present myself the best I can.

Maybe none of this drivel matters at all. You must carry the spirit of love in your heart, no matter what you wear, or what your circumstance.

# LITTLE LEAGUE
# BASEBALL, MEAT
# CLEAVERS AND
# HOTEL CALIFORNIA

*Italics indicate brief lyrics from Hotel California by the Eagles—a great song many people know the words to, however, this story does not in any way suggest that this song has anything to do with prison or crime. That should be obvious to all readers.*

We were both ten years old, wild and free, and as was customary after a little league baseball game, we avoided going back home immediately at all costs. Usually that involved riding our bikes all over town, buying pop and baseball cards at the grocery store or at a local bar or perhaps going to another player's home. This time, Cliff kindly invited me to his home. So, we rode our bikes from the baseball diamond in the center of town to the west side, mitts fastened to handle bars, and still in uniform. We rode possibly ten miles, but we had no idea about mileage back then, nor did we particularly care.

"Cliff, why did you stop in front of the State Prison gates?" I asked.

"This is where I live Carson."

"Why didn't you tell me you were in trouble Cliff?"

I hopped back on my bike, turned around and started pedaling back home at a brisk pace. Then I hear him yell at me, "It's ok Carson, my dad's the warden!"

*I thought to myself, this could be heaven or this could be hell.*

I took a deep breath, then came back and the guard smiled at Cliff and saluted him but he glared suspiciously at me while we were allowed to ride our bikes through the first set of gates into the minimum-security area of the prison. I didn't know what minimum security meant at that time, but I know we were inside the barbed wire, but outside the looming concrete walls. I noticed there were actually several average looking houses on the grounds, inside the barbed wire, with little yards, and I thought that was super weird.

He showed me his house—it looked like all the others although a little bigger, I guess. I do remember that he had a large box filled with what I estimated to be 100 baseballs (give or take 50), a rack of ten baseball bats, and baseball mitts galore. It was baseball playing heaven, that's for sure, and I thought Cliff was lucky—although I wasn't sure what the pressing need was for 100 baseballs.

"You wanna have lunch Carson?" Cliff yelled as he waved me into the house.

I nodded cautiously and went carefully inside. We sat down at the table and waited. Then a towering man appeared and at first, I thought it was a walking oak tree, but he was breathing and wearing either orange or stripes—I couldn't remember, but I do know I had to cock my head straight back to see his smirk. They say he was a trustee.

"You like beef?" said the towering oak.

"Um sure," I said.

Then he dropped a slab of meat on the table, and it landed with a thud, and said, "Thick or thin sliced?"

*We are all just prisoners here of our own device.*

Then I saw it and shivered from head to toe. The glistening meat cleaver in his aircraft carrier hands, descending down onto the clearly already dead meat sitting on the table in front of me.

*They stab it with their steely knives but they just can't kill the beast.*

"Got to go Cliff!"

*Last thing I remember I was running for the door. I had to find a passage back to the place I was before.*

I pedaled so fast; I was home in record time. It's been so long I've forgotten most of the details but those are the ones that stick like peanut butter on Wonder Bread. I am sure however, that never told my parents about this little adventure. No, never do that, otherwise I would be grounded for doing something so stupid.

They say you are the sum total of all your life experiences and when you die, they flash in front of you like movie scenes. I wonder if this will be one of those scenes. Either way, Cliff, if you are still around to read this, I don't know if I ever got to thank you for inviting me to the lunch I never ate at the Prison.

And I am not sure what life's lesson I learned on this occasion, but I am curious, where did The Eagles come up with their lyrics for Hotel California? Listened to it the other day, and perhaps I understand now why I am so connected to the lyrics—it is like Déjà vu all over again for me, from a previous time in a young boy's life.

Oh yes, and of course, I never told my parents about this. This is the only record of this event that exists in the world.

# COMMON SENSE AND
# NEW YEAR'S EVE

While I am an educated man and I have some wisdom in my occupation, that doesn't mean I always immerse myself in common sense. It's New Year's Eve and I should've known better, and it certainly would've been better to hire a professional on this night. But that didn't happen. I needed a little adventure on this special evening, the last night of 2016.

I adjusted my seat so that I was comfortable, in the correct position to accomplish all the duties necessary and I had my drink close—easily in reach of my right hand and my blue eyes were seeing clearly without a hint of red and I looked outside at the inky blackness and surged ahead.

It started out ok and it seemed quiet and I just kept going, hoping the freedom released by this adventure would take me to exciting, unknown places. I was confident that I would do fine. I had done this many times before, sometimes even on New Year's Eve. To clear my thoughts, I turned some music on, smooth Jazz/fusion—Down to the Bone. I immersed myself into the dark journey, buoyed with energy and careful concentration.

My peace shattered quickly when this asshole in the car

behind me had his bright beams directly shining high into my rear-view mirror, nearly blinding me. He kept following me, no matter where I turned and he adjusted his speed to match mine, even when I slowed or increased my speed. My heart leaped with the realization that this vehicle wanted to do me harm. Why else would he follow me for miles and miles?

Suddenly, he pulled up in the lane next to me, and I saw the pistol aimed at me, and I ducked, keeping control of the wheel and the road through peripheral vision, and the rounds splattered my driver's side window, shattering the glass and leaving it in a meshwork of shattered glass that I couldn't see much out of, except for the bottom. Taking advantage of few seconds of lull as he reloaded, I slowed down until my bumper was about a foot away from his rear tire and I decided the only way for me to survive was to PIT him. I learned the Precision Immobilization Technique back in the day, but this was the first time I'd used it for real. Once in position, I looked through the remaining clear glass and turned my car directly into his side, not braking, continuing my speed, causing his vehicle to be thrown to the side of the road, rolling several times, likely a lethal maneuver in most circumstances. I sped off, thankful that I could see no witnesses, but a softball decided to jump up and down in my gut when I saw the road ahead blocked by two cars in the northbound lanes. Thankfully the roads were deserted tonight, but not for long. The chase had brought us farther out into the country where the boys in blue figured there wouldn't be much action. Downtown was where all the drunk driving would occur.

I stopped but they already let off volleys of rounds into my car, through the windshield and thankfully their aim was bad—they were high near the roof. No means of escape, which would've been preferred, and I was trapped and realized I needed to shoot my way out of this fucking ambush. I pulled my Glock 19 out using a cross-draw on my right side and leaning back I saw their torsos, and correcting for the convexity of the glass I aimed low at the first man's pelvis, knowing that the trajectory through the glass would take the lethal wound to his chest. I fired multiple rounds, the first to break the glass and second to hit the target, and each target was then hit, faces down on the ground, the pavement washed with blood.

I took a deep breath, rubbed my eyes and didn't want to take my eyes off the page—this author had me spellbound with his action scenes, but I reached to my right, found my drink on the wide arm of my easy chair—a nice rich Bordeaux, perfect for New Year's Eve adventure, then proceeded to clumsily knock it over, and while trying to recover, threw the novel across the room, pages crinkled and smashed.

What a violent way to end my New Year's Eve adventure! I looked out at the carnage on the floor, red wine splattered everywhere, book with pages splayed and I just sat in my comfortable easy chair, looked out the window into that inky blankness, collected my thoughts and smiled. I was safe and happy this New Year's Eve.

# THEY TOLD ME I NEEDED TO GO TO THIS PLACE IN PARIS

They called it the Moulin Rouge. They said it was a famous place with great entertainment, so I bought some tickets before I left, like a good tourist, including train tickets from Bordeaux to Paris, the Louvre, Notre Dame and then of course the Moulin Rouge. If you are daring, you can refer back to my blog a few years ago to a little experience I had in Bordeaux: *Ze Flench Vin.* https://srcarson.com/ze-flench-vin/

So, after recovering from my last wine-dominated event in Bordeaux, I jumped on the fast train and landed in Paris. I really hated to leave Bordeaux, actually, but then I had tickets to these places in Paris and that would be a waste and all. Plus, I had to see what I could, drink lots of French wine and of course, see the Moulin Rouge after all those museums, Cathedral de Notre Dame, Arch de Triumphe, etc. Mon dieu!

So, I enjoyed all the cafes, and of course, trying to talk to the French people in broken French—some enjoyed my attempts to converse in their language, and some well, just didn't. Either way, it was fun just to sit at the café and drink your little espressos and watch all the young ladies ride around the streets in motor scooters, allowing their silky skirts to blow in the wind, similar to Marilyn Monroe. Yes, they were beautiful young women, not "things" or sexless "its".

So, then I took the subway up to Montmartre, and figured out how to get to the Moulin Rouge. On the way to finding a place to eat, I was interrupted on my gastronomic quest about ten times by people who would pop out of doorways with multiple locks on them and ask me, "Monsieur. Would you like a woman?" Of course, I thought, what a question to ask? So, I said, Yes, having a good woman as a companion is a great honor to a man. "Great, they said, Come with us, and it only costs 100 Euros for an hour." Oh, so that's what they meant. So, I told them, "no, I don't pay for a woman's company, they must pay me."

So that response stopped some of the people pestering me. But others persisted. After about the ninth proposition by these low-lifes, I was responding to them in a few short Russian or French words I know, demonstrating that I couldn't comprehend any of the junk that came from their mouths.

So, I finally arrived at the front ticket booth of the Moulin Rouge. Much to my chagrin, the line seemed to be a mile long, in front of the ticket booth. But then, I realized I had a ticket, so I thought I could bypass this obstacle called the booth.

So, I went up the guards at the front of the line and showed them my ticket. He laughed and said, "Oh monsieur, 1000 people in the line there just like you with the same ticket." Then, he ignored me. Then, I pulled out 20 Euros, and he already had been palm straight out before I pulled it out of my wallet. Anyway, that seems to get me right in, to the front of the damn place in 30 seconds!

While the thousands waited outside, I was in the Foyer of the Moulin Rouge theater. There was about 10 of 15 of us waiting before they opened the theater doors inside. I was the only American, it seemed, and the rest of the small crowd of 'VIP' clients, as I was apparently now labeled, were well-dressed Russians. Well, the ladies were wearing high heels and sexy dresses, but I didn't notice the men. So, they were a little obnoxious and the French employees were having none of it.

They opened the doors to the theater to let the VIPs (including me) into the empty theater. But the Russian men yelled, "We are Russian aristocracy and own much land in Moscow", or something like that, and therefore "so my group must go in first always!" The French men looked at them, laughed and said nothing, then walked to me and said, "Monsieur, come with us, you will be the first to enter the theater, and you can pick any seat you want."

Never piss off a French man who works in the Moulin Rouge, I think.

So they refused to let the Russians in, until I picked my seat. So, I went to the front of the theater and picked the table right in front of the main stage, and of course, right in front of a champagne bottle and glasses. Amazing seat, I must say. And I was chuckling inside because the French people had no tolerance of arrogant clients.

Before the show, they sat an Australian couple next to me, husband and wife, and I don't know who else. And the show started and oh my, the dancing girls were doing their kicks and struts, and I don't know what else not more than a meter or two in front of me. Very classy I might add, and well-choreographed. But the Australian wife, would not let the poor husband look at the excellent artistry and talent these ladies displayed. She kept saying, "Harold, what are you looking at?" Or, "you don't have to stare Harold!" I thought, damn, let the man enjoy! It's not like he's going to jump up there and dance with them or meet them back stage! Why did you come with him then, if he can't enjoy? So, I offered poor Harold lots of champagne.

And the professional dancing girls with their smooth long legs, and yes, I could see goose pimples on them from my vantage point, smiled at me while they danced and I smiled back. And then, when one of them made a mis-step, she laughed and the other girls released small giggles that people in the back could not hear. But I did. So, I took my glass of champagne and toasted her, and she blew me a kiss as the performance ended, or perhaps she blew a kiss to the whole crowd?

Turns out, her name was Francine, and she said told me she was a medical student at the Sorbonne, earning money during the summer. And she said, "Carson, you are funny, and a gentleman, and since you are American, you aren't familiar with the area, so after the show, some of the girls and I will go to a nice quiet restaurant with reasonable food and great wine. The owner gives us discounts. Would you like to join us? N'est-ce pas?

So, it was a nice evening in Paris.

# DRESS RIGHT DRESS, DRESSES AND LCWB

W e were good at it because we practiced it a lot. And if we weren't perfect, in those days, we would get our asses kicked. Or, we would receive corrective therapy when the marching was over. That corrective therapy often included lots of push-ups or squat thrusts, (now known by the less offensive term known as burpees.) The term *squat thrusts* apparently offends too many people, because I never hear it used anymore. But back then, the people training us didn't know what political correctness or safe zones were. Of course, these upperclassmen did understand that loud screaming in our ears was good for learning how to handle stress in not very safe zones. They loved yelling at us everywhere, and they especially loved to yell at us while we sang certain patriotic songs as loud as we could during what we used to call, "shower formations." By the way, those too are now illegal training techniques at this famous institution.

I did lots of squat thrusts, on demand, whenever asked.

Yes, after high school graduation I was appointed to a certain U.S. Military Academy in the mountains that shall remain nameless, but I did flourish there. But the topic at hand that came to mind today was marching. We were damn good at it, as I mentioned. Perfect lines, movements and impeccable uniforms. And we knew what the marching leader up front meant when he said things like, "Orwer...Harch!" That means forward march. Or "Bow Hase!" which translates to about face. And then of course there was the command "Hess Rye Hess!" which translates to dress right dress. The H sound was apparently used to make it sound like a primitive grunt sound similar to what body builders utter when deadlifting massive weights.

Dress right dress means, during the marching, while keeping your line perfectly straight, aligned with the cadet next to you and he next to the next guy etc., you immediately, on command, turn your head sharply to the right and stare into oblivion or at a wall, or the blue sky or whatever, no emotion, no facial expressions or sounds, until the command to look forward is given. You may wonder why I remember this command so well after all these years. Well you see, every day, at noon, a very accomplished band would play patriotic marching as several thousand cadets, in groups called squadrons, marched group to group to the mess hall to eat. It was quite a production, and I admit, I loved the pomp and circumstance, even if it was all choreographed just to get us hungry cadets to the massive chow hall that can serve 4000 people hot food simultaneously.

But there were certain times when *Dress Right Dress* came in handy and was sometimes pleasurable, ironically, for us young cadets. You see on Saturdays and Sundays, the general public was allowed to come and line up along the viewing walls near a certain famous chapel, and they all fought to see the pretty zoo animals on display, I mean cadets, as we marched the long way in front of that public viewing wall for their visual pleasure. But the truth is, it was our visual pleasure too! We were very good at picking out pretty ladies along the wall, dressed in their Sunday best, and we learned how to alert the guys in the perfect line, all staring to the right at these spectators, where the good-looking ladies were, so we could concentrate our eyes on them. We learned how to communicate like marching ventriloquists, without moving our lips, telling our fellow cadets where to feast their eyes, for the 20 or 30 seconds that we marched by. Such simple pleasures as this, we cherished.

We were the LCWB, or the last class with balls.

So you see, the zoo animals were also staring at the visitors and taking mental notes.

# BOY SCOUTS, BUGLING
# AND BOX TURTLES

I've read that the Boy Scouts have unfortunately taken on some bad press lately and because of some abuse scandals, they have filed bankruptcy. That's tragic for the kids involved and for the organization in general, because back in the day when I was a scout, it provided me significant challenges that helped prepare me for obstacles that would come my way in the future. In fact, without scouting I would've never learned how to swim or learn how to save people larger than me who were drowning, do the special ops silent swim or mile swim, blah blah.

So many stories to tell, but I must say, there were always lots of box turtles around our large forested camp surrounding a muddy lake. And then, there was that kid who was lucky enough to have a box turtle that had its' insides carved out so that he could use it as a neckerchief slide for his yellow neckerchief. Damn he was cool. The other scouts had basic ones made out of wood or metal their parents bought at the local Sears, but he was the real McCoy. His was made out of an animal. Must've been some kind of tobacco-spitting mountain boy.

I remember that he was the same kid who at the age of 11, went on his first campout—a 'camporee' competition involving many boy scout troops, competing against troops all over the city and county in events like map and compass, lashing logs into towers, building fires without matches, and I guess, well saving humanity. It was this skinny kid's first day and he inherited some old WW2 backpack from his grandfather that smelled like a moldy basement, so he proudly filled it with camping stuff you know like filled canteens, shovels, clothes, food and I don't know what else. I recall that this backpack stretched all the way down this little kid's butt while knocking on the backs of his legs and must've weighed almost as much as him. You see, all scouts had to climb up a large sand dune with all their camping gear in order to find the campsite. Poor kid was having trouble.

The others watched as he strained with all his strength up the mountainous dune, then when he almost reached the top, fell backward from the weight of the moldy backpack, rolling all the way down the dune to the bottom, upended, with his feet in the air at the bottom, like a box turtle who lay helplessly on his back with his little legs flailing in the air. The other scouts and scoutmasters kept going to the campsite, successfully negotiating the dune, but this kid had to keep trying, and falling backwards several times, until he finally made it to the peak exhausted. I am sure he was wondering if he was cut out for this hell called Boy Scouts of America, Troop 72, Pottawatomie Council, or whatever. By the time he made it to the campsite, the other scouts were already putting up tents. I always wondered what happened to that poor kid who started off so inauspiciously.

But one thing I remember about evening troop meetings at the gym and then various campouts was that there was always an American flag and patriotism, with saluting and of course, we needed a kid who could play the bugle because at the end of each event when we went home, taps always needed to be played by a bugler. Not a record player. And, at large gatherings we needed a bugler to play reveille to wake up all the campers in the morning, and also a bugler to play *To the Colors* as the flag was raised up the pole before breakfast in the mess hall. This was a special honor that we would bestow on a kid who could play the trumpet or bugle. The scout leaders told us it was an honor to be selected to play the bugle.

So, they volunteered me.

Of course, I it turns out I was the only one who could play the bugle that had no valves, as well as trumpet. One of the kids must've mentioned that fact to the scoutmaster, I don't recall. So, I became the troop bugler. It was a lonely job, but I guess someone had to do it. It had its perks, I guess, no pay, but it was a job no one else could do, and it was certainly better than cleaning latrines. Believe me, at 6:30 in the morning, no one enjoyed hearing my brass bugle go off with reveille, so that did not make me very popular. However, I did enjoy the rhythm of playing *To the Colors* during flag raising and it kind of gave me chills watching hundreds of other scouts saluting the flag. And taps, well, that was solemn, and for some reason, all us young scouts felt this. Well, at least I did, and I always tried to warm my embouchure (lip placement on the cold mouthpiece) so that I didn't make those occasional cracking notes from being cold. But it happened of course.

I guess I recalled this today, because my sister mentioned the playing of taps on Memorial Day. This is the day we remember those who sacrificed all for our freedom we all enjoy. I looked up the scout oath, while writing this piece and we all repeated it back then: *On my honor, I will do my best to do my duty to God and my country and to obey the scout law; to help other people at all times and to keep myself physically strong, mentally awake and morally straight.*

It was a nice oath to have and repeat and I understood it. But I wonder, what did they mean by 'mentally awake'? Avoid sleeping when the scoutmaster was talking? No, I think it probably meant be smart and don't do stupid things like play with fire or you'll pee your pants at night. And please pay attention and learn or you'll get dumped in the mucky lake at night.

And for those readers who were curious about the kid with the turtle neckerchief and the massive backpack that rolled him over and what happened to him, then, well, that kid was me. And that kid eventually became an Eagle Scout.

# THE INTERVIEW
# FROM HELL

I'm pretty sure that I know how to take a history from a patient, although I joke that it's much easier to cut first and ask questions later. My questions are posed to dissect out the basis of the patient's problem, taking the complaint and narrowing it down to the smallest differential possible. Like Doctor House, I believe I'm a detective sorting through carefully hidden clues, then while asking the correct questions, I listen to the response given by the patient and then carefully formulate a plan to verify the diagnosis and subsequently initiate treatment. Heck, I even look at their body language and their breathing pattern to guide me in the right direction.

I won't tell you how long I've been doing this, but I guess long enough to know that the more I know, the less I know, and I often pray to God to help me in the difficult situations. And yet, I'm confident enough in what I'm doing to know that the better I listen to the patient, the more likely it is that he or she will lay the answer right in front of me like a ridiculous steaming plate of lobster next to a cup of hot butter, accompanied by a crisp salad and a large pitcher of cold beer.

And without fail, patients are eager to answer my educated

questions because they want help and they want a quick and accurate diagnosis, and if testing is needed prior to treatment, they want the best test possible to efficiently nail down the diagnosis.

But all of this came to a screeching halt when Ms. X walked into my office.

"Hi Ms. X, nice to meet you. Have a seat. What may I do for you today?"

"Hi. I have Central sleep apnea, not Obstructive, and I need a home sleep study, not an in-lab study. That's why I'm here."

Taken aback a little by a patient making her own diagnosis without my input, then essentially ordering her own tests, I scratched my chin a little and thought about what the right approach would be. I figured I would use my finely honed interviewing skills to find out if she even needed any testing and that in fact, maybe, she had something different going on. She looked nervous and her arms were folded in front of her perfectly.

"Ok, what is bothering you about your sleep?"

"What do you mean? I have Central Sleep Apnea; I know it and I need a home sleep study because I know I won't sleep in a lab."

My patience was evaporating quickly, like the morning dew in Phoenix. I felt my patience try to morph into indignance, but I told it not yet please. Must have sangfroid.

"Do you snore?"

"Of course not. Why would I snore if I had Central Sleep Apnea?"

"Are you sleepy during the day?"

"You mean, do I have insomnia? No, I don't have insomnia. I told you I needed a Home Sleep Study."

Stubbornly, I refused to let her run the show and continued my now impatient attempt to get to the bottom of her real problem. But I could feel my leg start to move like it was running the 100-meter dash under my desk.

"So, when do you go to bed, and how long does it take to get to sleep?

"I told you, I don't have insomnia."

I amazed myself that I was able to continue without throwing her out of my office, an office that previously garnered a little respect from patients who sometimes paid me for my education and skill. But then, I realized, if I threw her out, I would hear about it in the papers or from her money sucking lawyer. So, I tried to get her to answer a couple more questions to narrow down the diagnosis that I already knew.

"What kind of work do you do?"

"What difference does it make? Why do you ask that?"

I was taken aback by her question. Why the hell wouldn't I ask whatever I wanted, within reason, to get to the truth? I stared at her, said nothing for a loud minute, and I felt my face start its' journey to flush town. I didn't feel I needed to explain each question I asked, but thought I would give her a generous benefit on just this one explanation.

"Jobs make a difference, for example, time commitments, late hours, stress etc."

"Not applicable here."

Her arms, already folded in front of her emaciated, coffee-stimulated body now seemed to caress her chest with increased vigor, and I could see her fingers blanch from the pressure. I decided I would save the last few precious moments of calmness I had by asking a quick double question to see if she responded.

"So, do you have a family history of sleep disorders, and how long have you been living at this altitude?"

"Why would you ask about my family history? And why would you care how long I lived here?"

Both of my legs were jumping now, supported on the balls of my feet, but they were controlled enough so that I knew she wouldn't see them or see my body vibrate, ready to explode.

"I ask these questions because I am trying to figure out

how to help you, Ms. X. For example, if there is a family history of Sleep Apnea or Narcolepsy it is helpful in the evaluation, or, if you recently moved to altitude from sea level, it could play a role in Central Sleep Apnea. But really, I don't have time to stop and explain to you all the medical reasons for my questions."

"You really have a condescending attitude doctor! "

I looked at her and wanted to tell her immediately to go jump out the window since I figured it was ten stories high and therefore would be effective in the job that she needed done. But I didn't. I just stared at her, relatively calmly, thinking of what to do next, knowing that this is a very litigious society; a society that has encouraged patients not only to sue whenever they could, but also that they had a right to sue at any time, and that they should at least report any physician who had a bad attitude to the state board. Hospitals also aggressively support this reporting to their administration with complaints, hoping to keep their patients happy when they rail against us horrible doctors, who after all, are the enemies of modern society. I excused myself, stepped out and left her alone for a little. I came back with a nurse practioner who pulled up another chair. I needed a witness.

"Why is she here?"

I didn't answer.

"So, have you ever been told you have a nervous condition or were treated for anxiety?"

"No, never. And that isn't applicable here." Then she hesitated as I stared at her. I stared her down as if she was just a dull rock taking up space, in dire need of being thrown through a window. I wanted her to tell me about her psychiatric problems, because I knew she didn't need a home sleep study at all. "Well, I guess I was on medications for a time a while back for my anxiety and depression, but that no longer applies now. I don't have anxiety!

No, she didn't need a home sleep study at all. Her problem

was psychiatric, but I ordered it anyway. Why? Well, the path of least resistance. Here's reason number 40 of why the cost of medical care just continues to rise: Make patients happy to avoid costly complaints to the medical board for absolutely no reason at all. Then, I would have to get lawyered up, spend hours and hours defending my completely professional en-counter with her instead of using my skills to save people's lives or at least make them better.

"Thank you for ordering the sleep study. After it is done, when will I follow up with you to discuss the results?"

"You'll follow up with my nurse practioner." I knew the study would be normal, and it was.

She will never see me again or waste my time. I hope her psychiatrist has some good meds for her.

# DO PARENTS SAY THE SAME THING NOW AS IN THE PAST?

For some reason, I dredged up some memories of things my parents said to me when I was a kid, mostly phrases or admonitions I guess, meant to teach, or perhaps intimidate or maybe just blow hot air, I don't know. And then, I wondered, are these common parental sayings that last throughout the years and therefore have become standard jargon for all parents?

You are probably wondering, how many years ago was this happening? Well, in the interest in my own security, and you know the paparazzi knowing too much about me, I will just say that I was a kid back when there were no cell phones, no email, and Al Gore had not yet invented the internet. (Who is Al Gore?)

1. **Eat it or Wear it:** I heard this at the dinner table once, when my cousin came over for dinner. My uncle told them, "you guys better finish everything on your plate or you're going to have to wear it the rest of the

day or evening." So, my astute parents remembered that phrase and used it on me about 1000 times and soon I didn't care whether I wore my broccoli or ate it. But they never said eat or wear it before church though. Must look good in church.

2. **Go Play in the streets:** Translation here is that of course, they wanted me out of the house, and when I heard this, I ran, and that leads me to number 3. But before I get there, yes, we played in the streets especially in mud puddles, rode skate boards down the hills, and drove our bikes behind DDT insecticide trucks.

3. **Come back when it is dark:** Always a good rule of thumb because as soon as they said, play in the streets, we ran all over playing ditch, climbing up on top of the school roof to play stick baseball, driving our bikes to the Monon Creek to catch ugly crawdads or around the state prison or perhaps to the store to buy baseball cards and gum with bottle deposits we turned in when we found them in the weeds around town. Sometimes there were playboy magazines near these old bottles in the weeds of empty parking lots. That was educational, but always wondered why people threw those magazines out. They seemed pretty valuable to me. Sometimes we got in trouble with the neighbors and they pulled guns on us for no reason. See: Dick Tracy and Chuck Roast blog from a few years ago. So, we came back at dark to eat because we had no watches.

4. **Dr. Seuss was a communist:** At that age I didn't know what a communist was, but I figured it was something bad, and apparently, they were red or something. I think they were going to drop a nuclear bomb on us, so we learned how to do bomb drills. I read his stuff once, but thought it was pretty stupid and didn't get the political undertones. I still don't.

5. **Children are to be seen and not heard.** This is

self-explanatory. So, we kept quiet in general.

6. **If you play with fire, you will pee you pants:** I think this was their way of telling us to be safe with matches and fire. I became pretty good with matches and fire in boy scouts and never peed my pants.

# I DID IT ON THE
# AIRPLANE AGAIN

I don't have a good explanation for it, but each time I fly as
a passenger, I can't seem to control these actions anymore.
It just feels so good and natural—and thankfully I haven't
been thrown off the plane yet, but if I do get thrown off, I will
scream as loud as I can and hold on to my seat arm with both
hands, trying not to laugh as they drag me by the legs off the
plane and into the arms of a money hungry lawyer who will
take a large chunk of my settlement.

But seriously though, I am not sure why I always do this
on airplanes, but I guess so far it hasn't bothered anyone. I'm
sure people stare though. Previously, it tended to happen at
bars, often stimulated by a beer or glass of wine, and embarrassingly it has also occasionally occurred while in the church
pew listening to the preacher. I must tell you though, that I
always kept one ear open to the sermon, clinging to the inspiring words while it happens.

Word vomit. That's right. As soon as I'm in my seat and
people are still struggling to put their luggage up above my
head, I whip out my black and white bound notebook and several black pens and we go at it furiously, pen and paper, words

flying silently but forcefully onto the pages, and I don't usually stop until we land or nature calls.

I wrote five or six chapters of my new novel on the trip to and from a medical conference, even though medical facts were occupying a significant part of my strained brain, but it seems the airplane brings out my creativity and I was able to switch quickly from left to squishy right brain and proceed to the thriller with larger-than-life characters filled with flaws, living in a story that holds on to you and won't let go.

Seems it won't let me go either.

Guess in order to finish this novel, I'm going to have to do some more traveling. But I wonder how much better I would've written if I had some red wine in my left hand in the airplane seat?

# BONE BRUISES, SIXTH GRADE TEACHER AND PATTY

It was in sixth grade. I'm sure of it. Mostly because I was in competition with a girl name Patty S, a tall blonde dream girl who always tried to beat me finishing tests. She smiled at me even when I beat her, which wasn't often, but oh my, when such a beauty smiled at me it made it all worthwhile. But then, she probably never frowned that I could remember. And she was a fast runner too. But not as fast as I was. I remember running everywhere, fast and long, whether it was through the neighborhoods playing ditch or capture the flag with my friends, around baseball diamonds, football fields, or away from the elementary school when the neighbors saw us climbing up on the roof of the school to play stick ball, then calling the cops on us poor innocent kids. Yeah, I was fast.

Then something happened. Not sure what—maybe I fell and injured myself, I don't' remember.

So, my Sixth-grade teacher, Mr. Leroy, who never smiled ever, somehow decided he was an orthopedic surgeon without going to medical school or something, and said something very devastating to me at the age of 11:

"Carson, you have a bone bruise on your heel. I am afraid to tell you this, but you will never be able to run again."

Now at the age of 11, that was pretty devastating news, I do remember that. *Never run again?* Sounds so final. Not only will Patty always beat me now, but my life clearly depended on the ability to run, and well this was my sixth-grade teacher, and I was supposed to respect his opinion because he was smart and older an all that. I don't remember if he examined me or anything, but even if he did, were sixth-grade teachers orthopedic or sports medicine doctors by default?

Of course, like everything else back then, you never told your parents anything because well, you didn't. So, for a certain time period, Mr. Leroy's statement that I would never run again, deeply imbedded in my mind and wouldn't leave and apparently, I believed him. I may have curtailed some of my sports activities and thought about my alleged bone bruise much longer than I should've and it became some sort of psychological anvil I now wore on my perfectly fine heel.

I think it forced me to do other things, like well, learn to play the trumpet. My father played the trumpet when he was in high school, so since he had an old smelly trumpet, he let me have that to make noise on, and I practiced it, thinking it would help me impress Patty somehow, or maybe Joanne, the Polynesian girl, and as time went on, I became fairly decent with it. However, trumpets are not a good instrument for parties and small gatherings. Guitars are, of course, but no one told me that, but I did know that only long-haired hippies played guitars.

This bone bruise thing was probably not much of anything at all, but Mr. Leroy, for some reason, decided to make it a big issue for me. Eventually I started ignoring this *you will never run again* silliness, and started running again in Junior high school and I found out, the natural skill I was blessed with came back and in fact, I joined the Junior High (Middle school) track team, running the half-mile and then mile. I did this mostly because no one at that age could run a mile, so I didn't have much competition, at least, in my school. But one day, I thought my Junior High track career would end quickly because a bunch of track athletes decided when the coach wasn't looking that they would bury me beneath the large foam bags under the high jump bar then pile on top of me as long as they could to see if I would scream or die or something. Turns out I did think I was going to die, but some kind soul finally pulled off the foam bags and the bodies on top of me just in time.

And sometime later, I broke the all-time school record in the mile run and went on to have a good running career in high school and college.

Mr. Leroy, if you are still alive and for some stupid reason you are reading this material, you were a worthless piece of crap for saying that to me back then, you moron.

After sixth grade though, Patty and I went to different schools and I never saw her again, but Patty, you were my first love and my inspiration, and although we never spoke about it, I am sure you knew it.

# KIDS SHOULD PLAY
# ON ROOFTOPS, NOT
# PLAYGROUNDS

Many of my readers have children and I'm sure all parents want their children to grow up to be strong, healthy and successful world beaters—even more successful than their loving, hard working parents. Of course, we all know that is only possible by feeding the little varmints large quantities of gooey, flaccid, bleached Wonder bread. At least that's what I remember from stupid TV commercials when I was young. Never liked that crap.

But I've noticed over recent years that the playgrounds are empty. Or at least partially empty, save for some circuit training adults who shouldn't be in tights, attempting to do pull ups or swinging from those parallel ladder things midway through their running, I mean jogging workout. Where are the kids? Inside playing computer games or Play Station or whatever they do electronically now?

Where is the cacophony of clattering bikes with baseball cards clothes-pinned to their bicycle spokes while they ride behind the fog produced by the anti-mosquito DDT trucks? Damn those were the good old days.

Ok, I admit that some parents would say I am out of touch with what is going on with kids today; they are active in organized sports such as soccer, baseball, football, cheerleading etc. Fine then. I'll have you know I used to know about kids too because I used to have some and worried about what was the best balance between work, play and safety in their lives too.

I still say the playgrounds are empty and bikes are replaced by cars and car pools and kids are the same of course, but much different now. And although they are smarter than we were with all this technology, I'm sure, they're also less fit in general. Just ask some of the military basic training drill sergeants.

I remember my mother telling me, "Carson, get out of the house and go play in the street." So I did. And I climbed onto roofs. In fact, there were only a couple of us neighborhood kids who were athletic enough to climb up the 25-foot exhaust pole just next to the corner on the other side of the gymnasium of Knapp Elementary School. Or maybe I should exaggerate and say it was 100-foot pole we shimmied, I've forgotten after all these glorious years, but it was a tall pole for us. The other kids watched us in awe after we climbed up on top of the gravel roof of the Elementary school and played baseball with sticks we had previously hurled up on the roof and the gravel rocks we would hit down to the playground below. Each hit from the roof was a home run of course, because the rock went out of site, "over the fence." And we said, "Hey Ernie, let's play two!" Then I think the others ran home and told their parents on us. Not sure if my parents ever knew, but I always came home for dinner.

Funny thing about roofs when I was young. Guess it was some type of primordial attraction I had for climbing trees and of course, that leads to climbing more roofs. Yeah, I know, it's the monkey in me coming out, but heck, you know, without monkeys there wouldn't have been a space program!

Seems the other roof that I enjoyed climbing up on was Grandpa's garage roof. It was a rickety old wooden garage, you know, the type that creak with the slightest wind and exudes that old musty smell. Thankfully, there was a gnarly old tree next to it, and I surely would climb it and straddle the triangle the gable made and talk to the workers smoking below on break by the restaurant grease pit on the other side of the fence below. Now I was the king of the roof back then! Seems no one could get me up there, not that I was paranoid or anything.

Sometimes, Johnny, the boy in Gramp's neighborhood, would be successful in coaxing me down from the roof, mostly because he had lots of gum, and always had seven sticks of gum in his mouth at time, "one for each year I is." I thought Johnny was cool, but it blew my mind thinking how much gum would be exploding his chipmunk cheeks when he was 18! So, of course, we ran down to the railroad tracks and put some dimes on the rails, stood back and watched the train come by, then picked up our enlarged and flattened dimes, now triple in size!

I know, that's enough of that reminiscing. But in the end, I must admit that it was a good childhood, full of independence and hope, mixed with danger and adventure. But at the same time, we accepted the realization that if you didn't work hard, you wouldn't succeed, and nothing would be handed to you. If you failed, it was your fault, and there's no one else to blame.

# WHERE HAVE ALL THE PUMP JOCKEYS GONE, PART 1

I made sure that I took almost my full hour of lunch at a local diner down the street, leaving within 5 minutes to spare before it was time to clock back in. I tried not to spend more than $1.35 at lunch if I could since that is what I made per hour that summer, but then that made no sense either if you think about it. I think that may have bought me a hamburger and coke, possibly fries. So, I was heading down the road at a pretty quick pace, glancing at my watch and proudly wearing my pale blue uniform shirt emblazoned with the STANDARD OIL COMPANY logo above the pocket that held my plastic pocket protector, holding my trusty tire gauge and of course a pen or two.

"Hey man, gimme a square!"

He looked like a two-legged Sequoia, completely obstructing the sidewalk in front of me. "Sorry man", I said. "I ain't got none." After I said that so quickly, I was shocked how easily I blurted out that hillbilly slang, and to what purpose, I'm not sure. But I said it.

"C'mon man. Y'all pump gas and even a baby with crap in his pants knows y'all light'em up all over the place and flick'em wherever you want even when you pumps gas."

The talking Sequoia had a decent point, I guess. My fellow pump jockeys all smoked heavy and when they weren't smoking, they were chewing and spitting with alacrity. For the most part the gas station uniform with the Standard Oil emblem was definitely cool, and I was sure my friends would be jealous of me if they ever saw me in it, but I'm not sure they never did. Not sure many had those kinds of jobs at that age actually. But now, that uniform was a curse because of a reputation that was well known in the world to all except me. I quickly looked at my watch and realized I was going to be late if I didn't start moving, and I'd be in trouble with the boss, but more importantly, I knew that at the age of 14, death was near, or if not death, at least a lot of pain. I thought about how they say your life flashes before your eyes like a movie before death, but I realized that I didn't have much life yet to take a movie of, and the flash would be more like a two-minute movie trailer. I'd hoped there was at least nice fireworks show on the beach or something.

"Sorry man, I'm late got to go." I knew if he took a swing at me for my lack of cigarettes and he missed, he'd never catch me if I accelerated, and so I sprinted a quarter mile faster than I could've at a track meet.

So, the tree didn't kill me and I was able to complete my afternoon shift, get on my bike and ride about 12 miles home and look forward later to experiencing some new and completely different pump jockey learning experiences that will soon follow.

Printed in the USA
CPSIA information can be obtained
at www.ICGtesting.com
LVHW050206230124
769429LV00042B/380